12-18-84

20452
12-6-84

CRONUS

William L. DeAndrea

CRONUS

The Mysterious Press New York

FIRST EDITION

This one is for BEN STANDLEY . . .
and high damn time, too!

Neither the town of Draper, Pennsylvania, nor any of its inhabitants or visitors, exists. Any similarities to actual places, people, or events is totally coincidental.

Moreover, there is no such plan as the Cronus Project. There is no such "Agency" as the one described in this novel.

There *is* a committee of the House of Representatives assigned to oversee the activities of various intelligence services, but the chairman of that committee is in no way intended to be represented by the character in this novel referred to as "the Congressman."

The FBI does not function as described. No American intelligence agency functions as described. Agents of the Soviet Union do not function as described. Terrorists don't even function as described.

This book is totally fictitious. Nothing like the events surrounding the Cronus Project ever happened, or ever could happen.

As anyone in Washington will be eager to tell you, should you be so foolish as to ask.

—W.L.D.

Chapter One

"IT'S NO FUN WITHOUT THE *BLOOD*." WALDO'S SOFT VOICE was petulant, and there was a pout on his loose, wet lips.

"Be quiet," Georgia told him. "You know what Leo said."

Waldo sighed. Yes, he knew what Leo said. They mustn't get blood all over the inside of the cab. The back of the ambulance was okay but not the cab. Leo had made him promise.

So instead of walking up to the place in the shady corner of the hospital parking lot where the ambulance driver liked to sit and eat his lunch, pulling the door open, and getting to use his big sharp knife, Waldo just reached through the window and grabbed him by the throat and squeezed.

It had been interesting, Waldo guessed, to watch the guy's eyes open wide, and his mouth, and watch his tongue come out, and hear the funny noises he made. It might even have been fun, if he hadn't been such a little skinny guy, who hardly could struggle at all. But it didn't give him that tingle he got all over, and especially down *there*, when he saw bright red blood spurting from somebody.

Waldo had seen a man run over by a car once, he'd been very close when it happened. Some of the man's blood had gotten on him. Geez, that had been exciting. Waldo had shaken all over, felt like he was going to explode. And he did, sort of. He'd asked Leo about it, but Leo just laughed at him. He asked

Georgia and Ramon and Roy and Candy, but Candy was the only one who'd tried to explain it to him. Waldo hadn't understood her too well. He couldn't see how what had happened to him had to do with men and women together.

There were a lot of things Waldo didn't understand. This whole business about the no blood. Ambulance guys get blood on them. Waldo knew that firsthand, because way back when he was thirteen, when Ma showed him about how exciting blood was, when she hit him with the rolling pin for playing with his thing, just came into his room, caught him just playing, called him dirty, and hit him with the rolling pin, and the blood rolled down him in a hot sweet wave, all over his body, and Ma jumping up and down in her nightgown . . .

Waldo stood with his eyes closed, seeing it happen again. Then Georgia swore at him and told him to get on with it.

"Sorry," Waldo said, and got on with the business of carrying the man to the green box they put the garbage in. He sighed again. He hoped at least Leo would give him credit for following orders. No blood.

It was a bright day, but this parking lot was behind the hospital and far away. On a Sunday, when all the visitors came, it would get filled up, but on a quiet Wednesday afternoon like today, nobody would notice. That was what Candy told Leo, and Candy should know—she'd been hanging around the hospital for weeks.

Waldo put the body inside the green box (there was a name for it, but Waldo couldn't remember what it was) then closed the lid. He had put the body in gently, facing away from the opening, because to tell the truth, the guy's face had turned a sort of purple-black that was pretty ugly to look at, and he didn't want the person who threw out the garbage to be surprised by it.

Georgia was standing by the back door of the ambulance tapping her foot impatiently. She was a small woman with short dark hair and the kind of nose that looked square from the side, and her neck was all ropy, and stuff jumped around in it when she was yelling.

Georgia wasn't yelling now, but she looked like she wanted to. She was dressed all in white, the way Waldo himself was, and against the white her face looked very red.

"Hurry up," she snapped. "I've already taken care of the intern."

She opened the door a little to let him see. Still no blood. Waldo was disappointed. It would have been okay for Georgia to make all the blood she wanted from the doctor guy who rode in the back of the ambulance, but she didn't. Her and her stupid ice pick. Waldo could see it sticking out of the guy's ear.

The doctor guy was black. Waldo always felt funny when they killed a black guy, because the League was supposed to help people who were . . . were *oppressed*. Waldo was very proud to have remembered the word. Black people were oppressed, and poor people and women and lots of other kinds of people, but sometimes they had to kill them. Leo had explained once, but Waldo couldn't understand.

Anyway, he picked up the black guy, and put him in the green box with the purple guy. Waldo laughed at his own joke. He wondered if purple people were oppressed and smiled again. Then he turned to go back to the ambulance so Georgia could tell him what to do next.

But Georgia was coming to meet *him*, and she looked really angry this time. Her face was redder.

"Idiot! You forgot to put this in." She slapped a small plastic rectangle into his hand.

"Oh," Waldo said as he took it. "I'll do it now."

Georgia made a mean face at him but said nothing. Waldo made one more trip to the green box and put the cassette (he was proud of that word, too) with Leo's message to the Pigs on it in with the bodies. It was Leo's message but Georgia's voice.

Waldo looked around slyly. Georgia was in the ambulance; she couldn't see him. Waldo reached into the box and pulled the ice pick from the black guy's ear. He stuck it into the dead guys a few times, but it was no good—an ice pick never made much blood in the first place, and people who were already dead would hardly ever bleed at all.

Waldo wiped the metal on the palm of his left hand, then put it back in the black guy's ear. He went back to the ambulance and got into the cab next to Georgia, who started the motor as soon as Waldo opened the door. Waldo couldn't drive a car. The idea alone scared him.

Now Georgia started to yell at him. She called him a moron. She said the next time Leo insisted on sending Waldo on an errand like this, Leo could go with Waldo himself. She said he'd wasted time, that they were going to be late.

She kept on like that all the way to the club.

Waldo just looked out the windshield and licked contentedly at his hand.

Elizabeth Fane swung a two-fisted backhand into the ball. It rocketed into the tape at the top of the net and plopped down onto the light gray artificial surface of the Lakeside Club's tennis court.

Lindsay Keith was smiling at her, his tan split by his white teeth. "You don't have enough control that way, Liz. Chrissie and Tracy and the rest grew up hitting like that. It's too late for you to start now."

"Shut up, Lindsay," she said firmly. "I've won the club championship two years running, and I'll do it again this year, too. *With* a two-handed backhand."

She shook her head as she walked back to receive service. Lindsay was a fine boy, socially acceptable and all that, but not really too bright. Good in bed, though. And just kinky enough to make him interesting. Still, he had to be handled.

"Just serve," she told him.

She watched him rake his sweaty black hair with his fingers, smiling indulgently all the while. The twit. A lock of Liz's own straight brown hair, two tones lighter than her summer tan, fell across her eyes. She tucked it back under her headband, crouched, rested the head of her racket lightly against her left hand, and waited for Lindsay to serve.

Soon after the rally started, Liz caught on to what Lindsay was up to. He wouldn't hit to her backhand at all, wouldn't let her practice what she'd set out to. Liz called him a bastard under her breath, and resolved to put a two-handed backhand shot into Lindsay's eye socket at the earliest possibility.

She was a better player than he was; it was inevitible that

eventually she'd be able to jockey him into a position where he had to hit the ball to her left. When it happened, Liz very nearly did put it in his eye socket. As it was, Lindsay managed to duck and turn slightly, so that the ball hit him on the temple.

He staggered, but he didn't fall. He held his hands to his head, and stood bent over, cursing. Liz stood with hands on hips, waiting for him to get over it.

Lindsay glared an accusation at her. "You did that on *purpose*," he said.

Liz asked him impatiently if he was all right.

"It hurts," Lindsay said.

"Maybe that will teach you not to fool around when I'm doing something important."

"Personally, *darling*," Lindsay said. He had to grind the words out. "Personally, I thought you would have learned to take a joke in twenty-two years of living." He took his hand from his face, revealing a round, red spot that showed promise of becoming a major bruise. Liz felt a twinge of regret. A little one.

It didn't show in her voice. "You promised to help me work on this. Now, are you going to keep your word, or should I look for somebody else?"

A voice behind her said, "Liz dear?"

"Mother," Liz said. "Don't you have your aerobic dancing today?"

"No, dear, I have to skip it this afternoon, remember? I have an appointment with Dr. Welkenheimer." Dr. Welkenheimer was the busiest, richest, and incidentally the handsomest gynecologist in the area. The fact that he was also a good doctor was an unasked-for bonus to his patients.

"I'd asked you to drive me, do you remember, dear? My car is in the garage." Sheila Fane pushed her oversized dark sunglasses up on her hair and smiled sweetly at her daughter.

"Of course I remember, Mom. I drove you here this morning, don't you remember?"

"You're right. Silly of me. Oh, well, it doesn't matter. You go on with your game—hello, Lindsay, have you hurt yourself?"

Lindsay shook his head and grunted a greeting.

Liz looked at him, decided he was a lost cause for the day,

and sighed. "No, Mom, it's all right, I'll drive you. Do I have time to take a shower first?"

Still smiling, Sheila Fane looked at her watch. "If it's a quick one."

"It will be, I just want to hose off. I smell like a herd of buffalo."

"Elizabeth!" her mother said. It was her invariable reaction when Liz was unrefined in public. Then she smiled, as if amused with herself for a lack of sophistication. Today's young woman would make this kind of joke.

Liz smiled back, kissed her mother on the cheek, then jogged off to the locker room. She showered quickly but thoroughly—as long as she was going, she might as well have the doctor examine her, too. Liz frequently slipped in on her mother's appointments. The doctor never seemed to mind, and it saved Liz the trouble of remembering the appointments.

Liz lathered, rinsed, and lathered again, enjoying the feeling of the sponge against her body. She liked everything about her body except her hips (they were, in Liz's opinion, hopelessly bony) and those two ridiculous bands of white in the middle of her tan. She simply had to find a place to sunbathe nude.

She shook water from her hair as she emerged from the shower. She felt much better—good enough, almost, to forgive Lindsay. She always felt better after a shower. Besides, one couldn't confront one's gynecologist smelling like a herd of buffalo, now, could one?

It took Liz a minute to dress—panties, shorts, halter top—and another ten to dry her short brown hair. She rejoined her mother less than twenty minutes after she'd left her.

"My," Sheila Fane said, "that was even quicker than I expected. We'll have plenty of time with the doctor now." They walked through the dining room to the entrance that fronted on the county road. Liz's car was in the lot across from it.

"I can't tell you how much I appreciate this," the older woman said. "Taxis are so unreliable."

"It's all right mother," Liz said. "I'm glad to do it." There was the slightest edge of impatience in her voice. Her mother's relentless politeness got on her nerves sometimes.

"Perhaps you can get back together with Lindsay again later," Sheila Fane suggested.

"I don't think so, Mother. I think I'll find something much more interesting to do with myself this evening."

The fat-faced old cow wanted more ice in her drink. Ramon wondered how she could tell the difference; surely the seven cocktails she'd had already should have made her mouth numb.

But apparently not. "Please, Raul"—he was known as Raul here—"tell them *lots of ice,* not two lousy lumps. Tell them it's for *me.*"

Ramon smiled brightly at her. "Yes, ma'am. I'll tell them."

"There's a good boy," she said contentedly, and went back to grazing on her salad.

Ramon could feel her watching him as he walked away; felt her gaze boring into his ass like laser beams. The short white jackets, the tight black pants—he knew why they made the uniforms like that. It was so old women who sat around these places could drool at the "good boys" they hired to bring them drinks and salads. Black good boys and brown good boys, tamed jungle dwellers.

Ramon was brown, his body small and hard like a jockey's. He had black curly hair, and a smile that experimentation had shown could increase his tips up to forty percent. He'd been working here for a month now, since the operation had begun, and in that time he'd been propositioned by five drunken women. He'd begun to run out of excuses to keep them off.

He never used to want or need excuses. When he had first started to work, at a place very much like this, not far from New York City, he'd been glad to make the ladies happy. Ramon had been only fifteen then, but the women had seemed younger, too. He'd been only too glad to make them happy when they wanted, take their money, bring their drinks.

Ramon could almost hate his younger self now. When Leo had first made the plan and suggested Ramon could work inside at the club, Ramon had refused angrily. He had been sufficiently degraded in his youth; his father had had his manhood destroyed, been turned into a grinning nothing, a lackey. Ramon would not willingly go back to that kind of life.

It was only when Leo had told him how much the plan depended on him, how he, Ramon, would get to fire the shot, that he had agreed to go along with it.

He was just leaving the bar when he looked at his watch and saw that the time had come. Ramon smiled as he abandoned the now ice-filled glass on a nearby table. *Let the old cow wonder what happened to her drink.* He walked rapidly across the dining room, leaving through the large glass doors by the Olympic-sized pool. He pulled a towel-wrapped object from where he'd hidden it in a bush. He nearly sprinted around the north wing of the club, smiling at the members at poolside but politely declining to take any orders. He would never, he thought, take orders from the likes of them again.

Past the pool, he broke into a run and reached his position exactly on time, hidden by the corner of the building, with a clear view of the entrance to the parking lot across the road. Right on schedule.

Schedule or not, though, he was almost too late. They were already in sight.

Ramon recited Spanish curses to himself. A small miscalculation in timing was probably inevitable, as Leo had said, but this was a bad sign—no one was supposed to be *too early*. That could ruin the whole plan.

Ramon took a deep breath. Well, by the Virgin, if the plan was to be ruined, it would not be ruined by him. He unwrapped his parcel, and pulled out the air gun.

He brushed some towel fuzz from the dull black metal of the barrel. He didn't want anything on the gun that might jam it. Then, from the pocket of his too-tight black pants, he worked loose the pillbox that held his ammunition. Three darts nestled in the box like shiny brown insects.

The insects had silver snouts—hollow hypodermic needles Candy had stolen from the hospital. The bodies were gelatin capsules filled with a powerful and fast-acting narcotic. The tails, one green, one blue, one red, were the nylon brushes from the tails of the .22 caliber darts that were the air gun's usual ammunition.

Ramon knew they worked; at Leo's orders, he had shot one into Waldo, and that great mindless hulk had keeled over in less than a minute. The only question now was whether he could put one in the proper target.

There were people around, going to and from the parking lot, but they'd expected that. Part of the reason for the ambulance was so they could get the target away in plain sight while delaying suspicion.

Ramon watched the two women as they walked to the parking lot. They were remarkably alike. The mother was a little taller, her daughter a bit more tan. Both had the same hair, the color of dark honey, the same lithe build, the same calm, strong features. The country club look.

Ramon took aim. *Well,* he thought, *let's start wiping that calm, superior expression off a few faces.*

They were turning to walk into the lot now, directly away from Ramon. The mother was slightly ahead. *Perfect.*

Ramon waited for two old men carrying tennis rackets to get of of his way. He took aim on Liz Fane's lovely bottom, and pulled the trigger.

And missed.

Ramon started to sweat. He opened the breech of the air gun, fumbled for another homemade tranquilizer dart and dropped the box on the ground, spilling the darts. Fighting panic as he began to pick them up, he had to be careful not to stick *himself* with one, or he would have some very difficult questions to answer when the club groundsmen found him lying here passed out with an air gun in his hand.

Ramon laughed at the idea in spite of himself. He was all right as soon as he did. He found one of the darts, the blue one, and gave up looking for the other. Thanks to his fumble, he'd only have time for one more shot before Liz Fane was out of range, anyway.

Ramon loaded, aimed, and fired in one smooth process, without thinking. The air gun made a noise like spitting.

This time it worked. Ramon heard the rich girl say *"Oh!"* at the same time he saw her reach for the back of a tanned thigh.

Right now, she'd be wondering what the wet stuff on her fingers was if it wasn't blood. She wouldn't know it was a drug, splattered on her body by the impact, the same impact that would force enough of the tranquilizer through the needle to knock her out.

It was happening now. Mrs. Fane had turned at her daughter's cry, and was now standing motionless, expressionless, as Liz waved like a willow in the breeze and then collapsed.

Ramon watched for a second, then went inside. Somebody, after all, would be needed to call an ambulance, once the word spread about poor Miss Fane's attack.

"How many Valium did you take?" Clifford Driscoll said. He put just the right mixture of concern and confidence into his voice. The people who called the Life Line had to be handled delicately.

"Four—no, fifteen," the voice on the other end said. Sleepiness was starting to take the edge off her panic.

"How long ago?"

"Couple minutes."

"All right, then. Angela? Listen carefully to what I'm about to tell you. Give me your address."

"No." She'd been adamant about that since the beginning of the phone call. Wouldn't tell him her last name, either. She wanted him to save her life, but he was going to have to work for it.

"Please?"

"No, I told you."

"Okay, forget it for now. Angela, I want you to—"

"Don't you want to know why I'm doing this? That's why I called, so I could tell you why I'm dying. Don't you want to listen?"

"Not now," Driscoll said. He heard Delia, who was sitting at the next console, inhale sharply, shocked. She did that every time Driscoll departed from the litany they'd learned before coming to work here. Always Listen to Their Troubles, that was a big one.

"Do this first," Driscoll went on. "Go to the nearest sink, and drink three big glasses of water. Don't hang up the phone. Just come back as soon as you do it."

"I don't want to drink water! I want to *die!*" Driscoll could hear the crying start.

"You see, Angela," he said gently, "I want to hear your troubles, but your voice is all clogged up. Go get the water, and it will make it easier for us to talk. Just leave the phone off the hook."

Delia let her breath go. Cliff was always surprising her. When he'd come to work here four months ago, she was intrigued by him, and attracted by his dark, intense looks; he wasn't handsome, exactly, but the dark eyes above the beard got your attention. Still, there was something about him, maybe those eyes, maybe the set of his broad shoulders, that made her decide there and then that she wanted nothing to do with him. That's why it was so surprising when he got her into bed within the week, and even more surprising when he moved in with her.

He was maddening. He broke all sorts of rules, but somehow he always got away with it.

Just the way, Delia reflected, he was going to get away with *this*. By sending her away from the phone, Cliff had insured that if his caller were to pass out, the line would remain open long enough to effect a trace. And if she actually managed to drink the water, it would dilute the drug, and maybe save her life.

Delia liked it, saving lives. Maybe she and Cliff would celebrate tonight. She smiled. Every time with Cliff was a celebration—maybe that was why she always forgave him. He seemed to know exactly how to please her, but he never did it exactly the same way twice.

But Cliff was talking again.

"Did you get a chance to drink the water?" he asked. "Good girl. Your voice sounds much better. Now tell me what the trouble is."

Angela took a breath with a catch in it, a sort of half sob. "I'm engaged to this guy, and I thought—I thought—"

"Angela, hold it a second," Driscoll said.

"Wha—what's the matter?" The girl's voice was slurred now, and getting sloppier by the second.

"I'm sorry, but I forgot your address."

"Oh," Angela said, then gave it to him.

Delia heard it over the monitor and had an ambulance dispatched almost before Angela had finished giving him her apartment number.

Driscoll kept talking to an increasingly incoherent Angela, until at last there was a little commotion on the other end of the line. The phone fell, and a male voice said, "Okay, we just got here, she collapsed as soon as she saw us. I think we can fix her up."

"Terrific," Driscoll said. Delia saw the light go out of his eyes as he disconnected the line and took off his earphone.

"Cliff," she said, "that was wonderful."

"Oh, sure," Driscoll said. "Another misfit kept alive to pollute the gene pool. You want some coffee?"

"Sometimes I just don't understand you at all," Delia said.

"It's probably not worth the effort. I'm going across the street to get some coffee, want some?"

Delia looked at him sadly, then gave up and nodded. "Sure," she said. "You know how I like it."

"Right," Driscoll said. He walked out whistling some cheery music. Delia sat waiting for the next call.

They were waiting for him outside. Driscoll saw them before he left the building, recognized them even through the metal security screen over the window in the door.

The Congressman's men. They had to be. They might dress in leather jackets and try to look like punks, or in rumpled clothes and try to look like drunks, but nothing could hide their general air of competence or the clear-eyed, vaguely handsome face they all seemed to have. Driscoll wondered, not for the first time, if the Congressman had gotten control of a genetics plant somewhere and was cloning these guys wholesale. The Congressman was a great one for experiments.

Driscoll stood there holding the door handle while he thought about things he might do. He could turn around and go back upstairs, forget the coffee completely. Delia would be confused and unhappy, but he'd gotten her used to that. Unfortunately, these two outside would simply wait until morning. They might see Delia with Driscoll and leave him alone for her sake, but they might not. She might be an idealistic, masochistic dreamer, but she deserved better treatment than being killed because she walked out of a building with Clifford Driscoll.

He could try leaving by another door. He laughed at himself as soon as he thought of that one. The Congressman's men were pros. They'd have all the exits covered. Worse, if Driscoll tried to sneak out the back way, they'd know he was on to them.

The only thing that made any sense at all was to walk out as if he didn't have a care in the world, and hope the men outside weren't ready to make their move just yet.

Driscoll would keep walking, that's all. He'd disappear. He'd done it before. He didn't want to go back. He'd kill these guys if he had to, but he wasn't going back.

Driscoll backed up a few steps, and walked briskly toward the door. He grabbed the handle again, pulled it open, and strode into the dark streets of Scranton. He kept himself from looking at the punk and the drunk by concentrating on the lights of the diner, walking quickly toward them as though a cup of coffee would save his life.

The night was hot and humid; the street seemed to be coated with something sticky that made it an effort to take the next step. Driscoll was beginning to feel sticky all over.

They waited until he was halfway across the street, then one of them called, "*Driscoll!*"

A feeling like a slash from a cold razor sliced down Driscoll's spine, but he didn't flinch or break stride. At least that's what he told himself.

The natural thing to do would be to take a quick look at

them. Of course. Middle of the night, back street, somebody yells—anybody would look, no matter what his name was. Driscoll gave a quick glance over his shoulder, then resumed walking.

The glance had been enough. They were beginning to follow him.

They were keeping up the charade, though. The drunk walked with a wobble, and his voice was slurred as he said, "Mr. Driscoll, hold on a second! Fella told me to give you something."

Driscoll kept walking. It was a wide street—the curb seemed to be in another country, with the door of the diner a frontier beyond that. The drunk kept talking loudly.

For just a second, Driscoll wondered if he might be mistaken. If he was being overcautious. Then he decided, so what. For as long as he could remember, it had been drummed into him that it was *impossible* to be overcautious.

Then it came to him, with the instinct born of training and practice. Why should an agent making a hard touch make a lot of noise? *To cover some other noise.*

As soon as the thought came to him, Driscoll heard the other noise under the rantings of the drunk—soft, quiet footfalls. Someone in sneakers coming rapidly across the street.

Driscoll was fairly confident they didn't want to kill him, though he might have preferred it if they did, if they just got it over with quickly. If they *had* wanted to kill him, they could have done it already, with a silenced bullet in the back. That was the standard method.

That gave Driscoll his only advantage. He was ready to kill these two and nine others like them, if it would get him out of this.

He waited until the last possible second, then spun rapidly clockwise, elbow out. A welcome pain shot up along his funny bone to the tips of his fingers as the elbow connected. A quick look over his shoulder showed him he'd miscalculated the pseudo-punk's height. The man was groaning, holding a broken jaw when he should have been choking to death with a smashed larynx.

Driscoll didn't mind. His victim would be out of action for the few minutes Driscoll would need.

There was no pretense now, no casual walk to the diner. He went into a low sprint, making himself a smaller target for bullets that didn't come. He stiff-armed the door to the diner, then launched himself into a sliding dive across the linoleum.

Sometimes the smart move makes you feet silly after you've done it. Driscoll scrambled to his feet to see that except for Louie, the counterman, he was alone in the diner; the agents he'd been expecting weren't there.

"Hey, Cliff," Louie said, "what's the matter? Did you trip or something?"

Driscoll didn't bother to answer. He ran to the counter, planted his hands on it, and vaulted over. "Back door, Louie. Quick."

Louie was puzzled, but he wasn't about to mess with a lunatic, especially since he'd already passed by the cash register. "Sure," he said. "Let's go."

Driscoll rolled his eyes. "Not you. Just tell me where it is."

"Oh. Sure. Through the kitchen." He pointed; Driscoll went.

The cook was asleep in a chair and never noticed him at all. The young bearded man didn't pay much attention to him, either. He was too busy making plans.

It would be impossible to get a taxi in this part of town at this time of night. His own car (Delia's, actually) would be watched. Buses, the airport, the train station, all too far away, all too irregular to be of much use, especially if he had to wait around for the next departure. Driscoll made a mental promise to himself that from here on he would memorize all public transportation schedules for whatever town he happened to be in.

He'd have to steal a car, and quickly. That would give him—he looked at his watch and saw it was three-thirty A.M.—a minimum of three hours driving before the car was reported hot, maybe more.

He'd definitely have to ditch the car by seven o'clock, but he could be in Ohio by then, if he crowded the speed limits. When stores were open, he could change a few more of the diamonds hidden in the heel of his shoe to cash. With the cash, he'd get new documents, with the documents he could go to a new place, and the chase would start again.

At the far side of the kitchen there was a door, three steps, then another door. Driscoll threw open the second door, breaking the latch in the process, and stepped into the alley behind the diner.

He made it five feet into the alley before the high intensity flashlight beam blinded him. Driscoll covered his eyes, then turned to run back into the diner.

"Don't do that," said a warm, deep voice. "I'd have to shoot you with this thing, boy. Wouldn't hurt you none—it's one of those tranquilizer dart things—but I need you awake."

Driscoll froze. He knew that voice, and he knew that the owner of it never, *ever* worked an operation in the field.

"Congressman," Driscoll said. His voice sounded hoarse to him, so he tried again. "Congressman."

He turned around again. The flashlight was pointed at the wall now, splashing enough light from the white-painted brick for Driscoll to make out the handsome face, and the distinguished gray-and-white hair above it. It also let him make out the nasty-looking weapon in his hand. Neither the gun nor the light wavered.

"In the flesh, Clifford," the Congressman drawled. "That *is* what you're callin' yourself these days, ain't it? Clifford Driscoll? We ain't tracked down the wrong man and come across you by luck have we?"

"No. Driscoll's my name now."

"Good as any, I suppose," the Congressman said magnanimously. "I'll call you that. Hell, you can even keep usin' it. Ain't got time to fix up new papers, anyway. Did you kill those two boys out front?"

"No," Driscoll said. "I broke a jaw."

The Congressman clicked his teeth. "I hope you ain't slippin'. Missed on the elbow trick you like so much, didn't you?"

Against his will, against all rationality, the man who called himself Clifford Driscoll felt ashamed, felt like an idiot because he'd failed. He'd only maimed a man, instead of killing him. It wasn't the first time Driscoll had felt that way; that feeling, and the self-hatred it engendered, were what had started him running.

"Well," the Congressman said, "it don't make no difference. We'll patch him up and keep him at work in the Agency. Still, it would have been nice for the old man here if you'd done them in. They managed to get told stuff they're too stupid to know. It's a problem. I don't like problems in my Agency."

Driscoll almost laughed. "I'm a problem," he said. "Why don't you have somebody do away with me?"

The Congressman *did* laugh. "Can't do that! That's against policy. You know better than that. If I could just haul off and have those two boys done in, it would make my life simpler all around." He took a step closer. "Besides, you ain't no problem, boy, you're a *re*source. A damn important one." He waved the gun toward the mouth of the alley. "Now come on, boy, we got us a little trip to take, and you're gonna take it, conscious or otherwise. We got work."

"You mean *you've* got work," Driscoll told him. "It must be something hot to get you out of Washington."

"Hot enough to scorch the President's britches, but he don't even know about it yet. I'll tell you about it once we get on the road."

"You can talk all you want to, but I'm out of it now. Kill me, Congressman, after you've told me. Kindly spare me that bullshit about 'policy.' Lock me up somewhere, with your tame Cubans for jailers. But I'm never working for the Agency again."

For the first time, the gun came down. The Congressman walked up to Driscoll and put his hand on his shoulder. Driscoll thought, *I could kill him now. I could put my hands on his throat and strangle him, here in a back alley in Scranton, Pennsylvania.* Driscoll made fists and shut his eyes. He shook off the Congressman's hand.

The Congressman put it back. "That's enough of that kind of talk, boy. You *got* to do this; you were born to do it—"

"You have the *nerve* to say that to me!"

"It's a simple fact. You were born to do it; ain't nobody else has a *chance* to pull this off, and it *must* be pulled off."

The Congressman's face lost all signs of deception. It wasn't his "sincere" face, the one he wore during those regrettable interludes when he had to make sure he got re-elected. It was his *real* face, animated by nothing but deeply felt belief. Driscoll was sure he was the only human being who had ever seen it.

The Congressman said, "Listen, you can chase around the country, pretendin' you're just like everybody else, tryin' to—hell, I'm fried if I know *what* the hell you're tryin' to do. But go ahead.

"Only not now. Because something's happened that might blow the lid off. The Russians today grabbed hold of the lever that can get them the biggest break in the Cold War they've had yet. It's this simple: Your country needs you, son."

Driscoll looked at him. There was something else he'd never seen in the Congressman's face, but he wasn't sure what it was. He decided at last that it was a ploy. He'd go where the Congressman wanted him to, but he wouldn't do the work. The dirty work. Work for the Agency was always dirty.

"Well, son?" the Congressman said.

"Well, what?" He shrugged off the hand again and walked away. After a few steps, he looked back at the Congressman, who had the gun up and aimed at him.

Driscoll smiled at him wearily. "Are we going to talk? Then let's go talk. And may you fry forever in hell. Father."

The Congressman smiled a that's-my-boy smile and led his son out of the alley.

It seemed to Driscoll that his father had always chosen small rooms for briefings. The Congressman said it was because a small room was easier to check for bugs; Driscoll didn't buy it. It was a matter of tactics. The Congressman tended to dominate any room he was in; the smaller the room, the more powerful the domination.

Aside from the fact that this room was in a Winnebago heading down Interstate 80, this was no different. The Congressman had his personality on full power, and Driscoll, who should have been used to it, still felt its influence.

"How'd you find me this time?" the younger man asked wearily.

"Contact lenses. We got your prescription, and we ran it down. You were smart to avoid gettin' lenses for both eyes at the same place, but you were dumb to buy assorted colors for the same eye in the same town. Makes a pattern, easy to spot, if you work it hard enough. I got a pair of your old spectacles with me, if you prefer."

Driscoll smiled ruefully. The old buzzard was still the best. And had him down pat, too. "Sure," he said. "Thanks. How long did it take you to find me this time?"

The Congressman narrowed his gray eyes. "Six little days, boy. Listen, that ain't good enough. I'm gettin' goddam tired of havin' to put five good boys to work findin' you all the time so I'll know where you're at when I need you."

"Then stop doing it. I want to have a *life*, Father dear. You planned me, trained me to be a monster, but it didn't take. I'll keep running until you get tired of chasing me."

The Congressman looked at his son and sighed. *Well*, he thought, *can't nobody's bright ideas all turn out perfectly.* And the boy did seem like a bright idea at the time, thirty years ago or more, when the Agency laid hold of that sneaky little thing who'd been screwing (in every sense of the word) secrets out of the Pentagon while working there as a secretary under the American-sounding name of Becky Underwood. Mr. Dulles once said (behind closed doors, of course) that little Becky had done more to hurt us during the Korean war than anybody outside of Mao Tse Tung.

But they caught her. Finally. By a fluke, no fault of Becky's. Of course, there was no question of a trial—too embarrassing. The plan was to make her talk, then have her just sort of disappear. That kind of thing was a lot easier to take care of in those days.

Only they couldn't break her.

They tried persuasion, hypnosis, torture. They tried to make deals. They promised her asylum. They promised her she'd be exchanged when the time came. She spit in their faces, sometimes literally.

The Congressman—he was the General then—got more frustrated and angrier by the minute. He had never been a man who would let go of something until he'd gotten some use out of it, but it looked like in this case he'd have to. It got so he went to sleep at night and woke up the next morning thinking of little Becky Underwood.

Part of the problem was he couldn't think of her as a Russian. She looked American, talked, acted, and even seemed to *think* American. There had been rumors, about this time, of the "American" towns the Russians maintained to train their agents for deep cover. It was obvious that Becky had been one of the star graduates. Not that they got her to admit anything like that. Or anything else. They especially wanted to get her to tell them about a "Cronus Project" they'd gotten wind of, but she just laughed at them.

Another part of the problem was the grudging admiration the General was developing for the woman. Here was an agent who knew what the business was all about—someone as smart, as tough, as dedicated as the General himself.

And more. She was a woman who liked the game, loved it, really, with the same passion the General did. He could see it in her eyes during the interrogations. She was doomed, and she knew it, but she was having the time of her life. She loved the gamble, no matter what the stakes.

If only, the General found himself thinking, *she really* were *an American. What a team we would be. What a power.*

It was her code name that gave him the idea. They'd intercepted it along with the Cronus Project business. Her code name was "Mother Russia." The more the General thought about it, the better he liked it. Her talents, her dedication, her *genius*, would never work for America. All right. Her flesh and blood would.

The General began to sleep with her, regularly. Little Becky went along; she'd been able to accomplish a lot by sleeping with men. Maybe she thought she'd be able to turn the General to her side. Of course, she should have known better, but maybe she was as stubborn as he was about getting something positive out of every situation. That was her mistake.

The General's mistake had been to stop sleeping with her after she became pregnant. She caught on then, and the battle was on, an eight month nightmare.

The Russians knew her well, knew she'd never break, so they neglected to provide her with a cyanide pill. That was *their* mistake. The General and the whole Washington staff of the Agency devoted themselves to seeing that little Becky didn't manage to hurt herself or her baby.

God knows she tried. They had to stop giving her silverware; they had to take away shoelaces, and anything else she might use to hurt herself. As the pregnancy progressed, she stopped eating, and they had to feed her intravenously.

It reached the point where they had to keep Becky tied spread-eagle on a hospital bed. But she beat them anyway. She smashed her brains out against the iron piping at the head of the bed. After thirty-one weeks, she'd died, convinced she'd won.

Only she hadn't. She was found in time by a nurse who'd come to check the IV. She found the bloody wreck Becky had made of herself and called the doctor, who happened at that moment to be talking to the General about what he saw as the questionable morality of what they were doing.

The doctor had no questions, though, about the morality of saving the baby. With the General looking on, beaming behind his mask, the doctor performed an emergency Caesarian section, and delivered Becky of a squalling baby boy.

As they were rushing him to the incubator, the nurse suggested they call him Macduff, but the General told her to hush up such nonsense.

Time passed; things happened. The General personally supervised the boy's education, and the youngster took to it like a frog to a lily pad. As the General had known he would all along. At the age of fifteen, the boy worked out a way to feed false information to the Red Chinese that the Agency was still using. When his son reached seventeen, the General put him to work, sent him to few fancy eastern colleges to infiltrate student radicals, co-opt them, make them unwittingly serve the General's purposes.

This was about the time the General became the Congressman. Watergate and all that happy horse manure had made Congress into a bunch of old ladies, who wanted to hold the President's hand over every little thing in the espionage field. There was no way the General was going to let them get away with that. He found a little jerkwater district in his home state, pretended it was a Central American republic, rigged the election, and wound up in Congress himself. A little judicious blackmailing got him put on all the right committees; specifically, it got him the chairmanship of the Intelligence Oversight Committee. The rest was simple. The Agency still ran; he still ran it; and he did it with a minimum of interference.

Unfortunately, all that messing around had left him too busy to keep an eye on his son. Something happened; could have happened to anybody, really, but it wound up with a couple of people getting killed, including this gal Clifford (might as well get used to calling him that for the time being) had been sort of sweet on.

Well, what the hell, he'd had to make her *talk* hadn't he? She'd planted a nail-bomb under the goddamn chapel steps, Clifford had to find out where it was. How was he supposed to know she'd have that kind of reaction to hypnotic drugs?

The worst part of it was that the boy convinced himself he didn't want to play the game anymore, and that couldn't be tolerated. The Congressman had talked to his son, but he couldn't make a dent in him. His mother's damn stubborn Russian blood coming out in him, or something. Though he knew nothing about his mother. The Congressman didn't want that confusing him.

So the congressman let him run. Until he needed him. Then he had to track him down, give him a figurative kick in the ass, and bring the boy's natural inclinations back to the top.

Because that was another way Clifford here took after little Becky. Deep down, he loved the game. The higher the stakes the better.

And what makes you so ornery and miserable, my son, the Congressman thought, *is that you know it.*

". . . So we're puttin' three things together, here," the Congressman said a little while later. "First, there's that kidnappin'. You need to hear any more about that?"

Driscoll blinked, then opened his eyes wide. He'd been thinking about Delia. He'd told his father they'd have to go easy on her—get her quietly out of town somewhere until "Clifford Driscoll" was done with his work. "It's been fifteen hours or so since they got this Elizabeth Fane, right?"

"'Bout that."

"No ransom demand? Or any sort of a demand? Any progress at all?"

"Not so's you'd notice," the Congressman said. He pulled a contraband Cuban cigar from an inside pocket, cut the end off with his pocket knife, and lit it. "Don't necessarily mean anything. Lettin' the family sweat, is all. Hell, boy, I don't have to tell you this."

"Just making sure. Have the police in—what's this town? Draper?—have they made any progress?"

"Oh, sure, they made progress. They been findin' bodies all over a hospital parkin' lot, and a homemade tranquilizer gun and darts at the country club. That's where I got the idea of greetin' you with one. They found a tape cassette with a message sayin' they killed those two poor bastards, and they'll kill Liz Fane if they have to and to stand by for further demands.

The Congressman bared his teeth in a silent snarl. Cigar smoke leaked slowly through it. It looked as if he were literally burning with anger.

"Ice picks in the ears," the Congressman said. "Strangulation. Witnesses said the people in the ambulance were a woman and a man. Okay, the woman could be anybody. But everybody who got a look at the man said he was a huge feller with red hair. Scars on his head. Baby faced.

"Ah," Driscoll said.

"Ah is right," the Congressman said. "That fellow always

seems to be around a certain person these days. Leo goddamn *Calvin*, boy."

Driscoll heaved a sigh. Leo Calvin was a one-man plague, a thorn in the Congressman's side for over a decade. Driscoll had crossed his path, but they'd never grappled head on. Leo Calvin was a terrorist, skillful and positively ruthless. He'd started young and never stopped. But one important thing happened along the way—he'd been bought by Moscow. Leo was one of the few terrorists of the early seventies (and Driscoll knew a lot of them) who was honest enough with himself to realize that the politics of the whole thing meant less than nothing. Leo just liked to hear the bombs go off, see the bright flowers of flame.

The Russians gave him money, and pointed out targets. Leo did the rest. Apparently, this had been going on for several years, though (the Congressman said) the Agency had only found out about it recently. The alphabet soup boys in Codes and Ciphers had recently gotten a line on an intercepted message that left no doubt that Calvin had become an old and trusted Comrade. They could convict him any time. If they could only catch him.

Driscoll couldn't make it add up. Rescuing damsels in distress wasn't the Agency's usual kind of job. He said as much.

The Congressman looked grim. "It is when her daddy holds the most important defense contract since little David went into the slingshot business."

"What do you mean?"

"I can't tell you."

"Give it a rest, Congressman." Driscoll was disgusted.

"I can't, boy. You ain't committed yourself yet. Once I tell you, you're in. Till the end."

"Oh, right." Driscoll's face twisted in a rueful grin. "How about that. Come on, you hypocritical old bastard, let's hear it."

"You ought to have more respect for your Daddy, Son."

"Tell me."

"All right. Welcome aboard. Ain't nobody else could do this. I'm not even sure *you* could."

"Enough butter, Congressman. You said it: I'm in. Let's hear it."

"All right. It's called MENTOR, but that don't mean anything. What it is is the slickest missile computer guidance system the world's ever seen. Works on single or multiple warheads. I've seen the tests—as soon as this thing goes into production, we'll be able to drop a warhead into the Chairman's bowl of borscht. You know why World War Three ain't happened yet?"

Driscoll knew what his father wanted to hear, but he was already angry at himself for being sucked in. "Dumb luck," he suggested.

The Congressman puffed on his cigar. "I can't deny that's a part of it," he said.

"The great work done by patriots such as yourself."

The Congressman jabbed the lit end of his cigar in Driscoll's direction. "You're laughin' behind that beard, boy, but there's a lot of truth in that, too. This is important work we do, and the sooner you realize that, the happier you're gonna be."

"I'm glad my happiness is important to you."

"Hell, you're my son, ain't you?" the Congressman said. "But to hell with that stuff." He waved a hand, sending the stuff to hell. "I'll tell you why we've been spared atomic war so far. It's because can't nobody be sure they can get away with strikin' first. Pre-emptive strike they call it. You shoot first, knock out all the other side's A-bombs, then finish them off at your leisure.

"Only trouble is, if you miss a few times, you're in a heap of trouble cause it don't take but one or two fusion fastballs comin' back to make a hash of a beautiful day."

"This was homework for me in kindergarten," Driscoll said. "MENTOR changes that?"

"You got it. This can make a pre-emptive strike ninety-nine percent effective, according to the computer simulators. That's way better than anything either of us have now."

The Congressman leaned back in his chair and blew out a gray cloud of cigar smoke. "And this girl's daddy, Herbert Fane, runs the company that's got the contract to manufacture the main circuit for MENTOR.

"The pressure on Fane is gonna be immense, now that Leo Calvin's got his little girl. And the Russians got Leo in their pockets. You know . . . uh, Clifford, that's why I need you handlin' this for me. I need the best, and I need someone I can trust completely. When it comes to those qualifications, you, my boy, are *it*."

"I'm touched," Driscoll said. As always, he liked the way the Congressman picked his words. *Handle things*. Cute.

"I tell you, boy, I'm afraid of what the ransom demand's going to be."

Driscoll raised an eyebrow. The Congressman was *never* afraid and never pretended to be. "So my job is to *handle* things so that the father doesn't hand over the secret of MENTOR to get his daughter back."

"Hell, no. They got the secret of MENTOR already."

"Ahh," Driscoll said.

"Dawn just broke for you, didn't it, boy? Hellfire, if the Russians didn't already have the damn designs, I'd tell Fane to hand it over to them, get his girl back (if that animal hasn't beaten her and drugged her and raped her and God knows what all into a sack of poke salad), and God bless him. There ain't no secrets anymore. Too many people in Washington with their goddamn consciences. They work for the government, but they follow their own *higher instincts*."

The Congressman's tone showed what he thought of higher instincts. "Hell, they'll go right from the National Security Council to *CBS News,* right to any old body on the street.

"No son, the only thing we got on the Russians with MENTOR is a three month lead goin' into production. Herbert Fane could make that evaporate like spit on a hot sidewalk. Send his workers out on strike with some stupid labor move. Get his factory sabotaged. We'd never get another place geared up to turn out the circuits in time. Do I have to tell you why we can't let the Russians have that system first?"

Driscoll shook his head. The cold logic of espionage had been another kindergarten lesson. You must base your actions on the adversaries' *capabilities*. You must assume that as soon as Russia can launch a preemptive strike with impunity, she *will*, *detente* and arms limitation talks notwithstanding. Once the United States had the system, they would be in a better position to talk to the Russians about MENTOR. That three month lead was also vital because it gave the geniuses who came up with MENTOR a chance to come up with something to counteract it.

And on and on. With slight modifications, the Russians had to be thinking the same way. The balance of terror must not tip, but if it does, it must be on your side of the scale. Driscoll wasn't sure he bought it all, and he was damn sure that even if he did buy it, he didn't like it. But there it was. A law of nature in the world he'd been born to.

"So what exactly is my job, Father?" Driscoll asked.

"You know what it is."

"I want to hear you say it."

"All right. Your job is to keep this girl's daddy from doin' anything that will imperil the completion of MENTOR's production schedule."

"Keep him from paying that as a ransom."

"Keep the Russians from catchin' up and passin' our schedules. Yes."

"So I'm to get the girl back."

"I don't care. Get her back, get Calvin and his boys to kill her. Kill her yourself. But don't drag this on. We ain't got the time for a two-year Patty Hearst fiasco. You do this *fast*, boy, whatever you do."

"I'll need help."

"Anybody you need. Unlimited budget."

"I want a utility man and a tapeman. The odds are pretty high that the ransom demands or whatever will come as tapes in Elizabeth Fane's own voice—much more dramatic that way. They'll want to make this play as a terrorist kidnapping, if they can. They'll be doing things pretty much along the lines of Hearst. I can make that work for us."

The Congressman fought to suppress a grin. His boy was back to normal.

"I'll also," Driscoll said, "want a lamb."

The Congressman grunted.

"You said unlimited budget," his son reminded him.

"I know what I said. You got specific people in mind?"

"I'll give you a list of names right after you tell me what else is on your mind."

"I don't know what you're talkin' about."

Driscoll mimicked his father's accent. "Hell, you're my Daddy, ain't you? I know when you've got something preyin' on you."

That gambit always made the Congressman smile. "For a while there, I was afraid you'd forgotten how to speak your native language, son. But you're right. There's something on my mind. It's a word that turned up in the same message that mentioned Calvin. *Cronus*. Looks like a code name for an operation. Mean anything to you?"

"K-r-o-n-o-s?"

"If you like. The code boys say you can bring it over from the Russian lots of ways. They like C-r-o-n-u-s."

"The code boys like Latin better than Greek," Driscoll said. "Cronus was the god of Time to the ancient Greeks and Romans. He was the father of the gods."

"Yeah, they told me that." The Congressman sighed and crushed out his cigar. "Still, it's appropriate. If this is what I think it is, your friend Leo Calvin is workin' on something the Russians been cookin' up for over thirty years."

Chapter Two

THEY MADE HER BEG FOR FOOD, THEN THEY DIDN'T GIVE her any.

"You've eaten too well, bitch," the woman from the ambulance had said. Her name was Georgia. Liz had seen her grinning face looming above her just before she'd passed out.

Liz whimpered behind her gag. She'd awakened to total darkness, unable to move. For an eternity, she was sure she was blind and paralyzed. It was no great comfort to discover she was bound and locked in a closet.

She'd cried for help; voices told her to shut up. She begged to know where she was, why they'd done this to her. At last, the door opened. Liz had squinted up into the light, into the face of a tall, impossibly thin man who had kicked her and again told her to shut up.

When the fresh pain of the kick had died away, Liz became aware of other pains. The burning where the rope chafed her, the dull ache of bruises from her fall to the pavement. And the pain in places she couldn't possibly have hurt falling down. Liz felt a sudden surge of nausea as she realized what they'd done to her while she was unconscious.

She began to cry, and they stood outside the closet, mocking her. She screamed at them to let her out, to let her go. They laughed. She cursed them, they laughed some more.

Hours went by. The voice of the man who had told her to

shut up (his name was Leo—at least, that's what the other voices called him) asked her if she was hungry.

She'd told him to go to hell, but as time went by, she realized just how hungry she was. The next time he asked her, she said yes.

"Make her beg for it," someone suggested.

Liz said please. It wasn't enough.

"*Pretty* please," said the voice called Waldo. His voice was a man's voice, deep and full, but the words and inflections were a child's.

Liz hesitated, but at last she'd made herself say it.

They weren't happy with that. They'd made her repeat things after them. "I am a fascist pig" was the mildest of them. They made her say hateful things, filthy things about herself.

Finally, the voice called Georgia said, "Open the door." Liz nearly collapsed in relief. Then Georgia pulled Liz's head back by her hair and stuffed a gag in her mouth.

"I'm sick of your voice, Daisy Mae," she hissed. "You've eaten too well already, bitch. On your pig father's money." She slapped a piece of tape over Liz's mouth, and left the closet, laughing.

Leo Calvin smiled at Georgia, congratulating her silently for a job well done. Leo raked some limp white-blond hair back from his forehead with a bony hand. Someone had once told him he resembled an albino Abe Lincoln. He liked that. Leo had a sense of humor. Besides, there were parallels. Lincoln had been a rail-splitter; Leo was a head-splitter. Leo liked that one, too.

Still, there were ways to split heads. One way was simple— he left that kind of thing to Waldo. The other way, the way they were practicing with Miss Fane here, was infinitely more fascinating.

He was going to remake Liz Fane with the time honored techniques of brainwashing. It was already well in progress. The first thing to do was to begin tearing down her self-respect, her money-bred habit of casual arrogance. Make her life too hard for her to deal with. Her begging for food after only twelve hours or so showed how *easy* she would be to break down. Leo had been well-advised about the girl, but the general principle held. The rich ones, the ones who'd had a soft life, always were the easiest.

The next thing to do would be to call her by a new name. Georgia had called her Daisy Mae, and that was as good a choice as any. It carried connotations far from the image Liz Fane had always had of herself, and that was important. Before Leo was through with her, his captive was going to be required to do things Liz Fane would never think of. That wouldn't be a problem for Daisy Mae.

The thing to do now was to get her used to the idea of doing things she never would have done before.

"Roy, are there any of those hamburgers left?"

Roy grunted, and kept looking at the newspaper accounts of the kidnapping. Roy was seventeen; black curly hair, hot green eyes. He reminded Leo of himself at that age; he had the same smouldering anger at the world and everybody in it. He didn't like to take orders; Leo knew that feeling, too. Roy had to be watched.

He walked over to the boy and snatched the paper away from him. "I asked you a question."

"I heard you. You've finally found something for me to do? Fetch you a hamburger? Think I can handle it?"

Leo sighed, then reached down and grabbed the boy by the front of his sweatshirt. He pulled him from his chair, then twisted until Roy began to choke. Nothing dangerous, just a little difficulty breathing.

"Whose house is this?" Leo asked calmly.

"My—my grandfather's." Roy had to make an effort to force the words past the twisted cloth.

"And where's your grandfather?"

"In Florida."

"You grew up in this town, didn't you?"

"Y-you know I did." Roy's green eyes were wide now. They kept darting side to side as if he expected someone to tell him the answers.

"People know you. Idiot." Leo's voice was still smooth as ice. "If they happen to make you, where do you think they'll come look?"

"Here."

"Right. Here. Listen, Roy, you're doing an important job for us." Leo gave the sweatshirt another twist. "You have to buy our food. You have to deal with the salesmen who come to the door. We need you. Do you understand that?"

Roy nodded. His face was red, darkening toward purple.

"Good," Leo said, then smashed the boy across the face with the back of a bony hand. He gave the sweatshirt one last twist, then shoved Roy back down into the chair.

"Something else you have to understand. I don't like to explain things. Makes me angry. Now. Do we have any hamburgers left?"

Roy was rubbing his cheek with one hand, his throat with the other. He looked up at Leo with a mixture of fear and resentment.

"I asked you a question."

"A couple," Roy said. His voice was hoarse.

Leo smiled. "Good. Get one. We're going to feed our prisoner. You get to do it. Do you understand?"

Roy risked a small smile. Leo said, "I see you do."

Roy went to the kitchen and got the hamburger. He came to Leo for instructions, but got only a smile in return. Roy nodded soberly, and walked to the closet.

Liz was awakened by the ungentle hand that ripped the tape from her face. At first she thought it was part of the nightmare she'd drifted into when she'd passed out from weakness and fear. Then she knew it wasn't. This was the *waking* nightmare again.

"Dinner time," said a voice. She didn't have a name for this one yet. It was nasal and contemptuous. It said, "Do you like hamburgers?"

Liz wanted to giggle. Of all the questions. Then she wanted to cry. She was so afraid. So hungry.

"Oh," she said. "Yes, I do."

"Good, Daisy Mae, because that's what we've got for you."

"Thank you," Liz said. "Now, if you could just let me get my hands free . . ."

"No way, piglet. I'll feed you. Only one thing."

"Wha-what's that?"

"Your mouth has to earn it first."

He grabbed her by the hair and pulled her to her knees. Liz cried out. She was about to ask him what in the name of God he wanted, but the slow, tearing noise of a zipper being undone answered her before she could even say the words.

Liz started to cry, tight little screams of frustration and rage and fear. Her tormentor giggled.

He slid down and joined her on the floor of the closet. He put his hands on her and began to slide them around the ropes that held her.

"That's the way it is, Daisy Mae. All we've got on the menu is a two course meal. And I've got all night."

The hands got bolder. Liz continued to cry.

Clifford Driscoll had learned that the secret to really successful deception was to tell as small a lie as possible, then stick to it. If he had tried some elaborate plan to get close to the Fanes, it would have taken too long and probably would have failed.

As it was, he simply shaved off his beard, put on the wire-frame glasses his father had brought him, put on a suit and tie, and showed up at the front gate as Clifford Driscoll of the Defense Department. He showed them nice credentials, and told them he'd been sent from Washington to give any assistance he could in bringing about the safe return of Liz Fane and especially to handle any aspect of the problem that touched on Mr. Fane's MENTOR contract.

The only outright lie in any of that was the part about the Defense Department, and the Congressman already had that covered in Washington in case someone took it into his mind to check.

The guard, a rent-a-cop, posted no doubt to prevent the rest of the family from being kidnapped, looked long and suspiciously at Driscoll before raising his walkie-talkie and calling in to the command post in the house.

With a sour look the cop gave Driscoll back his credentials and opened the gate for him. Driscoll smiled at him and told him to have a nice day.

He was ready for more of the same at the main house, but he got a surprise. A couple of surprises, in fact. The first was the house itself. It was a handsome old colonial, painted a chaste white with blue trim, but it was nothing like a mansion.

The second surprise was the girl who answered the door. His first thought, that Elizabeth Fane had somehow been returned, he dismissed as ridiculous. His second thought, that this was a sister, he knew couldn't be right. The Congressman would have told him.

His third thought was that he'd better stop staring. He was out of practice; if he couldn't control himself better than that, everybody around here was likely to wind up dead. Including himself.

The girl was laughing at him. "No, I'm not. I wish I was. Or I wish she was here to answer the door instead of me. You know what I mean."

"I think so." He reached for his pocket. "I'm Clifford Driscoll. From the Defense Department. I called this morning—or rather my office did."

"Yes, Uncle Herbert has been expecting you. I hope you don't mind waiting a few minutes. He and Aunt Sheila are being consoled by the bishop."

Driscoll could see the differences between this girl and the one in the photograph in his pocket now that the initial shock had worn off. His hostess was taller, darker, and a little older than Liz Fane.

"I get the impression you don't think the bishop is going to be much help, Miss . . . ?"

"Oh, I'm sorry. Payne. Robin Payne. Or at least that's what it is now. There was already a Roberta Fane in Equity, so I had to change it."

She led him into a dark little sitting room that looked so much like the waiting room of a prosperous medical practice, Driscoll half expected her to show him a magazine rack and leave him alone. Instead, she closed the door and sat on an overstuffed chair identical to the one Driscoll had taken and looked at him intently.

"I shouldn't have laughed when you came in," she said. "Liz was my best friend growing up, and she and Uncle

Herbert and Aunt Sheila are the only family I have since my parents died."

"Ah," Driscoll said. "You're her *cousin*. That accounts for the resemblance."

"That's why I laughed—everybody who's come through the door has done a big double take when they see me. Even the bishop, and he's known me since I was a little girl. Of course, he hasn't seen me since I went to New York five years ago, but still. It used to happen back then, too. Even today, we're sometimes mistaken for each other on the phone."

She fingered a string of pearls at her neck. Driscoll had noticed, during his long experience with crises, that people tend to dress up for them, almost as if wanting to look good for the big meeting with disaster. Robin Payne (born Roberta Fane) was more evidence for his theory. She wore a white silk blouse, pearls, a dark gray skirt, and black stockings. Sitting down now, she had eased her feet halfway out of sensible black pumps. There was absolutely nothing wrong with the girl's looks, and in an outfit like that, which let those looks speak for themselves in a dignified way, she was smashing.

"But I know it's not funny, really. Nothing can be too funny with Liz in danger. I shouldn't have laughed."

"Don't worry about it," Driscoll told her. "In a situation like this, a little laugh now can help prevent gibbering hysterics later."

"How do you know?" she challenged. "Do you do this sort of thing a lot?"

"Not recently," Driscoll said. "But enough. I've had my share of gibbering hysterics, too."

"I don't believe you, Mr. Driscoll. But thank you for trying to make me feel better. Can I ask you a question?" She frowned.

"Sure."

"What the hell are you *really* doing here, Mr. Driscoll?" She spat the words at him. Before he had a chance to answer, she went on. "I know my uncle has some big contract with you people. Some new tank or a jet or some other way to kill people. What does that have to do with Liz? I don't want you to use her as a pawn in some macho political *game*. This situation is bad enough without . . ."

She went on with it. *The flush that comes to her cheeks when she's angry is really pretty,* he thought. He also thought, *It's a shame, lady, but a pawn in a political game, macho or otherwise, is exactly what your cousin has become.* He suppressed a sigh. Coming into this assignment, facing the fact that his father had roped him into another one, Driscoll had already gotten a preliminary idea of what he wanted to do. Now, looking at this actress-cousin of the kidnapped girl, he was formulating a way to accomplish it.

He apologized to Robin Payne, an apology no less sincere for being silent. He would have been happy to leave her out of it, if he'd had the time to think of a better way. But there was no time. There probably was no better way. *God help me,* Driscoll thought, *but, Miss Robin Payne, I've got no choice but to make you a pawn in a political game, too.*

She was a fair-minded girl. Driscoll expected her to end her tirade with a "So there!" and march from the room. Instead, when she finished, she fixed him with a bright brown stare and said, "Is there any response you'd like to make to that?"

Driscoll calculated that the best response would be an air of patience lightly strained by irritation. "Would it do any good?" he asked wearily.

"I just want Liz to be safe. I know how you military people think."

"I'm not a military person," Driscoll said. "I want your cousin to be safe, too." Lord, how he wanted her to be safe. For his own sake, if for no other reason.

"Besides," he went on, "if your cousin is a pawn, or turns out to be one, it will have been the kidnappers who made it happen. I'm just here to help. Your uncle's contract may figure in this. If that happens, I'm supposed to help things along as well as I can. All right?"

Her eyes were skeptical. "I'd like to believe you," she said.

"I'll settle for that," Driscoll said. He smiled at her.

She smiled back, shyly. "I guess I came on a little strong.

But I *do* want Liz to be safe. Oh, I'm terrible. Would you like something to drink? I'm not used to being a hostess."

Driscoll was saved the bother of refusing when Herbert and Sheila Fane entered the room. Driscoll rose to greet them as Robin performed introductions.

Herbert Fane was a burly man, bald with an iron-gray fringe. He was being stoic. His face was set so firmly that Driscoll almost felt his own jaw ache. When the two men shook hands, Fane forced the word "Driscoll" past his teeth with a sharp nod of his head.

"So kind of you to come and help us," Sheila Fane said. Driscoll gave her the usual load about its being his job, but that he'd do what he could.

"You can't do anything!" she suddenly exploded. "Nobody can do anything! Don't you think I know what's going on? Don't you think I know what's happening to my daughter? Admit it— you're *helpless!*"

She opened her mouth as if to go on, but stopped short. Her face, tight with anger, suddenly softened and collapsed into a mask of infinite sadness. She put her hands to her face and left the room.

Robin Payne jumped up and followed her out, with an apologetic look over her shoulder. Herbert Fane asked Driscoll if he'd like to sit down.

The industrialist rubbed his eyelid with a finger. He looked like a man who hadn't slept in a week. Avoiding Driscoll's eyes, he said, "I *do* feel rather helpless, Driscoll."

"It's natural. But you're not helpless, really. The police, the FBI, me if I can—we'll help you work out a way to get your daughter back. They wouldn't have taken her if you didn't have something they wanted in exchange."

"But who knows what they want?" Fane protested. "The FBI told me today about some terrorist group they think may have done this. They're not sane."

"They know what they want, Mr. Fane. You'll hear from them." *And that,* thought Driscoll, *is a promise.*

Fane wasn't convinced, but Driscoll made appropriate soothing noises until Robin returned. The young actress told her uncle that Aunt Sheila was feeling calmer now. "I think she'd like it if you talked to her a little."

Fane closed his eyes and exhaled, as if trying to think of something to say to his wife. He got to his feet, asked Robin to show Mr. Driscoll out, said they'd confer at a better time, then left the room.

"Couldn't wait to get rid of me," Driscoll said.

Robin smiled at him. "We've all used you as a whipping boy this morning. It's just that when something like this happens, you can't help feeling responsible. Especially Aunt Sheila. She's got this idea in her head that if she hadn't asked Liz to drive her to the doctor's office, this never would have happened."

Driscoll nodded. That doctor's appointment would have to be looked into, but there was no sense bringing that up here. He had something more important on his mind.

"You could make it up to me," he suggested. "The whipping boy stuff, I mean."

Robin tilted her head and looked at him. "Are you about to ask me to dinner or something?"

"That's *exactly* what I'm going to do. I could sit around the Holiday Inn, but I'd rather have someone nice to talk to."

"Uh-huh," Robin said. "Also someone you can pump for information on the victim's family."

Driscoll made his manner serious. "That's right. Somebody intelligent who can give me straight information, not tainted by panic, about the family. It could be important. You said you wished you could help."

"I did?"

"You said you wanted her to be safe. You said that three times. This is your chance to help." Driscoll smiled again. "Besides, I don't see how you can resist. You pay taxes, don't you?"

She rolled her eyes. "As who doesn't?"

"All right then. Dinner tonight—you pick the place. The most expensive place you can think of. Your Uncle Sam will pick up the check."

"Your tax dollars at work," Robin said.

"Something like that."

"Okay, Mr. Driscoll, you and Uncle Sam have a date. Seven-thirty?"

Driscoll said seven-thirty would be fine.

She walked him to the door. "I should warn you, I was raised as a rich girl in this town. I know some expensive places. Uncle Sam is going to regret this." She smiled at him, a friendly, bright smile, and offered him her hand.

Driscoll smiled and took it. *Not as much as you will,* he thought. Pawns never wound up enjoying the game.

Driscoll looked at his watch again, then down past the Holiday Inn sign toward the beginning of the curving driveway. Nothing. He bit his lip and cursed the world at large. They were supposed to be here at one o'clock, and it was now seven minutes after one. How the hell was he supposed to accomplish anything if the Congressman couldn't get his troops together for him in time? Now that he was into the damned operation, Driscoll wanted to get *on* with it.

He looked at his watch again. It still said seven after one. He could press another button to change the digital display and count off the seconds that were wasting, but that would only make him angrier.

What the hell was the matter? Had Vi been caught? Was Jake too old for this sort of business? Maybe Miles had defected or something. But that was ridiculous. As long as Miles had enough work to do, he was happy, and the Congressman always gave him enough work to do.

Then the whole train of thought became ridiculous, because there they were. It was, as promised, a Chrysler limousine, dark gray, with windows so tinted as to be almost opaque.

It pulled up, and Miles got out, ran around the front of the car, and opened the door for Driscoll. Like everything Miles did, it was perfect, a quintessential little jewel of chauffeuring.

Miles was a contemporary of Driscoll's. The Congressman's son had recruited him off the campus of one of the fancy

eastern universities; he had taken to Agency work like a baby
to milk—Driscoll sometimes got the impression that Miles
wouldn't have minded at all being the Congressman's son. Even
more unsettling, Driscoll sometimes thought Miles suspected
the truth about Driscoll's own relationship with the old man.

Driscoll smiled inwardly. He would be delighted to step
aside for Miles; the only problem was, Miles wasn't what the
Congressman had in mind. Miles was a damned good forger,
an expert lockman, and an excellent infiltrator (as evidenced by
his performance as chauffeur). He was good at assaults and
armaments. But he wasn't a planner. He was a valuable tool, but
he had to be used with skill.

Driscoll stepped into the soft interior of the limousine.
Viola greeted him with a curt nod. "Driscoll," she said. Viola
was a thin, angry black woman, a veteran of the Black
Liberation Army, and an experienced bank robber, safecracker,
and all around felon. She had never actually murdered
anybody, and that was her luck. Vi had never decided what kind
of luck. On the one hand, she was still free and alive, which was
more than she could say of most of her former comrades,
including Hamilton, once her lover and the one who had
finked on her in the first place.

On the other hand, she was working for the government
now, the same one she'd tried so hard to overthrow. She was a
lamb. That was what she was here for now, that and her general
usefulness undercover. But mostly she was here to be a piece of
dark meat thrown to the wolves if things got too hot for the
white folk. It was the kind of job that could end abruptly. Still,
the pay was good. Damn good. She had enough saved up to
keep the daycare centers she'd opened in New York and L.A.
and Atlanta and Oakland going even after these damn ofays
got her killed. And she'd had some fun in the meantime.

Driscoll nodded back. He took Vi on her own terms, and
she respected him for it. He was one of the few whites she
would shake hands with, and she offered him a bony hand now.
He took it, and they both nodded again.

Sitting across from Vi, who occupied the jump seat, was
Jake Feder, the tape man. Jake had a shiny Miami sunburn,
topped by sparse white hair. He wore a navy blue blazer and

belt, white shirt, pants, socks and shoes. A light green cigar sprouted from his mouth.

"Hello," he said heartily. "About time you got to Uncle Jake. The General tells me your name is Clifford this time around. So hello, Clifford. Shake my goddamn hand, you snot, I'm getting tired of holding it out here, and my circulation isn't what it used to be."

"Hello, Jake." He took Jake's hand. It was a hand of enormous skill. Jake Feder was a loud, obnoxious, vulgar old man, but he was also a legend in the world of electronics. He had spent years with CBS Labs, helping them develop the long-playing record, video character generators, and dozens of other developments. Now, he was an independent consultant based in Miami ("to blend in with the other old Jews," Jake explained). He had been working for the Congressman (whom he still referred to as the General) since the closing days of World War II. It was only after getting the General's okay that Jake had gone ahead and roasted his particular part of Richard Nixon's goose over the infamous eighteen-minute gap in the Watergate tapes.

"So tell us what this is all about," Jake said. "My equipment is in the trunk bouncing around."

"Don't unpack it yet," Driscoll told him. "None of you is here on orders. I asked for you. This is going to be a rotten job, and it may take a long time. If anybody wants out, this is the time to go."

They were all silent. Driscoll suddenly remembered the Agency magic phrase that would let them reply. "Without prejudice," he said.

"I'm in," Vi said. "Ain't nothing rotten I ain't already done or had done to me."

Miles, still playing chauffeur, picked up his speaking tube and said, "I'm with you all the way, sir."

Jake Feder laughed. "Cliff, you must be crazy. When the General called and told me I was going to work with you, I jumped at the chance. What am I supposed to do now? Leave? And miss one of your famous Mind-Fuck Follies? Not a chance. Come on, what are we going to do?"

Driscoll looked at the back of Miles' head, and the alert,

competent faces of Jake and Vi. Something was wrong, either with them or with him. God knows *he'd* get out if he had the chance. They couldn't wait to get started.

He took a deep breath, leaned back against the soft leather of the car seat, and obliged them. "What we're going to do," he said, "is to drive Leo Calvin and his friends crazy. We're going to create a situation where they have to bring the girl to us— and that's all *anybody's* going to be able to do. The girl's father, the police, the FBI, the press, they won't be able to do a thing. We simplify the problem until it's only the kidnappers and us. Then we crush the kidnappers."

Jake stuck his cigar back in the middle of a big wolfish grin. "Sounds good already. How do we go about it?"

Driscoll closed his eyes. "The first thing we do," he said, "is steal some cars."

Chapter Three

INTERSTATE 80 AT NIGHT, WHERE IT CROSSES CENTRAL
Pennsylvania, is like a four hundred mile tunnel. Woods close
in over the top of it, and you can't see a damn thing outside
your headlights. *It's funny,* Cary Wilkis thought, *thirteen years in
the saddle driving over the damn thing, and I never noticed how dark
and spooky it is along this stretch of road. Wonder why. Ha!*
Cary knew why. It was the damn cargo. Life was tough for
independent truckers in general, especially independent truckers who'd mortgaged a good part of their income for ten years
or more on a new cab-over-engine Peterbilt tractor with every
option he could think of. He couldn't afford to be too choosy
about what he hauled, and generally he wasn't. He'd carried
dynamite, toxic chemicals, even swinging meat. Swinging meat
was the worst, because the heavy sides of beef or whatever
tended to keep going when the driver wanted to stop, giving
him a friendly nudge into a crowded intersection, or a tire-
tripping crater in the road.

Harry Swanson'd been busted up that way. Swinging meat
kept him going straight when he should have been stopping,
and he'd wound up going over the edge of a bridge that had
been washed out by a flash flood on some little piss of a creek
somewhere in Arkansas.

It was the kind of decision you had to make, that was all. Be
safe, or make a better living. Cary had always said there was no
legal cargo he wouldn't refuse—hang the danger.

That still went as far as Cary was concerned. It wasn't the danger, damn it, it was—well, damn it, he was scared. And angry at himself for *being* scared.

Because the whole thing was ridiculous. It wasn't swinging meat, it was *dead* meat. The fact that all the meat was stacked up and wrapped in green plastic inside boxes, or that the meat had once been human had nothing to do with it.

After all, they *were* dead. They *were* secure in their pine boxes. They *were* locked in the back of the reefer. They weren't going to get out.

Cary chuckled at the thought, but at the same time, he reached out and turned up the volume on the radio. WOWO, Fort Wayne, Indiana. Eleven-ninety on your dial. If you were a trucker and liked rock, you listened to WOWO. If you liked country, you listened to WWVA, out of Wheeling, West Virginia. If you didn't like either, you weren't much of a trucker. Both clear channels; you could hear them all over the country at night. Of course, Cary had a great stereo setup in the cab, with speakers on either side of the driver's seat, and two more in the back, in the ceiling over his little bed. (Not that he'd used the bed much—he wasn't doing much sleeping with a cargo or corpses. He'd violated his principles and was flying across the country this trip on greenies, but he was beginning to think that hadn't been one of his all-time best ideas either—an imagination that doesn't get any sleep is a very difficult animal.)

Cary could have played taped music in the cab; he had hours of it. All his favorite stuff, beautifully recorded, too. He didn't have to listen to the tinniness of the AM radio. But (and he gave himself a rueful chuckle about this, too) he wanted to hear the announcer. He wanted to hear another person's— another *living* person's—voice.

He'd tried the CB a few times, but at a quarter to four in the morning, or whatever the hell time it was, nobody in range had his ears on. The last comeback he'd had was about two-thirty, a four-wheeler. Usually, he made it a point of honor not to talk to anybody who called him good buddy (which no longer meant what it had before nontruckers started to learn about CB), but Cary had been more than a little sad when this guy said his last ten-four, and pulled off the interstate outside of Mercer.

Again, he tried to scold himself out of that bad feeling. It seemed to have a fingertip stroking the bottom of his spine before it took a good hold. *Hell,* he told himself, *they can't come and get you. You solid on that?* He decided he was. *Okay, what's the problem, then? It can't be what they look like—in the first place, you didn't see them, and in the second place, there ain't a one of them been dead more than a week or so. None of them died in a horrible way. These are A-number-one, prime, choice stiffs you're hauling here. All kinds of folks who left their bodies to science. Wasn't their fault that all the stiffs happened to wind up in Seattle, and science needs them in medical schools in the East. Why hold it against them? All you gotta do is get them to Newark, New Jersey. They'll be doled out to the medical schools from there, and you can get back to Sue in time for her to still remember your face.*

Cary nodded. "All right, then," he said aloud. He felt a little sheepish, but it felt good to say. "All right," he said again. He smiled, and started tapping his high school ring against the steering wheel in time to an Eagles song.

His mood outlasted the song by about ten seconds. Then his amphetamine-stoked imagination took over again. He was just sitting there, listening to a commercial for an all-night doughnut and coffee place in Fort Wayne, thinking it sounded like a good idea, and speculating on how many people were listening to the commercial who had never been to Fort Wayne, Indiana and never would, when his imagination hit him with this one: *What if one of them* isn't *dead?*

The bad feeling had his spine in a tight fist, now. *Imagine it,* he thought. *Imagine it was* you. *You'd been in a coma or something, and now you wake up. It's really cold, and you pull your blanket tighter to you. Only it isn't a blanket. It's a plastic sheet. And you hear this rumbling sound—from the truck, but you don't know that. And you pull the sheet away from you, and what do you see? The lid of a box . . .*

Cary reached out and turned down the expensive air conditioning in his expensive rig, but he knew that it wasn't the cold making him shiver.

"Jesus," he whispered. "Jesus, I will never take a pill again.

Or make a joke about a funeral. Or drive dead meat. Or read anymore Stephen King. But Jesus, make it *stop*."

Because he couldn't get rid of it. The pills and the bodies in back had taken over his whole brain, and he wasn't just imagining what it would feel like, he was *feeling* it. Cold and alone and bewildered, and scared enough to drive himself crazy.

He probably would have cracked up and added one more to the number of corpses in the rig, but the Dodge saved him. It was a few years old, a canary-yellow Dodge Volare wagon, and it had its nose into the tangled mess that passed for a shoulder on this part of the road, and its ass end sticking smack in the middle of the eastbound lane. A man and a woman were putting out flares.

It was probably the color of the thing that brought him to his senses—if it had been a black car, he probably would have taken it for a hearse, and the flares for hellfire, and taken the exit for the cemetery right then and there. But hell, nobody dreams nightmares about canary yellow cars. It had to be real.

They needed help, too, so that made it nice. He had a tool kit, and he ought to be able to do something for them if the problem was minor. He had the CB to call for help if he needed to. Besides, it would give him an opportunity to get back down to earth, talk to a few people. Let the greenies wear off. Get the sun closer to coming up.

Cary pulled the rig to a stop before reaching the car. He saw now that the man, stocky and on the tall side of medium, was white. The woman, thin but not weak-looking, was black. Ordinarily, Cary Wilkis would have avoided a situation like that, but not tonight. Tonight he wouldn't have cared if it was a woman screwing a trained rhino. He just wanted to talk.

They were running up to the truck now, waving their arms, as if they weren't sure he was going to stay stopped. Cary started to grin. Looked as if they'd been a little nervous, too, wanted to see somebody.

He opened the door and climbed out. "Howdy," he said. "What seems to be the tr—"

He stopped because he was back in the nightmare. The woman raised a hand with a gun it it. The gun spit like it was mad at him, and something was sticking out of his chest. He pulled it out and threw it away, but that was only a second before his legs turned to licorice, and he spun heavily to the pavement. He wasn't able to move anymore. Soon he wasn't able to see. Then he wasn't able to hear. Then he just wasn't.

Coming back from the dead was nothing like Cary had imagined it. He didn't get scared right away—first, he got out of the car and threw up. Tranquilizers and greenies are a bad combination. Then he realized he had been in a car (the canary-yellow Volare), and then he knew he had been tranquilized. His brain must have kept working while he was out.

He figured he might as well keep it on the job. The sky told him it was just a little before dawn, so he hadn't been out too long. An hour, hour and a half. The pain in the side of his face told him he'd hit the pavement pretty hard.

Still, he was in pretty good shape for someone who'd had his truck hijacked. *Hijacked*, he thought. *Shit.* Then he started to laugh. His imagination again, trying to make up for the crap it had put him through last night. Cary was laughing so hard, he had to get back in the car to sit down.

He just wished he could get a look at those clever bastards when they saw what they'd stolen.

"Come on, honey," Miles said, "give me your hand."

"You're sick," Viola told him.

"She doesn't mind. Look, this is not a pleasant job. Would you like to do it instead?"

"Uh-*uh*."

"All right, then."

He got back to the job. Even death and the stiffness of refrigeration couldn't hide the fact that the young woman on the table had been attractive, possibly even beautiful. It was hard to say—no one's beauty could survive after rigor mortis had come and gone.

None of that mattered of course. Driscoll had put in an order for one corpse, the same age, race, sex, and general coloring of Elizabeth Fane. The Congressman had put the Agency to work, and they'd found one in less than two days. A college student done in by a bad heart. A little mix-up in the paperwork, and Honey here had lost her name, and become Jane Doe number sixty-four, eligible for shipment to the medical schools of the East. The truckdriver hadn't known it, but he'd been tracked across the country—not constantly, but frequently enough for Driscoll to know when to send Miles and Vi out to greet him. It was just as well the driver decided to speed across the country (in more ways than one), because Miles was getting anxious.

It had been four days, and nothing from the kidnappers. To Miles, it was imperative to have Operation Shell Game (Miles' unofficial name for it) completely set up before Calvin and his bunch sent their first message.

Driscoll had been maddening. "They have to make the first move," he kept saying. "Relax. We've got to do this right."

Of *course* they had to do things right. But the men who worked for the Agency had to be *fast* and right. Driscoll should know that. He *had* to know it. Nobody got to be that special to the Congressman without having the knowledge in his bones.

Driscoll was—Miles conceded it grudgingly—a damn good agent. Better, he admitted, than he himself could ever be. That was the reason he irritated Miles so much. All that talent, and such a bad, antiproductive attitude. Why did he take these long leaves? Why didn't he do his share of the day-to-day work of the Agency? With his brain, he could do a lot to help his country.

Miles had finally gotten the fingers of Honey's hand open and reasonably limber. The warming had made the body blossom with the smell of death, and Vi had backed away across the basement of the hastily obtained small factory building they were using as a headquarters, as if to distance herself from it. For someone whose lover had shot and killed six policemen from ambush while she looked on, Vi was too damned fastidious about death and dying, if you asked Miles.

"Vi, bring me the form and the ink, please?" Ordinarily, to take fingerprints from a corpse, the best thing to use was a roller. These, though, had to be substituted for some that had been taken from a living person. On the living, a stamp pad was used, and an expert could tell the difference.

Vi's usually dour expression deepened as she approached the table. Miles could see she was breathing through her mouth. She handed him what he needed, and started to back away.

"Not yet, Vi, I need your help."

"Why? You're the one who likes playing with dead bodies. I'm just letting you have all the fun for yourself."

It wouldn't do to show the anger he felt. Miles understood the concept of the *lamb*, and he knew how important it was. They were just so hard to *work* with sometimes.

"Vi, just hold the form steady, all right? We had to get paper the right age, to start with, and I went nearly blind faking the rest of the security form. We've only got five of them, and if I mess them all up because the paper slips, we've wasted a whole day."

Vi looked at him for a long second, then held the paper flat on the table. Miles remembered to thank her. Then he lifted the body so that the right hand would bear on the table at the proper angle. He propped it up that way and slowly and carefully he took the impressions.

Vi watched him in a kind of horrible fascination. "Do you think that truckdriver is all right?"

"Mmm-hmm," Miles said. "The Congressman got us the information that the guy must be taking drugs—we adjusted the dosage of tranquilizer in the gun accordingly. He's probably awake by now—we took too long at the truck. I was afraid he was going to wake up, start up the car and catch up to us."

"You would have killed him if he did, though, wouldn't you?"

"Fortunately," Miles said, "the question didn't come up."

"You would have. Wouldn't even have blinked. That's why I let the air out of one of the tires."

Miles smiled at her. "That was excellent thinking, Vi."

"I've seen too much killing. Shit, I used to like it. Used to cheer my man Hamilton on."

"Anybody can get too much of a good thing," Miles said. He was bored with the topic. He saw himself as a soldier. The name Miles *meant* soldier, that's why he had picked it for his cover name, his *nom de guerre*. The Congressman had told him that first time, when he'd taken him into the Agency, that he would be a soldier, one that got frequent opportunities to fight for his country. The promise had been kept, in spades. As a soldier Miles followed orders, secure in the belief that his country was worth the hardship.

"You are sick," Vi said again.

He couldn't expect her to understand. Even in the Agency they laughed at him about it. Called him a Boy Scout. And they, though they didn't want to admit it, worked under the same rules he did. Vi was just a mercenary. She'd made her best deal to save her life, and that was that.

"All done," he said.

"Don't have to do the other hand?"

"No. Fane Industries' security department only takes right hand prints if you're right-handed and left hand if you're left-handed."

"Well, that's good news. I'm gonna get some sleep. If I can."

"Sure. It's been a long night. Just help me get her back in cold storage, all right?"

Vi scowled, but she went to open the top-loading refrigerator the Congressman had scrounged for them off some forgotten government warehouse.

"You're sick, Miles," she said. "The only one sicker than you is Driscoll."

"Nice of you to say so," Miles said drily. "What makes him so sick?"

"He *thinks* of this stuff."

Driscoll had been feeling the same way about himself. The feelings were reinforced by the fact that having thought of a plan, he now had to start putting it into effect. Not the detail work on getting the corpse, or preparing the document switch—Miles was eminently competent at that sort of thing.

Driscoll, on the other hand, had assigned himself the task of bringing Robin Payne into it. That, he thought, ought to be sickening enough for anybody.

He remembered looking across the table at her. She was lovely in something dark blue and shiny, not especially low cut, but loose enough for her skin to play hide and seek when she moved. When she walked, the slit skirt gave a teasing display of her legs. She had on diamond earrings and makeup. This was a very sophisticated lady Uncle Sam was buying dinner for tonight.

On the surface. Driscoll only had to hear her laugh, or notice how she'd take a sidelong glance at him to find out how one of her conversational sallies had gone over with this government big shot, to know that inside, she was incredibly clean and undisillusioned. Driscoll reflected bitterly that he never met that sort of people anymore. Except when he wanted to ruin everything for them.

True to her word, Robin had picked an expensive place to eat, the Sportsman's Inn, a steak-and-wild-game place about forty-five minutes from town. Robin had ordered pheasant; Driscoll had a venison steak. When the meal came, she offered him a bite.

Driscoll raised an eyebrow. "Is that done here?" The role-playing instinct nature and the Congressman had developed in him cut in smoothly, providing the perfect touch of light banter. It left his emotions untouched. He could turn them off completely, if he needed to, replacing them with new ones more likely to achieve what he wanted to achieve.

"We'll be discreet," Robin said. She quickly put a piece of tender white meat on his plate.

"Very good," Driscoll said, chewing. "The venison is excellent too. Like to try some?"

"No, thanks."

"I'll be discreet," he promised.

Robin looked embarrassed. "It's not that. . . . I've never been able to eat it. My father and my uncle used to go hunting—not far from here, as a matter of fact—and my father would bring the meat home, but every time I took a bite, I thought of Bambi."

"Cows have big sad eyes, too, you know," Driscoll said.

Robin laughed. "How did you know it was the *eyes*? That's what I always see, Bambi's big sad eyes. But what do cows have to do with it?"

"I'll bet you eat steak."

She laughed. "Maybe I won't anymore."

They ate and talked about her career. She was up for a part in a road company of *Amadeus* and she was naturally excited about it. She asked him about his work, but he managed to duck the questions and turn the conversation back to her. She had never been married. "All I ever meet is actors," she said, "and I don't want to marry an actor. One obsessive neurotic per family is enough."

"Meaning you."

"Of course, meaning me. We all go around suffering and sacrificing for Art"—she indicated the loftiness of the subject with a toss of her head—"but the public thinks of us as toys. The thing that really makes us neurotic is the sneaking suspicion that they're probably right."

"Everybody needs to forget his troubles for a while now and then." They'd finished their coffee by now; Driscoll signaled for the check.

"Yes," Robin sighed. "They do. Thank you."

"For what?"

"For taking me out. For letting me talk about myself. It must have been terribly boring for you."

"Do I look bored?"

"Goodness, what a gentleman. But I really needed this. Not that I've been forgetting about poor Liz—she's been in the back of my mind right along—but at least I haven't been chasing my thoughts in a circle the way I do back at the house. I'm driving myself crazy."

"It must be terrible for her parents."

"You saw them this afternoon. I wish I could do something for Uncle Herbert and Aunt Sheila, but what can I do?"

"You can help."

"How?"

"Let's go somewhere private and talk about it."

If that had been a come-on, Robin decided, it was the most tasteless one in history. She didn't think Mr. Clifford Driscoll would stoop quite so low.

But then again, maybe he would. There was an intensity about him, an air of energy-not-in-use that purred in him, the way the engine in a Jaguar she had once owned would purr impatiently whenever she drove below the speed limit.

If he was determined to free Liz, and if he thought Robin could help, she owed it to her cousin to hear what he had to say. Besides, she was intrigued by him, liked his company. If he'd suggested they go dancing somewhere, she would have played along with that, too.

She took him to her uncle's cabin, the one he had shared with her father in their deer-hunting days. It took awhile to get to, but you couldn't beat it for privacy.

"Everything is hooked up," she said as they drove up the gravel road to the cabin. "Uncle Herbert comes here pretty frequently. He says it's to relax, but he's always got a fat briefcase with him when he leaves."

Robin used her key and let them in. She hit a couple of switches just inside the door, and lit up what had always struck Robin as a set designer's idea of the perfect cabin in the woods. Rustic, but fully equipped, from the microwave oven on the kitchen wall, to the heat lamp in the bathroom.

"Sit down," she said. "I'll see what's in the refrigerator." She opened it, took a look inside. "Figures," she said. "Beer or ice water?"

Driscoll smiled. "If we're going to have beer, I might as well take my tie off."

"If you're going to take your tie off," Robin countered, "you can just drink it from the can. So there."

He got up from a wooden chair to take the can from her, popped the tab, and took a swig. "Us macho men always drink it this way." His face became serious. "Come on, sit down. Let's talk."

Robin nodded, then perched on the edge of the cabin's small bed. "All right," she said. "You were going to tell me what I could do to help."

Driscoll hesitated. It was all part of the con—he had to be reluctant and sincere and honest. That was the approach his instinct and experience told him would work on this particular individual. But he was too good an agent to be able to kid himself into believing that was the whole reason.

He was hesitating because this was the final cut, and he just didn't want to do it. Things were in pretty sad shape when he started waffling over involving the person who was the focal point of the whole plan. He hadn't wanted to do this, but now that he was in, he couldn't look back. The Objective was what he had to concentrate on. He'd learned that at his father's knee. "The Objective at any cost, boy. Keep the cost as low as you can, but do what you have to to win. 'Cause if you don't win, any price you paid was too high."

All evening, he'd been looking for something contemptible in this young woman; some smugness or callousness or stupidity that would place her solidly among the expendable. He'd found nothing, except perhaps for her damnable niceness.

It took a fool to be nice in the world as it was. To be nice meant maintaining an insulation of ignorance about the way things worked. And for a nice person, there's always the danger that you may wind up in the middle of some very not-nice people and events.

Nice people hurt more than people like Driscoll.

Driscoll would have laughed, but it would have ruined the reluctant-honest-sincere pose the professional half of him had been maintaining while he thought. He really was the king manipulator, wasn't he? He'd almost maneuvered himself into writing a woman off as worthless because she wasn't part of his lost and dirty universe.

To hell with it. It was a job that had to be done. Because he was already lost, because he'd been soiled too deeply ever to come clean, he could do it.

Robin was talking. ". . . can't do anything until you tell me what it is you think—are you listening to me?"

"Of course I am," Driscoll lied. "But before we talk about

what you can do, I have to tell you a few things you're not going to believe."

"Try me," she said. "This is the girl who believed in Santa Claus until she was twelve."

Naturally, Driscoll thought grimly. *She'd want it that way.* "All right," he said, "but whether you believe any of it or not, I want you to promise me you'll never talk about these things to anybody."

"Oh, I get it. The first thing you're going to tell me is that you're a spy."

"I'm not playing a game with you, Robin," he said. *Another lie.*

"You *are* a spy? I've thought you were since this afternoon, but I figured I must be crazy."

"No," Driscoll said. "I'm not a spy. I have been a spy. A spy is someone who gathers secret information. My job is arranging things."

"You don't sound as if you like it much."

"I was drafted."

"And right now you're arranging to get Liz released?"

"I'm arranging to get her back."

"That's what I said."

Driscoll shook his head. "Your cousin will never be released. That's the first thing you won't believe. They'll draw this out as long as they can; make it look like an authentic terrorist kidnapping as long as they can; then they'll kill her."

"My God," Robin said, "if this isn't an authentic terrorist kidnapping, what in the world is it?"

Driscoll's voice was very soft. "An act of war," he said.

Robin's laughter was almost a shriek. She had very nearly taken this maniac seriously. "The *Russians?*" she said. "You think the *Russians* have kidnapped my cousin? Why? Do they want her to teach them tennis?"

"An American named Leo Calvin is almost certainly the person responsible for your cousin's kidnapping. He has been in the pay of Moscow for close to ten years; before that he was a run-of-the-mill terrorist. But he is now definitely working for the Russians. And now you know more than any of his accomplices probably do.

"This is one of the things you have to be quiet about. If you start talking about any of this, you will be silenced. It's not my department, and I don't know how far they'll go, but you will definitely be silenced."

"My God," Robin said again.

"As for why the Russians want your cousin kidnapped, it's to slow down the manufacture of a new missile guidance system your uncle's company has developed."

Robin was looking at him with round eyes. "Is the whole government as paranoid as you are?"

Driscoll's smile was sad. "Even paranoids have enemies," he said.

Robin said, "Hmph. I suppose I had better tell you I am very active in the nuclear freeze movement."

"Many nice people are," Driscoll said.

"I suppose you all think we're dupes of Moscow."

"Of course you are."

"Why? Because we want to make sure the world isn't destroyed in a nuclear war?"

"Hell, no. Because you want to make sure that if there *is* a nuclear war, only Russians will survive it."

She looked at him as if he were a specimen under a microscope. Driscoll was glad to see it. Curiosity and irritation were a potent combination, and it looked as if he'd hit on a subject that could arouse them both in strong proportions.

"Listen, Driscoll—" she began.

"Call me Cliff."

"Cliff. Do you honestly think Russia is behind the nuclear freeze movement?"

"Depends what you mean by behind. Did they start it? Probably not. If they stopped having anything to do with it, would it go away? Definitely not. Do they have people here spending money and supplying ideas to keep it stirred up and in the press? Absolutely."

Robin was disgusted. "Oh, for God's sake."

"They'd be crazy if they weren't doing it," Driscoll insisted. "Anything that keeps us divided, anything that lowers our ability to fight back is good for them. If their society was open enough to allow demonstrations, I'd be over there trying to screw *them* over."

"If that's the attitude everybody has, we're all doomed."

"Robin, don't get me wrong. If there could be a bilateral, verifiable arms reduction system, I'd lead the parades. The Russians will never go for it. And before you tell me we should meet them halfway, ask the people in Afghanistan and Poland, or the passengers on Korean Air lines flight 007."

"Or the people in Vietnam or Nicaragua." She stood up. "Take me home. I feel sorry for poor Liz if this sort of thing is the best she's got to help her." She took his beer can from him (it was still mostly full), emptied it in the sink, and disposed of the can.

As she passed him on the way to the door, she was lost in the disappointment of it all. Part of the reason she had moved out on Uncle Herbert had been his constant recitations of the same speech Driscoll was trying to give her now. Somehow, she'd thought Driscoll would go deeper than that, and she might enjoy digging down to learn how deep.

And she was even more disappointed because she had been fooled into hoping this damned ideologue, this close-minded fascist, would be able to do something for Liz.

With her hand on the knob, she said, "Don't worry, you won't have to have me silenced. I won't tell anyone. I'm not fond of being thought crazy."

When he grabbed her wrist in a strong hand and spun her around, she was too surprised to scream. Her New York-acquired reflexes, though, were in full operation, and she struck his face with a right-handed slap that had the full power of the spin behind it. It left a bright red mark on his cheek, but she might have blown him a kiss for all the reaction he showed.

Then she saw his eyes, bright and hot behind the glasses, and it occurred to her to be afraid.

"Listen, little girl," he said between clenched teeth, "people will think you're crazy if you talk about it, huh? What do you think it does to you to *live it*? This is *my world* we're talking about. I didn't ask for it, and I don't like it, but God help me, I know it inside and out.

"Do you think it's an accident that the ruler of Russia is a former head of the KGB? I envy you if you can. You just go on marching in your demonstrations, and hating those of us whose sad fate it is to crawl around in muck to make it possible for you to do it. It's so unpleasant to think about.

"But it's going to be hard to forget, because my world has reached out and hauled your cousin into it. She'll never be the same after this. Neither will your uncle or your aunt. Neither will you. But the sooner we free Liz Fane, the weaker the effects will be.

"I admit this. I've seen things, and I've done things, that I don't like to think about. But keep this in mind—if anyone is going to get your cousin loose, it's going to be me. Because I know how to fight dirty. And anybody who's not willing to get down in the mud to fight dirty is at the mercy of anybody who is."

He took a deep breath, then looked down at the hand that held her wrist as if he had never seen it before. He let go of it immediately. "I—I'm sorry," he said, and now his voice was soft and human again, not the snarl it had been a second ago. "I had no right to lay hands on you that way. I really am sorry."

Robin rubbed her wrist and stared at him. "It's okay. I laid a hand on you, too. I really touched a sore spot, didn't I? It's funny, though, I just never thought of a spy as somebody who had feelings."

Driscoll opened his mouth, but Robin went on. "I'm sure it's a tough job, but I have a hard time buying this cold war stuff. If that makes me a naive fool, so be it, and no hard feelings I hope. Okay?"

Driscoll shrugged and smiled.

"But you were going to say something a few seconds ago and I didn't let you," she went on.

"It doesn't matter."

"Cliff, don't be like that."

"No, that's what I was going to say. It doesn't matter who's behind the kidnapping—and the murders, let's not forget the murders—the way we attack them is the same. The only reason I told you we think the Russians are behind it is to give you some idea of how important this is to the government. It was supposed to reassure you."

Robin looked at him. He really *did* live in a different world if he thought learning that this was not only a family crisis but possibly the curtain raiser for World War III would be reassuring.

"It didn't.work," she said sourly.

"No," he said, "we got sidetracked. But there's still the job to do, and you have a part."

"Fighting dirty," she said.

"Not your part. I promise." *Another lie. Maybe.*

"What do I have to do?"

"Tell me everything you know about Elizabeth Fane and the people around her."

"Is that all?"

"No. I'll want you to go back to New York for a few days. And later I might want you to make a tape recording for me."

"And keep quiet about it."

"About *everything*."

"I can stop anytime," she insisted.

"If you want to." One more lie wouldn't hurt.

"All right. When should we start?"

"Yesterday." Robin made a face. "All right," Driscoll went on. "As soon as possible. Tomorrow morning? I'll call you."

"Is it that important?"

"At the risk of being trite, I'll tell you the truth: Every second counts."

"Then let's just stay here and get started. I've never spent the night with a spy before."

"I'm not a spy," Driscoll said. He took out a pad and a notebook. And even as he hated himself for pulling the kidnapped girl's cousin into his dark world, somewhere in the back of his mind, the Congressman's son was congratulating himself: *Objective accomplished.*

Robin had bought magazines to read on the trip, but she left them on the bus unread. All the way to New York, on the cab ride uptown from the Port Authority Bus Terminal, she'd been far too involved with worries, doubts, and second thoughts to be able to read.

It was obviously insane. She wasn't a spy or an agent or whatever it was he wanted to call himself, and she never wanted to be. His plan sounded crazy enough to start with; it couldn't work. It just couldn't. And Robin didn't want any part of something that would get Liz killed.

And yet it sounded so *plausible* when he said it. Maybe it was because he believed it so much. He had this Holy Mission thing riding him, and Robin thought that must be a pretty uncomfortable load to carry around. God knew she sometimes felt the weight of her career on her back, and that was just one woman's ambition.

Despite her worries, that ambition and long habit had put her on automatic pilot as soon as she got back to the Ansonia.

The Ansonia was an old, ornate gray-white architectural fantasy on Broadway and Seventy-third Street. It had once been a fancy residential hotel; then the neighborhood deteriorated, and it became a shabby place for people who were just getting by, i.e. struggling actors. Robin had read about it in a mystery story years ago and had made it part of her career dreams.

Unfortunately, by the time she'd been ready to come to the City, the Upper West Side had become fashionable again, and the Ansonia had rescued itself from the sex clubs and bathhouses that had taken up residence, and regained its former glory as a fancy residential hotel. Robin was struggling, but not starving; she had a trust fund, and ample money for a one-bedroom in the residence of her dreams.

She felt rather guilty about it. An actor who is starving gets a lot more respect from other struggling actors than somebody who is eating well on non-show-business money. Robin missed a lot of the companionship she'd counted on. Sometimes she thought she'd look into getting an apartment in the Bel Nord, on Eighty-sixth Street, which was the current place to be, but she always decided against it. In the weird world of New York real estate, her seven-hundred-dollar-a-month apartment was an incredible bargain now; they'd have her committed if she gave it up.

Robin got her mail from the desk and leafed through it in the elevator. Nothing of interest. Not that she was expecting anything.

Inside the apartment, she called her answering service. Robin used the Up-West service, a switchboard place staffed almost exclusively by starving actors, musicians, and artists.

It was a nuisance, sharing a message box with eight or nine other actors, especially when you got an idiot like this one today, but it was part of her childhood picture of the Noble Struggle for Art, and she needed to keep *something* from that image.

"Hello, this is Robin Payne. Are there any messages in box four-fifty-eight?"

"There are messages in there, Sweetie, but none for you."

The *bastard*. Nobody but an actor could be so rotten (and, face it, nobody but a gay actor could be so bitchy), and nobody but an actor would know exactly the right thing to say to raise, then crush the hopes of an actor waiting to hear about a part.

This wasn't the first time, either. The first time, she'd been about ready to cry; now she was just mad. If he did it again, not only would Laughing Boy get an earful, his boss would too.

On a large scale, there were the people who took her cousin. On a small one, there was the boy at the answering service. Robin felt tired and dirty just thinking about them. If you offered her a nickel for the human race just then, you'd have had a sale. Dirt cheap.

She decided to take a shower and wash some of it off. She ran the water, took off her clothes, and stepped under the spray. She decided she could take it a little hotter, and adjusted the temperature. She shook her wet hair back, grabbed the sponge, and began to wash herself. And every place she touched—neck, breasts, belly—seemed to burn with the memory of the touch of Clifford Driscoll.

For hours last night, they had been all business. He asked her a million questions about Liz, Lindsay Keith, Herbert and Sheila Fane, the people at the plant (as though Robin were going to know much about any of them), and, it seemed, anything else that crossed his mind. Driscoll didn't take any notes, but he listened intently, and he had no trouble catching the smallest word that might have been inconsistent with some other small word she'd said an hour before.

When at last she was out of answers, he'd smiled at her and said, "That's all for now. Thanks."

Robin hadn't thought she'd been of much help, and said so.

"You never know," Driscoll replied. He tapped his temple. "I've got a lot of stuff up here now. Now when a situation demands something, there's that much data I won't have to wait around for."

"Are you going to remember all that?"

"Haven't failed yet. Your tenure as an agent is off to a great start. You're a good observer and a brave lady."

"Me? I'm a chicken."

"Chickens don't turn their backs on the country club life and try to make it as actresses. I know your uncle didn't like it. I know he doesn't give you any money."

"I don't want it," Robin insisted. "I wouldn't take it. It's not like I'm destitute, you know. My father left me some money. You probably know that too."

Driscoll grinned sheepishly, then nodded.

"And I don't see where what I've done was anything special—"

"Liz never could have done it," Driscoll said quietly.

Robin looked at him. She managed to keep her jaw from dropping. Somebody else knew. This . . . this *stranger*, without hearing Liz's patronizing comments (and sometimes just plain mean ones) about Robin's acting, without seeing Liz's boredom with the routine, and her resignation to a marriage with the impossibly vapid Lindsay, had seen what Robin had always known but had never put into words. Liz was *afraid*. Draper, Pennsylvania was too easy, too comfortable, to leave, and Liz knew it, and was constantly angry with herself over it.

Driscoll was staring at her as intently as he had been during the questioning; Robin was sure he could tell what she was thinking. That was comforting, too. There was no need to explain. She simply said, "Thank you."

"I just tell the truth, ma'am." He came to her and gave her a little kiss. Then he pulled away, and looked at her as though she'd bitten him. He said, "Mmm," in a surprised way and kissed her again, and this time she felt it too, and went on feeling it for a long time. The bed in the cabin came in very handy.

The best thing about him was that he *cared* so much. He wasn't the deftest, or the most imaginative, or the longest-lasting lover she had ever known, but he was the most sharing. She had been with men, sometimes actors, but most often not, who took lovemaking for a performance. She once caught one, an accountant, appropriately enough, counting the strokes. Too many of them seemed to want applause or something when they were done.

There was none of that with Clifford Driscoll. He was aware of all her needs and desires, sometimes before she was herself. In the heat and darkness of the cabin, with his sweating body wrapped in her arms, she could almost believe she loved him. And that was *really* ridiculous. She'd have to make it a point to keep reminding herself of that.

Robin turned off the shower, whipped her head around to get rid of some of the water in her hair, then reached outside for the towels. She wrapped one around her head and one around her body, and went to the bedroom to dress. She turned the radio on for company.

Bad timing. A song finished and the news came on. Robin hated to listen to the news. Drugs and war. The Carribbean and the Middle East. Then something closer to home.

"The fiancé of a kidnapped debutante is hospitalized today after a beating at the hands of unknown assailants," the announcer said. "Lindsay Keith, fiancé of Elizabeth Fane, who was the victim of a daring daylight kidnapping two days ago, was attacked outside his apartment in the small Pennsylvania town of Draper. A police spokesman says Keith was beaten by somebody who 'knew his business.' Keith suffered a broken leg, and numerous other injuries. Authorities refused to speculate on a possible connection . . ."

Robin tuned out, mentally and physically. She nearly twisted the knob off the radio in the attempt to get it to be quiet. She ran to the front door of her apartment, made sure both locks were locked. She wedged a chair under the doorknob, the way people did in the movies. She ran back to the bedroom, locking the bedroom door behind her. She put a chair under that knob, too. She sat stiffly on the edge of the bed, staring at the door. The towel fell from her body, but she didn't notice. She concentrated on the sound of her own breathing, as if to reassure herself that it continued. It was ragged and uneven, and she worked on bringing it under control.

Finally, when the tension had eased enough so that she could inhale without hurting her chest, she stood slowly and walked around the bed to the telephone.

About that same time, Driscoll was talking to his father in Washington. "You," he said, "have a strange sense of humor."

"What are you talkin' about, son?"

"You didn't want to talk to me in your office—okay. I wouldn't be surprised if somebody had it bugged . . ."

"I would," the Congressman said. "I have Jake Feder go over it at irregular intervals. I just felt like stretchin' my legs."

And he wanted to stretch them by walking around the Watergate, that symbol of all bungled covert operations, more especially the one that had made things tougher on all the intelligence services. The Congressman was fond of quoting Talleyrand on the subject—"It was worse than a crime, it was a blunder." Driscoll reminded the Congressman.

"Well," the older man drawled, "I guess we could all stand to learn a little humility, now and then. But that ain't the reason I like to walk around here. Mostly, it's because up close, you can't tell how ugly this thing is the way you can when you see it from a distance."

It was hot and muggy as only Washington in August could be. Driscoll had driven down from Pennsylvania in an air-conditioned car, and the air of Washington had hit him like a hammer when he'd stepped outside. He had a headache. What he wanted to do was get back in the car, get back to Draper, and get on with the project.

He didn't see any reason not to, either, except that the Congressman was being contrary again. Driscoll had done what he needed to do—bring the Congressman up to date on the operation and submit a shopping list—but the old man still wanted to talk. Driscoll hoped the old man wasn't slipping—one hearing used to be plenty for him; his brain could absorb anything and immediately extrapolate matters to their logical conclusion.

The Congressman, for his part, was hoping his *son* wasn't slipping. It wasn't that there was anything wrong with Clifford's plan—it was simple, and it had the great advantage of not having to fool the enemy. It only had to get past the innocent bystanders.

There wasn't anything wrong with the way his son had handled the girl, either. Hell, telling her what amounted to about ninety-eight percent of the truth had been a brilliant move. The Congressman doubted *he* would have thought of it. Provoking an argument, then apologizing; taking offense; putting on the tormented man act; all classic moves to get a civilian on your side.

But the boy was feeling it too much. That was bad. When the Congressman, just being helpful about a routine detail that must have slipped the boy's mind had said, "And of course you planked her before you wound things up for the night, didn't you?" Clifford had become distant, ice-cold despite the August heat. He hadn't answered.

Well, that meant of course that he *had* planked her. He was too good an agent to have neglected that. Dealing with civilians, bringing them in on an operation, was a dangerous thing, and it was a fact proven by experience that civilians were more loyal, and therefore less likely to be dangerous, to somebody they had slept with. For all the "sexual revolution" and all that crap, there was still, for women especially, more involved in lovemaking than slapping bodies together. As long as that fact remained true, it was a stupid agent who didn't use it to help secure the Objective, and to help keep himself safe.

But Clifford was acting as if he were *ashamed* of doing the smart thing here, and that was bad. Agents weren't civilians, and the minute they started acting like them, their usefulness was over.

The hell of it was, the Congressman couldn't even ream him out about it. Or, at least, he didn't want to until he knew for sure how well the boy was holding things together. He didn't want to give him an excuse to run out again. Not that he could bring himself to believe his son would leave in the middle of an operation. He just wasn't taking any unnecessary chances.

He had decided to keep the boy around for a few more hours, talk to him, maybe get a better idea about just what the problem might be.

"Let me just get a few things absolutely straight in my mind, son. Not so young anymore. D'you mind?"

"What do you want to know?"

"Well, on your list here, you write down that Jack Feder wants some video equipment to dub Beta-format cassettes on to inch-wide tape. Why's that? I thought we were going to work on a strictly audio basis."

"We are. But I learned something from the cousin last night that will lead us to a better source of audio. Seems Liz Fane's fianceé—Lindsay Keith—is a video nut, and likes to take tapes of things all the time. So there's a lot more source audio for her on these VTR cassettes than there would be anywhere else." He paused for a moment, gave his father a sour look, then said, "There are a lot of tapes of the two of them making love. At least, that's what Liz told her cousin. That will be a help when we make our own message."

"Why's that?"

"Because if you don't know the difference to start with, sex sounds just like pain."

The old man took off his jacket and folded it over his tie. "Damn uncomfortable city. Well, that sounds good. How are you going to get hold of those tapes, boy?"

"Miles got started on that early this morning. He didn't do anything irreversible, just enough to keep Keith in traction for three weeks or so. We'll make sure the apartment stays vacant, and we've secured constant access to the tapes."

"Fast work," the old man said approvingly. "But why didn't you—"

"*Don't even say it, Congressman,*" Driscoll hissed. His eyes were hot.

The Congressman laughed and patted his son on the back. "Don't worry boy, I wasn't goin' to ask you to kill him. I was wonderin' why hurt the poor bastard at all. Why not get him to cooperate?"

"You know better than that, Congressman. One civilian in on the operation is already too many. You taught me that your—"

Driscoll stopped again and looked at him. The old bastard. That lousy old bastard. He was *testing* him. Testing *him*, for God's sake, after he'd been dragged back kicking and screaming at the old man's orders.

"If you think I can't hack it, Father, now is the time to tell me so."

The Congressman's expression was bland. "Oh, you can hack it, son. The question in my mind is if you *want* to hack it."

"I'll get the goddamn job done. Whatever it takes."

"I'm happy to hear you say that. Like I told you before, ain't nobody else I can trust to do it."

"I said I would do it. I don't have to like it."

"It's easier for a man when he likes his work."

"Go to hell," Driscoll spat.

"Eventually. But you want to get back to work, don't you? Anything else you want to talk about?"

"Yeah," Driscoll said, knowing that there was nothing that could be said. He violated a District of Columbia ordinance and spat on the sidewalk. "Deliver the stuff to the address I gave you. It's an electronics factory—small shop. Herbert Fane more or less drove it out of business. Miles is pretending that he's going to open up something there. He's got a lease on the place. The trucks can drive right up—no security needed, as long as the stuff that gets delivered is packed in nice anonymous crates."

"You testin' *me,* now, boy?"

Driscoll shrugged. "You're the one who wanted to talk. I was just trying to oblige you. Anything else you'd like to discuss? Or can I get back to Draper, and the business of saving the world?"

"Oh, hell, boy, you know the world comes first. Just make a little time for your daddy every now and then."

Driscoll nodded, and turned to walk away. The Congressman's voice called, "Oh, and son?"

Driscoll turned to face him.

The old man smiled. "Keep up the good work."

Driscoll walked through the humidity to the car. He got inside, started the engine, then turned on the air conditioning. He rolled down his window to let the first hellish blast that came through the vents get out the window. Then, as the air became cooler, he rolled the window up, and adjusted the vent so that the breeze blew on his face. He locked his door, made sure the others were locked, then closed his eyes and took off his glasses to feel the cool air on his eyelids. It felt good, but Driscoll didn't indulge himself for too long. His father's men had once caught up with him when he was washing his face in a country stream. Since then, Driscoll had vowed he would never again be taken with his eyes closed.

He opened them now, put the car in gear, and headed north. Miles greeted him when he arrived. As always, Miles' attitude toward Driscoll was an odd combination of deference and hostility. Driscoll attributed it to Miles' respect for anyone the Congressman had confidence in, coupled with irritation that Driscoll didn't want to see espionage and counterterrorism as a kind of boy's adventure story, with the agents, especially Driscoll and Miles, playing the parts of a rollicking band of Musketeers, shoulder to shoulder and forward to the fray and similar nonsense.

Driscoll wouldn't play that one, so he was forced into a different kind of game, one that had him playing the teacher while Miles was a promising, but insecure student. It all got rather tiresome after a while.

"Welcome back," Miles said, as Driscoll emerged into the cool gloom of the safe-house factory's garage. "How's the Great White Father?"

Driscoll looked at him. Was Miles being funny? Or had he somehow tumbled to the relationship between Driscoll and the

Congressman? Driscoll decided that innuendo wouldn't be Miles' style in that case and answered his question in the spirit in which it had probably been intended.

"About the same," he said. "The stuff will be coming in soon. Make sure Jake is around to receive it. What's new here? Have Leo Calvin and friends made any moves?"

"No," Miles said. "They want to give Fane time to get good and desperate, it seems. But *you* got a phone call. Robin Payne."

"Ah," Driscoll said. "She's heard about Lindsay. Good job on that, by the way. I take it you didn't let him have a look at you."

"Of course not," Miles said. He looked mildly perturbed at the comment, and Driscoll was irritated at himself. Tempered praise was not the right way to handle Miles. He always discounted the praise, and took the tempering as a reproach.

"How was she?" Driscoll pressed on. "How did her voice seem?"

"Dead," Miles said. "No emotion at all. I think the news hit her hard."

It was supposed to, but Driscoll didn't bother to mention it. "Tell me all of it," he said. He saw a frown start to form on Miles' face, so he added, "I know you taped it, but I want your impressions, too."

Miles nodded. "All right, here's how it went. I picked up the phone and said, 'Five-six hundred.' Then she asked for you. I told her you were away for a while, but that I had been assigned by you to answer this emergency number, and that I would help her in any way I could. Then she told me about her cousin's fiancé and asked me if I knew what had happened to him. I told her I did."

Miles allowed himself a small grin at the irony. "Then she said she was afraid she'd be next and she didn't know what to do. She said again that she wanted to talk to you."

"What did you tell her?" Driscoll said.

"Just to stay put, keep her doors locked, and that I'd have you get in touch with her as soon as possible. I didn't try to talk her out of the idea that the terrorists might have everybody on a little list or that she was in danger herself."

"Terrific," Driscoll said. "Absolutely perfect, Miles." *There,* Driscoll thought. *That ought to do for untempered praise.*

"I'm not as stupid as I seem, am I?" Miles said. That was another thing. Miles would always offer Driscoll opportunities to insult him. These must never be picked up.

This time, Driscoll just ducked it. "I'd better go make that call."

Jake Feder was just screwing the bottom plate back on a recorder phone. "Here," he said, "use this one. Guaranteed bug proof for twenty-four hours." Driscoll took the receiver from him and dialed.

Robin thanked God when she heard Driscoll's voice. Driscoll told her to relax. Robin started to babble all her reasons for being afraid, but Driscoll cut her off.

"We know all about it," he told her. "Don't worry about a thing. We're watching over your aunt and uncle here, and we've got people watching your building now. You won't see them, but they're there. If you leave, they'll follow you, so you don't have to make youself a prisoner if you don't want to."

Robin yelled at him. "*Are you crazy?* Nobody is getting me out of this apartment!"

"All right. Stay in. I hope you have enough food." She assured him she did. "Good. If anyone calls you, answer the phone," he went on. "If it's something normal, say you have a cold, and that's why you're staying in. If there's anything out of the ordinary about it, call the number I gave you, any time, and Miles or I will help you out. You'll only have to put up with this for one day—"

"How do you know *that?*" Robin demanded.

"Because tomorrow, I'm coming up there to get you. We have to go back to work. You're still going to help us on this, aren't you?"

"It looks like I have to," Robin said sadly. "They're liable to get me if I don't help you get them first."

"It might not be as bad as all that," Driscoll said.

"I'd prefer not to take any chances, if you don't mind."

"That's always a good plan. I'll be up there sometime late in the day. I'll see you then. Everything will be all right."

"I hope so." Just before they hung up, she said, "Cliff?"

"Yes, Robin?"

"You be careful, too, okay?"

That was how Driscoll happened to be in New York, in the Ansonia Hotel, making love to Robin Payne ("Planking her to reinforce conditioning," his father would say) the night Miles and Vi were stealing the body of Jane Doe #64 and taking her fingerprints and putting her in the recently delivered refrigerator.

And now, the next morning, as she sat beside him, quiet and brave as he drove the rented car back to Draper, Driscoll was thinking that his two female fish, the live one and the dead one, had been hooked and boated. Everything was in place.

Now everything waited for Leo Calvin to make his next move.

Chapter Four

LIZ WAS PAST HOPE NOW. FOR THE FIRST FEW DAYS, HER heart had leapt at every sound from the street, every step on the floor. Any second, someone would come and get her out of this stinking closet, free her from these crazy people.

Now she knew that no one would find her—that her world would always be an unlighted space about four feet square, opened occasionally for someone to give her a beating or to stick a needle in her. She had memories of people talking to her at times, but she was unclear about what they said to her.

She was past fear now, too. The terror of the first few days had passed, replaced by a numb apathy that was a disguise for despair. Fear had proven unprofitable. All the things she had been afraid of—that she would be tortured, that she would be raped, that she would be brainwashed—all were coming to pass.

Liz guessed she might be due for another shot, because she rarely thought about things like this. She rarely thought. Most of the time now, on this sixth day of her captivity, she answered to "Daisy Mae" without hesitation, and sometimes even found herself thinking of herself by that name. She did whatever they said, repeated what they told her to say. She tried to please them.

It must have been working. They let her out of the closet once in a while now. They blindfolded her and gagged her when they did, but she got a chance to straighten out her legs now. The legs had grown numb, too. She was taken out twice a day to use the bathroom, instead of having to foul her closet as she had done the first day. The other times she got to leave was when they wanted to use her sexually. That was heaven. She got to lie down on a bed, on her back or on her stomach, it didn't matter which. That was such a pleasure, it didn't really matter *what* male or female hands and mouths and whatever were doing to her. Liz would lie there, sometimes tied, sometimes not, and feel the cloth, smell the clean sheets. Sometimes this even made her feel so good she could feel the stirrings of response in herself.

The rest of the time she spent in a half-dream, images of violence linked with childhood memories. She remembered the scene at the Tennis Club, the sting in her thigh just before she passed out (an eternity ago), and wondered where her mother was, if anything had happened to her mother. Then she'd feel her mind sliding back to the time her mother had spared her from her father's wrath when she had led her cousin Robin through some of the loopholes in the plant security system when it was first being set up. Why couldn't Mother have protected her *this* time? And Liz would feel abandoned and start to cry. At times like this, she would almost *want* to be Daisy Mae. Daisy Mae's life was tough, but it was all her own. Daisy Mae didn't depend on people, only to be let down. She wasn't rich but powerless. She had nothing to resent. It was a great comfort to be helpless and *accept* it. It took so much of the pressure off.

And she (Liz or Daisy Mae, for this it didn't matter) slept a lot. Some of that, she supposed, was due to the drugs. A lot of it was because there was nothing else to do. Her brain just shut off on her. It was a relief, and for a few blissful seconds just after waking, she would remember nothing, not her past life, not her life in the closet. Just an absolute comforting blankness. It was the best time of the day.

The door of the closet opened. Automatically, Liz cringed. It was not unknown for one of them to open the door and begin hitting her without a word. This visitor was one of the ones who had done it, the boy, the one who had made her blow him before she could have any food. She could tell by his voice (she was learning all their voices) when he said, "Give me your arm, Daisy Mae, it's Happy Juice time." He always called it Happy Juice.

She gave him her arm, felt a cold swipe of alcohol-soaked cotton, felt the needle go in, then the warm pressure as the liquid diffused through her tissues, another swipe with the cotton, and he left her alone.

Soon, her brain began to loosen, began to feel less like crushed rock packed into her skull and more like a comfortable toy, one that didn't make too many demands on her. She could feel herself returning to that friendly void that wasn't quite sleep.

She never quite got there. The closet door opened again, and this time, it let in light. There had never been light in the room before when the door had been opened. Between being blindfolded and being locked in the closet, Liz had been six days in darkness, and now she blinked painfully in the light, wanting to shut her eyes tight against it, at the same time wanting desperately to see *something*.

It was a woman—Liz could tell that much. She had blond hair, medium-short, and she wore a white blouse and khaki pants. The light was too vicious for Liz to stand any longer— she turned away before she could make out any of the woman's features.

The woman said, "Hi. Are you all right, Daisy Mae?"

It was a new voice. It was soft and low and pleasant, and none of the voices she'd heard here, men's or women's, had been any of those things. And none of them had said "Daisy Mae" as anything but a sneer, an insult. This woman said it as though it were a joking nickname among friends.

Then the woman's actual words got through. Was she all right? Liz didn't know whether to laugh or cry; she tried to do both at once and succeeded only in making little choking noises.

"Here," the woman said. "Give me your hand. Let's get you cleaned up."

Liz had a million questions—more—but she'd been con-ditioned well. Without a word, she offered her hand to the blond woman.

It was difficult for Liz to walk—her legs were stiff from her long day in the closet. The blond woman, though considerably smaller than Liz, supported her and cooed encouragement as she led her across the floor.

In all her fantasizing and mental vaporings over the last six days, Liz had never speculated on exactly *where* these people were keeping her, except for one vagrant fancy that she had died and gone to hell. The fact that the site of her captivity seemed to be a perfectly ordinary wood-floored one-family house left her dumbfounded. Pale yellow walls. Colonial furniture. It seemed *wrong*, almost impossible that the things she had experienced should have happened here.

Liz and her companion passed through a room and along an upstairs hallway. There was no one in sight, but Liz's isolation-sensitized hearing detected sounds behind doors. She was being watched by people who were being careful to keep themselves out of sight.

"Here we are," the blond woman said. She pointed to a wooden door identical to all the others in the hallway. "My name is Candy, by the way."

"Candy," Liz repeated dumbly.

"That's right," the woman said. "I see you're still blinking, so protect your eyes. The light in here is pretty bright. All the tiles, you know."

Liz dutifully closed her eyes and let herself be led across the threshold. She opened them at the sound of roaring. She blinked a few times, but her pupils were already getting back the nearly forgotten habit of adjusting, and soon she could look around without pain. The bathroom. And the woman was filling the bath for her. Adding bubble bath. Liz suddenly became aware of six days of accumulated filth on her body, and suddenly that tub full of hot, scented water was all she wanted in the world. She looked longingly at the blond woman. Candy. She had to remember that. Candy.

Candy smiled at her. Her face wasn't anything special, Liz thought, but she had a pretty smile.

"Come on," Candy said, "Get those filthy clothes off."

With a gratitude that almost hurt, Liz shed the clothes she'd worn since she'd left the Lakeside Club—the people who'd used her sexually hadn't even removed them from her, just pushed them up or down or aside.

As she dropped her things, Candy picked them up and put them in a plastic bag. "We'll be getting new clothes for you," she said. "Now get in the water."

Liz nearly fainted as she stepped in. That was how good it felt. She was lightheaded and comfortable as she'd never hoped to be again. A hot tub in a white-tiled bathroom in a nice family house. Liz was filled with the sudden desire to die here in the tub, while this was still going on. She relaxed.

Candy, meanwhile, had taken off her blouse. She draped it over the towel rack and said, "I don't want to get this wet while I wash you." Her chest was large for such a small woman, Liz thought. The bra she was wearing was definitely necessary.

Candy wet a sponge at the sink, then knelt on the bathrug beside the tub. She began to wipe Liz's face. Her touch was gentle, but Liz winced all the same.

"I'm sorry," Liz said. "Somebody punched me in the nose."

Candy nodded. "Waldo. He can't get off unless he sees blood, and somewhere along the line, he learned that a punch in the nose is the quickest way to produce it. That's what I'm trying to do now, wash the blood off your face."

Liz remembered it now, all of it. The heavy body and the animal breathing and the tongue licking her face. She shuddered.

"There's . . ." Liz swallowed and began again. "There's a woman, too. Harsh voice. She—she pinches." Liz raised an arm through the bubbles and looked at the butterfly-shaped bruises. Seeing them somehow hurt more than having them made.

Candy nodded again. "Georgia. She pinches. Don't worry, it won't happen again."

Suddenly, Liz grabbed Candy's bare shoulder with a sudsy hand. Words started to tumble from her mouth. "Candy, you've got to get me away from these people, they're crazy, they're going to kill me, we've got to get the police, stop them—"

Candy's face grew very grave. She looked intently into Liz's eyes and said, "Daisy Mae!"

"Y-yes?"

"You don't understand. *I* am one of these people. We have

a hard and important job to do, and that makes us do things. We have our faults, but we're not so bad really."

"I hate you!" Liz screamed. *"Hate you! Hate—"*

Sadly, Candy shook her head. "That kind of talk will get you put right back in the closet."

Liz shut up instantly. *Oh, God,* she thought, *not the closet.* She began to beg Candy to forgive her. Hot tears ran down her face.

Candy put a finger across Liz's mouth. "Shhh," she said. "You don't have to cry." Candy leaned over and kissed Liz softly on the lips. "Everything will be all right," she whispered. "Just be smart and things will be fine. I promise."

The FBI man narrowed his eyes. "We haven't worked together before, have we Driscoll?"

Driscoll had known this was coming. If the FBI had a political kidnapping specialist, Fenton Rines was it. He even taught future agents how to deal with such things at the FBI school at the Marine Base in Quantico, Virginia. The Congressman had warned his son that Rines was certain to be put in charge of the investigation for the Bureau; the only thing that hadn't gone according to expectation was Rines' not showing up until yesterday. Driscoll thought he'd be seeing him a lot sooner.

Still, now that he was here, he was worth waiting for. He was tall, taller than Driscoll, with a friendly face and a firm handshake. He wore a gray suit and a blue tie over a trim frame. His eyes were blue, and his dark hair was combed straight across a bald pate to make one of those half-circle hairlines. He looked like a mathematics professor, or the president of a small town bank.

According to the report sent to Driscoll by the Congressman, Inspector Fenton Rines was forty-three years old, the last sixteen with the Bureau. He was the kind of man the FBI would have drafted, if they had the authority to do things like that. Rines covered all of J. Edgar Hoover's requirements under several layers of excellence. He had better than twenty-twenty vision, he was a college graduate and a veteran (Marine Corps), and he had graduate degrees in accounting *and* law; the FBI required only one or the other. On top of that, Rines had even practiced law for a year or so in his uncle's firm before joining the Bureau.

He had done good work, especially during the turbulent sixties. The Director never hesitated to give Rines the toughest assignments and the most visible ones. Whatever it was—antiterrorism, intelligence gathering on the hottest college campuses of the sixties, or less political assignments—Rines did his job quietly and efficiently. The Director had been very proud of him.

If J. Edgar Hoover had lived another two or three years, in fact, Fenton Rines might very probably have been Deputy Director of the Bureau, and in position to move up. Rines would never have allowed the Bureau to be used the way it had been during the Watergate coverup, Driscoll reflected—if nothing else, helping a President scrambling to stay in office was, in Rines' opinion, beneath the dignity of the Bureau.

If Rines had a flaw, it was his tendency to be overzealous in his devotion to the Bureau. He tended to be vocally angry over what he saw as the erosion of respect for the Bureau. None of his comments ever made it as far as the press—he wouldn't have lasted long as an agent if that had happened, no matter *how* good he was—but they got to important people. Three Presidents had heard that Fenton Rines thought the Freedom of Information Act had been a big mistake. Legislators managed to hear that he thought the oversight committees in the House and Senate were overzealous and made life unnecessarily difficult for everyone in what they liked to call the "intelligence community," and especially, in Rines' unsecret opinion, for the leading citizens of that community, the FBI.

Driscoll conceded that Rines probably had a point. As chairman of the House Intelligence Oversight Committee, Driscoll's father made a great show of making the Bureau and the CIA and the DEA and everybody else toe the line, the better to cover the activities of his own boys, the outfit so secret it didn't have initials.

Rines had once accused the Congressman of coming down especially heavily on the FBI. Rines was sick of it.

"I don't know what you're talking about," the Congressman had replied pleasantly.

"I'm talking about deep, unauthorized domestic covert operations."

"Why, those things are *illegal*," Driscoll's father had said.

"I know, Congressman. But they're still going on. And since they *are* illegal, they must be going on with your knowledge. All I'm asking is that you give the Bureau a fighting chance to do its job as well as the people you've already given the go-ahead to."

The Congressman had frowned. He was tempted to recruit Rines for the Agency on the spot. No one in the community had come this close to things before. The feeling was strengthened when Rines said he had been clipping newspaper articles of unusual events, and that a lot of them formed a pattern. He mentioned three possible covert operations, two of which were actually Agency projects. The Congressman decided against dropping the truth on Rines, because he suspected that the agent was too attached to the Bureau to say yes.

"I think you have quite an imagination, Mr. Rines," the Congressman had said.

Rines had smiled at him. "All right, sir," he had said, preparing to leave the office. "I'm at your mercy—you can probably have me dismissed over this. In fact, I advise you to do it."

"Why's that, Mr. Rines?"

"Because I'm not going to bother you anymore until I have proof of what's going on. It will take awhile—I have my regular job and all that—but I'll get it. When I do, I'm going to show it to you. That will be my lever to get more leeway for the Bureau out of you."

"If you find proof of abuses," the Congressman had told him, "I want to see it, of course."

"You'll see it, I promise." With that, he had wished the

Congressman good afternoon and departed. The Congressman watched him go, and sighed. Rines did too good a job for
the country to have him thrown out of the FBI. Or killed, which
was also an option. Still, some day, he might turn out to be a
nuisance that had to be dealt with.

Driscoll hoped this wasn't the day. He had enough to worry
about wondering from one second to the next if Rines would
pick this moment to find some proof and blow Driscoll's little
living theater production right off the stage.

He might do it, too. Driscoll had seen Rines in action,
during his college days. Rines had investigated the terrorist
group Driscoll had been keeping company with. Rines had
questioned him twice.

Driscoll had weighed forty pounds more then, and his hair
was lighter and he wore a beard. He also wore colored contact
lenses instead of his glasses, and he had affected a Boston
accent. So he wasn't overly afraid of being recognized. But
there were going to be many unusual events going on here, and
Rines might well put them together.

As it was, working aboveboard and within the law, Rines
had come within a day of discovering a bomb plot that Driscoll
had to crack using every trick he'd been taught and a few he
invented on the spot.

When Driscoll had learned where the bomb was (and the
girl he loved was worse than dead—he chased the thought from
his mind) . . . when he knew where the bomb was, it was
Rines he called with an anonymous tip. Rines got the bomb
defused, and everyone was saved, except the girl, of course.
And Driscoll. It was then he'd started trying to hide from his
father. Maybe he should have hidden better.

"Have we?" the agent said.

"Have we what?"

"Worked together?"

"No," Driscoll said. "I would have remembered."

"You look familiar."

Great, Driscoll thought. *Wonderful.* Still, he managed to
smile. "Come on, Rines, what are you doing, practicing? Take a

look at my file. I've been working in Asia for the last eight years."

"Your file?" the Inspector said innocently.

"Yeah, the one you got from the Defense Department. What the hell, I've got one on you."

Then Rines smiled knowingly. Driscoll relaxed, realizing now that he hadn't been recognized. At the same time, he felt a bit of irritation, because he knew he'd been taken in.

"All right, Mr. Driscoll," Rines said. "I just wanted to know if we had a bureaucrat on this case, or a real professional."

"Did you find out?"

"Yes, I did."

"Well, I hope you're happy with the answer."

"That depends. There are frequently frictions and hurt feelings when people from agencies with different priorities get together on a case."

Driscoll shook his head. "Not in this case. Our priorities are going to keep us friendly."

"I hope so."

"I guarantee it. Look, I'll do some nosing around, but I'm not really here to investigate anything. That's your job. My job is to take the situation in hand and babysit the girl's father. Make sure a certain piece of hardware gets built in his factory on schedule." It occurred to Driscoll that this was the longest string of true statements he had made (to anyone but his father) in five years.

"Excellent," Rines said. He smiled like an astronaut, happy and wholesome. "I don't want anybody to do anything spectacular without mutual consultation."

"Count on it," Driscoll said, breaking the string.

"Good. Let's go in and talk to the locals."

The muster room of the Town of Draper Police Department could have been a grade school auditorium. There was a stage, a blue-green curtain, flags of the United States and the Commonwealth of Pennsylvania, and about seventy-five fold-down seats made of bright red Masonite or plastic, or something. Whatever it was, it was cold and slippery.

Actually, from what Driscoll had seen, the whole building could have been a grade school. Or a modern courthouse. Or a medium security prison. Every public building erected between 1955 and 1965 looked like this, Driscoll reflected. White, imitation stone tile floors, bare brick for outside walls, pseudo-burlap inside. Not enough light. He wondered what the holding cells looked like.

The chief of police kept referring to it as "the New Headquarters." "That's right, Mr. Driscoll," he would say, "I joined the force here in 1959, one year before they opened the New Headquarters."

That was the only remark the chief made that was addressed to Driscoll. He was polite enough, but he didn't have much attention to spare from Fenton Rines, a top FBI man, for God's sake. Driscoll, as far as the chief knew, was a bureaucrat, and therefore didn't count.

That was fine with Driscoll. This get-together had been called to coordinate all the various authorities who were looking into the Liz Fane case. Driscoll was surprised when they invited him. He would just as soon have skipped it, but it would have looked strange if he weren't there. He would attract less attention sitting in front of them, nodding like a Washington functionary. He concentrated on looking interested, if slightly above it all. Every once in a while, he nodded. He might as well have been invisible.

The chief was nominally the host of this gathering, but Driscoll suspected that Rines was behind it all. His suspicion was even stronger now, after the little chat out there in the lobby. Anyway, if Rines hadn't taken total charge yet, he would now. The chief certainly wasn't making it difficult for him. He started out by asking Rines if he had had a chance to read all the reports as readied for him by him and Captain Roedale of the State Police. He didn't say, "Please, *please* say they are good," but the message got across.

Rines smiled his bank-president smile. "Yes, excellent. I'm right up to date. And the local office of the Bureau tells me you men are doing a very energetic and efficient job."

Driscoll could see the fear slip off the chief's shoulders like a wool overcoat. The man's name was Fred Anderson. He was burly without being especially tall, and he had gray-black hair combed to the right, where it exploded into a fizzy mass that clung to the side of his head like foam on beer. He wore a white shirt with the sleeves rolled up over hairy forearms, sending a message to these Washington big shots that he was a hard-working man.

Which he was. Driscoll had gotten copies of those reports, too, and the locals were all doing good work. Everything they'd found had been negative, but eliminating possibilities is police work, too, and just as useful in the long run. Anderson was honest beyond question, and he was competent or better for all the stuff a local police chief is usually called upon to handle. Rines had told Driscoll (after accepting him as a fellow professional) that Chief Anderson had done a very nice job on the murder of a drifter whose armless and headless body happened to wind up in Draper.

But terrorist kidnappings were out of Anderson's league, and he was a good enough cop to know it. He called for help loud and clear at the first legally permissible moment, but that didn't mean he had to like it.

Anderson was angry with himself. Roedale was giving him a dirty look—full of State Trooper pride, he supposed. Well, they were a good outfit, funny hats and all, but they weren't the FBI.

This was the biggest thing that had ever happened in this town. Reporters were still pouring in—they'd filled up the Holiday Inn, and all the other places for five towns around. One guy, from a San Francisco paper (doing a compare and contrast with the Hearst thing) had even asked him for a shakedown in the jail.

They were all getting antsy. Reporters, even the ones from the local paper and radio station, could get very put out when somebody they thought ought to be talking to them wouldn't. These national guys were vicious. Damn it, if Fred Anderson wanted to hear somebody call him frightened and nervous on national TV, he would have run for President. The fact that he *was* frightened and nervous had made it all the worse.

It was nice, at least, to know that the FBI, in the person of one of its top agents, was behind him. It gave him confidence, something he was going to need when he faced those hyenas at a press conference later this afternoon.

That was the current item on the agenda, the press conference. The chief read them his opening statement; everybody said it was fine. "Then I'll introduce everybody, and throw it open for questions."

"Very good, Chief," the FBI man said. "Just be ready for some tough stuff. Don't get rattled. Don't be afraid to say 'No comment' to as many questions as you have to." He looked around at the gathering. "That's something for everybody to remember. Even me. *Especially* me." He grinned sheepishly. "I've let the press get to me a time or two. It never makes the job any easier, does it?"

So here was the big FBI man, relaxed among pros, not worrying about the *dignity* of the Bureau, and the other tight-assed things they usually were worried about when Fred Anderson had had anything to do with them. It occurred to the chief that Rines might have done it on purpose, to make the local yokels feel at ease, but he dismissed it from his mind. Besides, it didn't matter. A federal man's bothering even to *fake* respect for a local cop was rare enough to mark this as a special occasion.

Anderson felt so good, he was ready to dismiss the meeting right there, but they still had things they wanted to talk about, specifically the attack on the kidnapped girl's boyfriend. Captain Roedale reported that nobody in his department was hearing or turning up anything to suggest that it hadn't been the terrorists who'd done it.

"Statewide, even," the captain said. "With all the police and press attention this town has been getting, most of the hard boys who work this area are staying home." He looked sourly at the chief. "I bet crime is way down here lately, aside from the Fane-related things."

The chief took a second to fight down the impulse to call Captain Roedale an asshole. Only Fane-related crimes. Two murders, a kidnapping, and a first degree assault, that's all. He ran a hand over his head. "Thanks, Roedale. I guess there's a bright side to everything, huh?"

Then the chief decided to use some of his new-found confidence. "One thing, though," he said. "I'm not completely sure the Lindsay Keith thing *is* Fane related."

Fred Anderson wasn't confident enough yet to say something like that without trying to read faces to see how it had gone over. Rines looked interested; Roedale didn't bother to hide his disgust. Driscoll made it a tie. The quiet guy from the Defense Department sat there with the face of a corpse, one who had died of boredom. If Anderson didn't see him blink every once in a while, he would have been tempted to call for the coroner.

The FBI man said, "Would you like to elaborate on that for us, Chief?"

"Uh, sure." He shuffled through reports. "Here's the medical report on the kid. See this?—only one broken bone, left shin. The rest of the stuff is deep bone bruises. Done with shots with a blackjack down the length of the body, probably. We used to see a lot of stuff like that back when there was trouble over unionizing the mill."

"The mill?"

"Yeah. Used to be a coke refinery around here. Strip mining laws basically put it out of business years ago. It was a lucky day for this town when Herbert Fane decided to move his operations here. Bought the whole mill property, too, even though he doesn't use much more than half of it—"

"How about the beating, Chief?" Rines said gently.

Christ, Anderson thought, *I've been rambling like an old woman.* He made a face at himself, and went on. "Anyway, back in the mill days, there was a lot of trouble over union things, and people on one side or the other were being put in the hospital pretty regular. That's when I saw this kind of beating. Takes a pro to do it—hurts like crazy, lays you up—hell, cripples you—for weeks, but doesn't really do much lasting damage."

Roedale was getting impatient. "So? Nobody thinks the people who snatched the girl at the country club were amateurs, Chief."

"That's just it, though. Different kind of pro. These bastard terrorists don't give a shit for anybody. They wasted the ambulance driver and the intern, probably didn't even know their names. Why were they so considerate of Lindsay Keith? I mean, we don't even have much of an idea about why they knocked him around in the first place, but as long as they were out to hurt him anyway, why didn't they blow him away? It doesn't make sense, to me."

The chief took a breath. There. He'd said it and gone out on a limb. He may have been just a small-town cop, but what the hell, that didn't mean he didn't have a brain.

It looked like his little idea had gone over pretty well. Roedale even was forced to concede that Anderson might have a point. Driscoll still didn't say anything, but he looked at the chief and nodded as if to say the same thing. Rines said that it would bear looking into—he'd put men on it right away. They discussed nuts and bolts routine matters of the investigation for a while—how long to keep the road surveillance up, allocation of personnel for a raiding party, when and if they had somebody to raid, who would man the hot-line phones, and how information would be distributed—then the party broke up until four o'clock and the press conference.

Rines caught up with Driscoll in the half-brick hallway. "What do you think of the chief's theory?"

"I didn't know you could be drafted into the FBI," Driscoll said.

"Come on, I just want to know how it struck you."

"It struck me that Fred Anderson is a smart cop."

Rines nodded. "And a good one. He's fighting through all the hype of the press and his awe of the Bureau."

"Oh," Driscoll said with a grin, "you noticed."

"It happens all the time. It's a pain, but cops like Roedale are worse—they think the Bureau consists of nothing but glory grubbers. Which, I admit, we have our share of. Still, when it comes to a crunch, I think I'd rather have Anderson backing me."

"Actually, I think it's more to the point to ask you what you thought of it."

"Just what I said in there," Rines protested. "You heard me. It's worth looking into."

Rines reached the door first, held it for Driscoll. It was hot and humid enough outside to be Washington weather.

"Thanks," Driscoll said. "I heard you. I also agree with you. However . . ."

"However *what?*"

"However, if you didn't spot it as soon as you saw the report, you must have bought your great reputation from somebody else."

"Of *course* I spotted it," Rines said. "That doesn't make the chief any less smart. Besides, we're running checks on everybody, anyhow. It's just that now we'll give more attention to Mr. Lindsay Keith."

"Think there's anything to it?"

Rines shrugged. "That somebody else beat Keith up? Eminently possible. As the chief says, they don't often leave survivors. That the kid was in on it?" He shrugged. "That's a lot of pain to take for a cause."

Driscoll nodded. In his experience, people, extremists, even agents, were more willing to suffer at the hands of the enemy, no matter what the propaganda gain that might be obtained from a staged injury engineered by your own side. An important part of the psychological gratification of being a martyr was showing some son of a bitch he couldn't get your respect even by killing you. Driscoll knew some people who'd take a beating for show, but they were real sickos, and valuable for that reason. Certainly none were civilians like the Keith boy.

A kid in a suit who carried a tape recorder looked at them for a few seconds, frozen in mid-stride like a hunting dog. He came out of it, and made for them, pretending he wasn't in a hurry to get them cornered.

"Mr. Rines, Mr. Driscoll?" he said, slightly breathless. "Tom Ivery, WLTN. The local station, you know. Just a couple of ques—"

They cut him off. "We're saving everything for the press conference at four o'clock," Rines told him. "Sorry."

Driscoll had to admit the kid had discipline. He held his enthusiasm in at the risk of possible internal injuries. He caught his breath and said, "I'll let you go on one condition."

Driscoll sized the kid up. Twenty or so. Big. Kind of fat,

kind of clumsy. No dope, in any sense of the word. And on top of his job—the fact that he'd known Driscoll on sight, after all his efforts to keep a low profile (the name "Driscoll" hadn't been in anybody's newspaper) proved that.

"What's your condition?" Driscoll said.

"Somebody has to call on me at the news conference. All the big networks are going to be there, the magazines, the wire services. You're all going to be looking at Leslie Stahl—you won't call on somebody from a little local FM'er unless you promise to. So promise to. That way maybe we all make the network news. Or talk to me now. Or I'll chase you with my tape recorder everywhere you go."

"Anything but that!" Driscoll said. "All right, kid. What's your name again?"

"Tom Ivery."

"All right, Tom, I'll see you get called on."

"Thank you."

"Right," Rines said.

"I'll leave you gentlemen alone now."

"Good," Rines said.

"Thank you."

"*Beat it!*"

Tom Ivery gulped, nodded, and strode away, holding on to whatever journalistic dignity he could.

When he was out of earshot, Rines looked at Driscoll and said, "That kid's got it already."

"Got what?"

"The journalistic outlook. One eye on the story, but the good eye on the career."

"Yeah," Driscoll replied. "Good thing law enforcement people never have to worry about things like that." Rines started to take a breath to reply, but Driscoll cut him off. "So. Now all we have to do is improve each shining hour until the press conference."

"No problem for me," the FBI man replied. "I've always got reports to read. You do too—you're getting copies of all our unclassified stuff."

"I know, and thanks. But I think I'm in the mood to read

something a little bit lighter. I'll just take stroll over to the public library. I'll see you later."

Rines looked dubious; nobody read for pleasure in the middle of an investigation, it was ridiculous. Still, he bought it finally, shrugged, got in his car and drove off to the Holiday Inn on the edge of town.

Driscoll, meanwhile, strolled two blocks past dress shops and drugstores, a barber shop, a luncheonette, a deli, and Bogner's Bootery, "Shoeing Draper for Over Sixty Years." Driscoll had to stop and look at it. There were good leaf designs around the windows, and carved wood (or formed plaster, he couldn't tell which) for the frames. Wing tips and designer sneakers competed for attention. The sneakers won, only because they were so out of place.

They were out of place, in fact, in the whole town square, which could have been a movie set labeled "small town, c. 1921." The last time Driscoll had passed through this part of town, it had been night, and he hadn't appreciated it properly in the darkness. The square was about a hundred yards on a side, and the whole thing sloped gently upward toward the north and City Hall. There was a gazebo in the middle, big enough, no doubt, to hold the town Marching and Chowder Society Band for Fourth of July concerts. City Hall was marble, three stories, with a White House-style portico, complete with fluted columns. The bank was white marble, too. The rest of the buildings were immaculate wood and whitewash—the post office, the Old Police Station (which was now a daycare center— the cells probably came in handy, Driscoll reflected), and his destination, the library, a long-ago gift from Andrew Carnegie.

The air conditioner didn't date back to Andrew Carnegie, but for all the noise it made and all the good it did, it might as well have. Driscoll took off his jacket and loosened his tie. The woman behind the desk smiled fatalistically at him from behind a small leaf fan. "We keep trying to get the city council to fix it up, but there's always a new traffic light they want to buy, or something. The heat's pretty good in the winter."

"I'm sure it is," Driscoll said politely. "Which way to the card catalogue?"

"Just around the corner from the desk. If you need

something on microfilm, just let me know, and I'll get you all set up."

Driscoll squeegeed sweat from his forehead and grinned. "Don't tell me," he said, "you got federal money for the microfilm system."

"Exactly right. Are you with the government?"

Driscoll shrugged. "I'm not *against* it." Not at the moment, anyway.

"I wish I could tell somebody in Washington that without air conditioning the microfilm gets all sticky and the emulsion comes off. Waste of money."

"Welcome to bureaucracy."

"Yes, I know what you mean. If you need anything, just sing out." Driscoll was going to ask whatever happened to silence in the library, but decided that the air conditioner had probably made that problem irrelevant.

He pulled a drawer marked *Mu–Na* from the wooden cabinet, placed it down on a slide-out shelf, and flipped to a section marked *Myths and Legends*. He got a break right at the beginning of the alphabet. *Words from the Myths*, by Isaac Asimov. Decorations by William Barss. Houghton Mifflin, 1961.

Field operations for the Agency often involved a lot of spot research like this. Driscoll, at an early age, had worked out a prime directive for doing it: Find out if Asimov has written a book about it. Driscoll's father had given his ten-year-old son Asimov's *Foundation Trilogy* to read. The stories of the decline and fall of a galactic empire were supposed to serve as a sort of a painless introduction to power politics.

Driscoll learned even more when he began to read Asimov's nonfiction. The man was a compulsive explainer, and damned good at it, too. Whether he was writing about the history of France, the Bible, Shakespeare, or science (or any number of other topics), Asimov was always clear without being too simple, detailed without getting bogged down in arcana. And since Asimov had published close to three hundred books, there was always a chance his explanation compulsion had lit on the subject you wanted to know about.

His only failing, as far as Driscoll was concerned, was that when he waxed political, as he did from time to time, Asimov still tended to see the world in terms of liberals and conservatives. Driscoll found that quaint. In Driscoll's world, the political parties broke down into Smarts and Deads.

He sighed, opened his collar a little more, and turned to the index to see what the good doctor had to tell him about Cronus.

Cronus, it seemed, was a second generation god, one of the Titans, the children of the original two gods of the Graeco-Roman universe; Gaea, goddess of the earth, and Ouranous (the Romans called him Uranus), the sky god. Cronus led a revolt of the Titans against their father. The revolt was successful, because Gaea armed her son with a scythe, with which Cronus drove Ouranous away.

According to Asimov, the name "Cronus" might predate the Greek language itself, perhaps a relic of the language of the people who lived in Greece before the Greeks. The similarity of the name with *chronos*, the Greek word for time, led to identification of Cronus as the god of Time. Even now, we picture Father Time as carrying a scythe.

There was more about Cronus a few pages later. After his victory, Cronus took to wife his sister, the Titaness Rhea. (Who else was there? Driscoll thought). But they didn't live happily ever after. Old Ouranous, from his exile, made a prediction, or maybe it was a curse. One of Cronus' children, he said, would treat him the way Cronus had treated Ouranous.

To Cronus, this seemed all too possible, so he swallowed up his children as soon as they were born. This saddened Rhea, so that when she bore Zeus, she didn't surrender him up to be swallowed. Instead, she wrapped a large stone in swaddling clothes and gave that to her husband to swallow. Zeus was raised secretly on earth. When he was grown, his mother helped him trick Cronus into taking a drink that forced him to vomit up Zeus' brothers and sisters (who, as Immortals, remained unharmed inside their father). Asimov didn't say what happened to the stone.

Cronus' children ganged up on him, just as Ouranous had predicted, banished him, and took up residence on Mount Olympus, and the rest is history. Or legend, at least.

Driscoll checked the index to make sure there wasn't anything else about Cronus, then closed the book. He pushed his glasses back up his sweat-slick nose, and asked himself what it all meant.

Not the myth itself, of course. Historians, literary people, psychiatrists, and the gods knew who else had been arguing about that for centuries, and probably had a few more centuries to go before they exhausted the topic.

Driscoll's concern was what it meant to the Russians. According to the Congressman, the Russians had had something to do with something called the Cronus Project thirty years ago; now the phrase had begun to turn up in intercepted communications again. Was it the same operation? Or were the Russians just recycling project names?

Driscoll doubted they were. Possible confusion in intelligence background summaries militated against using the same name for two operations. On the other hand, thirty years or so is a long time to keep *anything* going, especially an intelligence operation.

Of course, that alone could explain it. It seemed perfectly appropriate to Driscoll that the Russians (or anybody) should name a thirty-year operation after the god of Time.

Or it might be something as simple as the scythe Cronus carried—the scythe standing in for its smaller cousin the sickle. As in hammer and.

One thing Driscoll had to keep constantly in mind was that the name might not mean *anything*, except that somebody in Moscow was a mythology freak. Hurricanes are named after people (girls only for a long time) because a guy wrote a novel about someone who worked at a weather bureau who decided to name a storm after his girlfriend. And ever since a wartime America located the Manhattan Project in Tennessee and New Mexico, American code names haven't meant much.

But the Russians tended to get romantic about their attempts to screw up other countries. The last thing he had worked on for his father was countering a Russian plan to cause a meltdown at a reactor in France. He'd managed to pull it off, even if it did mean he had to do his damnedest to get a Socialist French Government elected before he could be sure the

Russians would back off. But that was beside the point at the moment. The point was, the Russians had called that one the *Vulcan* Project, after the god who ran the Olympian forge and the furnace that went with it.

So while there was no guarantee, Cronus might, just might, mean something. If Driscoll could figure out what it meant, that could possibly give him a little edge in figuring out what Leo Calvin had in mind for Liz Fane.

He would have to think about it—hell, he *would* think about it whether he had to or not. Because it had gotten hold of him, somehow. It kept telling him there was something there, though he couldn't say what. Something more (or less, if you like) than intellectual curiosity bound him to the question.

Which reminded him: He'd have to have another talk with the Congressman about this Cronus business. In the trailer the other night, the old man had been cagey in an uncharacteristic way about things. Something else to worry about.

Right now, though, he had to deal with the press conference. He had just enough time to get back to the hotel to shower and change and make it back to the New Headquarters in time to keep his promise to young Tom Ivery.

Back home in Durham, Cary Wilkis sat in the house watching game shows on TV and sipping a beer. He had a long, lucrative trip coming up the end of the week, so he was treating himself to a few days off.

He'd been driving since the hijack, stuff he couldn't afford to turn down, so this was his first chance to see his wife and get over those goddamn pills. For about the thousandth time since just before the hijacking, he promised himself never again.

He was getting better, though. Now his hands only twitched a little. He finally understood the term "crashing"—he really did feel as though he'd been dropped from a high cliff someplace. He'd even dreamed that once or twice while he was sleeping it off. That and other dreams.

Cary shook his head, hard, like a cocker spaniel trying to

shake water off his ears. *Forget dreams,* he told himself, *it's nothing.* He picked up the paper and turned to the sports section. He tried to get interested in the question of how good, if at all, the Duke University football team was going to be this year. The article concluded probably not very. Reading it didn't do Cary any good, anyway. He hadn't done any dreaming about Blue Devils yet, but he knew now it was coming.

"Shit," he said aloud. Sue stuck her head in from the kitchen. She had a concerned look on her face, but she didn't say anything. *She probably thinks I'm nuts,* Cary thought. *Maybe she's right.*

Because despite the hijacking, everything had been okay. At least it seemed that way. Cary had changed the flat tire and then just drove the car they'd left him in to the nearest State Police barracks and told his story. Everybody'd had a good laugh over it, then the troopers set out to find the truck. He gave descriptions of the man and the woman, best he could, but of course he hadn't seen much.

They found his truck in no time, pulled off on a county road that was pretty deserted at night. Cary had wondered how the damned thing could be more deserted than Interstate 80, but he didn't say anything. They dusted for prints and all that, but with no optimism that it would do any good. The manifest checked with the cargo (they forced a rookie trooper to go in there and count boxes)—ninety-seven on the list, ninety-seven on the truck. The rookie said he was glad the hijackers at least had the good grace to leave the refrigerator on in the trailer. That was another big laugh.

But something bothered Cary about it, though he didn't know what at the time. The feeling came back when the stiffs were unloaded at the destination. It niggled him for another day or so.

Then, while he was drinking a cup of coffee at a Roadway in Delaware, he got it. He'd seen the inside of that trailer back in Seattle, seen those pine boxes being loaded into it. They'd stacked up even. *They'd stacked up goddamn even.*

There was no way you could get ninety-seven to do that. He'd taken a pencil and a paper one night and tried. The closest he could come was seven stacks of five and ten stacks of six, but that still left two over. Besides, there was no five and six about it. All those stacks, if Cary could believe his eyes or his memory, had been the same height.

The question was, *could* he believe his eyes or his memory? He just didn't know anymore. There was a lot of speed between him and his memory of recent events. Nobody seemed to want more bodies than he had on the truck. Nobody'd tried to give him any back, either. He could have *sworn* the manifest called for ninety-*eight* boxes on that goddamn Dracula Express he'd been driving, but when he'd spent his own money on a phone call West, nobody at the place in Seattle would admit to knowing what the hell he was talking about. Hell, they didn't even want to admit he'd picked up anything at all, but he got that much out of them, at least. But as far as numbers went, they didn't know, didn't much care, and damn well weren't going to stop what they were doing and go look for it. Cary had hung up angry and confused. Also scared. None of which had gone away yet.

Cary faced it. Either he was crazy, or somebody had stolen a body. Gone to a lot of trouble to do it, too, and cover up that they'd done it. It wasn't right. It was—Cary groped for an unfamiliar word—*sinister*. Stealing bodies. He shivered. And if they hadn't stolen one, they'd *added* one. That was even sicker.

Unless, of course, I'm crazy. Which is where I came in, he thought.

Either way, he had to know. Which meant he had to get somebody who knew what the hell he was doing to look into it for him. Which meant he had to tell someone. The decision now was whom to tell.

That much was something he could handle, and he felt better getting it reduced to that. He'd start thinking about whom he wanted to tell right after he had a beer. He got up and went to the kitchen to get it. He figured Sue would be pleased not having to bring it to him. He was right.

Tom read over the list of questions he had prepared for the press conference. He realized he was probably going to get to ask only one, and maybe none at all, but he had to be ready—if he went in there with only one question prepared, he knew damn well somebody from CBS or somewhere was going to ask it, leaving him to stand there and swallow like a yokel if he ever did get called on.

He realized he was supposed to be a professional journalist. He should be able to make up questions on the scene. Actually, he figured he probably could, but this could be his big break, and he wasn't going to take any chances with it.

He was nervous, there was no denying that. He had a terrible time getting the new alkaline batteries into the station's tape recorder (couldn't have *that* going dead in the middle of the press conference), and he'd dropped one of his backup pens, which had rolled under an antique transcription machine that Mr. Littleton, the owner of the station, had never gotten around to junking. He would have to be very careful with the two pens he had left. What good is a journalist if he can't take notes?

After he'd gotten everything squared away, he still had a half hour to kill before he could decently leave for headquarters. Even then, he'd be pretty early for the press conference. *Bad planning*, he thought. Now all he could do was to sit there and wish his forehead wouldn't sweat so much when he got nervous.

He became aware of the Beautiful Music being played on the newsroom monitor. That's what WLTN played all the time. Beautiful Music—the kind of stuff you hear in a dentist's office. Right now, they were playing a castrated version of Bobby Bloom's "Montego Bay."

Tom smiled in spite of himself. "Montego Bay" was the guidance casing machine song. The bracket/wheel cover assembly machine worked to "In the Year 2525" by Zager and Evans. All the machines at Fane's (where Tom had worked summers home from college alongside his father, who had done this backbreaking, mind-numbing work for twenty-five years) worked to a particular rhythm. Tom found he could make a fortune on piecework if he just found the song that fit the rhythm of the machine he happened to be assigned to, then just hummed it to himself all day. It drove him crazy, but it made him enough money so that he could devote his time at school to the college radio station (in addition to classes, of course) instead of having to work part-time to meet expenses.

He had made in the factory, in fact, roughly three times per week as much as he made now as the News and Public Affairs director of WLTN. That part didn't bother him so much as it did his parents, with whom he still lived. His father saw it as a rejection of him, but it wasn't. Tom's respect for his father had grown immensely after he'd seen what his old man had put up with all those years in order to take care of his family. Tom's mother had an unwavering eye for the bottom line. If job A brings in x dollars a week, and job B brings in $^2/_3$ dollars a week, no one but a fool would pass up A for B, and don't try telling me anything different young man. When Tom tried to talk about things like personal satisfaction, and the *potential* money to be made in broadcasting, his mother said, "Where are you going to go from this dumb little station?"

Which was indeed the rub. Four years ago, when Tom had tried to get a summer job at WLTN, Mr. Littleton told him he couldn't afford to give him one, but that Tom should come see him after graduation, and he'd see what he could do. And Mr. Littleton had been as good as his word. Better. He'd offered him the job.

The only trouble was, WLTN wasn't a real radio station anymore. Oh, they still played the same kind of music, but sometime during Tom's senior year, Mr. Littleton had fired all the disc jockeys and replaced them with the Monster. The Monster was a rented machine that did everything automatically. Music, announcers, national commercials, all on tape cartridges that you fed into the Monster at the company's instructions. You were supposed to feel good knowing that dozens, probably hundreds of radio stations around the country were playing exactly the same thing at the same time.

Tom's was the only live voice heard on WLTN these days. He did a fifteen-minute newscast at seven A.M., and another at six P.M. He also engineered sometimes, looked for stories, and swept up. He fed the Monster, too. He might as well have been back dancing with the machines in the factory. Except that the

Monster had no rhythm of its own, just the syrupy, borrowed rhythms of the canned music.

Oh, every once in a while he'd send out tapes and a resumé to stations in bigger towns, and he read the help wanted ads in *Broadcasting* like a dirty story, but nothing every happened. They'd take a look at the resumé, see he'd worked for a college station and for a dog-ass little five-thousand watt automated FM station in the middle of Pennsylvania, and slip everything right back in the envelope and return it to him. He had his long hoped-for job in broadcasting, but he had to live with the fact that it just didn't count.

He was discouraged and he was broke and his options seemed about equally divided between suicide and going back to the factory, which to him represented the same thing.

Then Liz Fane had been kidnapped. In broad daylight. She and her abductors had vanished without a trace; there was a Washington connection. This was a big story. Oh, God Almighty, it was a *big* story.

That was all it took, Tom knew. Just one big story. He was sorry for Liz (whom he knew slightly—in Draper, everybody knew everybody at least slightly) and for her family, but what the hell. Dan Rather had probably been sorry when President Kennedy was shot, but sorrow hadn't kept him from riding the story from his job as an obscure Texas reporter to the absolute heights of the industry.

Tom wasn't aiming for a network anchor post, at least not yet. All he wanted was something a step up from Draper and WLTN. He wanted to get into real radio, and maybe get a raise to $x/2$, to show his mother some progress at least.

Please, Tom thought, *I'm never going to get another chance like this. Just let me do something with this story.*

Just . . . *something.* Something that would let people know who he was. That he could do the job. A lot of that depended on the press conference this afternoon.

Tom looked at the clock and decided it was okay to leave now. He picked up his tape recorder, checked his press credentials, notebook, and pens, and with one last *please,* went out to embrace his future.

Through some sort of screw-up, they had been led out to the stage before the chief was quite ready. Reporters had tried to get a few questions in, of course, but Rines had told them no questions until after the chief read their joint statement. After a few more tries, the press decided the FBI man wasn't kidding, and went milling around talking to each other.

Rines nudged Driscoll, who was seated next to him. "Look at the Ivery kid," he said. "Pretty popular with the big shots, isn't he?"

Driscoll saw that the local boy was mixing right now with people from CBS and CNN, and enjoying every minute of it. "What the hell," Driscoll said. "He's local—he knows the town. He can save the New York reporters a lot of time. And Ivery has spread around a few favors among people who might be able to help him out some day."

Rines nodded. "That makes sense. Everyone needs contacts, even us, right? Still going to let the kid ask a question?"

Driscoll let the comment about "even us" go by. For some reason, Rines kept trying to elicit replies from Driscoll that would include him, at least implicitly, in some Fraternal Order of Federal Investigators. Driscoll didn't want any more of it—it had been a mistake to tell the FBI man as much as he had this morning.

"Sure," Driscoll said. "I'll let him ask one. We promised, after all."

"Yes, we did," Rines said. "Wouldn't want to lie now, would we?"

Driscoll refused to be strung along. "Absolutely not," he said. He wondered if the agent had finally recognized him, from their encounters long ago. If that weren't it, he wondered just *what* Rines was up to. All Driscoll could do was tough it out and let the Congressman know that Rines was acting coy.

The FBI man got a gleam in his eye, and Driscoll could tell Rines had another double-edged remark for him. Driscoll was saved hearing it by the entrance of Chief Fred Anderson.

The chief's statement consisted of an announcement that new men, additional men, he should say, had been assigned to the case at all levels, bringing to one hundred fifteen the number of federal, state, and local officers working full or part time on the Fane kidnapping.

The rest was all negative. They had not heard from the kidnappers, although they had received messages purporting to come from the Ku Klux Klan, the Weather Underground, the Irish Republican Army, and a Puerto Rican independence group. These calls had been investigated, and had been found to be hoaxes.

Driscoll suppressed a smile. What the chief wasn't telling them was that all four calls came from the same number; the same person, in fact—a sixteen-year-old high school drama student from the next county, who "wanted to give my ability at characterization and dialect a *real* test." The only reason she remained at liberty right now, instead of playing a command performance at the county jail, was that the chief didn't want the publicity.

Anderson went on to say that there were no suspects except for the busboy at the country club who disappeared about the same time the kidnapping took place; that there was no evidence except for the air gun, which had been innocent of fingerprints; and no results from the highway roadblocks that had been up over a week. It seemed to the investigators that either the kidnappers had gotten away before roadblocks could be set up or they were still in the area.

He concluded by saying that the bodies of the driver and the intern had been released, and were being sent to their families in other states. The Fane family were cooperating fully, in the absence of instructions from the kidnappers to the contrary, but their first concern, of course, was the safe return of their daughter. A concern, he added, shared by all.

Finally, he introduced Special Agent Fenton Rines of the Federal Bureau of Investigation, Captain John Roedale of the Pennsylvania State Police, and Mr. Clifford Driscoll of the Department of Defense, who would be glad to answer any questions.

There were plenty of them.

UPI wanted to know how they knew all the phone calls claiming responsibility for the kidnapping were hoaxes. The Chief pissed him off by saying that investigation had revealed that they were, and that was all he was going to say about it for now.

Gannett wanted to know if they thought this kidnapping was politically motivated. Rines said that was impossible to answer in the absence of any message from the kidnappers.

KYW of Philadelphia asked Driscoll what the hell he was doing there. Driscoll got a small laugh by saying, "I've been trying to figure that out myself," then went into his number about Fane being a prime contractor for the government, and his being there simply to help in any way he could. The other agencies were kindly keeping him informed, so that he might be of more help.

There were a few follow-ups to that one. Was he calling the shots for the Fane family? Definitely not. Was he on the scene because the kidnapping indicated a breach of security involving a government contract Fane Industries might be working on? "That's being investigated as part of FBI routine, I'm sure," Driscoll said. Out of the corner of his eye he saw Rines nod agreement. "There is nothing to my knowledge that would make it anything *more* than routine." Again, Rines confirmed it.

The New York Times wondered whether, if there was a possibility the kidnappers hadn't left the area sealed off by State Police roadblocks, there had been any consideration given to a house-to-house search of the area. Roedale explained why it wasn't feasible. The explanation took fifteen minutes, boring everybody, including the guy from the *Times*. It boiled down to three reasons. One, Draper was a small town, but it wasn't *that* small—there would still be thousands of houses to search. Two, unless everybody happened to be at home and willing to cooperate when the searchers got there, the local judges would have to work around the clock getting out warrants. Three, there were not enough people to search the whole area at once. The gang, assuming they remained in the area, could simply move from place to place ahead of the search. No, the captain said sadly, until and unless evidence narrowed down the area of the search, a house-to-house operation was out of the question.

It went on that way for an hour or more. The reporters knew what was going to be said, they had been through this thing before. All they were doing was looking for justification to write "Chief Anderson said" after descriptions and comments they already knew by heart.

When things began to wind down, Driscoll nudged the chief and asked him to call on Tom Ivery.

As Driscoll looked at the chief's face, he thought a cop should be able to hide his thoughts better than that. The man was obviously thinking, *Tom Ivery? The local kid? What the hell is* he *doing here?* Maybe because he was watching, Driscoll seemed to be the only one who noticed.

Anderson turned to the crowd and pointed. "Yeah, over there. Tom Ivery." Heads craned to look at the young man in the back. Except for the network stars, he was the only reporter the chief had called by name.

Tom rose slowly, hoping his legs wouldn't shake. He concentrated on making his voice sound good. "Tom Ivery," he said, "WLTN News." A pro touch, that, getting the name of his station on the air, and on everybody's tapes.

"I have a question for Mr. Driscoll."

Driscoll stood at the microphone and nodded for him to go ahead.

Tom looked at his notes. He hadn't had to use a backup pen. "Mr. Driscoll, you said earlier that Herbert Fane is a 'prime government contractor.' Would it be fair to say Mr. Fane's company is working on an important government project right now? And if so—"

Driscoll smiled inwardly. The reporter's magic phrase, "and if so." Use it judiciously, and you can stack questions ten feet high.

"And if so," Tom Ivery said, "how far would the Defense Department go to protect that project, if it were to be jeopardized by the current situation?"

Driscoll's hidden smile turned bitter. *How far would you go to get a sensational story, you little twerp?* he thought. That's what I get for trying to do an unambiguous good deed for once in my life.

Okay, now he had to answer the question. He did what any

good public servant would do in a similar situation. He buried it under obfuscations. Of course Mr. Fane was working on an important project. Two minutes on why Fane Industries' work gained the company a constant stream of important projects. Getting Liz Fane home safely was everybody's top priority. Three minutes on that. Finally, Driscoll used the bureaucrat's magic word, the one that countered "And if so."

"It would be *counterproductive* to speculate on matters that may never arise," he said sternly, then sat down.

He was furious with himself; he should never have let himself get into this, because even though he'd blown a lot of smoke, and would get through the rest of the press conference, Driscoll knew he'd done something to reduce his own options.

Now the reporters, and therefore their readers, would boil it down to this: Driscoll had been asked if they would let Liz Fane die to protect some weapons system (*secret* weapons system), and Driscoll hadn't said no.

Not that he knew what else he could have done. Liz Fane wasn't mentioned in the question; if he mentioned her in the answer in anything more than the pious generalities he had used, it would have been seen as a case of the wicked fleeing where no reporter pursueth. *"Mr. Driscoll! Are you saying the Defense Department has actually considered letting an innocent kidnap victim* die *to keep a government secret?"* That sort of thing. Accompanied by large helpings of shock and consternation.

Driscoll had to face it. Once Tom Ivery opened his mouth, Driscoll was screwed no matter what he did. And the fact that he'd been taken like that by a kid not yet dry behind the ears didn't do wonders for his confidence in being able to handle Leo Calvin.

Leo was happy. Waldo could tell. Leo smiled a lot, but most of the time he wasn't happy. Now he was, though, because of something he had seen on TV. A bunch of people talking, big deal. At least to Waldo.

But Leo had made the happy smile he hardly ever made,

with real light in his eyes, and with his bottom teeth showing, too. Then he turned off the TV and told Candy to bring Daisy Mae. It was time to make the tape now. Candy was happy, too.

Waldo was sad. He didn't want to watch a bunch of people talking, he wanted to watch Tom and Jerry cartoons, the way he always did. Yesterday, Jerry (that was the mouse) had hit Tom the cat in the face with a great big frying pan, and Tom's head took the shape of the pan. That was fun to watch. Waldo figured it probably wouldn't work in real life, though. That was sad, too.

Waldo was sad because he couldn't figure out what was going on with Daisy Mae. Was she in the Closet, or was she okay? Leo used to put Waldo in the Closet when he wasn't good, but that hadn't happened for a long time, now.

At first, Daisy Mae was in the Closet. When people are in the Closet, you don't have to be nice to them. When you feel that funny feeling, and need to see the blood from them, you just *do* it. Daisy Mae had come in very handy, then.

Then, the other day, Daisy Mae was suddenly *okay*. At least, she could walk around the house with them and see everybody's face. But then, after about a day, she had asked Leo one little question about some tape or something (maybe the same tape Leo was talking about today, Waldo guessed), and before you knew it, she was back in the Closet.

That part was okay. Leo had to be strict. Leo had explained to Waldo, but Waldo had forgotten the reasons. But what got Waldo mixed up was that when Waldo told Leo he wanted to see blood, so could he now? Leo had said *no*! He said the Closet would be enough for her this time. Enough for her, big deal! What about Waldo?

Waldo was also sad because he was remembering stuff again. He was remembering a *lot* of stuff. He remembered a name—Walter Donnely—that was him when he was a kid. And (this was the worst) he remembered being *smart*. Sitting in a school and reading books and talking to other kids (why couldn't he remember what they *said*, though?) and being able to count out his lunch money. And nobody laughing at him. At least not too much. They didn't now, either, but that was because Leo only let nice people meet him.

He remembered Ma. And the funny feeling and the rolling pin. He was sad that he never saw Ma again after that night.

Waldo was sad because he was mixed up and confused. And because he had the funny feeling all the time now (and it had been a *long* time, too), and if he could just see some blood, it would be better. He kept trying to tell this to Leo, but Leo just didn't *listen*.

And that not only made Waldo sad, it made him scared. Leo was his friend. But what if he wasn't anymore? Waldo shook his head and said "No" right out loud. They looked at him for a second, and he grinned sheepishly at them. They went back to what they were doing.

No, he said to himself this time, Leo would always be his friend. He promised.

But, as he watched them fix up a machine for Daisy Mae to talk into, Waldo knew one thing. With or without Leo's permission, Waldo was going to *see some blood*.

Real soon, too.

Chapter Five

IN MOSCOW, A MAN LAY IN A BED. IT WAS HIS OWN BED, IN his own bedroom. He would not go to a hospital. When a man in his position went to a hospital, his orders were no longer necessarily followed. His subordinates started looking to make themselves agreeable to the favorite to succeed him. He might as well be dead, for all the good he did the State. A sick man's lingering only made more prolonged and bitter the inevitable power struggles.

So he would not go to a hospital. He would have the hospital brought to him. That was not good, and missing the May Day parade had been worse (because the West had seen he wasn't there), but it was the best he could do. He could not give orders to Nature. Unfortunately.

He watched liquid, slightly pinkish in the summer light, trickle through a tube into a needle in his wrist. He paid little attention to the summaries read to him by his aides. They would be out feathering their own nests the instant he dismissed them. Who knew what ends they were serving with these so-called impartial reports?

An aide finished his reading and was dismissed. The sick man didn't even bother to give him any orders. He watched more liquid flow into him. It looked so pale—how could that be keeping a strong man alive?

That was how the Western press referred to him—"Soviet

Strong Man." For a moment, he had an image of himself, muscles rippling under a garment of leopard skin, as he wrestled with a ferocious bear. He started to laugh, but it turned into a cough, then faded to a wheeze.

He fought to stay alert, then picked up the buzzer to tell the nurse to admit the next caller. A few seconds later, a young man in uniform entered carrying a dispatch case under his arm.

He told the soldier to open the case, but he read the contents himself. This was the only part of the workday he cared for anymore. This was the report from Borzov in Special Intelligence.

He could trust Borzov. His old comrade was content where he was; he was older still than the man in the bed; and he had no sons or nephews through whom to experience ambition secondhand. They had conceived the Cronus Project together; now that it was finally beginning to bear fruit, Borzov was delighted.

The sick man was elated, too, for a moment. The young woman they had had abducted was ready to communicate with the authorities, to pass on the "terrorists'" demands. Which would, of course, be followed. The very structure of a Cronus operation insured it.

That was what had excited him all those years ago, him and Borzov. It was a blind spot in American society—you couldn't avoid noticing it from even the most cursory study of their culture.

And any warrior soon learns that the place to strike the enemy is at his blind spot. It would take much preparation, more work, and a great amount of time and expense, but it would be worth it.

Time was the essence of international struggle. This Fane girl had been first because it was time to use her. To buy time for Soviet factories to catch up with (and, with luck, to pass) the West in implementation of the MENTOR system.

They had sent one hundred agents out on the Cronus Project back at the beginning. Sixty-two had failed. One had been diverted to another assignment before disappearing. Five had completed phase one of the plan, but had been unsuccess-

ful with phase two. That left thirty-two potentially viable
Cronus operations. Thirty-two instances where the Americans
could be tripped up. Crippled, confused. Thirty-two victories
in the war of weapons and ideas. Enough, finally, to end
America's Cold War on the Motherland for all time.

Because each Cronus operation was discrete. It couldn't be
linked to the others, even if the Americans broke an occasional
code.

He had never quite been able to make his predecessors in
the Chairmanship take the first step and actually give the order
for a Cronus operation. When he himself assumed the Chairmanship, he saw the wisdom in waiting for the proper time.

Time. He smiled. Borzov, that old, dusty scholar, had
named the project "Cronus" for several reasons, but the time
element kept thrusting itself forward.

But the man in the bed didn't have time to wait anymore.
He would not survive another year, he was sure. This was his
gift to his successor, to the Motherland; he would prove to them
that the Cronus Project worked. That America could be
crippled by its use again and again, when the times demanded
it. That Cronus was a precious resource that should be used.
Judiciously, to be sure. But used to make true the famous
promise of one of his predecessors. He believed it when the
little man uttered it; he was sure of it today.

We *will* bury them.

He handed the paper back to the soldier and sent him
away.

The Chairman lay down to a peaceful nap.

Herbert Fane sat at the breakfast table eating like an automa-
ton. His arm moved in a fixed arc, plate to mouth. Egg.
Sausage. Egg. Sausage. Toast. Coffee. Egg.

Sheila Fane looked at him and fretted. Since her daughter
had been kidnapped, all her concern seemed to concentrate
itself on her husband, perhaps because he was here and
available to receive it; she had decided very early on that she

must never allow herself to think what might be happening to her daughter.

But she knew what was happening to her husband. He was eating himself into another heart attack. He might as well go on a diet of salt and cholesterol exclusively. It worried her terribly. She *needed* him; he simply must not endanger himself. Not at a time like this.

But it would take some thought before she would be able to do anything about it. She had made Herbert Fane her project in life, studied his likes and dislikes and little idiosyncracies. She'd devoted herself to pleasing him. It was an old-fashioned attitude, perhaps, but then she knew her husband liked that, too. And their marriage had been entirely successful. Sheila Fane had seen to that. Herbert's first marriage, though it ended with the death of his first wife and not through divorce, could never have made him as happy.

Having studied the man so closely and for so long, Sheila Fane knew she mustn't do anything that could remotely be considered coddling or sentimentality.

Like most American men, Herbert was ashamed of his emotions. He tired to deny, even to himself, that they influenced him at all, and resented it mightily if anyone ever pointed out the obvious. It was a small fault, easily forgiven, and usually easily gotten around. But this was a sensitive time and a dangerous one. She had to get Herbert out of this round of unthinking excess, or he wouldn't be able to think clearly about *anything*. Especially poor darling Liz.

She thought she might have a way to distract him with something. It couldn't make him any worse if she tried it. Not while he was eating, though. She kept silent while he pulled more sausage from the serving plate to his own dish. She watched him eat, and left him alone with his thoughts.

His thoughts at the moment were about her. Why didn't she *do* it? Why wouldn't she tell him all the things he'd done wrong, the things he should have done to keep his daughter safe? God knew the list was long—he recited it to himself constantly.

At the lower fringe of consciousness, he noticed he was out

of sausage again. Automatically, without thinking or tasting, he resumed eating.

He had done it to her, after all. The second day or so, after the initial numbness had worn off, he had railed at Sheila for leading her daughter into a *trap,* what kind of mother would let her only child be kidnapped from under her very *nose,* for God's sake, how could she be so criminally stupid—

But he was the one who had been stupid. He knew that now. He'd known it even as he had been saying it, really. But he had felt so helpless, so useless, so downright afraid, that he'd turned on his wife. Just to show himself he had some kind of power over *somebody,* if only the power to make her cry.

Which she had duly done. They had made things up again, of course, but now, along with the helplessness and the frustration and the fear, Herbert Fane felt guilty and weak. He had given in to an evil impulse that Sheila was strong enough to resist.

Herbert Fane was a proud man. It could be he was being punished for his pride. He was proud of having made a lot of money, all on his own, too. Now the money had made his family a target for God knew what.

He didn't even have to *be* here. He was rich enough; he could have lived anywhere. It seemed to him that people with money never got victimized in their protected little colonies. Once or twice, Sheila had even said she might like to move to Palm Springs or the like. Fane had replied by saying he had to be close to the factory; that absentee ownership always made workers nervous; that it was good for efficiency and for business that he had enough faith in his business and his workers to make a lifelong commitment to the town they shared.

All of those things might have been facts, but they were lies just the same. Because none was the *real* reason Herbert Fane stayed in Draper. The real reason was that he *liked* being the richest man in town. He liked being consulted by elected officials before they proposed a measure in Town Council. He liked the feeling that Draper, Pennsylvania stayed alive (when similar towns around the area were dying) solely because of the factory *he* owned. He enjoyed charities depending on his name.

He enjoyed everyone's knowing who he was. He liked seeing his name and picture in the newspaper.

Fane's jaws worked mechanically on untasted food. Well, he thought, everyone, not just in Draper, knew who he was now. His name and picture were in more newspapers than he'd ever dreamed of. He was an object of pity to people who never heard of him. And his daughter was . . . what? He didn't even know if she was alive or dead.

He reached out again, but there was no more sausage. He'd polished off the eggs and toast long ago. He swallowed the last cold drop of coffee in his cup, then looked around, at a loss.

His eyes met his wife's. He'd been avoiding them till now. Hers were filled with concern. He thought without self-consciousness that he was lucky to have her. He hoped she knew it without his saying so. That sort of thing sounded so . . . so *foolish* spoken aloud. Herbert Fane couldn't bring himself to do anything that might make him appear foolish. He didn't like to be laughed at. Only Liz had ever laughed at him without making him angry.

Sheila Fane said, "I heard from Robin."

"Robin," he said, blinking his way out of his thoughts.

"Roberta, dear. She wants to know if she should come back and stay with us again. I think it would be a good idea."

"She'd be better off if she stayed in New York," Fane said. "Unless she wants to be another exhibit in the sideshow. Or she wants the publicity. Wonderful opportunity for her. She finally found a use for Liz. She prob—"

"*Stop it!*"

Fane stared at his wife. He had never heard that tone from her before. He hadn't known she was capable of it.

She went on, quieter, but just as intensely. "Herbert, you must stop. I—I am in danger of losing my daughter. My only child. I have no intention of losing you, too."

"No chance of that," Fane said. "We're virtual prisoners here, well guarded."

"That's not what I mean, and you know it."

"Well, damn it, what *do* you mean?

"You are being bitter and hateful. I have never known you to be that way before."

"They've never kidnapped my daughter before."

Sheila Fane swallowed. "Yes, dear. I know. But try to save your hatred for the people who kidnapped her. Don't use it all up on Robin. Or on me. Or even on the authorities. I know *I* want to tell Mr. Driscoll the things I said to him the day we met were the result of guilt and panic."

"Driscoll." Herbert Fane grunted his disgust. "You didn't hear him on television yesterday. He doesn't even care—"

"That's not the point, Herbert, is it? I'm sure he's doing his best for Liz."

"It's not his job to do his best for Liz," Fane said. "He's got the whole defense program to worry about."

"All right, then. Maybe so. But in the thinking I've been doing over the past week, I thought frequently of Mr. Driscoll. I thought, what if it comes down to a choice between my daughter or my country? Driscoll may have to make that decision."

Tears came to her eyes. It was another astonishing sight.

"What if . . . what if *I* had to make it? Herbert, it's a hard decision," she said. The rest was swallowed in tears.

Fane rose, walked around the table, helped his wife to her feet, and held her. "It's not going to come to that," he said. "It's just one little circuit. I'll junk it if I have to to get Liz back. The country will get by without it."

Sheila Fane, that dignified lady, continued to cry on his shoulder. If he felt guilt before, he was practically drowning in it now. He opened his mouth to tell her he was sorry for the way he'd been acting, for making her suffer his share of grief when she had her own to carry.

But the moment passed, and his self-imposed strictures returned. He did the best he could.

"Robin can come if she wants to," he said.

Sheila Fane, as she was used to doing, decoded her husband's hidden emotions. "Robin will be pleased," she said. "She really does want to help."

"I said she could come," Fane repeated. The hidden message in that one was don't embarrass me with sentiment. Sheila received it loud and clear.

They heard the telephone ring. They froze and looked

toward the sound—that had become a habit since the kidnapping. Fane felt dread and hope fighting to a draw in his mind. He told himself (as always) not to be foolish. It might be nothing. It probably *was* nothing. Some enterprising journalist (and may they all go to hell, Fane thought) who had ferreted out the unlisted number. Perhaps it was another call from Robin.

Fane reflected that he might have been angry at his niece simply because she called on the phone. He was not prepared to feel kindly toward anyone who made that telephone ring for anything other than news of his daughter.

The phone rang twice, then stopped. Henrietta had been dusting in the parlor and answered it there. After the first three or four heartbreaking calls, the Fanes had stopped answering the phones themselves.

They waited for Henrietta to report to them. They looked at each other, afraid to speak. There was no way to measure time like this—it seemed to take up his whole life, stretch into his whole future. Finally, Henrietta shuffled in.

Moving nothing but her jaw, she said, "It's Police Chief Anderson, Mr. Fane. Says he's got news. Wants to talk to you personal. Or Mrs. Fane."

Herbert Fane ran for the telephone. He could hardly hear himself speak—blood was roaring in his ears. Hope and dread were starting a newer, more frenetic battle.

"Yes, Chief." He practically shouted it. "What is it?"

Anderson sounded as if he were yelling across rapids, but Fane made out the words. "We've heard from the kidnappers," the chief said. "Your daughter's voice is on the tape."

Tom Ivery had awakened at four-thirty that morning, a half hour earlier than usual. He'd been too excited to sleep, anyway. *All three* networks had used the answer to his question on the evening newscasts. Dan Rather had even left in the question, though they cut out the part where he'd identified himself.

Still, it was something. It even impressed his parents, who

beamed on him as though they'd urged him to follow this course over his natural shyness, instead of sniping at his resolve and self-confidence every step of the way.

Well, what the hell. He knew what made them do it. He even understood it. The thing to do now, though, was to work this into something that would lend him enough security so that his parents would never feel the urge to do it again.

And this morning, he was sure he could. As he shaved, he looked in the mirror and said, "Tom Ivery, CBS News." The mirror became a TV screen. War-torn Beirut appeared behind his right shoulder. Then he decided that that was a pretty big step, and tried, "Tom Ivery, Mutual News, Detroit." That sounded good to him, too.

He was brought back to earth when he nicked himself at the corner of the mouth with the razor. He laughed at himself. It occurred to him that it was when daydreams suddenly become *possible* that they become funny. The sad ones are the impossible ones.

He smiled through the rest of the shave, stopping only to wince at the styptic pencil. Then he finished dressing, went to the kitchen and poured himself a glass of orange juice. He stepped outside, took a second to enjoy the summer sky, unlocked his 1979 Dodge Colt (he'd bought it back when he was making x dollars at job A), threw his jacket in the back seat, then got in and drove to work.

WLTN was on the eastern edge of town, out by the lake, on the other side of the woods from the Fane Plant complex. At this time of year, the sun rose directly behind the transmitting tower, making the red blinking aircraft warning lights in the gridwork seem feeble and ridiculous by comparison.

He parked his Colt right next to Vince Mangiamolli's old Chevy. Vince fed the Monster at night. He was the station's chief engineer by virtue of having an FCC First Class Radio-telephone Operator's license.

It was venerable broadcasting lore that engineers were weird. Tom didn't know if the lore was created to describe Vince, or if Vince had decided to live up to the lore. Either way, Vince fit the description. He had long hair and a long moustache. He wore a patterned vest over a white shirt, winter and summer. He rarely said anything but "Hi," "Okay," "Uh,uh," and "Holy shit." He sat in the booth, looking like Wild Bill Hickok, feeding the Monster, and reading classics. Any Penguin book with a black cover was for him. Plato. Montaigne. Dickens. None of it ever made its way to his vocabulary, but he read it all.

The station itself was a converted one story, six-room cottage. Tom used his key to open the door, stepped in, and kicked something down the corridor. A white rectangle. An envelope, with something more than paper in it. It had probably been dropped through the letter slot.

He went to pick it up, calling out, "Hi, Vince!" One thing about working at an automated station was that you never had to worry about yelling when someone was on a live mike.

He heard Vince's "Hi," in return, but didn't register it. He was concentrating on the envelope. It was addressed to TOM IVORY in blue ink. There was no further writing on it. And there was a smaller rectangle inside. A tape cassette.

Tom dropped the ·envelope, then stooped to pick it up again, using his fingernails to touch only the edges of the paper. He carried it into the engineering booth and put it down on the console. He pointed to it and asked Vince if he knew anything about it.

"Uh-uh," Vince said. He looked up from his book. La Rochefoucauld.

"Hold this by the edges, Vince. Don't make any fingerprints on it."

Vince shrugged. "Okay," he said.

Tom picked up a razor blade from the splicing block on a now-unused reel-to-reel tape machine. He sliced vertically through the envelope, a perfectly plain, cheap, business-sized one, next to the edge of the cassette. He took the envelope by one corner, and shook the cassette free. It was a cheap model, sold by millions all over the country. The label was blank. Tom sent Vince to the newsroom for the cassette player, and sat staring at the gray plastic box in front of him while he waited, as if he expected the cassette to self-destruct in five seconds.

Vince returned. Holding the cassette by the corner, the

engineer loaded it into the machine. Tom nodded and told him to hit the play button.

There was a silence as the leader ran through, followed by the characteristic background hiss of cheap tape. Then there was the hollow clunk of a microphone hitting against something.

"This—" a voice began, then stopped.

"*Go ahead!*" said another voice, in a fierce whisper.

The first voice spoke again. "This is Elizabeth Fane speaking on behalf of the League to End Oppression."

Tom began to think CBS might not be too big a leap after all.

Vince let out a blast of air that fluttered his moustache like two pine branches in a storm. "Holy shit," he said.

"Look, Mr. Rines," the kid said, "I want to cooperate. I *am* cooperating. But I've got a newscast to do in less than an hour. Will you give me some time to get it ready?"

The FBI man thought it over. There was no sense keeping the kid off the air. The chief had made a couple of copies of the tape, or rather the engineer had, under close supervision by Rines and Anderson, after the cassette had shown up negative for prints. No prints on the envelope, either, except a few of the kid's, and he'd admitted picking it up. It'd had his name on it, after all.

"It had his name spelled wrong," Driscoll pointed out. As a courtesy, Anderson had told him the news when Ivery called him. For someone who kept saying he wasn't an investigator, Rines thought, Driscoll was Johnny-on-the-spot whenever something happened.

"So it had his name spelled wrong," Rines said. "Does that tell you something?"

"It *suggests* something," Driscoll said.

"What's that?"

"That the tape didn't come from anybody local. Anybody

from Draper who wanted Tom Ivery to have the tape would probably have spelled the name with the *e*."

Rines nodded. "I've got you now. This is probably from somebody who decided to send it to him after seeing him on TV yesterday."

"Yeah," Driscoll said amiably. "Seeing him make an idiot out of me, you mean."

Rines suppressed a smile. Ivery had gone out of his way to thank Driscoll for seeing that he got called on yesterday. Journalists really pushed this no hard feelings business for all it was worth.

"It suggests they're still inside the roadblock, too," Driscoll said. "It wasn't mailed, and I doubt they'd want to risk the roadblock twice to deliver it in person."

"I thought of that already. Roedale is going to keep the roadblocks up. Now that the kidnappers have gotten the tape delivered, they may try to sneak out."

"Where did Anderson go?"

"He had some errands. He's bringing one copy of the tape to the State Police lab. I'm keeping the original, sending it to the Bureau."

"There'll be a stink about that."

"Tell me about it. There'll be a stink in Washington, too, when they find out I'm giving a copy back to the kid."

"What else could you do? According to the tape, if the tape isn't played at noon on this station, the girl is dead." Driscoll looked thoughtful. "By the way, Rines, has anybody thought to find out if that's really Liz Fane's voice? And not, say, another drama student?"

"Of course," the agent said. "Something else the chief is working on. He's going to go play the tape for the Fanes and see what they think. I'm going to join them when I'm done with the kid here. Care to join us?"

Driscoll surprised him. "No thanks," he said. "Got some administrative stuff to take care of."

They talked about Ivery for a while. "His career stock is rising all the time," Rines suggested.

Driscoll smiled. "And his stock with the chief is falling."

Rines laughed. Anderson had been irked, maybe even

hurt, that a nice local boy he'd known all his life would start pulling First Amendment responsibilities and *the public's right to know* on him. When Ivery had told him he should be happy he hadn't played the tape on the air before calling him, Anderson had been close to apoplexy. That was when Rines suggested he get in touch with the parents.

Rines and Driscoll sat in Ivery's newsroom, a converted day room or parlor. Rines turned up the volume on the burlap-covered monitor and listened to Ivery's newscast.

He did it up, telling how the tape had been dropped through the mail slot of the WLTN studios on Lakeside Drive, how the envelope had been addressed to him, how he and engineer Vince Mangiamolli had checked to see what was on the tape, then had notified the authorities who were now investigating. He mentioned them all by name.

He recapped the case, from the snatch itself, to the beating of Lindsay Keith, to the press conference yesterday, to now. He managed to work in a few quotes garnered from Rines and Anderson that very morning during the questioning.

"He does learn fast, doesn't he?" Driscoll said. Rines just frowned.

The voice on the monitor went on to describe what was on the tape. "The speaker," Ivery said, "purported herself to be Liz Fane, and it seemed so to listeners among officials and reporters who knew her voice—"

"If he means himself and Anderson, why doesn't he just *say* himself and Anderson?" Rines complained.

"Reporters—big-time reporters—are too modest to do things like that," Driscoll replied. "I still want to know what it sounds like to her parents. Make sure they're absolutely positive."

"I know my job, Driscoll."

"—named her captors as a group calling itself the League to End Oppression. She quoted them as saying they stood for, quoting now, 'The end of American militaristic imperialism,' and 'Peace and freedom for all peoples.'

"The voice claiming to be Miss Fane said she was healthy and well treated, and that she would be released when the demands of the League to End Oppression were met.

"Speaking without emotion, the person on the tape begged the parents of Elizabeth Fane to meet all the demands, and to see that demands made on others are met.

"The first demand was that the tape be played in its entirety on this station at twelve noon today. The tape promised further communications. Stay tuned to WLTN for details as they become available.

"In world news, Russian sources said that rumors concerning the health of the Communist Party chief are false and unfounded. Speaking at the Kremlin—"

The phone in the newsroom started to ring. Driscoll nodded toward it. "Now comes the deluge. On the phone there is the first drip."

"I didn't know reporters got up as early as this."

"I don't know about you," Driscoll said, "but I'm going to be unavailable for comment for a while."

"I wish I could," Rines said. "Hell, I bet I won't even get time for breakfast." He sighed. "Ought to be used to that sort of thing by now. Anyway, this ends speculation about whether it's a terrorist job or not."

"You never thought it was anything else, did you?"

"Of course not. People who kidnap for money want it over with as soon as possible. Only somebody with a political axe to grind wants to draw things out and make everybody suffer."

"'Healthy and well treated,'" Driscoll quoted. "What do you think they had to do to her to get her to make that tape?"

"I don't even want to think about it. She didn't sound natural."

"The lab will tell us more," Rines said. Then, something from the monitor caught his attention, and he started to laugh.

"What's so funny?" Driscoll demanded.

"Ivery. He's doing local stories now. He's not only disappointing the chief, he's using him for hot news."

They listened. ". . . Chief Fred Anderson said that the dead cat, which had been found on top of a fire hydrant on Averal Avenue, had had its throat slit and it's eyes gouged out.

"The Chief also said—"

They'd already heard what Anderson had also said. Rines

cut the volume on the monitor. "Fortunately, the cat killer is the chief's worry."

"Yeah. Is there anything more to be done around here?"

"Oh, lots to be done. I'm going to take the kid and the engineer over their stories a few more times. We're going to give this place a lab job when my men get here from Washington. Lots of things."

"Anything I can help with? Anything that will be fun to watch?"

"I doubt it. Why?"

"I've got bosses in Washington, too. They're going to want to talk about this."

"I'll bet they are," Rines said. "Will you be available if I need you?"

"Is Anderson going to hold another press conference?"

"Not if I can help it. But you're going to want to know what the demands are when they come in, aren't you?"

"I certainly am." Driscoll's tone implied there was nothing in the world he wanted more. "I'll be at the hotel, if you need me."

Driscoll looked at Jake Feder's hands. The white gloves the sound man wore hid the wrinkles and the veins, so there was no way to tell they were the hands of an old man. They flew over the console, punching buttons and sliding volume controls the way Artur Rubinstein's flew over piano keys.

He paid no attention to Driscoll at all, except to tell him not to touch anything. "Oil on your hands, gets on the tape, eats away at it. Makes a difference, an expert can tell. And we're dealing with *video* tapes here, they're even more sensitive. Now get out of my way and let me work."

Driscoll let him work. Jake Feder hit a button. The picture on the television monitor nearby went from black to a jumping confusion of colored lines, then locked on to an out-of-focus close-up of the naked bottom of Lindsay Keith.

Lindsay ran out of the picture, revealing Liz Fane lying

naked on the bed in Lindsay's apartment. For this tape, Keith had positioned the camera at the bottom of the bed at a slight angle, so that it pointed at her body over her right foot when she spread her legs.

Which, after a little kissing, she did. She pushed Lindsay Keith down between them, and then she forced his head down to where she wanted it.

"Ah, good," Jake Feder said. "Now maybe we'll get something we can use, without this asshole kissing her face and muffling it."

This was the fifth tape they'd watched, the eighth sexual act between Liz Fane and her fiancé. Miles had stolen the tapes the day before yesterday, after hospitalizing their owner, but Jake refused to see them until he knew *exactly* the kind of thing he'd need. "Ten years, I'm not able to have a woman," he'd said. "I'm not going to watch two kids *shtupping* and get jealous and frustrated until I've got a job to concentrate on instead."

Fair enough. That meant he had to wait until Driscoll had something from the real kidnappers to respond to, and that had happened today. Everyone had been listening to the noon broadcast of the tape received that morning. Tom Ivery was in his glory as he introduced it. Rines and Anderson had been there, though God knew why. Driscoll had been back at his little impromptu headquarters here, giving instructions to a confused Robin Payne and a stolid Miles.

Right after the tape played through, there had been a phone call to the station. A woman's voice told station-owner Littleton, who had come back from the Bahamas for the occasion, that Chief Anderson should look in the front seat of his car.

They had left a second cassette while Anderson had been in the station. Looking at it, he assumed it would carry the kidnappers' demands. He was right.

"This is Elizabeth Fane speaking for the League to End Oppression. The League has taken me prisoner to force Herbert Fane, my father, to make reparation for his war crimes. Specifically, the crimes committed against the Peoples

Republic of Vietnam, the people of Nicaragua, the Palestinian People, and all oppressed peoples who have suffered because of American imperialism backed by weapons created by my father and his fellow war criminals.

"I am a prisoner of war; the League will hold me until my father meets all the demands of the League to End Oppression on behalf of his victims. I am unharmed, and will stay that way if Herbert Fane makes these reparations. If he should fail to do so, however, the League will be forced to try him in absentia, and execute his sentence on me, to make him feel the anguish he has caused the helpless victims of American imperialism.

"I understand and accept this.

"Here are the demands.

"One. Herbert Fane must make a complete and unequivocal confession of his crimes, including a description of all the terror-weapons his company has developed, and all the places they have been used by the American military. This confession is to be run in its entirety on at least one network television newscast, and the others must announce its showing. This must happen within a week.

"Two. Herbert Fane and his company must stop immediately all work on military contracts. This means especially, but is not limited to, the MENTOR missile guidance system. Any continuance of work on this project, or cooperation with the government of the United States in moving men and materiel concerning these projects will be cause for immediate sentencing and execution.

"Three. Herbert Fane will distribute three million dollars from his personal holdings, among the following organizations and groups: The American Communist Party. The Socialist Labor Party. The Underground Defense Fund. The New American Re-education Compound . . ."

There were about fifteen such groups, all on the extreme left. The first two were the only ones that didn't practice or condone violence. The money was supposed to be distributed within two weeks.

"When all the demands have been met, I will be released unharmed. There will be a communication at that time.

"This concludes the message from the League to End Oppression."

The part he was playing demanded that Driscoll drop everything and go hold the girl's parents' hands. He did so, and amazed everyone by advising Fane to order an immediate stop on the military contracts at Fane Industries as the tape had demanded. "After all," he had said, "it's been the position all along that nothing is more important than your daughter's life."

Rines had looked him over suspiciously; the Fanes got in each other's way trying to thank him. Fane had ordered the work stoppage immediately, allowing Driscoll to get the hell out of there and back to his real work.

It didn't matter, anyway. He calculated that the plant would be back in operation in two days, tops. The time lost would be more than made up for by the propaganda value of the delay.

It would be a busy two days, though. Driscoll met with his three assistants from the Agency and worked out a plan and a schedule. Then he'd called Robin in and sent her off with Miles. Vi had a job of her own—she had to case the Fane Industries offices.

Driscoll and Jake Feder stayed in the shop and worked on their answering tape. They were in their ninth hour of watching sex between Liz and Lindsay, and they had approximately forty seconds of usable cuts of the kidnapped girl's voice, mostly groans and gasps. But it wasn't enough—to make this work, they needed words. Sentences.

Jake Feder moved his head slightly from side to side, as if in unconscious imitation of young Lindsay Keith up there on the screen. "Look at that," he told Driscoll, whose eyeballs felt as if they had been freshly painted with mucilage. "He looks like a kid trying to get the last of the ice cream out of the dish. Do you young people like to do that shit? No kidding? If I ever tried to do that to my Ethel, God rest her, she would have had me arrested.

"Besides," he went on, "when I used to have sex with women, I would at least *talk* to them, for God's sake. I would at least say, 'Was it good for you, darling,' 'You want now a sandwich,' *something* that would give the idea I knew I was with a *person*."

Driscoll sighed. "Let's just watch the tape, Jake, all—"

He stopped because there was finally something worthwhile on the audio track. Liz Fane suddenly reached down and grabbed her boyfriend by the head, pushing him down, digging her red fingernails into his scalp.

"Oh, *God!*" she cried, and the words sounded as though they had been twisted from her. "Please . . . don't . . . stop . . ." She said that a few times. She was nearly crying. Her voice became rhythmic and uncontrolled. "Stop . . . don't . . . don't . . . don't . . ." Then she cried out.

"I guess you young people *do* like it," Jake Feder murmured. On the screen, Lindsay Keith's face reappeared, looking into the camera wearing a big, satisfied grin.

"Bingo," Jake said. He punched a button and the screen went dark. "That ought to do it, right, Clifford?" He called him Clifford every chance he got, presumably on the theory that it got on Driscoll's nerves.

"That'll do fine, Jake," Driscoll said. "You edit up a background track. I'll see if Vi is back."

He found her on a cot in the de facto living quarters in the back. "All set, Vi. Just make a few comments on the tape for us, and we'll be ready to go."

"Ain't we gonna need your little girlfriend?" She sat up suddenly, the way she made all her movements. She began to fluff her Afro with her fingers.

"Not this time," Driscoll told her. "There'll be plenty of time for that. How did it look at the factory?"

"How well can you climb a rope?"

"I'll get wherever I have to go."

"Good. You just follow me, boss. I'll get you inside the building. After that, it's in your hands."

"Fine. Let's get that tape over with. I want to get some sleep before we take off."

"You got that right," Vi said. "This is going to be a long damn night."

In the control room, Jake sat Vi down in front of a

microphone and had her read from the statement that Driscoll had prepared. He watched the dials as she spoke, adjusting the slide controls on the mixer board. Sometimes, he would close his eyes and tilt his head back, listening.

Once he changed microphones, saying, "Driscoll tells me it's okay if they recognize your voice, but why make it easy for the bastards? You'll use this mike, it's got a better treble response, and I'll attenuate and pull out some of the mid-range frequencies, so it will still sound like you, but it will take them a little time to place you."

Vi scowled at him. "Sure, old man. Whatever you say."

Finally, Jake was happy. Vi went to take her nap. Driscoll stayed with Jake while he mixed the final tape and transferred it to cassette. Both listened to it more intently than music critics listening to a new classical recording.

"It'll go," Driscoll said at last.

"Of *course* it'll go. To spot that as something we whipped up will take a sound man as good as I am. And better than I am, they don't come."

"Right," Driscoll said. He had very little patience with people once their jobs were done. "You get back to Miami now. Be home to take the call when you get asked in as audio consultant on this case."

"Yeah. Who's going to ask me?"

Driscoll shrugged. "You've done work for the FBI before. I *hope* Rines will think to call you in. The Congressman is working to prime them for that down in Washington. If they don't call you in, I will."

Jake promised to be ready. He went in back and packed his things.

Robin sat in the darkness of the southbound Trailways bus and looked out at the rain.

It had been cloudy since the afternoon, but the rain hadn't started until the bus was in the Lincoln Tunnel. It was strange— she'd gone into the tunnel during a muggy summer night, and emerged in the middle of a violent thunderstorm. It was like a horror movie.

Not that it wasn't horrible enough, with poor Liz reading those messages in a zombie voice. Then Driscoll sending her back to New York, only to have her turn around and head straight back to Draper again. "I want someone to see you getting off that bus from New York," he'd said.

If he wanted someone to see her, though, why did he arrange things so she'd get back in the middle of the night? The middle of a night she wouldn't want to be out in if she were an otter, on top of it.

And worst of all, he had to send that *Miles* character along with her. Not her idea of the ideal traveling companion. All the way up, whenever she tried to get some answers out of him, all he'd say was, "Mr. Driscoll knows what he's doing."

Robin was starting to have her doubts. For example, what was the big idea of Miles getting on the bus with her (having dumped the car in New York) but instructing that they weren't to talk to each other, or even acknowledge the other's existence?

For a few seconds, she allowed herself to believe that Clifford Driscoll might be jealous, but that was ridiculous. His attentions to her over the last week or so were welcome—oh, who was she trying to kid?—they were fantastic! It was as if he had a direct line to her mind. And she didn't think she was flattering herself in thinking Clifford was getting something out of it, too. But it was easy to see she had come to want and need him more than he would ever need her.

Besides, Miles was such a fish. He wasn't ugly, or anything, but he was so *devoted to his duty* (whatever that was) that he was about as sexual as a statue. Furthermore, he would never mess with Mr. Driscoll's plans, of which Robin had so obviously become a part. He was sitting three rows behind her. She could feel his eyes on her.

She just wished she could figure out what the plans *were*. Why this shuttling back and forth? And why had she had to make that phone call to Aunt Sheila, and tell her all those lies?

A flash of lightning lit up the interior of the bus. It gave Robin a photographic view of herself. In her anxiety, she'd been twisting a Kleenex with her fingers, and had worried it to shreds. *Great,* she thought, *I go back to Draper with a lap full of lint and a mind full of fear.*

And not unjustified fear, either. Clifford had been very calm and reassuring this afternoon about how he felt she was no longer in danger, how the beating of Lindsay Keith had been an "isolated incident." Robin didn't care how isolated it was. It only had to happen one more time.

Still, she did want to help Uncle Herbert and Aunt Sheila, to comfort them as much as possible. And the only way to do that was to go back to Draper.

And, God help her, she wanted to be in Clifford Driscoll's arms again. Damn him.

She fell asleep that way, listening to the rain splatters and rumbles of thunder, with desire and curses mingling in her mind. She woke up at every stop. At Fenster, the last one before Draper, she stayed awake. It would only be about twenty minutes or so. She looked at her watch. That meant the bus would arrive in Draper about three-fifteen A.M., only about twenty minutes behind schedule. Rain or no rain, that wasn't much worse than usual.

There was no more thunder and lightning now, just a relentless, vertical fall of heavy drops. The driver pulled off the highway and headed for the gas station that was the city's bus stop.

"Draper," he said. "All out for Draper."

Robin got unsteadily to her feet, stretched, brushed uselessly at the tissue fibers on her pants, grabbed her bag from the rack, left the bus, and sprinted across the shiny blacktop of the deserted station for the phone booth. Once inside, she watched Miles look around. When he saw no one was around, he nodded to Robin, then disappeared into the rain.

Robin shuddered. Miles might be a creep, but now that he was out of sight she missed him. She knew he was supposed to be watching her from hiding, but she felt better when she could see him. She looked at her watch—there were certain intervals during which she wasn't supposed to call (something else she didn't understand), but now was okay. Robin shook water from her hair, then put a coin in the phone and dialed.

The phone purred in her ear. Five rings. Six. Seven.

Finally, there was a click, and a man's voice said, "Guard Station."

Robin relaxed. "Mr. Jackson, this is Robin Payne."

"*Who?*"

"Roberta," she said. "Roberta. Mr. Fane's neice."

Mr. Jackson had a deep smooth voice, unchanged from the days her uncle would bring her and Liz to the plant for a day to see the big machines work. "Miss Roberta, I thought it was you. Your uncle said you would be callin' me about this time. What'd you give me, your actin' name?"

"Yes, Mr. Jackson, I'm sorry."

"Don't be sorry, it's a nice name. See it on a movie screen someday." The guard chuckled. "But you don't want to stand around jawing. Where are you, at the bus station?"

"That's right."

"Okay, Gambrelli don't live but a minute from there. I'll call him right away, have him pick you up, bring you to your uncle's house."

"Thank you, Mr. Jackson. I hate making extra work for anybody."

"Don't worry about it, Gambrelli's happy to make the overtime. He's got another daughter gettin' married this year."

Robin smiled in spite of herself. She thanked Mr. Jackson and hung up. As she waited for the car, she thought, *Well, I'm back. And I'm in the middle of something the enigmatic Mr. Driscoll has dreamed up.*

She was, she suspected, *directly* in the middle. Right, she thought, where he wants me.

They had been sitting on the roof in the rain for a good half hour before Jackson went to the back of his station to answer the phone. When he stood in the front of it, he could see the skylight they would use to enter; that was one of the things Vi had spotted during her reconnaissance this afternoon.

The rest was easy. The shutdown had reduced the number of night-shift eyes that might see them. Fane Industries had

had to file their security plan with the government, and everything that was available to the government was available to Driscoll through his father. They had gotten through the fence, or rather over it, with the aid of a device that deadened the alarm circuit for a ten foot stretch, while convincing the computer that controlled the security systems that it was still intact.

They used a similar gimmick on the skylight. It had been all wired and ready to go, but they had to wait for Robin's phone call to divert for a few precious seconds the one kind of security equipment they couldn't damp out—the man's eyes.

Vi landed on the floor noiselessly. Her thin body seemed strong out of all proportion to its weight. Driscoll made a wet thud when he landed. He wiped his rain-stung eyes with a towel he took from a small gym bag, then handed it to Vi, who did the same. He pointed in the direction of the personnel office.

They had ten minutes before the inside guard would check that office or the corridors leading to it—if he stuck to his schedule. Here at Fane Industries, they used a modern version of the clock-key security system. The inside guard had to appear at specified times at small keyboards (really computer inputs) built into the wall around the office complex and punch in a special code that changed nightly. If he punched in the wrong code, the alarms cut in. If he was two minutes late, they did the same. The guard could, of course, turn in an alarm any time he saw something suspicious.

Robin's call had come at one of the fringe moments. They would just barely have enough time. He and Vi virtually sprinted for the office. Driscoll was pulling a key from his pocket as they arrived at the door.

It was a Rabson Nemesis lock. It wasn't supposed to be possible to make a master key for that kind of lock, and on behalf of the government, he hoped nobody would start thinking otherwise. Once inside the office, he went to the security files. As Robin had told him, there was a special section for members of Mr. Fane's family. It was a good thing he had gotten that bit of information; the special section was at the end, marked "miscellaneous." He would have found it, but it would have taken more time than he had to spare.

Now Driscoll pulled the file on Fane, Elizabeth S. (daughter) partway out of the drawer. He wiped his gloves on the inside of his thigh, because that was the only part of his clothing still dry. He reached inside the black gym bag in which he had carried the anti-alarm gimmicks and a few other tools, and brought out something sealed between two pieces of plastic. He peeled the plastic back, and brought out the sheet that bore the name of Liz Fane, but the fingerprints of their Jane Doe. He pulled Liz Fane's authentic fingerprints from the file, and replaced the old form with the new one.

Vi had been standing by the door, watching. She held a knife in one hand and a silenced pistol in the other. The tranquilizer darts would be no good here. They were pretending to be terrorists now. If they were discovered, they had to *be* terrorists. They could leave no one alive to say he had seen them near this office. Once again, Driscoll was amazed at how easily he and Vi had accepted the cold logic of counterespionage, how ready they were to sacrifice an innocent life, if necessary, to the Objective.

And, he thought, if you stop daydreaming and get the hell out of here, it will be less likely to become necessary. Driscoll replaced the file, then closed and locked the cabinet.

He had just used the supposedly unobtainable master key to relock the office when he turned around and saw the floor of the hallway gleaming in the dim service lights.

Rainwater. Little puddles of it making a trail from the skylight directly to this door. They had marked their path as effectively as Hansel and Gretel, revealing their destination as plainly as a neon sign.

Driscoll did some simple arithmetic. The guard would come into this corridor in about two minutes. The water would never evaporate in that time.

He had to wipe it up. He signalled Vi to get going. She looked at him defiantly. Driscoll broke his own rule and spoke, telling her, "*Move!*" in a harsh whisper. Vi shrugged, then took off.

Driscoll pulled the damp towel from the bag, and began to scamper down the hall like Quasimodo, stopping at each puddle just long enough to spread it around. The results were gratifying. Once thinned out, the water began drying in streaks even as he wiped, evaporating into the dry, air-conditioned atmosphere of the building.

He was wiping up the last puddle, the big one under the skylight when he heard the whistling. "Stormy Weather." The inside guard was amusing himself while completing this section of his appointed rounds.

Driscoll stuffed the towel back in the bag, drew his gun, and dropped into a crouch, both hands on the gun for better accuracy.

Under the whistling, he could hear the guard's scuffling footsteps.

The gun began to waver. Sweat mingled with the dampness of rain on Driscoll's forehead.

God damn it! God damn it to hell! It was no good. Hastily, he stuffed the gun back in his belt, slung the bag over his shoulder, and clambered up the rope. He had a bad moment when the skylight seemed to be stuck, but he gave it an extra shove, and it came open without spilling much more water into the hallway. He pulled himself through the opening onto the tar and gravel roof, directly into four inches of standing water.

He ignored the cold discomfort of it and began to remove the electronic device to reactivate the alarm. A sudden idea made him stop. He looked through the frosted glass to the hallway below. The guard wasn't in sight yet, but that didn't mean he was still out of earshot.

Driscoll had no time to weigh things. One question: Was it worth the risk? One answer: Probably. He acted. He pulled his gloved right hand back across his body and delivered a backhand blow with the edge of his hand to a panel of skylight glass.

Too soft. Nothing happened.

Driscoll made a face, then drew back his hand to try again. The danger was that he would strike the window too hard, showering the guard with slivers of glass.

He swung again, and made a nice clean crack in the glass panel—just the kind that would let water in during a heavy rainfall—enough to account for that puddle on the floor.

Now Driscoll went ahead with restoring the alarm. If his

calculations were correct, there was no danger that the crack in the glass would set off the alarm when it was reconnected. It wouldn't be a total catastrophe even if he turned out to be wrong—the alarm would be blamed on a water-caused short circuit.

His luck held, though, and the alarm was reconnected with silence. He sprinted across the roof, coiling the rope he'd climbed as he ran.

He rappelled down the side of the building fast enough that he could feel an uncomfortable heat through his gloves. He landed on the flagstone walk, glad he didn't have to take the time to mess over footprints he would have left in the soft earth.

He ran the path to the fence, climbed over, reconnected the alarm there, then ran off into the trees surrounding the factory. He reached the road, wet and breathing hard. From a stand of trees about a hundred yards up the road, he saw car headlights blink three times.

He felt himself beginning to relax. Vi had made it. He walked toward the car as she drove toward him. He opened the door, threw the bag in the back seat, and climbed in.

"Where to?" Vi said.

Driscoll leaned back and closed his eyes. "Headquarters. I can't go back to the hotel like this. What time is it?"

Vi looked at her wrist. "Quarter to four. I hope you don't expect me to clean this car out. Mud from the woods on the outside, mud from us on the inside, later for that."

"Don't worry about it. It's an Agency car." Driscoll let go another big breath. "Twenty-five minutes."

Vi took her eyes off the road for a second to look at him. "What's the matter? You act like you never did anything like this before."

"Just drive."

"What did you do, kill the guard?"

"No," Driscoll said distinctly. "I did not kill the guard. Now shut up, Vi, I mean it."

Vi scowled at him, then her face softened into a thoughtful look. She nodded, as if in agreement with something, but kept quiet and drove.

She knows, Driscoll thought. *I didn't kill the guard. But Vi knows, as I do, that I* should *have killed the guard. It was the percentage move, the right thing to do to attain the Objective.* Which, it turned out, he wasn't so ready to sacrifice innocent life for after all.

All right, he had (most likely) gotten away with it this time. And he had Vi's approval, apparently. Not that her approval meant much. Vi worked these operations with the full knowledge that she was paid three times as much as Jake or Miles or any normal agent because as a lamb, it was eminently possible *she* would wind up sacrificed before the operation was over. It stood to reason she'd be glad to see any signs from Driscoll indicating he might be reluctant to do it.

It didn't make *him* glad at all. It was softness, and there would come a time when softness would destroy him, if he wasn't careful. And possibly, if he lost sight of the Objective, it might hurt the whole country.

He thought about it back at the hideout. He barely acknowledged the presence of Miles, who reported success with his own mission and wanted to know how theirs went. He thought about it while he changed clothes and drove his rented car back to the Holiday Inn.

The worst part of the evening came later, after his shower, after he'd gotten into the too-soft motel bed and turned out the light. He went over the whole sequence of events, again and again. He berated himself for every wasted second, every bit of added risk.

But no matter what he tried, he couldn't change one thing: He was irrationally, but undeniably and profoundly, *happy* that he hadn't killed the guard.

The implications of it terrified him. The rain was over and the sun was up before Driscoll achieved anything even close to sleep.

If a tragedy accomplished nothing else, Robin thought, it made people take a long close look at their priorities. She'd been awakened this morning (about half past eleven) by the sound of Uncle Herbert's yelling at the telephone.

That had happened before, though not too often. What was unprecedented was what he was yelling *about.* Uncle Herbert had been chastizing a subordinate because the subordinate had made the phone ring to tell Uncle Herbert there was a crack and a water leak in the skylight of the office wing of the factory.

This was the same Uncle Herbert who had fired a supervisor for not telling him the vending machines in the cafeteria were ripping off the workers, and had kept him fired for four days, before cooling off.

Now, he didn't want to be bothered with the factory. Robin dreaded facing him over lunch.

She got out of bed and dressed, putting on a light blue cotton dress. Loose at the shoulders, very Sissy Spacek. She did her hair back with combs. It was funny. Back in New York, she *never* wore dresses for everyday. In Draper, she wore them all the time. Of course they were cooler, but it got hot in New York, too. Maybe it was the town itself. This was a pretty Sissy Spacek kind of place.

But there was more to it than that, this time. It was almost as if she were overcompensating for being—and she grimaced as she thought it—a spy. She had something more than a suspicion that whatever had happened at Fane Industries early this morning had had more than a little to do with her carefully-timed phone call to the guard. And she knew damned well that whatever it was had been more than a cracked skylight.

Robin faced the fact that she had agreed to help Driscoll, in part because she thought it would be *exciting.* Robin had never done anything exciting. She was too young to have really known what Vietnam and the protests against it were all about, but she was sure being in that turmoil on either side had been something important that felt, oh, dangerous. For some people in some places, the protests and counterprotests *were* dangerous; that wasn't the point. The point was that not having something important and a little dangerous in her background had struck Robin as a serious lack to her as an actress. Then

Clifford had come along (talk about dangerous) and offered her exactly the sort of thing that would let her fill that void.

She didn't feel that way anymore. Being a spy, even a non-risk-taking, peripheral kind of spy, was hard, ennervating and nasty work. So many details to keep straight. *What lies have I told to whom?* As an actress, she had to play one part at a time. In Driscoll's world she had to play a different part with everyone she met. And in a strange way, every single one of them was some part of her. No wonder she wanted to dress wholesome. She wanted to prove to herself that wholesomeness was still a part of her, too.

She was just reaching behind her to button that last button when Sheila Fane knocked on the door. Robin told her to come in.

Aunt Sheila smiled sadly at her. "I'm glad you're up, dear," she said. "Let me get that for you."

"Would you? Thanks." The button attended to, Robin said, "Did you want me for anything, Aunt Sheila?"

"I just wanted to make sure you were awake. It's nearly noon now, and Mr. Driscoll is coming over for lunch at one o'clock." She frowned. "Is something the matter?"

Driscoll is the matter, she thought grimly. *If he had told me, I could have been prepared for this.*

"No," Robin said. "It's—well, it's just that I couldn't help but overhear Uncle Herbert being angry this morning. Is he really up to having visitors? Are you, for that matter? I don't know how you stay so calm through all of this. I couldn't."

Aunt Sheila closed her eyes, and for a second allowed Robin to see how weary she was. "You could do it if you had to, Robin," she said. "Someone has to remain calm, or this would eat us all up. Devour us. But don't think I don't think of it. I'll be thinking of this for the rest of my life. However it turns out."

Robin heard herself say the obligatory, stupidly optimistic words. "It'll turn out fine, Aunt Sheila. Everything will be all right."

Her aunt smiled at her again, even more sadly than before. "All I can do is hope you're right," she said. "Come downstairs soon, won't you? Your uncle is eager to see you."

Despite Robin's doubts, that turned out to be the truth; an

understatement, if anything. Uncle Herbert was sitting on a sofa in the parlor looking off somewhere into time and space. Robin didn't think she had ever seen him in the parlor before— he was either at work or in his study. He didn't notice her for a few seconds, but when he did, his fact lost its dead stare and attained true sadness. He rose and almost gave her a hug, but at the last minute contented himself by taking hold of her upper arms.

Robin, in a way, was glad he had chickened out. If old, undemonstrative Uncle Herbert had actually gone so far as to give her a hug, she would have demanded he be fingerprinted for identification. If he had broken down and cried (at least in her presence) she would have had the imposter arrested on the spot.

Then he said, "Robin. I am very happy to have you back here. Thank you for coming. I—I think it's very important for us to be together now—as a family . . ."

As he tapered off, *Robin* started to cry. She hugged her uncle. And she felt like a louse. About everything.

She took control of herself after a few seconds, grateful that her uncle hadn't complained about her as a damned emotional female, the way he had about the females in his household in the past.

"Thank you, Uncle Herbert," she began, not really know-ing where she was going with it. The doorbell saved her from having to go anywhere.

As Henrietta ushered him in to join them, Clifford Driscoll smiled politely and asked them all how they were.

Robin flinched, waiting for Uncle Herbert to say some-thing along the lines of, "How do you think I'm doing, you silly ass?" but he was still subdued. He muttered something about doing as well as could be expected. Aunt Sheila thanked Driscoll for coming. Robin just said hello.

Lunch was ready, so Aunt Sheila showed them into the dining room. The conversation over salmon croquettes was, in Robin's opinion, pathetic. They had nothing to talk about except Liz and her plight, and by some kind of telepathic consensus, that was out during the meal. Robin had to admit that even *she* would be hard pressed to come up with a topic to discuss in public with Clifford Driscoll, and she'd been *sleeping* with him, for heaven's sake.

Aunt Sheila tried; she asked him how he went into government service. Driscoll smiled his little polite smile (so different from the smiles she'd seen when they were alone together) and said it was a family tradition. Then Aunt Sheila had asked him if he knew this or that acquaintance of hers and Uncle Herbert's, and though he'd heard of a few of the Defense Department ones, he'd never met any.

They wound up talking about the weather, for God's sake. It was deadly there for a while, until Aunt Sheila came up with another idea.

She approached it indirectly, asking Uncle Herbert what they should do about the Draper Community Fund Dinner scheduled for Sunday evening, and then turned to Driscoll to explain that as usual, her husband was the chairman.

"But Herbert, we can't go, of course. If . . . things don't change, we won't want to, and if they do, we'll be away somewhere. Liz will need a change of scene after all this."

So Liz was back in it after all, consensus or not. Robin was surprised. Aunt Sheila was usually very perceptive about that kind of thing.

Uncle Herbert said, "Of course you're right. I'd forgotten about it completely. I'll call Nate Jeffers later this afternoon." He was still being quiet and mild mannered. Robin was beginning to worry about him.

And speaking of telepathic, Robin felt the *improving* gaze of her aunt upon her, the one that had always gotten across to her How Young Ladies Should Behave. As always, it prompted her to Do the Right Thing.

"I'll be happy to represent the family," she said.

"Why, thank you dear," Aunt Sheila said. "That will be a great help to us and to the organization."

Clifford Driscoll, of all people, protested. "I think it might be a good idea to see what Chief Anderson and Mr. Rines think. We don't want to put Robin in any danger."

That went without saying, as Aunt Sheila and Uncle Herbert hastened to assure him. Forget it. Why take any chances?

"As long as I don't have to make a speech or anything, I don't mind going just to show that the Fanes aren't beaten by this thing."

Robin paused for a moment, listening to her own voice, and deciding that, much to her surprise, she really meant it. She had always thought of Uncle Herbert and Aunt Sheila and Liz as only the next best thing to a Real Family, but now here she was, absolutely overflowing with Real Family Spirit.

It made her playful. "Besides, Mr. Driscoll can be my escort. He'll make sure I'm safe."

Uncle Herbert said, "No, Roberta, please." He hadn't called her Roberta in twelve years. He hadn't ever said please to her before. "Unless Mr. Driscoll really thinks it's safe."

Driscoll smiled and said, "We'll see how it looks at the time."

"All right," Robin said.

They took their coffee to the parlor. Uncle Herbert reverted to form by telling the women they probably would like to leave the men to talk business, but even that was tentative. It was as if Uncle Herbert wasn't sure of anything anymore.

Driscoll said he didn't mind if Aunt Sheila and Robin stayed. They were deeply concerned in this; both were smart and cared for Liz. "We need all the good minds on this we can get, Mr. Fane."

So they stayed, but there was nothing any of the good minds could think of to help the situation. Uncle Herbert was doing all he could to comply with the terrorists' demands. The plant was shut down. He was having his financial people work on raising the money. "It's not easy to get three million dollars in liquid assets together on short notice, even for a rich man, Mr. Driscoll."

But they were getting there. Uncle Herbert figured he would be able to begin distributing the money to the groups named in the tape beginning two days from now.

"Have you heard from any of these people?" Aunt Sheila asked. It had been arranged for the FBI to contact the various groups. Robin had figured out why. For one thing, the FBI was likeliest to know how to get in touch with left-wing radicals in a hurry—they were probably keeping them under surveillance.

For another, the FBI wanted to sniff around and find out if any or all of the people named were involved in the plot.

"We've heard from a few," Driscoll said. "One outfit, a San Francisco group called SOFA . . ."

"SOFA?" Aunt Sheila said.

"Stamp Out Fascism in America. They said they rejected kidnapping as a political tool, that assassination was sometimes justifiable, but never kidnapping. Especially kidnapping for ransom. So they turned down the money."

"They turned it *down?*" Robin was incredulous.

Driscoll flashed his real smile. At least, she thought of it as real. "Integrity is a flower that grows in all kinds of soil. I think someday I'll sent them a few bucks myself."

Then he adjusted his glasses and gave a pompous little cough, and the smile was gone. "Everybody else is accepting the money. The Communist Party and the two socialist parties did go so far as to say they were taking it only because it might help your daughter. Which it might."

"It might," Uncle Herbert echoed. "So it goes out. I'm saving my confession for last. My war crimes confession."

Aunt Sheila laid a hand on his arm. "Herbert . . ."

He didn't shake her off, but he didn't pay any attention to her, either.

"That's the worst of it, Driscoll. The contract means more to the government than to me, though I hate having these punks tell me how to run my business. I can spare the money. But the idea of my going on television and saying I'm a criminal and a murderer . . ." He let breath out from between his teeth.

"*They're* the murderers. Destroyers. Cowards. Their fight's with me, not with my daughter. She's never oppressed anybody. What has she ever done to deserve this?

"For that matter, what have *I* ever done? Or my wife? Or anybody? I was poor; I was a 'worker.' One of the 'people.' I didn't whine about it, I did something about it. I built something. I *built* something! I saved this town after the mill closed, ask anybody. Ask the workers, why don't you?"

This is good, Robin thought. *This is what's been driving him crazy, holding all this resentment in.* None of what he said was very original. Or, Robin thought, very enlightened. But the important part now was that Uncle Herbert was opening up—getting things off his mind. He wasn't waiting for answers, which was just as well, because there probably weren't any.

That, she suddenly realized, was the full horror of terrorism. The people who did it had reasons, but the effects of their actions were reasonless. Terrorism struck like lightning. It most often blasted the high places—rich people, and government officials, but it could strike anywhere. Robin was no expert, but she read newspapers. Children in Ireland, in the Middle East. Black people in America. Those two poor men in the ambulance.

What must it be like, she wondered, to be so involved in a cause that people no longer counted? She shuddered. It was bad enough to know what it was like to get in the *way* of some of them.

Suddenly, her eyes met Driscoll's, and she felt a sick sensation slither up her back. Was *he* like that? He said he'd do whatever it took to get Liz back. Limited by what? Terrorists could work for governments, too. Most often, they did. Was she infatuated (or, God help her, in love) with one of these people?

Uncle Herbert was still involved in his therapeutic speech. "I'll bet these people have never built *anything*," he was saying. "All they can do is tear down. They've been doing it for years. And you people let them."

Driscoll's voice was very soft. "We try to stop them, Mr. Fane. The Defense Department, the FBI, the CIA, police departments everywhere. When they do anything more than talk or write, we try to stop them."

"What?" Uncle Herbert demanded. "What are you doing to stop them?"

"All we can." Driscoll's voice became even softer. "Just as you are."

There was a noise from outside. Someone was pounding on the door, ignoring the bell entirely. Since the parlor was just off the hallway and near the door, and because Uncle Herbert needed to be doing something, he yelled, "Forget it, Henrietta," and went to the door himself.

Driscoll followed, and Robin, curious, followed him.

Her uncle had opened the door to a guard, one of the men on the front gate.

"Someone threw this over the fence and drove away," the guard said. His face was red and sweating. With his fingertips he held a small cardboard box, about the size of a box of Milk Duds. The box was wrapped in brown paper and heavily taped. It was addressed to Herbert Fane.

He reached out impatiently and grabbed the box from the guard.

"Fingerprints!" the guard squeaked.

Uncle Herbert turned a dead face to Driscoll. "Well? What should I do?"

"Don't worry about it," Driscoll said. He spoke gently, and Robin could have kissed him for it. "It probably didn't make any difference anyway. Everybody knows about fingerprints, now."

Herbert Fane sighed. He turned back to the guard. "Go," he said. "Back to your booth. Call Chief Anderson from there. Tell him I'm going to open this."

"The chief's not going to like—"

For a moment, Robin thought her uncle was going to hit the guard, but he just screamed for him to go. The guard, remembering who paid him, fled.

"Okay," Driscoll said, getting calmer as Uncle Herbert got more excited. "Let's open it. But let's not take any more chances. I'll do it."

Driscoll took out a pocket knife, and working with great care, cut the wrappings and removed the package. Robin could see now it was textured white, the kind of box jewelers put necklaces in.

Driscoll put the box down on the table. Again using his knife, he flipped the top off the box.

There was something black in the box, and something white. The black thing was easy to recognize—a tape cassette.

The white thing was harder to identify. They all stood and looked dumbly at it. Then Aunt Sheila, standing behind Robin, gasped. Suddenly, Robin knew what it was.

A mangled human finger. A woman's pinky.

Robin kept thinking, *I want to scream. I want to faint.* But she didn't. She stood there staring down at the thing until Driscoll took her by the shoulders and turned her away.

"Come on Robin, we have to help your aunt and uncle."

"What?" Robin said.

"Look after your aunt and uncle. Come on, help me get them out of here."

Robin closed her eyes tight, opened them, and looked around her. Aunt Sheila was standing still, eyes wide open. "They can't," she muttered. "They promised."

Uncle Herbert was crying, beating his fist on the table and screaming *no* over and over.

Help them, she thought. *They need God to help them, not me. We need God to help us all.*

Chapter Six

LEO CALVIN PICKED UP THE PHONE AND DIALED. "GO GET Daisy Mae," he told Roy. The boy gave him his habitual sullen look, but he moved. Roy hadn't talked back, or said much of anything to Leo since the throttling.

Leo watched him go. Stupid, vicious boy. Freedom fighting had turned out not to be exciting enough for him. He sulked around the house, and seethed when they sent him out on some errand. Roy would have to be attended to.

But there was time for that. The boy's grandfather was away, there were no friends to come looking for the little snot. Nobody would miss him until school opened, and maybe not even then. In any case, that was still two or three weeks away, time enough to take care of things.

There were more pressing problems. Much more.

Roy ushered Liz Fane to the phone. She had become a model prisoner in recent days, not attempting to make any noise, not attempting to unseal her windows, not even checking to see if the door to the room she now shared with Candy was locked when she was there alone.

She dressed as they did, now—jeans and T-shirts, no bras, work clothes, army fatigues. Only Roy, because he lived here, and Candy, because she still went out to work, had other clothes.

Today she wore a T-shirt that said "Another Shitty Day in

Paradise," which Ramon had gotten once in Puerto Rico. It was tight on her, and showed the beginnings of indentations below her ribs. The hypnotic drugs they kept her on seemed to deprive her of her appetite. It didn't matter; she wasn't going to starve to death.

Liz Fane's eyes were wild, staring and sunken. The mere threat of the closet was enough to send her into hysterics. She began to whimper whenever the door to that closet was opened for any reason.

Her head twitched frequently from side to side, as if she were trying to chase down some random, unrecognized sound. Her hands twitched, too.

Her healthy, whole, untouched hands.

"Daisy Mae," he said sternly.

"Yes," she said.

He held the phone out to her. "Here," he said as she took it. "Talk to your father."

Liz Fane clapped the receiver to her ear with such force that Leo thought she would knock herself unconscious. *"Daddy!"* she screamed. *"Daddy!"*

Leo's lips tightened. He rubbed his long nose. He figured as much. Still too soon. She was placid, she was tractable, she was thoroughly cowed. But as a personality, she still existed somewhere behind the drugs and the pain.

He watched Liz Fane's face dissolve into confusion, then disappointment, then tears.

"Candy," she said. "I—I thought . . . he said . . ."

Leo got tired of looking and took the phone away from her. "All right, Candy," he said into the phone. "Come home."

"I told you it was too soon," she said.

"Yes, you did. You were right. Come back."

"How is she? How badly is she broken up?"

"She is crying quietly. Come back here and make her stop." He hung up the phone, banged it down on the hook. *Bad,* he thought. *Have to show control at all times.*

He'd had one hundred percent control until yesterday afternoon. The operation had gone perfectly. As late as yesterday morning, he'd received word that Ramon had landed safely in Cuba. And that he'd been safely taken care of.

In fifteen years and more of this sort of operation, Leo had learned that leaving loose ends lying around was inviting catastrophe. He had learned, in fact, to tie up the ends as soon as they became loose.

Ramon had had to leave. He realized that. He had been seen, was known by people. He was the only suspect the opposition had in the case. When Leo had praised him warmly in front of the others and told him he was being sent to Cuba for safety and reward, he had nearly glowed, he was so proud.

That was good. Leo didn't want it to be said he'd never given his people anything.

Ramon had been smuggled through the roadblock in an ambulance from the hospital where they'd gotten the one they'd used in the kidnapping. Ramon had been in back, wrapped in bandages by Candy. The paperwork (also arranged by Candy) said he was a burn patient being transferred to a hospital in Philadelphia. Once past the roadblocks, it had been easy to get him on a plane to Miami and a boat to Havana.

Once there, of course, Ramon got a little surprise. He'd expected to become a Hero of the Revolution. He wound up as fertilizer in a yam field.

That had been yesterday morning.

But yesterday afternoon, the opposition had made its move. Some brilliant mind in the opposition had made its move, and for the first time in his adult life, Leo Calvin was baffled.

Leo Calvin's father had been a plastic surgeon, his mother a grade school principal in the town he'd grown up in, a comfortable suburb just east of Buffalo.

Leo had been an idealist, at least through his teen years. His parents were active in liberal causes, so that all through his youth he heard the right rhetoric. His parents told him that the government had to rearrange things so that the poor would not be cheated—they told him lots of things. He forgot the baby talk they put it in, but the message was clear. They planted it, and it took root.

Then one day he noticed that his father never waited in

line at the bank. The bank manager would come out to greet him, glad to see him. Glad to see the next installment of the money Dr. Calvin earned for helping women make a liar out of nature. It wasn't a very big thing, but it was a start. It got him thinking, asking questions that his parents could never successfully answer, like why was it the only black person who ever entered their house was the cleaning lady?

Leo Calvin laughed, remembering how that younger version of himself had felt so betrayed. He was still an idealist when he entered high school, but he was an angry young idealist.

His anger expressed itself, one day, over a fairly mundane liberal-conservative split on a school board matter. The conservatives won, thanks to the work of a particularly obnoxious, childless businessman who was only on the board to see that none of his tax money would be spent on schools.

Leo decided not to let him get away with it. One night soon after the vote, he went to the businessman's house and burned down his garage, with his thirty-five thousand dollar Mercedes in it.

That was the start of something. Because Leo was never suspected of causing the fire, never even questioned about it. And as days, then weeks went past, he had trouble remembering that he had done it for a reason. He was too absorbed in the sensation of having *done* it. Of having used power he had found there for the taking.

He indulged the urge to feel that way again when he went away to college. He found there that a person bold enough and clever enough could always do exactly what he wanted. He could close the college down, and he did. He could have burned the college down, but chose not to. He could cow faculty and intimidate administration. And be loved by students.

And he did it all for the *right causes*. His parents challenged him during one of his rare visits home. Why did the riot start, son? We've heard the administration was about to give in to your demands, at least most of them. Why did three young men and three young women die in a riot?

Leo sneered at them openly, now. He'd been sneering at them inwardly since shortly after that day at the bank.

He didn't tell them the real reasons. The thrill of power; that was the real reason. His parents had lived the lives of ineffectual idealism for so long, they wouldn't even recognize the *secondary* reasons for the hard-headed practicality they were.

A demonstration that was well reasoned, sincere, and earnest would be ignored. A noisy, colorful demonstration was worth two minutes on the local news. A riot made the network. And a riot that resulted in deaths lingered for weeks in the headlines; had a grand jury named to investigate it. It lived in the public mind for years.

Instead, Leo attacked his parents where they lived— "What's the matter? Don't you want the war over? Don't you want social justice?"—until he almost had them apoligizing to him.

As time went by, Leo entered the third stage of his development. That was his realization that it was *all* a waste of time. That the North Vietnamese, whom he met on a trip to Hanoi in early seventy-two, were just as corrupt and vicious as the South Vietnamese. More so—the North won, didn't it?

He realized that poor people were just as selfish and hypocritical as rich people; just nastier because their lives were less comfortable, and therefore more bitter.

The better he got to know people, the easier it was to loathe them. All of them. All people.

And the easier it got to manipulate them.

That was the part he liked. The manipulation. The power. He could move into a stable situation and unsettle it. He could take a possible problem and turn it into hell on earth for all concerned. He could be smart enough, and ruthless enough to make escape impossible. Except on *his* terms.

He never wanted to be a media celebrity like the Chicago Seven and the others. They had only been dabbling in the power, anyway, getting off their political rocks while the tide of guilty little white kids was running with them, then selling out at the earliest sign the tide was ebbing. Becoming stockbrokers. Flacks for gurus. Unsuccessful politicians living on rich relatives' money. Jesus freaks.

And he'd been too smart to live the lives the more

committed had led. Running, hiding. Starving. Robbing banks to buy guns. Using guns to rob banks. Fools, all of them.

Of all the great radicals of the sixties, only Leo Calvin had realized one salient fact—his talents were eminently marketable. *Forget* causes. Causes were a joke. Leo would keep doing what he liked doing, and he would make enough money doing it to live securely and comfortably between jobs.

Logic dictated that he approach the Russians first. They had already footed the bill (indirectly but substantially) for many of his activities, of that he was sure. He approached his most faithful (and most secret) money man, a Wall Street broker, and laid it on the line. The contact had looked thoughtful and had said nothing, but within a week, a meeting had been arranged between Leo and the "Agricultural Attaché" of the Russian Embassy in Washington.

True to his mission, the attaché cultivated Leo, and the deal was made. Deaths, disappearances, urban violence, labor unrest and all sorts of politically related woes followed. Life had been interesting and comfortable.

Leo liked to plan his operations from the beginning. He would get a message from his employers telling him what the final result was to be, but he would get there on his own.

He had welcomed, though, the opportunity to join the Cronus Project. It was, in his expert opinion, the most audacious and farseeing terrorist plan ever conceived. Leo, who had studied the great practitioners of his craft, knew that this had to be the brainchild of the sick man in Moscow, and Leo's admiration for the Chairman's talents grew even larger.

Leo fitted into the plan perfectly, removing one of the last awkward parts of the mechanism that had been building for some thirty years—the question of who would actually put it into effect. The plan had originally called for the reassignment of agents from other projects in America, but this way was better.

Of course, it hadn't necessarily been planned as the kidnapping of Liz Fane, this sobbing Daisy Mae of theirs who was now being led back to her room, asking in whimpers where Candy was. Not necessarily her at all. Cronus had been in preparation since long before she was born.

But Liz Fane was the chosen target. Moscow had told him her name, given him his deadline, and let him go to work. He'd recruited from the hungry and hidden terrorists of the decade before, coming up with Georgia and Candy, who were the remains of a botched bank-robbing spree, and Ramon, who had been thrown out of the FALN for being too unstable.

Candy was actually a qualified nurse, with dozens of forged identities. She and Ramon had been the first to arrive, ordered to find a safe house and to scout out the territory. The safe house had come complete with this overprivileged juvenile delinquent who thought terrorism was all bombs and gunfire, and who had no patience for the subtle terror of uncertainty and waiting.

Georgia had come in later, with weapons and other equipment. Leo could have used his own contacts, but it was always better to let one of the temporaries handle traceable things. Georgia might become a problem after the project was over. She had been visiting Leo in bed fairly frequently over the last few days, no doubt as some sort of revenge on Candy for the attention she had to pay to Daisy Mae.

Leo didn't mind. Georgia was no beauty, and she had a tendency to bite, but Leo didn't sleep much, anyway, and sex passed the time. The trouble was, Georgia showed signs of beginning to enjoy it. There had been a slight softening in her, some tenderness in what she had been doing with him, and it had Leo worried. He made it a matter of policy not to kill associates unless absolutely necessary. If Georgia kept this up, she would make it necessary. He didn't relish the prospect of trying to do it, either. Georgia was a skilled and remorseless assassin.

Waldo was merely an enthusiastic one. He had killed a guard at a mental hospital (to see blood), then wandered off. Leo had found him and more or less adopted him. He felt for Waldo a combination of the feelings a hunter would have for his dog and his trusty rifle.

Leo wished he knew his opponents as well.

Well, he knew one of them, or rather, he knew that one of

them was a black woman, whose voice sounded oddly familiar. He couldn't place it just now, but it would come. She had such a fine deep voice, and a wonderful way with the familiar rhetoric. "Crimes against the People" sounded much more convincing in this woman's voice than it had in Liz Fane's. And the menace. The sounds of moaning in the background, pleading with someone to stop.

Leo could not be fooled on something like this. Those cries were being forced from someone under severe physical stress. And the voice could well be Liz Fane's. It truly could.

And there was someone among his opponents who could make the familiar rhetoric sing and do tricks. When he heard the tape on the radio—and there was no need for them to force the media to play *this* one, Leo was sure—he had listened closely. Through his anger, he had to respect the talents of the black woman (and who *was* she?) or whoever of her associates had composed that little speech.

"This is the New America Liberation Army." Moans in the background, punctuated by stifled screams. "We decry the fascist fraud perpetrated by the United States Government and the Pig Herbert Fane in an attempt to exploit the disappearance of his daughter to the detriment of the working people of this area, in a vain attempt to escape the justice of the New America Liberation Army."

That had been a classic bit right there, Leo thought. It seemed to be written in true terrorist style—elevated beyond the writer's capabilities, pretentious, and angry.

"The daughter of the Pig Fane is in the custody of the New America Liberation Army. The so-called 'League to End Oppression' does not exist. The Pig Herbert Fane shall ignore the fraudulent so-called demand put forward secretly by the United States Government to cheat the workers of their pay.

"The workers shall be put back on their jobs immediately. They will be paid for the time they were locked out. The New America Liberation Army supports true social justice, not the so-called democracy of fascist America or the so-called socialism of fascist Russia."

That was to explain why they wanted to get the missiles back in business, Leo thought.

"The Pig Herbert Fane will meet these demands. The workers will return to work with no loss in pay. Herbert Fane will assign to his workers seventy-five percent of his stock in Fane Industries. All employees will share equally in this disbursement. The workers will receive all rights and privileges of stockholders in any corporation."

Leo had shaken his head. Another nice touch. A play for the asterisk in the minds of the populace. "Well," they would think, "of course the NALA are terrorists, and therefore murderous scum,* *but* at least they really seem to be for the *workers*, and not just Negroes and Puerto Ricans and women and faggots and junkies and the poor and other inferior types." They wouldn't say that, but they'd think it.

"Pig Herbert Fane will assemble *four* million dollars of the People's money, which he has stolen, and await instructions. It will be paid, not to ineffectual political groups, but to the New America Liberation Army, who will use it for the People.

"An extra million has been added to the fraudulent demand to punish the Pig Herbert Fane's complicity with the government's attempted fraud."

The black woman left the best for last.

"We include proof that the New America Liberation Army has custody of the daughter of the Pig Herbert Fane. We will furnish one proof of the same kind per week until our demands are met."

They'd sent the "proof" to Herbert Fane, but Leo realized he was the one who had gotten the finger. Somebody—Fane, the government, someone hired by one or the other—had finally learned the rules of this game. From now on, Leo's work would be a lot more difficult, but a lot more interesting, too.

Starting tomorrow (or maybe with the night shift today) the MENTOR system would go back into production, with only two days shaved off its lead. That would not do.

The opposition had scored heavily with a surprise counterattack. This was a war for public credibility. A war to make Herbert Fane do what Leo wanted him to do. It would, of course, be harder if Fane was in collusion with the black woman and whoever she represented, as she had accused Fane of being in collusion with LEO.

Except Leo *knew* he wasn't. He had unimpeachable assurances.

The accusation, true or not, lent verisimilitude to the second tape.

Leo would have to so discredit the "New America Liberation Army" that going on with the charade would be a public relations disaster for the government. Leo would have to pin this solidly on the government, so that they would be the heartless monsters who played charades while an innocent girl was in danger. He would have to convince Herbert Fane that the government was playing around with his daughter's life.

It wouldn't be easy. The opposition had thought things out well. They had even managed to make the fingerprints check out, according to the scoop just offered up by Tom Ivery. Leo would like to know how they'd done it.

They had intangibles going for them, too. Drama. Their tape had been far more dramatic than his. That would be fixed. Surprise. And the asterisk factor.

Leo thought about his options. He could cut Daisy Mae up like a frying chicken, match them "proof" for "proof." But if they were saying already that the fingerprints offered by the opposition matched, it would be a waste of time. They'd say any body part that *he* sent didn't match, and that would be that.

He had established to his own satisfaction that he couldn't risk putting Daisy Mae on the phone live to her father.

All this assumed, of course, that Herbert Fane was not making public relations moves himself, that he really did give more than the proverbial rat's ass about his daughter's fate.

If that assumption were false, Project Cronus, at least in this phase, was doomed, and Moscow would see that heads rolled for it. Still, Leo was losing no sleep. The assumption *had* to be good. No terrorist ever had better information, or a better psychological picture of his subjects than Leo did now. That was a large part of what Cronus was all about. He *knew* that Herbert Fane was an insensitive, often incompetent father, but that he was, in his own clumsy way, a devoted one. Leo had that from a source he knew he could trust.

No, this pilot project for Cronus wouldn't fail on any misjudgment of Herbert Fane's personality. It would stand or fall on Leo's talents, his genius at his chosen profession. And Leo *wanted* Cronus to succeed. It promised so much for the future.

Somewhere in Draper, Pennsylvania, that night, the KGB agent who had been responsible for this facet of Cronus lay awake, thinking.

Thirty years on this project, literally day and night. Away from my home. Away from the life I thought I would lead. I am tired now. Tired of the constant deception, though I have managed at times to play my part so well that I have forgotten it was a deception.

Most of the time, before the plan came to be put into effect, I could simply be who I have become over these years. I know I can never again become who I was.

I still believe in the cause. The Revolution. I do my duty; what I was trained to do. If it involves allowing Leo Calvin and his monstrous following to have their way, I will do it, and willingly.

But these new developments have me worried. Is there some other group of terrorists, trying to steal the thunder of what they perceive as a rival group? Or just some opportunistic criminals, trying to promote money out of the misfortunes of others? And how, wearing my everyday mask, am I to respond to it?

That must be decided. And this threat must be dealt with.

Because I am a soldier, and have been since I was a child. I regret the deaths of the ambulance driver and the intern, and the mutilation of whoever it was who lost the finger that mysteriously matched the fingerprint it could not possibly have matched. I deplore the fact that Elizabeth might have to be killed. Despite what the Americans might think of us, I am not a monster.

But I am a soldier, and as a soldier I know that this is war. A cold war is no less a war than any other. And it is an inescapable reality of war that the innocent suffer and die. There is no way around it. I wish there were.

But the driver, the intern, the nameless girl have met their destinies. Elizabeth and others, perhaps many others, will meet theirs. Perhaps I will.

I'm not afraid of what may happen to me, or of what I may be forced to do. That is not why these new developments bother me.

I am afraid for the plan.

Because the plan is real, for me. For me, the plan is all that is real. I have devoted my life to it. I have given it thirty years. Nothing must stop it from succeeding.

Had I remained a soldier, remained in the Motherland, I might have done many things for my country. But I did not, and the Cronus Project is my one service, my life's work. Thirty years of it.

I will not see it wasted.

Feeling better for having the matter clarified and the decision made, the agent lay back and went to sleep.

Clifford Driscoll wasn't sleeping. He sat against the padded headboard, with two oversoft motel pillows behind him to keep his bare back from sticking to the plastic covering. He wore a pair of gray sweat shorts and his glasses.

He wasn't expecting visitors, so the knock on the door surprised him. He sprang to his suitcase and grabbed his gun, a thirty-two automatic. It wasn't the same gun he'd carried on the burglary last night—that was stowed safely at headquarters. The thirty-two was a compromise, a decent weapon that still might be owned by a young executive or government official, his two most common covers when forced to work for his father.

A quirk of his personality that he acknowledged without analyzing led him to spend all the time he was on the run *from* his father totally unarmed.

He was working now, and he didn't like surprises when he was working. Moving silently in bare feet, Driscoll went to the side of the door. Slowly, quietly, he pulled back the slide to put a bullet in the chamber.

The knocking came again. A little louder, this time, impatient.

"Who is it?" His tone was one of surprise and curiosity, just what a visitor might be expecting to hear.

"It's Robin."

Driscoll shook his head in disgust. He eased the mechanism back, but held on to the gun.

"Are you alone?"

There was irritation in Robin's voice. "Of course I'm alone. Who would I bring with me to visit *you*? Are you going to let me in or not? I don't want to make a scene in the hallway."

By this time, Driscoll had restored the gun to the false bottom of the suitcase. He swung the door open. "Enter, dear lady."

Robin didn't appreciate the whimsy. Her jaw was tight, her eyes hooded by worried brows.

"You can see why I asked you if you were alone," Driscoll said. "I'm decent, but I'm hardly dressed for company."

"But it's okay for *my* company, is it?"

"I'll put something on, if you like," he said quietly.

"No, it doesn't matter. I just have to talk to you."

"All right, sit down and talk."

Robin sat in one of· the room's two wood-framed brown-cushioned chairs and crossed her legs. She was wearing the same summer dress she'd had on when he'd been at the Fane place this afternoon. With all the turmoil, the coming and going of police, FBI and the press, she probably hadn't gotten a chance to change. The dress was soiled and sweated in, and Robin knew it and didn't seem to care.

Driscoll didn't either. This girl's honesty and innocence had an allure for him that he found very hard to stifle. He found everything on this operation to do with what the Congressman called Practical Human Relations (i.e., use them and get rid of them) very difficult.

He asked Robin what she wanted.

"What are you trying to do to us?"

"I'm not trying to do anything to you."

"You sent that package today, didn't you?"

"Witnesses said a black woman in a car delivered it."

Robin made a fist and hit herself in the thigh, hard. "Don't play these games with me!" She took a breath. "Don't you care about anybody?"

Driscoll sat on the edge of the bed right across from her and looked her in the eyes. "The more truth I tell you," he said, "the harder it's going to be for you to get out of this."

Robin raised an eyebrow in scorn. "Get out of this? You've already told me I was in for the duration. Don't you remember? Or was that all pillow talk? Was that it? You were just trying to scare me into bed with you, I bet. Well, congratulations, you won."

"Stop it, Robin."

"*I will not stop it!*" She hit herself in the thigh again. "I thought Uncle Herbert was going to die this afternoon, I swear to God. And Aunt Sheila's been locked away all day. I wish she'd let the doctor give her a sedative."

Driscoll looked bland. "Why won't she? Everybody has to get some sleep."

"*I* don't know," Robin said. "I was on the doctor's side, trying to talk her into it. Even after Uncle Herbert took one, she refused."

"Yes," Driscoll said, "he was fairly calm when I talked to him."

Driscoll told Robin that her uncle had called him after the doctor's injection had made him calm enough to know what he should do, and that he had told him that there seemed to be little choice but to follow the instructions backed by the gruesome proof of the severed finger.

"But, Driscoll," the industrialist had protested. "You heard the tape. These people claim I'm in on some kind of plot. What if the first group feels that way about *this* situation?"

"Yeah," Driscoll said. "Good point." He'd paused for a moment, pretending to consider, then came up with the suggestion he'd had ready for days.

Herbert Fane should call a press conference—his first since his daughter's kidnapping. There, he should answer any and all questions put to him, no matter how specious or hostile.

"Can you handle that?"

"I honestly don't know, Driscoll. If I do it soon enough, before the medicine wears off, maybe."

He'd had the press conference within the hour. He denied being involved in anything other than trying to get his daughter back unharmed. In response to a question from Tom Ivery, he specifically denied the possibility that anyone could have tampered with the fingerprint files in his Fane Industries security department. Special Agent Fenton Rines, who was lending moral support, added that reports from Washington matched up.

(Driscoll had attended, but had effaced himself at the back of the crowd. He came away with two impressions—one, that Tom Ivery was possibly too smart for his own good, and two, that he was very glad his father had managed to get things handled on the Washington end.)

There were a few other tidbits. Fane admitted that the voices on both tapes sounded very much like his daughter. Rines said they had no leads at this time as to the identity of the black woman who had delivered the second tape. He also announced that the FBI was having voiceprint analyses of the tape done not only by their own people, but by two world-renowned audio experts, Chester Garland of New York City and Jacob Feder of Miami, Florida.

That was all, but it was plenty for the media to work on. Bios of Jake and Garland. Speculation as to which group of terrorists (or whatever) was the McCoy. Speculation about which (if either) of these that old tough buzzard Fane might be in cahoots with.

And one more thing, also Driscoll's idea, also kept for days in his mind until this moment. Something designed to supersede and end all speculation in the last matter.

Herbert Fane announced that he was willing to take a lie detector test. The press could pick the expert or experts to conduct it. He wanted the group that actually had his daughter (almost certainly the NALA) to know he had no part in any hoax. The machine and the press would prove that, and once that had been taken care of, he could await further instructions telling him how to get his daughter back, which, he reminded them again, was all he was interested in.

The test would take place tomorrow (nobody can move

faster than a newsman on his way to call somebody's bluff), about the same time the plant would reopen.

Robin was silent for several seconds after Driscoll stopped speaking. "So the lie detector business was *your* idea."

Driscoll nodded. "It seemed like the only thing to do. Once everybody knows your uncle had nothing to do with this, it's up to the bad guys again."

"Why did my uncle call *you?*"

"He said he thought I had a good head on my shoulders. He said he trusted me."

"*Trusted* you?" Robin's eyes went wide.

"That's what he said. He also said you seemed to like me, and that you were a good judge of character."

Robin hit her thigh with her fist again, so hard that she made Driscoll wince. "God *damn* you!" she said. "You're a magician, Clifford Driscoll! I came in here to get a few facts from you, and you distract me with tales of your brilliance."

"I'm sorry," Driscoll said.

"I said don't play games with me! You knew you were doing it. You always know! I wish to God I knew *how* you do it. You're some kind of evil—" Her voice choked off; apparently her imagination failed her for what kind of evil thing he was.

"I'm sorry," Driscoll said again. This time Robin said nothing. "What do you want from me? Remember, I warned you."

Robin was petulant. "Warned me about what?"

"The truth. That it can be dangerous."

She gave a short, unhealthy laugh, like a sour note on a cornet. "I've agreed to help you; and I'm stuck. My word means something to *me*, Mr. Driscoll, whatever way things are done in your world. But if I'm going to keep driving myself and my only relatives crazy for you, I've got to know why."

"You haven't done anything. I asked you to help make a tape, but we haven't had to use you for it."

"Yet," she said.

"Yet," Driscoll conceded.

She leaned forward over her knees, as if to look at the man on the bed through some sort of moral microscope.

"Where did the finger come from?" she said.

"From someone who didn't need it anymore."

Robin stared at him.

"For God's sake, Robin," he said. "We got hold of an unclaimed body with the right sex and age and blood type. We didn't kill anybody. We're not like that."

"It's still disgusting," she said.

Driscoll shrugged. "Maybe so. I was actually pretty proud of it, considering what I could have done to achieve what I'm supposed to be doing around here."

"You—your superiors would let you—what's so funny?"

"Nothing. My superiors. Go on." He wiped the smile off his face.

"Your superiors. They'd let you just kill some innocent person—another *American*, for God's sake—just because you wanted to use a part of her body?"

"Let me, hell! They'd give me a medal if it worked. If agents got medals."

"Then you don't," Robin said.

"Don't what?"

"Don't care about anything."

Driscoll sighed and stood up and walked over to the sliding glass doors to enjoy the view they afforded of the parking lot.

"I don't know about that," he said. "I care about you."

"Bullshit."

"I care enough about you to tell you enough to get us both killed," he said, still talking to the glass. "In fact, if this room were bugged—by anybody, including my 'superiors'—we'd be as good as dead right now."

He turned back to face her. "Caring about somebody is not a luxury a person in my position should indulge in."

Robin was standing now, brought to her feet by the mention of bugging. "Oh, my God, Clifford, I never thought," she said, then "God damn you, how could you take a chance like that, you're supposed to be a professional! We should have gone outside when you knew I wanted to talk. God *damn* you!"

The rest of it was swallowed up in tears of anger and fear.

Driscoll was by her side in a second. "Hey," he said. He took hold of her as he had that night in the cabin, strong hands grasping upper arms. "Hey, Robin. I said *if*, remember? Stop worrying. The room's not bugged."

"How—how do you know?"

"I know. I've checked. I check every time I come back here. I've got electronic gizmos to check with.

"Look," he went on. "You can't have it both ways. If I'm really such an evil magician, I'm not going to take a risk like that. And whether you believe it or not, I wouldn't let you take one either."

Her eyes were liquid and wide, but unwavering. "Until you needed me to," she said.

Driscoll looked at her for a long moment. Finally, he said, "Yes, if it makes you happy. Yes, I would risk your life to attain my objective. My superior's objective. Be ready for it. Don't trust me. Just don't sell me out, either. I'm evil and I'm dangerous, and it was the worst day of your life when you met me. Do we understand each other?"

Her eyes were still steady. "Yes, Clifford, I understand."

"Good," he said, then pulled her to him and kissed her.

Robin had come to straighten a few things out with Driscoll. She hadn't planned to let him manipulate her again, to let him put her through all the emotional changes and leave her confused and vulnerable. He wasn't supposed to make her afraid.

She didn't want him to kiss her, until he did it. Then, she closed her eyes and shared it even as she called herself a fool. She didn't want him to lift her and put her on the bed, or to take her dress from her shoulders and kiss her there, kiss her everywhere the dress no longer covered. He drove her crazy with his hands and mouth and body until she didn't care who he was or what he did for a living, as long as he was her lover and he kept doing this.

In a strange mixture of loathing and ecstasy, she cursed him, but the curses repeated themselves and became meaningless, except as love cries.

And in the last instant before her sensations took over her

brain, and she was no longer able to think in words, she was sure of two things about the man in her arms.

He was definitely evil. And definitely magic.

Waldo's room was in the basement. It was a neat room with wood walls, shiny, smooth wood. There was a TV and a record player and a little bathroom, but Waldo was only allowed to use the bathroom.

When they'd first come to Roy's house, Waldo had slept down here on a couch that opened out into a bed. Waldo liked to see it work, and he learned how to do it, and kept opening it and closing it until Leo made him stop. Leo did something to the couch that made it so it wouldn't open. Now Waldo slept on a mattress on the floor.

Waldo used to need a light on before he could sleep, but not anymore. Leo had explained it to him once, in the house in the woods where they stayed between the busy times. You are stronger in the dark, Leo said. The night hides you, and no one knows who you are. Darkness makes weak people afraid, but it makes strong ones stronger.

Waldo lay on his mattress, hugging the dark around himself, making himself stronger. He needed to be strong, because he was going to do something *bad*. He was going to disobey Leo.

He'd already done it once this week, when he'd seen the kitty's blood. Tonight, he was going to do it again. He didn't know what it was, but lately the blood called to him more and more.

It was this house. He didn't like what was going on here. Leo didn't have any time for him anymore and neither did his other friend, Candy. She was always spending her time with Daisy Mae, and at night in the room they had, they made strange noises together.

Georgia had never liked him, and Roy made fun of him all the time. Or he used to, until Leo made him stop. But Roy still made nasty faces at Waldo when Leo couldn't see.

So Waldo was alone. He hadn't even been given anything to do for the Oppressed (*I still remember that word,* he thought proudly) since they took Daisy Mae away in the first place.

He didn't want to disobey, but he felt bad all the time, except when there was the blood. Tonight was another night for blood.

Waldo listened in the darkness. He listened hard, but he couldn't hear any sound, not the TV in the living room upstairs, anyway. That meant everybody was on the second floor, at least. If it was late enough at night, they would all be asleep. Waldo went to the top of the steep basement stairs and listened some more. Still nothing but house noises and his own breath and heartbeat.

He went back down and got his shoes and put them on his feet. He didn't tie them. Waldo could tie his own shoes, but not in the dark. He walked over to the couch where he used to sleep, and climbed up to the back of it. Above the couch, high up in the smooth wood wall, was a window. It slid open from one side or the other side, but it wasn't big enough for a big person like Waldo to get through.

But Waldo had been sliding the window back and forth one day (since he couldn't play with the couch anymore) and he found something out. The *whole window* could come out. Waldo had been scared at first, but he learned with a little trying that it was just as easy to put it back in. He just had to remember to push the little trigger things in the corners.

With the windows and the screens out (they worked the same way) the hole was big enough for Waldo to squeeze through. He took them out and put them down gently on the couch. If he broke one, everything would be ruined, so he was very careful. Then he reached his arms through the hole and braced his hands against the wall outside.

Then he stopped. He had forgotten something. He stepped back down to the couch (being careful to avoid the windows) and ran back to his mattress. He reached under his pillow and got his big knife. Waldo wiped his forehead and said "Whew!" under his breath, just the way he'd seen people do on TV. He would feel pretty stupid if he went out and tried to see blood without his big knife with him.

He put the knife outside first, because it hurt him if he tried to crawl through the window with it in his belt. Then he reached outside again, and pulled himself through. He picked up the knife, wiped it on his shirt, then tucked it in his belt. Waldo stuffed the ends of his shoelaces inside his shoes. He didn't want to trip over them.

The blood was calling to him very strongly. Maybe the night made the blood strong, too. Waldo wanted to follow it, but he forced himself to wait. He listened from outside, but he couldn't hear anything in the house. He couldn't see any lights either, but that didn't make any difference, because the shades were sealed up, and he wouldn't have seen any, anyway.

When he was satisfied everyone was asleep, Waldo went to the street and let his feelings take him. The blood was calling him; it almost sang to him. He could smell it in the air. The breeze was warm with it. The stars shone red with it.

Waldo wondered what kind of blood it would be tonight. Another cat? A dog, maybe? Maybe a wild animal. There might be a raccoon around, there were enough trees in this neighborhood.

Waldo walked down the end of the street, and around the corner. He heard something from far away. A car motor. He didn't want anyone to see him, so he hid behind a hedge. He waited and watched.

A car drove into view. It was on a cross street, and parked at the corner at the end of the block. Its motor kept running. Waldo could see a light come on as a car door opened. A boy about the same age as Roy, with yellow hair that shone in the light, got out of the car.

He stopped and looked back into the car. A voice in the car said, "You sure you don't want me to drive you the rest of the way?"

The boy with yellow hair said, "Nah, why should you catch the fallout when my old man yells at me? Besides, I could use the fresh air, it's only a couple of blocks."

"But there's two groups of terrorists running around, Pete," the boy in the car said. "One of them might kidnap you."

Both boys laughed. Pete said, "I come home with this

booze on my breath, my father will pay them to come and take me away. Go on home now, I'll be fine."

They said good night to each other, and Pete started walking down the street. Toward Waldo. Waldo had to bite his lip to keep from crying out with happiness.

A person. Oh, Leo, you can put me back in the Closet, if you want to. A person.

Pete whistled as he walked down the street, then stopped. He was probably afraid he was going to wake the neighbors up. Finally he got close to where Waldo was waiting. Waldo stepped out in front of him.

"Hi," Waldo said. He could feel a big smile stretching his face.

"Whoa!" Pete said, stepping back a second. "You scared me, man."

"I'm sorry," Waldo said. "I want—"

"I don't have any money," Pete said. "I spent it all tonight."

Waldo was hurt. "I don't need any money, honest."

"You're lucky," Pete said. He smiled. His smile was kind of silly, and his eyes were a little red, but he was a handsome boy.

"I just want to say hi," Waldo said.

"Okay, hi. Nice night. Now, if you'll excuse me, man, I've got a father eager to yell at me for staying out late and drinking."

"Oh," Waldo said. He thought of Leo. "I'm sorry," he said again. He stepped aside.

Pete walked on. "Yeah," he said, "Good night."

"Good night," Waldo echoed.

Then he grabbed Pete from behind, threw a forearm around his neck and held him there while he got the big knife from his belt and used it.

"Oh," Waldo said under his breath as he saw the blood that had been calling to him all night. "Oh." He held Pete close to him and looked over the boy's shoulder as the wetness, black in the bluish light of the streetlamp, washed over his hands.

Waldo felt strong. He loved Pete. Pete wasn't strong anymore though. He went limp in Waldo's arms. Waldo placed him down on the sidewalk and watched, fascinated as always.

What made it jump out like that? It was like the blood wanted to be free, the way Waldo wanted to be free from the basement.

Finally it stopped. Waldo dragged Pete off behind a hedge. He whispered, "Good-bye, Pete," then headed back to Roy's house.

Waldo was smiling. He felt warm. He felt strong. This was the best one ever, because he got to know the person a little first. Other times, he just went and saw the blood of whoever Leo told him.

But Pete was all his.

It was wonderful. Waldo couldn't remember ever being so happy.

He was still happy when he got back to the house. So happy, in fact, that he forgot. In his joy, he forgot all about the windows that he had left on the couch.

Moves and countermoves chased each other through Leo Calvin's brain. The thing to do was to regain the initiative, to force the opponent's hand as he (they, she, whatever) was trying now to force his.

The door opened and Georgia walked into Leo's room. She wore an old terry robe and was smoking a cigarette. Leo didn't like to see her this way in the light—Georgia was at her best rigged out for battle, not for bed.

"Leo," she began.

"Georgia, I told you I have to think tonight."

"To hell with that," she said shortly. "We've got a problem."

Hearing her voice so competent and urgent led Leo to think that perhaps Georgia was rigged out for battle after all.

"What is it?" he said.

"Waldo. He's been out. He's done something. I told you using that dummy was a mistake."

"What do you mean he's been out?"

"I mean out of the house." She didn't add "asshole," but her tone did it for her. Georgia had been alone from a very early age (to hear her tell the story, what little of it she let slip) and had developed impatience and contempt for most people under most circumstances as a result. She had been grudgingly respectful of Leo till now; she would never have let him become one of the few men ever to have touched her if she hadn't.

He still needed Georgia. She was his fiercest warrior, and the second best brain in the operation. It was important that he retain her respect. He'd have to be careful.

He decided to match her brusque professionalism. "Tell me about it."

It worked. Georgia gave him a grim nod that said, "That's more like it."

"I was going to the bathroom," she said. "Heard glass break downstairs. Nothing wrong on the first floor, so I checked the basement. Turned on the light and found Waldo sitting in the corner trying to hide behind his mattress."

Leo was up off the bed, now, dressing. "Go on."

"Right. Anyway, I saw a big hole where the window should be—the dummy was smart enough to learn how to take the windows and screens out. Broken window on the couch. Probably stepped on it coming back.

"Went to the corner and pulled the damn mattress off him. He'd been outside, all right. Dirt and blood all over him. Not his blood. I checked. He's got a few scratches on his ankle, but nothing to cover the front and arms of his shirt with blood the way they are. He's offed somebody, and not too long ago, either. The blood wasn't even too sticky, yet."

It was Leo's turn to nod. "What did you do?"

Georgia snorted. "What I should have done was taken that goddamn pig sticker from him and put him out of our misery. But I didn't; I tried to find out what he did, but he wasn't answering. He just cowered away in the corner. Kept saying 'Don't put me in the closet, don't put me in the closet.' Also a couple of 'Don't tell Leo's.'"

She shrugged. "I left him there. You're his daddy, maybe you can get something out of him. I don't think he's going to get out of here again—he's too scared to do whatever it is he does instead of thinking.

"But to hell with what he's going to do. What are *we* going to do?"

Leo grabbed his chin. What, indeed? It only took two seconds to realize that there was really no choice. Waldo had undoubtedly killed someone, recently and nearby. The body would be found, and there would be an investigation; considering the climate around Draper, Pennsylvania these days, a particularly vigorous one. There would certainly be a canvass of the neighborhood—that much was police routine.

Time to run, Leo thought. Fortunately, this had been among the courses of action he had been considering when Georgia had come in. What was it the military called it? *Strategic withdrawal to previously prepared fallback positions.* Exactly.

All right, now. This was a good opportunity to repair whatever damage had been done to Georgia's respect for him. "All right," he said crisply. "We're pulling out. Wake the others. Get them dressed. Bring essentials only, and all the food we can carry. Put them in the van." The van had been in the garage since the beginning of the operation. It was stocked like a fallout shelter—canned water, dried food, portable sanitation facility, bedding, first aid. It would see six of them through several weeks of camping out nearly anywhere, especially since Candy had a small flat in town—a dummy address for her job at the hospital.

Five of them would last even longer. That was something else to be attended to.

Georgia went to attend to her job; Leo went downstairs to deal with Waldo.

He was still cowering in the corner when Leo found him. Tears flowed down Waldo's face.

"Leo, I'm sorry, I'm sorry. I didn't mean to be bad, I couldn't help it. . . ."

"All right, Waldo, stop crying. What did you do?"

Leo's voice, calm, if not exactly kindly, seemed to reassure Waldo. The man on the floor sniffed, then said, "I had to do it. I had to see the blood. It was *strong*! I couldn't help it."

Leo was suddenly stern. "It's a good thing for you you're telling me the truth," he said. Leo played a hunch. "You killed that cat the other night, too, didn't you?"

Waldo looked up at him with wide round eyes. Leo knew *everything*.

"Didn't you?"

"Yes, Leo, I'm sorry, *don't put me in the Closet*, please—"

"Maybe I should," Leo said.

"Oh, no, please, don't, I'll be good, I won't disobey you anymore."

"You'd better not. I'm the only one who really cares about you, don't you know that?"

Waldo nodded. He tried to speak, but he only made sounds.

"Good," Leo said. "Well, you're going to have to be punished, anyway."

"Not the Closet, *not the Closet!*"

"Not the closet. Give me your knife."

"My big knife?" Waldo sounded crushed. He hadn't thought of this possibility. This was almost as bad as the closet.

"Yes, your big knife." He put out his hand.

Waldo pulled out the knife and handed it over. Leo tucked it in his belt.

"You'll get this back when I'm convinced you can follow orders, Waldo. Is that clear?"

Waldo assured him with words and sounds and gestures.

"Good. Now, tie your shoes and come upstairs with me."

Waldo hurriedly knelt and did as he was told. He had a little trouble at first, because of the ends of the laces being tucked in his shoes. He got them out soon enough, though, and got two neat bows tied in no time.

He followed Leo up the cement stairs, happy things hadn't been worse.

The cellar opened into the kitchen. The rest of them were already there, working by flashlight. Candy was cool and efficient, pulling cans from shelves and putting them in bags for Georgia and Roy to take to the car. Elizabeth Fane was slumped in a chair in the kitchen, her head cradled in folded arms on the table. Her eyes were open, but glassy, and Leo thought he could hear her humming softly.

"I gave her a pretty big dose," Candy said, still emptying shelves. "I don't want her to start screaming on us, or run away."

"No, we've had enough trouble with people straying

tonight." Leo turned to Waldo. "You do what Candy tells you. Remember, you're on trial."

"Yes, Leo," Waldo said meekly. Leo barely heard him. He took a quick tour of the house, making sure they didn't leave behind anything they might need. He wasn't concerned with anything that might incriminate them. It didn't matter, and there wasn't time to wipe their fingerprints off everything even if it did.

He saved his own room for last, picking up the cassette recorder as he did so. Then he went back downstairs. They were just finishing up in the kitchen. Candy was helping Daisy Mae to the van, supporting her with an arm around her waist and making little coos of encouragement in her ear.

Good. They'd be out of here in ten minutes. The authorities would arrive sometime today, possibly tomorrow. They'd know the League to End Oppression (Leo smiled) had been here, and after they read the fingerprints, they'd know the names of the members. But the trail would end here. They wouldn't know where the League had gone, wouldn't even think of looking for them in that place.

It might be that Waldo had unwittingly pulled off a masterstroke, something that would get the situation off dead center. There would be a tape about this, too, as soon as Leo decided the best way to exploit it (and as soon as he found out exactly whom Waldo had killed), and it would shake things up, re-establish credibility.

After all, the first requirement of a terrorist is that he be terrible, and mindless, uncomprehending violence like Waldo's might be the most terrible thing of all.

Roy came back into the house to pick up the last bag of groceries.

"Leave that," Leo said.

The boy looked into Leo's flashlight beam, eyes bright, a smile of suppressed excitement on his face. *This is more* like *it, isn't it kid?* Leo thought. *This is what being a terrorist is all about—blood-soaked colleagues in the middle of the night, speedy evacuations one step ahead of the pigs. This was it, this was fun.*

"We've got to get something from the cellar," Leo said. "I need you to help carry it."

"Sure, Leo," Roy said. "What is it?"

"I told you not to ask me questions." He pointed at the cellar door. "Go."

Roy shrugged, too happy to make an issue of it. He opened the door and turned on the cellar light. He started to go downstairs.

"Wait!" Leo said. "Turn around for a second."

Roy opened his mouth, then closed it again. No questions, the boss had said. Obediently, he turned around and faced him.

Leo pushed him sharply with both hands in the middle of the chest.

A look of surprise and hurt passed over the boy's face before he went over. *That's how the victims feel, boy,* Leo thought as he watched it happen.

Roy fell hard, then bounced down a few more steps before he used up all his momentum. He lay there groaning.

Leo sighed. Kid must have kept the back of his head up. He went down the stairs past the boy's body, took Roy's head, wedged it against a stair post, then pulled Roy's shoulders sharply toward him. He stopped when he heard the crack. He walked back upstairs past the body. He turned the light off behind him, then left the cellar.

Georgia was at the wheel of the van. She looked a question at him. Leo nodded. She started the engine and the five of them (counting Daisy Mae) drove off.

That was that, Leo thought. A lot of the operation was traceable to Roy—vehicles, phones, things like that. Now Roy would be right here for the authorities to find. One loose end, neatly tied off.

The authorities will be able to tie off a lot of loose ends when they find this place, Leo thought. *But when they've got the knot completed, they'll find it's the knot to a blindfold, and it's around their own heads.*

Leo couldn't see the sky through the painted windows of the van, but he knew it would be daylight soon. Still, they should have plenty of time to reach the new hideout by dawn. And Roy, through the media, would tell their confederate where they were. This message had been arranged long ago. Body in the cellar, fallback hideout. Body on top floor, operation canceled, confederates in flight.

No necessity for canceling now. Time to go back on the offensive. He was beginning to see a way to do it. He felt good. He started to laugh.

And next to him in the back of the van, made suggestible by the large dose of hypnotic drug, Daisy Mae started to laugh, too.

Chapter Seven

IT WAS LATE AFTERNOON BY THE TIME TOM IVERY GOT out to the Fane Industries plant. It had been a busy day, and Tom had been on the go since five A.M., but he had no intention of stopping. He was living on cold hamburgers and adrenaline, and thriving on it.

This was incredible. It was beyond his wildest dreams. A kid just out of college, working for an automated FM station in the boonies, was in the middle of one of the biggest stories in years. Not just in the middle of it, right on *top* of it. Big stories kept coming to him, begging him to break them.

This morning, for example, the body of Pete Westrum was discovered behind a hedge, and that led to the discovery of the abandoned hideout. Of course, TV got the best stuff there—the bloodstains in the cellar, the various ropes and manacles left behind, the used hypodermic needles, stuff like that. The chalk outline on the stairs marking the location of the body of Roy Ralkis, whose grandfather's house it was.

Pete had been a good kid; B student, cross country team, like that. Worst thing he ever did was drive his car too fast. He'd had to come home with Rocco Accarella, a friend, because his father had taken Pete's car away in the wake of the latest ticket. The police theory was that Pete had somehow stumbled on the terrorists (whoever they were—LEO or NALA, this was confusing everybody) in some secret nocturnal activity, possibly moving Liz Fane to some other location. The other theory was that they moved because they had killed Pete, and knew the investigation would get to Roy's house eventually. The only trouble with that was it left the terrorists a little short of motive.

Roy Ralkis had been a punk and a troublemaker from earliest childhood, and nobody was going to miss him, not even his grandfather. Especially not his grandfather, whom Roy had been embarrassing, terrorizing, and sometimes physically abusing for the last two years or so since his parents died. Roy apparently had fallen down the cellar stairs and broken his neck and had been left behind by his comrades. It was obvious that Roy had been a full accomplice to whatever this group (whichever one it was) had done.

The salient factor for Tom though, was that he was able to get exclusive interviews with relatives of both boys. Tom had actually dated Pete's older sister, Martha. Through her, he was able to get the whole family on tape, including Mr. Westrum saying he had been planning to yell at Pete when he got home, then breaking into tears.

Tom was also able to work a few neighbors and find out where in Florida Roy's grandfather was, and to get him on the phone for another interview. The old man had said all the right things, shock, can't believe it, he was always a good boy, etc., but the relief that floated behind the words was unmistakeable. Tom had framed it just right when he'd put them on the air, contrasting the boys' attitudes toward life, comparing the ways they'd died.

The Westrums had decided they wouldn't give any more interviews, so the networks came begging to Tom for a tape of his. He gave it to them, to anybody who wanted it, but only on the condition that they billboard in "in an interview with Tom Ivery, of WLTN radio in Draper," and Mr. Littleton had backed him up on it.

Mr. Littleton had backed him up to the hilt, allowing Tom to interrupt the Monster at will for late-breaking stuff. He also let Tom add his sister Alexis to the payroll, to watch the wire and work the phones.

There had come a moment at about eight-thirty that morning, when Tom's memory flashed him a picture from years ago, at the playground of the elementary school. Tom was a big sixth grader, sweet on Martha Westrum. To make points with her, he showed her little brother Petey, a second grader, how to shift the wings and the nose weight of a balsa wood glider to make it fly straight or in loops.

It was the weirdest thing. Tom had felt hollow, all of a sudden, as though his head might fall right through his body, and his vision was filled with greenish splotches. He'd had to sit down until the feeling passed.

He chalked it up to fatigue—after all, he'd been going on this for three and a half hours, already, and the day was barely started. He got himself a cup of very bad station coffee, and soon his professionalism reasserted itself enough so that he could make that great deal for credit on the Westrum interview.

Tom had already decided that as soon as this was over, he would be going to New York and visiting some of those names he had been accumulating since his debut (he thought of it that way, now) at the press conference.

Not *everything* came up roses, of course. He'd thought of something that might possibly be a big story, and had checked on it, but it didn't work out. It had occurred to him that Liz Fane had a cousin who had grown up here, and who'd been known to hang around town sometimes. He knew that from certain angles, she looked something like her cousin, and she was supposed to sound like her, as well. Tom had checked into the possibility that *Roberta Fane* was the voice on the tapes, but the audio experts said they had already checked that, and the answer was absolutely not. Furthermore, Rines had told him that though Liz's cousin was in town now, she had definitely been in New York, guarded by government agents during the times the rival tapes had to have been made. He'd even offered to let Tom see the reports. Tom took him up on it, more because he'd never seen an official government report before than any serious reason. The reports (approved, Tom noticed, by the House Intelligence Oversight Committee Chairman) confirmed what he'd heard.

Tom used the story, of course, and he still numbered it among his scoops, but negative stories are always less impressive than positive ones. It was the same thing with the other story—Herbert Fane passing his lie detector test with flying colors. Nobody is interested in who *didn't* kill Cock Robin.

Anyway, that took up most of the day. By a quarter to three, he'd left the station to do what he'd planned to do in the first place, a feature story on the reopening of the Fane plant, with a sampling of worker reaction to the idea that the terrorists (NALA) were trying to wrest control of the company away from the capitalist who had founded it and have it turned over to them.

Lack of breakfast (and lunch) overtook him en route, and he made a quick stop at McDonalds before he continued to the plant. There was only a half hour left in the day shift when he arrived, but he figured it ought to be enough time. He could always come back tomorrow. Barring further bizarre developments, of course.

Tom drove past the old abandoned coke processing plant that had been part of the steel mill complex Fane had taken over, and on to the fence that marked the area that was still in use for Fane's electronics operation. Security at the inner gate had been tripled from what Tom had known in the days when he'd worked machines there. He had to show three kinds of ID to guards who had known him all his life before they would let him in the gates for a visit he had arranged with the plant manager after consultation with Fane himself.

One thing hadn't changed, though. Tom had been feeling an uneasiness way out of proportion to the hangup at the gate, and now he smiled to himself as he realized what was causing it.

It was his old friend and dancing partner, the Lower Casing Forming and Stamping Operation, a two-story tall vertical press that came crashing down with sixteen tons of pressure with every stroke.

It took that much force to shape the thick steel that protected the submarine guidance system Fane built for the Navy, but that sixteen tons business was the subject of much humor—another day older and deeper in debt, that kind of thing.

But the Obscene Machine (the insider's name for the LCFSO) worked to a different rhythm altogether. It was a reggae beat, the *fsssssh-chka-BOOM-chk* of Montego Bay. Tom had made a lot of money once he'd discovered that, singing himself hoarse against the roar of metal moving to a Jamaican beat.

He'd had to sing that loud in order to make himself aware he was doing it. No one else could hear him. Everyone who worked in that end of the plant had to wear ear protection, like the guys with the flashlights who worked at airports, parking jets. Communication took place by way of sign language exclusively. The noise was audible much farther away, without actually being obnoxious. From where Tom was standing, it had been just enough to get on his nerves without actually making him aware of it until he'd taken the time to think about it.

When they finally let him in, Tom went to the other side of the building, where he could get workers' voices on tape. He spent about three quarters of an hour getting interviews, following a particularly vocal quartet of workers out to the parking lot at closing time.

He got a good mix of opinions. About seventy-five percent said they would like some kind of say in the running of the factory, whether it involved stock transfers to them or not. Overlapping that, about twenty percent said they thought workers should be given a piece of the company after a number of years of loyal service. A surprisingly high (to Tom at least) twenty-five percent didn't want any part of running the company. "I just want my paycheck at the end of the week," one twenty-year veteran said. "If I'd wanted to make decisions, I'd have gone into business for myself."

Some things were unanimous, or the next thing to it. They all expressed sympathy for Mr. Fane. Practically all of them believed the group that had sent the finger were the real kidnappers. None expressed happiness that their cause was being championed by terrorists. And, except for one worker, who would never make the air (he thought "Fane should tell both of them terrorist bastards to go fuck themselves") all the workers agreed that Fane really couldn't do anything else about the situation except what he was doing, other than hoping for the best.

The best thing about the afternoon, though, was Tom's father, who kept beaming on his son like a lighthouse, following him around suggesting whom he might interview next. *The bum has made good,* Tom figured his father was thinking. Hiring his sister didn't hurt, either. No more insults at home from now on.

If he ever got home, that was. Right now, Tom got back in his car, waved good-bye to his father, who was still smiling at him, and headed back to the station to edit his audio. He wanted to get his feature on the six o'clock news, and he had to hurry.

In different rooms on different continents, two old men read reports and thought and worried.

In Moscow, the Chairman lay in bed. His health was no better; the reports sent him about the now-confused Cronus Project were probably making him worse.

The really maddening thing was that the Chairman was sure he knew who was behind it all. There was only one American clever enough and determined enough to think of such a ploy as the false terrorists, and brazen enough to make it work. The General. They had been colleagues in World War II, enemies ever after. And, the Chairman was sure, fellow scorners of the possibility of detente on anything but the most superficial level.

The Chairman lay back against his pillows and made a rasping noise in his throat that was supposed to have been a sigh. It so alarmed his attendants that the Chairman had to spend precious minutes, the last minutes of his life, they might well be, convincing them that no, they had not heard his death rattle quite yet, and that the various vultures they had been cultivating would not fight for his power beginning tonight.

Powerless doctors. Shamans. What good did they do him? Let the ambitious bastards wait for their chance to climb over the Chairman's corpse to a good position in the Ministry of Health.

When they were gone, and he picked up the thread of his thoughts, the Chairman was moved to sigh again, but he suppressed it. He didn't want to have those fools all over him again. But the emotion called for *something*. He cursed them, instead, and felt better for it.

The thing was impossible. As good as the General was, good enough to scare the Chairman with his Russian-like talents and determination to make his country prevail, the General could not have been behind this. In the long run, the Chairman's old friend had been too American to succeed in the game. Too much the democrat.

He had emasculated himself by giving up his post as head of the Agency (the one that not even the American press had been able to reveal the existence of) in order to work undercover for the continued health of the whole American espionage program as a supposedly hostile member of Congress.

It was a bold and clever move (the Chairman would have expected no less), and it may well have been necessary. The Chairman had always believed that the Americans were their own worst enemies, next to the Chairman himself.

But necessary or not, it had had the effect of removing the General from the international arena. Besides, he was watched. Not a constant surveillance—the Chairman's agents in Washington did have other responsibilities, after all—but a fairly consistent monitoring of the activities of this Southern Congressman. If the General were to decide to come out of retirement, it would not take the Chairman by surprise.

But the person who opposed them in this small Pennsylvania town that history was supposed to come to know as the place the Chairman's plan had had its first victory was *not* in retirement.

Whoever he was (or she), he seemed to think like one of the Chairman's men, act as decisively as one of the Chairman's men. Not at all like an American.

But that was the great hope the Chairman held. No, the great certainty. No matter how much he had learned from the KGB, the adversary had to be American enough to be blind to the secret of the Cronus Project. The Chairman had designed the plan to take advantage of that very American blind spot. Cronus would work, the Chairman thought. The setback was real, but only temporary. The Americans would not have MENTOR operational before the Soviet Union would.

The Chairman would bet an apple pie on it.

The Chairman began to laugh at his own joke, but the laugh turned into a wheeze and that brought the future Ministry of Health down upon him again. It took threats of GULAG to get them off him.

When they were gone, he thought again of his little joke and treated himself to one last chuckle before drifting off to sleep.

In a suburb of Washington, Clifford Driscoll's father sat in a small apartment on an unpretentious side street. He was in a reclining chair, shoes off, feet up, relaxing as the heat and vibrating motor reached into the muscles of his back and pulled the tension from him.

He took a sip from a glass of sour mash whiskey, then put the glass down on the table beside the chair and picked up another set of intercepted Russian communications.

He looked it over with speed that came from long practice. *Damn it,* the Congressman thought. *Here it is again. Cronus and Leo Calvin mentioned in the same message again.* That was the third one this week; they must be having kittens over this back in Moscow.

The Congressman leaned back in his chair, closed his eyes, and made wishes.

He wished the code boys could crack something more in these goddamn Russian dispatches besides proper names. And while he was at it, he wished that if they couldn't succeed, they'd be a little more humble as failures. He might have gotten that message across, finally. The last time he told them they had to do better, they'd gone into their usual routine, a big song and dance about how this was a code as well as a cipher, and how the computer had broken the cipher, so that now they could very accurately get the names of things mentioned in the orders, which was usually much harder to do, but they still didn't know what these orders entailed. The Congressman had cut it short.

The only important news was that they couldn't do it. He'd elaborated on that theme for a while. They wouldn't forget it.

He wished that somehow he could pick up the messages themselves farther down the line, instead of when they came into the Russian Embassy in Washington, or that they could track something from there to Leo Calvin. The Congressman wanted to know where that dangerous bastard *was*.

Well, hell, boy, he told himself, *you don't want too much, do you? Just the answer to the whole case.* He shook his head at himself. He *must* be getting old to wish things like that.

But most of all, he wished he could trust his son.

That was a strange wish, and the Congressman knew it. His life was based on not trusting anyone, but the boy who now called himself Clifford Driscoll had been the one and only exception to that.

Not that he expected the boy to turn traitor or anything— that was not possible. But ever since they'd had their little walk around the Watergate, the Congressman had been receiving confidential reports from Miles, who was under instructions to watch Driscoll as closely as possible without getting in his way.

Miles had followed orders, as always, and as always, had done a thorough job. All in all, things were going well. The factory was back in operation, and the ball was in Leo's court. The more moves he made, the better chance he had of losing his balance, and that was all to the good.

But.

Even allowing sixty-five percent leeway for Miles' under-standable jealousy of the boy, Clifford was doing some remark-ably impractical things. Miles seemed to think Driscoll was sweet on the girl, which was ridiculous. Miles *knew* (because Clifford had told him) that Driscoll had risked the whole operation because he'd shied away from *killing* somebody, for Christ's sake.

There was one last thing, which the Congressman knew for himself. In his reports to his father, Clifford was talking more and more about securing the return of Elizabeth Fane, and less and less about making sure that the MENTOR system went into the missiles on schedule.

All right. Robin was still in line, and it didn't look as if she had stopped him from doing anything that needed to be done. The raid on the fingerprint file had worked, and the deception was pretty well accepted, except by those (like Leo Calvin) who knew better. As far as finding the Fane girl was concerned, it would have the result of attaining the Objective automatically, so that was all right, too.

So far. But the way it was starting to look, the man he had placed in charge of an operation that even the Congressman himself couldn't define the importance of (the Russians had been working on Cronus for *thirty years*, for Christ's sake), was maybe going soft, getting his priorities screwed up. It was frightening.

Even more frightening, perhaps, because the Cronus Project, whatever it was, affected his son so personally. The pretty, clever, fanatical little girl, code name "Mother Russia," who'd infiltrated the Pentagon as "Becky Underwood" had been part of the Cronus Project.

She had died, beat her brains out against the bedstead, rather than tell the Congressman anything about it. She'd failed to kill their son by only a matter of minutes.

Cronus.

It had to be big. It had to be important. It had to be more than just a kidnapping in Pennsylvania.

The Congressman had come to grips with it in its earliest stages and had failed to stop it, or even find out what it was. His son was an unintentional by-product of the Cronus Project. And now here it was again.

Driscoll was faltering. He didn't know any of the background of the case. No, he didn't know any of his *own* background, wasn't aware it connected with the case at all.

Maybe it was time he found out.

Maybe the story of his birth would shock him back on course. Maybe it would remind him of a lesson he seemed to be forgetting—that it was a great tragic paradox of a decent civilization that at times, the most desperate times, it can be defended only by a select group of people who are willing to act savagely.

Or maybe the news would push the Congressman's son over the edge, into total revulsion, or worse (from the Congressman's point of view), ineffectiveness. The Congressman had trained his son to be a special kind of weapon against a special kind of enemy. He couldn't afford the time to train another.

The Congressman took another sip of whiskey, then looked angrily at the glass and drained it. He got up from the recliner, went to a special closet in his bedroom, and he picked up the scrambler phone.

He listened to the phone ring, then heard the signal that told him the phone had been answered at the same time it told his son to attach his scrambler-decoder to the receiver.

Finally, the noises on the line became intelligible. "Hello, Congressman."

"Hello, son. I want you to come down here. First thing in the morning."

"All right, I'll drive down. Things are getting pretty hot up here, you know—sure you want me away from Draper if things pop?"

"We'll get a helicopter, fly you back in a half hour if we need to. You just come on down. We've got some talkin' to do. Put it off too long already."

"Are you unhappy with my work?" There was no emotion whatever in his son's voice. That alone told the Congressman something.

"Your work is fine, stop fishin' for compliments. There's just some intelligence you should get face to face."

There was a silence. The Congressman listened to the buzz of the scrambler on the line. Looked like he'd given his son something to think about.

Finally, the young man spoke. "As I said, I'll be there."

"Good." It was probably the most sincere word the Congressman had ever spoken in his life.

And as he replaced the receiver, he made one more wish. He wished with all his might he was doing the right thing.

Orders for the nurses at the hospital were strict. No one was to talk to Lindsay Keith about the kidnapping of Elizabeth Fane, or about the beating someone had given the boy himself.

Candy had scrupulously observed the ban. As much as they wanted to know what Keith had to say, she and Leo both knew that it was more important for her to maintain her cover than it was to debrief Keith. Now that Roy had been eliminated, Candy was the only one of them who could move freely about town to buy supplies or pick up news. Even so, she had to leave and return to the new hideout under cover of darkness.

The temptation to make Keith talk was not especially great. He was a whiner, the kind of patient who, against all logic, blamed the nurses for his being in the hospital. His pillow was always too hard or too soft. He always needed the TV adjusted or had some equally unmedical problem.

And he wanted to be a hero. Or rather, he wanted to be *thought* of as a hero, and he got quite resentful when the FBI, for example, didn't treat him with what he felt was proper respect.

He kept making passes at the nurses, even though he was too beat up to be able to do anything about it if he succeeded. He had a different approach to each of them. To Candy, he had offered a variation of the let-me-take-you-away-from-all-this approach: "You're so confident and skillful, the way you take my temperature and all. I realize now that Liz . . ." and then, without actually saying anything outwardly nasty, he'd compare his kidnapped fiancée unfavorably with working-girl Candy, and finish by suggesting they get together sometime to discuss ways of making things fairer.

Candy managed to smile only by thinking of what little chance this fool had. And by thinking that one positive service they'd perform for Liz Fane would be the ultimate busting up of her relationship with Lindsay Keith.

Candy had no problem reconciling her nursing past (and, with forged credentials, present) with the more usual elements of the terrorist life. She really didn't think of herself as a terrorist; didn't think about herself much at all. She had always lived in the present; faced with a choice, she made it, and went on. No patterns, just occasional surprises. Whims were as good as plans—better, because you could always count on having a whim.

For example, she'd gone into nursing because back in those nearly forgotten days when she'd had a family and a real name, people always joked about her signature—"C. Barton." That little fact took her into nursing school, and that took her into New York's Bellevue Hospital. She worked hard, then forgot about her job when she went home. She lived alone, went on occasional dates, took her vacation in a different country every year, and saw no reason her life wouldn't go on that way forever.

Then one night they brought Peter Gonzalez to her hospital floor. Peter had burned off half his face while constructing an incendiary bomb that was intended for an Eastern Airlines ticket office and which would somehow further the cause of Puerto Rican independence.

Candy had forgotten how that was supposed to work, but she would never forget the effect Peter Gonzalez had on her. He showed her, by his very existence, something mysterious and exciting. *He* had plans, and an almost suicidal commitment to the future the plans were supposed to bring about.

Candy remembered looking into his good eye and wondering why his face hadn't been burned from the inside long before this by the fire inside him.

By the second night, they had made love. In the hospital bed, with the guard outside, saline solution flowing through needles into his arms; none of that mattered. A surprise. Candy learned she had a need for excitement and adventure, after all, things she was incapable of generating for herself.

By the fourth night, she had helped him escape, drugging the guard and forging the papers that let her wheel him out the front entrance to the waiting arms of his comrades.

Two hours later, Candy was gone too, tending to Peter in the back of a private plane flying (in stages) to Mexico. She learned the skills of the underground there, and took to it as if it were just another course of study to be mastered.

And, thanks to Peter's sister, Pilar, Candy had another of her surprises. Candy was a lesbian. For heaven's sake. She'd never been aware of any attraction to women, but once it happened, she knew she would never be happy with men again. Men were too . . . too *moment*-oriented. Women could relax and let it happen, over and over—or never, if that was the mood they were in.

As Peter recovered, he became more involved with his dreams of Revolution. He had less and less time for Candy. He seemed to be glad she and Pilar had each other.

Peter and Pilar had been killed. It was inevitable—that was another fact that Candy faced. Sooner or later, everyone in the underground sells out or dies violently. If the brother and sister hadn't fallen in a shootout with Mexican police, Peter would have blown them all up with another bomb, or worse, grown old and weak, and ended up giving names and addresses to the police of one country or another.

Candy went on, adjusting as she always did. She had made contacts during her time with Peter; she used them, and made more. Eventually, she met Georgia, and through her, Leo Calvin. And here she was, dusting off her old nursing skills, being happy that she hadn't lost them. Not liking her patient. Not that it mattered, of course.

Her patient was watching a morning news show. They happened to be doing a summary of the Liz Fane case. It gratified Candy to see how far the press still was from learning anything important, despite the fact that they now knew from fingerprints in the house that Georgia and Ramon had been there. Georgia had been a hotly sought fugitive for years, ever since a bombing at a draft board that killed four people, so she didn't mind if the police knew she was in this or not. Ramon's fingerprints were on file only because of a car theft he'd committed at eighteen, but he was gone, so that didn't matter, either.

Still, Candy would remain in character, and, in character, would follow orders. She went to the television and turned it off.

"Leave it on," Lindsay Keith whined. "I want to watch it."

"You're not supposed to be upset by this sort of thing," Candy said.

"I'll be upset if everyone keeps treating me like a child, for Christ's sake."

Candy said nothing.

"Come on, turn it back on, please? Nobody's let me see or hear anything about it since I came here." He even sounded like a child. Then he smiled. "Come on, I want to see if I get mentioned, or if the bastards ignore me again."

Candy thought he was disgusting, but decided that his honesty should be rewarded. She hit the switch, and the picture returned. They had reached the point in their coverage where they discussed the rival claims of the groups calling themselves LEO and NALA.

They played excerpts from the tapes. From the one Leo had written, they heard Liz Fane calling her father a war criminal in a dead voice. From the bogus tape, Candy listened to the black woman spit threats while a voice in the background that sounded just like Liz Fane's moaned and screamed, and said " . . . stop . . . don't . . . please . . ." in a helpless voice.

Candy concentrated on that second tape. She had a suspicion that had been growing since the first time she'd heard it on the radio. Candy listened again, trying to get enough of an impression to decide.

She was concentrating so hard, she almost didn't see the look on Lindsay Keith's face. He was turning pale so quickly that the Nurse C. Barton part of her had her rushing to his bedside to check vital signs.

Keith threw her off. "That's not pain," he said, in a strangled voice. He pointed with his chin toward the TV set.

I knew it, Candy thought. *I was right all along.*

She forced herself to stay calm, to put the right degree of bewilderment in her voice. "What do you mean, it's not pain?"

If Lindsay Keith had any scruples about discussing his sex life with a stranger (which Candy doubted), shock had wiped them away.

"It's sex," he said. "When I ea—when we have oral sex, that's exactly what she does. One time I drove her crazy. She kept asking me to stop, but when I did, she threatened to mutilate me. She was always doing things like that."

Candy nodded. She knew. She'd heard Liz Fane make that noise, too. She heard it, in fact, nightly. Liz Fane, despite differences in environment and wealth, was Candy's sister in a special way. Candy had suspected it from the very beginning, when she had come to Draper alone to size things up for Leo. Their advance information had suggested it might be the case. Now, Candy had been proven correct.

Candy was sure that in her own mind, Liz Fane was blaming it on fear, blaming it on panic, blaming it most of all on the hypnotic drugs. And it was true that an important step in mind control is to get the subject in the habit of performing sexual acts he or she would have considered repugnant before. Sexual inhibitions were strongly tied in with the sense of self— as with changing the name, when you change sexual habits, you damage the subject's grip on her own identity, leaving a vacuum for the controller to fill.

But all rationale aside, Liz's or Leo's, Candy knew one thing. Liz Fane, despite money and loving parents, had not been happy. Certainly Liz Fane's picking this fool in the hospital bed to marry had little to do with self-respect. Liz Fane had hated herself because the life she was living was unfulfilled and unfulfillable. Inside the little rich girl was an image-smasher waiting to be let out.

Candy was sure she had opened the door. In time, Liz would step through. She was already on the way. It may have been the drugs, but then none of Candy's lovers. had ever responded to them as Liz Fane had. Candy was almost sorry to contemplate the time when the ransom was paid and they let her go. Or killed her. Leo hadn't mentioned coming to a decision about that yet.

But Candy had a job to do.

"You're not making any sense," she told Keith. "If she's having such ecstasy with her kidnappers, why don't they say she's joined up with them? How come they want people to think they're torturing her if they're not?"

Lindsay Keith tried to shake his head, then settled for the grimace of pain the effort produced. "You don't understand," he said. "They've got my *tapes*."

"Your tapes?"

"They must. These are the fake ones, the phony terrorists. Somehow, they've gotten hold of my tapes."

"What tapes?" Candy said. She tried to sound casual.

He told her. His adolescent mind had found it amusing to video-tape his sexual sessions with Liz. Disgusting. But undeniably the source of the voice on the rival ransom tapes. No wonder the audio experts had been fooled.

"All right," Candy said. "That's enough of this foolishness." She snapped off the television, and ignoring her patient's squawk of protest, took the control out of his reach. Quickly she left the room and walked down the hall to the drug cabinet. She had been careful not to fool around in there—it was dangerous. The cabinet was audited regularly, any discrepancy followed up with vigor. Candy couldn't afford to be discovered. The drugs they used on Liz, the amphetamine that was keeping Candy alert now, after no sleep last night, were obtained through other sources.

Still, this was an emergency. She'd find some way to cover. She removed some narcotic from the closet, put it in a little paper dose cup, and returned to the room.

Keith was still sulking. He insisted she turn the TV back on.

She handed him the cup. "After you take this," she said.

He eyed her. "What is it?" he demanded.

"Pain reliever. Stronger than what you've been getting. Doctor's order. You've asked for something stronger, haven't you?"

He shrugged and swallowed the pills.

Candy said, "That's good," and left him. The pills would make sure he wouldn't talk to anybody for the next five or six hours. He'd talk, then, but to the people Candy wanted him to talk to.

Candy paused. What she contemplated wasn't supposed to be done without permission and orders from Leo first. But thanks to Waldo's indiscretion, things were different. There was no time to get in touch with Leo, no way to do it all in daylight. And waiting might waste the opportunity.

It was Candy's decision (or whim) that the opportunity was too good to pass up. Therefore, she'd accept the consequences, whatever they might be. That taken care of, Candy went about her rounds, competently.

She refused to look at a clock. It wouldn't do any good, anyway. She was scheduled for lunch at eleven-thirty, and she couldn't start putting her plan into effect until then.

But when she got things going, the League to End Oppression would be making some important gains in the credibility department. Candy was sure of that.

Miles sat in Jake Feder's control room, reading manuals, trying to learn about electronics. He didn't touch anything—he didn't want to take a chance of hindering Jake in the future by messing with things he didn't understand. But it would be good to know something about what Jake did. A good agent learned as much about as many things as possible. It made a better liar of you.

Miles was also practicing patience. That was his main shortcoming. He just wasn't cut out to sit around and let the opposition make the next move. Since patience was what the job most often demanded, Miles had tried for years to cultivate serenity.

At times like this, though, he would settle for acceptance or even tolerance. Anything but this gnawing need to DO SOME-THING! that would have made his fingers twitch in frustration—if he weren't practicing patience.

He looked back at the manual. ". . . connect patch A to either red channel B or . . ." He threw it down again. He couldn't concentrate on crap like this.

He couldn't concentrate on the operation, either, because he kept thinking of THINGS HE COULD BE DOING! and that wasn't his job. It was *Driscoll's* job. That was the way the Congressman wanted it, and one thing Miles would never think of doing was disagree with the Congressman.

The best thing to do would be to talk. Unfortunately, there was no one around here to talk to. Driscoll had been called to Washington (he'd left early this morning), the Payne girl was home working on her aunt and uncle. You had to be careful talking to her anyway, because she was an amateur, and you didn't know what was safe to tell her.

Vi was here, but she was worthless to talk to. She kept walking around, sitting, getting up and walking around again. She made black noises every once in a while, saying "Mm, mm, mm," in an exasperated way.

The only time she said anything was when she asked Miles, "Did you ever think of what you'd do when you got out of this business?"

The thought of getting out of the business was so absurd, Miles had gone into the control room to escape her. God knew what she would come up with next.

Suddenly, a small box screwed to the cinder block wall began to give off a series of sharp double rings, like an English telephone. Miles could hardly believe it. Someone was breaking into Lindsay Keith's apartment. There was SOMETHING TO DO! at last.

Putting an alarm into Keith's apartment had been Miles' idea. He did have them, occasionally. Driscoll, to give him his due, was even willing to listen to them, as long they didn't involve policy. He'd listened to this one, and nodded at Miles.

"Yeah," he'd said. "Do it. Of course, if they get that far, and find out about the tapes, we're probably sunk anyway, but catastrophes are like baseball games—you can appreciate them more if you know all the details." Miles supposed Driscoll had thought that was funny.

Miles had installed a pressure alarm under the floor of Keith's apartment. He'd done it while the ambulance was whisking the kid away to the hospital after the beating Miles had given him.

Miles had already put some time in placing tiny, all but undetectable taps in the phone lines of the Draper Police Department and Fenton Rines' temporary FBI office. That was another of his ideas.

It was the phone tap that made Miles think that someone's entering Lindsay Keith's apartment was not necessarily the catastrophe Driscoll had predicted it would be. The taps, and the constant monitoring of all official radio channels, even the ones the public wasn't supposed to know about, let alone have access to. That was one of the advantages of working for the government—you were always right up to date in the latest technology.

The point was, though, that none of this fancy technology had produced anything. Miles couldn't believe that after all this time the cops would go back there (they'd had a look around before Miles had taken the tapes away) without the event turning up in some communication somewhere.

As if on cue, a light went on and a tape recorder started to work, indicating that a call had come in on one of the special kidnap hot-lines at the New Police Headquarters. Vi entered the control room at the same moment.

"I heard the alarm," she began, but Miles shushed her and hit the monitor button.

". . . thing about the Fane case," a voice was saying. It was a woman's voice, disguised with a harsh, whispering tone that compelled attention.

"I've heard that voice," Vi said.

"Quiet," Miles said. He leaned closer to the speaker.

"What is that, ma'am?" said the voice of a bored police officer. Miles figured he was probably being punished with telephone duty for not giving out enough parking tickets.

"I can tell you something about the Fane case," the harsh voice repeated.

"Yes, ma'am," the officer said. "Name and address, please."

As Miles thought, it hadn't even been worth asking. "Tell Chief Anderson to play the terrorist tapes for Elizabeth Fane's boyfriend. Tell him to ask Keith about *his* tapes."

This wasn't the usual kind of phone-in tip—"I saw Liz Fane in the audience on *Family Feud* last night"—this could really be something. Miles heard the alertness awaken in the officer's voice.

"Yes, ma'am—ask boyfriend about tapes. Could you be more specific please? And may I have your name and address ple—?"

He stopped because she hung up on him. The officer kept the phone to his ear long enough to curse, then hung up himself, presumably to try to find Chief Anderson.

Miles didn't know how long it would take to find the chief. He thought, though, that on something like this, Anderson wouldn't want to move without being accompanied by Rines, and maybe even Mr. Driscoll of the Defense Department, and they were both out of town this morning.

So Miles had time, but not much of it. He reached for the scrambler line to Washington, even as Vi said, "Rines' office is getting a call." She punched a button. "Same lady, too," Vi said.

Miles punched in a code, then his identification code, and practiced patience with all his might while the computer digested it and decided whether it would let him speak to the Congressman.

Cary Wilkis answered the front door and wondered what the right way to receive an FBI man was. Offer him a beer, or what?

He was beginning to regret the good-citizen impulse that had led him to make a ruckus about those uneven stacks of bodies, and this tough-looking guy in the gray suit with the watch-your-ass-boy smile on his face was reinforcing the feeling.

He'd begun with the cops in Pennsylvania, and that had started a runaround that had ended when the ICC had sent a guy around to talk to him. Very polite fella, too. Never said Cary was nuts, even though he obviously thought so. He just said that since all the paperwork was in order on both ends of the run, and no one was complaining other than Cary himself, there was really nothing anybody could do. The guy said he was sorry, and if there was anything further they could help him with, he should let them know, and thank you for being a good citizen and a credit to the Interstate Highway System, good-bye, and God bless you.

What had been left unsaid was that if Cary bothered them with any more of this graverobbing bullshit, they'd pull his ticket so fast it would burn up from the friction, and maybe they'd have him committed, too. The message got across just the same. Cary had shrugged, and figured he'd done his duty.

He'd never haul stiffs again (he repeated this promise to himself constantly) and he'd never stop puzzling over what had happened this time, but as far as officialdom was concerned, Cary was just as glad to have heard the end of it.

Only he hadn't.

The call from the FBI had come while Cary was making love to his wife, and if that wasn't enough to ruin an enjoyable experience, Cary couldn't tell you what was.

It was this guy Rines. Cary had heard of him on the news. He was in charge of finding this rich girl who'd been snatched off a country club. So he wasn't any small potatoes.

Now there he was on the phone telling Cary he wanted to fly down to Durham (!) so that they could have a "little talk." He told Cary not to worry, he wasn't in any trouble.

Cary tried to believe that, but he had a hard time. Of *course* they would tell him he wasn't in any trouble. If the FBI was coming to send you to the Federal pen, what were they gonna do? Call you on the phone and say, "You're ass is grass, boy, and I'm the lawnmower, so sit tight till I get there"?

Cary was too nervous to run, so he'd sat tight. Now, here the man was, looking stern and uncorruptible and probably not the kind of guy you offered a beer to. Except that if Cary didn't offer him one, he wouldn't be able to have one himself, and he was going to need a beer to face this.

So he offered, got turned down as expected, swallowed, then opened the door wide to let the FBI in.

For several days, Fenton Rines had been too busy to talk with Austin Tressa, his friend in the ICC. Big case, keep hopping, things like that. If Austin hadn't been so persistent, if this truckdriver hadn't been so persistent, Rines most likely would have never heard of the uneven stacks of coffins. And Rines had a hunch that in one way or another, that would prove to be a very important little piece of information.

So he'd taken his earliest opportunity and flown down here to talk to Cary Wilkis, to make sure he had all the details of the story right, and to get whatever additional details might be available.

Austin Tressa had been amused by the whole thing.

"Look, we know what time he left Seattle; and we know what time he wound up at the Pennsylvania State Police. To get from one to the other in that little time, he *had* to have been eating greenies like jellybeans. So the whole thing is probably a drug-induced nightmare."

He chuckled, then went on more seriously. "Still, he *was* hijacked, and there *were* some pretty weird elements about it. The story about the boxes was the frosting on the cake that made me think this was your kind of wrongo, Fen. I hope it makes you happy."

"Bears looking into," Rines said. "Thanks."

"Don't mention it. Ever going to tell me what you're collecting these things for?"

"Someday, maybe. I'll buy you dinner if I ever get back."

Rines was positive the steer to Wilkis was worth at least a dinner. The guy was simple, but he wasn't stupid. He was nuts, maybe, but absolutely sincere. Rines' experience told him to believe what the trucker said. And that led him to some interesting speculation.

If a body was stolen, how was it that no record remained on anybody's documents that it ever existed? Simple answer—the records had been gotten to. Changed. Destroyed. Except the simple answer wasn't so simple. It took *juice* to mess around with official documents on that sort of scale. Money or power or both. We're talking the Mafia, here. The Russians. The Vatican. Or the U.S. Government.

And *if* a body was stolen, whose body, and why? No way of telling. But if it had been the body of a young woman, say, the idea of someone's using it as the prop-finger in a dismember-ment horror show sort of leapt to the mind.

Rines frowned.

"Something wrong, sir?" Cary Wilkis asked.

"No. Nothing at all. Go on."

Rines went on thinking. He could listen and think at the same time and never miss a word. The trouble with the body theory was the fingerprints. Rines didn't really see how they could have made the fingerprints on a finger from a body obtained at random match those in three different files, one of them the Bureau's own. The voiceprints were a problem, too, but more easily solvable (or maybe ignorable) to the agent's mind.

The one thing he was sure of involved the tranquilizer gun that Cary Wilkis had been hit with. Regular hijackers would have hit him on the head, or tied him up and left him while they drove off with the truck. Terrorists would have killed him. They always killed people—that's why they were terrorists. They only went in for fancy stuff when they needed their victim alive. Liz Fane, for instance. Even in her case, the darts had been homemade, jerry-built.

No, the use of a tranquilizer gun on the truckdriver screamed *professional agent.* And the fact that they'd taken the risk of not killing him, to Rines' patriotic mind, spelled *American* professional.

American professionals, however, who broke laws left and right, and who (as far as Rines could tell) reported to no one.

It went together, sort of. If it didn't exactly make a picture, it at least made a shape. Rines had the feeling that he was just one or two more facts away from keeping his promise to the Intelligence Oversight Committee Chairman.

Any day now, Special Agent Rines would walk through the door with evidence of clandestine American domestic operations. It would be interesting to see the look on the Congressman's face when he did.

As he drove to Washington that morning, Driscoll had found his mind occupied by, of all things, a gynecologist. Dr. Leon S. Welkenheimer, the handsomest and most successful gynecologist in that part of Pennsylvania, presented some intriguing problems.

The rush of events usually didn't allow much time for it, but Driscoll found it useful at times to review the elements of an operation whenever he got the chance. It was more important than usual with this case, because important events had occurred before he had known anything about the case.

Driscoll had treated himself to a private sardonic smile as that thought crossed his mind. He could almost hear his father's voice saying, "Well, whose fault is that, boy? You stay away from me, make me go huntin' you down, you're always gonna be reactin' to enemy moves. Come back to work for me on a regular basis. You'll get to do plenty of instigatin'."

No thanks, Driscoll had told the voice. *I've done too much instigating in my life as it is.*

What he wanted to know was who had instigated the kidnapping of Liz Fane. Not whose idea it was. The Russians wore that hat very becomingly. But who had given the go-ahead signal? Who had been the finger man?

Because that kidnapping had been exquisitely timed. It seemed fairly obvious that the Hispanic waiter had fired the dart. He'd disappeared, after all, and the FBI investigation had found all his credentials and background stories to be incredibly brazen lies.

But how had he known when to be in position to fire that dart? He hadn't been eavesdropping on Liz Fane and her mother, that was certain. He had been taking drink orders inside the clubhouse right up till five minutes or so before the time the dart had been fired. Driscoll had read the transcripts Rines had been sending him—his favorite interview was with the woman club member who had seemed less upset with the idea that the waiter had been part of a kidnap plot than she was because he hadn't brought her her drink before he left to fire the dart. "But I'm always so careful to *tip* them enough," she'd said.

The ambulance business had taken timing, too. It wouldn't have been smart for the red-haired man and the woman to have spent too long driving around after slaughtering two people to get hold of it, no matter how much care they'd taken to see the bodies weren't found until hours later.

They had to be just the right distance away from the club parking lot when the dart struck. They didn't want to be sitting parked somewhere, waiting for Liz Fane to collapse. That might plant details of their appearance and actions in the minds of too many witnesses. On the other hand, they had to be able to arrive on the scene before the real ambulance showed up.

None of it called for split-second timing, but it damn well called for *timing*. Somehow or other, LEO had known about what time Liz Fane would be leaving the country club.

And that brought him back to Dr. Welkenheimer. The doctor certainly knew that Liz Fane invariably tagged along when her mother had an appointment with him, getting him to work her checkup in at the same time. He also knew Sheila Fane had an appointment with him that morning. Mrs. Fane had even told the FBI (and the doctor, maybe ingenuously, maybe shrewdly, had confirmed it) that she called Welkenheimer's office that morning to make sure it would be okay to bring her daughter along with her.

So he had known those things, and he had been in a position to find out anything else he needed to know. Driscoll, who had masqueraded as one, once, for an assignment, knew from experience that women tell gynecologists things their parents, husbands, priests, best friends or God would never hear. A woman had told him, for instance, that she was passing minor state secrets to the Russians to make her former lover (who worked with her at the Pentagon) look bad and lose his job. It had turned out that the minor state secrets had been less minor than she supposed, and her former lover had been about to become a permanently misplaced person.

But all that was beside the point. The main thing was that Dr. Leon S. Welkenheimer was an unusually promising candidate to be a Russian agent working deep cover on the Cronus Project. Whatever that was.

Deep cover—that is, spies working patiently to rise to positions of influence as ordinary, seemingly loyal Americans so that they can be more effective when finally called to begin their covert operations.

Dr. Welkenheimer would be a perfect candidate, assuming that the Cronus Project had had Herbert Fane, or at least Fane Electronics, as its target from the beginning.

That wasn't an impossible assumption, either. The file on Herbert Fane showed that he had been on the way to the top since before he'd graduated from RPI. He'd seen the potential of the transistor before practically anybody else, and had a head start on everybody but Bell Labs, where the transistor had been invented, when he went into business for himself in 1949.

Korea had been a big boost to his business (and to that extent, Driscoll supposed, Fane *was* a war profiteer), and it had just kept growing when the war ended. The company had had a slight setback in 1954, just around the time Driscoll had been born, when Fane's first wife died of botulism poisoning contracted from a can of paté, and the industrialist had gone into a deep depression. The depression didn't end until months later when he met Sheila Kirby, a decorator who'd come to try to get him to hire her to re-do the offices at his factory.

According to Rines' reports, she hadn't gotten the job, but about a year later, she'd gotten the boss. Fane snapped out of it, got his business in high gear again, and he had been blissfully happy ever since. Some romantic at the FBI (Driscoll hadn't known there were any) had actually used "blissfully" in the report.

Fane had bought the Draper plant in 1959; Liz was born a few years later. Fane had continued to grow richer and more successful over the years. Fane Industries was the only company the FBI could think of that had *never* turned in a government project late or over budget.

This was the kind of man Moscow would keep an eye on. America did it, too. His father had copies of CIA files on thousands of young Russians of promise. Who might be turned. Who could be of propaganda value. Who might become dangerous. Who ought to be killed.

It was not unreasonable that the Russians would devote a full-time, self-financing spy to Herbert Fane, to be close to him (or at least his family), getting to know the vulnerable spots, readying contingency plans. Then, when a high-value item in the game of international politics comes up, something like MENTOR, say, and Herbert Fane is the key to the whole thing, you'd be ready to strike instead of worry.

It wasn't unreasonable at all. There was only one problem with it.

It was impossible.

At least, it was impossible if the spy you're talking about is Dr. Leon S. Welkenheimer. Rines and his men had Welkenheimer's whole life on paper, and there was just no way. He had never, so far as they knew, ever in his life associated with anybody left of Hubert Humphrey; he had no unexplained absences; he behaved nothing at all like a spy, or even like a mole.

Besides, the FBI report said, he was carrying on affairs with three of his patients.

That was the clincher. A gynecologist who messes around with his patients is asking to be killed by a jealous husband. Because, as the old joke goes, a gynecologist is the only man alive who can tell a woman to take off all her clothes, touch her wherever he wants, then send her husband a bill.

But in some ways worse than that, he's asking to be disgraced, or thrown off the roster. No gynecologist who was working as a spy for the Russians would dare do it. He would be dead meat the minute the Russians found out. They had no interest in preserving someone who has destroyed his own usefulness, or has even risked it. Useless agents can still talk. Moscow would prefer they didn't. Nobody becomes a spy without knowing this.

So, unless Welkenheimer was a self-destructive idiot of historic proportion, he was not Driscoll's theoretical mole.

Driscoll puzzled over it all the way to Washington.

If Welkenheimer wasn't the spy, who, if anyone, was?

If there were *no* deep cover spy arranging for the Fane women to be crossing the sights of the homemade dart gun at that particular time, how had the plan *worked*? Or did the opposition really have God on their side, after all? Could it be that, Cronus or no Cronus, this was not brilliant timing at all, just dumb luck? Driscoll couldn't believe it, but it wouldn't go away.

And most maddeningly of all, should he even be spending time thinking about this? Granted, a solution to the question of who the spy was (was there one, though?) would shoot him to a resolution of all his problems in practically no time. Once Driscoll got his hands on someone, he could make him talk. He knew that and would always know it. No matter how hard he tried to forget it.

But turning someone up, someone he couldn't really be sure even existed, was such an incredible long shot, it seemed a waste of time to speculate about it.

Besides, within the limits of the assignment as stated by his father, he was already a big success. MENTOR was back in production; America would keep that three-month lead. *"God Bless America" plays in the background; the flag raises; four handsome young people in uniform (the Air Force is represented by a woman, the Marine Corps by a black) salute. The audience wipes a tear from its eye.*

Driscoll realized that he really didn't give a shit about MENTOR anymore. If the leaders of the world decided to blow us up, we probably had it coming, anyway, and one missile guidance system more or less wouldn't make that much difference.

What had come to matter to him was the ordinary lives of ordinary people, something he knew only academically, the way he knew the life of ancient Rome, or the life of New Guinea tribesmen. He wanted to keep people like Leo Calvin, and, God help him, people like "Clifford Driscoll," who were so far from everyday life they didn't even have real names, from causing the fear and frustration that had poisoned so much of the world.

In this operation, Driscoll had become a counterterrorist, and he was beginning, in a perverted kind of way, to like it. He knew he was putting the people behind the Cronus Project through the same kind of torment they usually inflicted on the innocent. He used their own methods, up to a point, and he hurt people, and used them shamelessly when he wasn't hurting them. (Pictures of Robin Payne in tears and in passion came to his mind.)

As much as Driscoll hated his father, there was one thing he admired about him. He had never, in seriousness, tried to wrap the flag around his dirty work. The Congressman's god was a pragmatic one—we live here, we like it, this is what we've got to do to keep it—and he never tried to sell his son anything else.

But over the last couple of weeks, the man who called

himself Clifford Driscoll had caught an intriguing whiff of something, something he'd never known before; hadn't ever really believed existed: principle.

It was a strange feeling to think that as he went about the business he'd been trained for, that of pushing people and events until they lined up in a way that suited him, that he might this time actually be pushing in the direction of something good. That he might be the instrument of a rough but poetic justice over the terrorists of the world.

It was an unprecedented thought; he liked it. He held onto it all the way into Washington.

Chapter Eight

"SIT DOWN, SON," THE CONGRESSMAN SAID.

No game this time, Driscoll thought. *No sidelong glances with double or triple meanings. No leisurely strolls along the Potomac. All business. Not especially pleasant business, either.*

Driscoll sat.

"You're doin' a good job up there, boy," the old man said. "Mainly."

"You didn't bring me down here to tell me I was doing a good job."

"Mainly," his father said. He smiled sadly. "But, no, I didn't bring you down here to tell you you're doin' a good job." The Congressman opened a steel drawer in his desk. It took doing—there were three keys and an electronic combination involved before it would open. He took a folder from it, an old one, big enough to hold the bedsheet-sized printout from the Agency's first computer, a vacuum-tube giant that took up half a building and could do less than a modern pocket calculator. Driscoll hadn't seen a folder that size since he was seven years old—that file had been in there a long time. Not that it hadn't ever been taken out. It was worn and bent from frequent handling.

The old man lay the file down on the desk, but didn't open it. He drummed his fingers on it, looking at it as if he were

trying to decide whether or not it had been a good idea to take
it out of the drawer.

Maybe it was another game after all, Driscoll thought. He
was in no mood to play.

"Well, Father, why *did* you bring me down here?"

The Congressman drummed one last beat on the folder
and looked up to meet the younger man's eyes. "I brought you
here, son, to tell you about your mother."

The statement had no meaning for Driscoll; in context, it
made no sense at all. He had to make sure he hadn't mistaken
two other syllables for that incredible word.

"Did you say my *mother*? *My* mother?"

"That's what I said."

"Jesus Christ." It wasn't even an exclamation; he was
calling on Jesus because He might be the only person capable of
understanding a miraculous occurrance like this one.

"Jesus Christ," Driscoll said again. "Why? After all these
years, why?"

"Because now it matters," his father said. "What's wrong,
didn't you ever wonder about her?"

Driscoll couldn't remember the last time he'd cried. If he'd
wanted to ask, the Congressman would have told him it had
been when he was four years old. After that, he'd made it a
point to train his son out of the habit. It wasted energy, and it
took time.

Driscoll wasn't crying now, but it was a close thing. His eyes
burned, and his throat got so tight it hurt, just the way it had all
those nights in his childhood when he'd lain awake wondering
(but not crying) over his mysterious mother. The one his father
would never speak about.

Had she loved him? Was she pretty? Why did she go away?
Maybe one of the ladies his father brought in to teach him and
take care of him had been his mother in disguise.

There were a lot of them; they never lasted more than
three months. Driscoll realized now that the General, now the
Congressman, had wanted to keep his son from forming an
attachment to anyone but himself. *How well you succeeded,*
Driscoll thought. His throat got a little bit tighter.

But none of his teachers made him feel the way he had

learned from his reading that a mother should have made him feel. When he was ten, the ladies stopped coming, replaced by a succession of stern men who had no interest in him except to see how much knowledge they could pound into his head. This project had been eminently successful, too. The only women he dealt with were those his father brought to him to complete his sex education.

If Driscoll had been allowed the company of other children with home lives anything close to normal, with mothers of their own, it might have been worse for him. Fortunately (*Fortunately!* Driscoll thought) all his relationships with others had been homework assignments, carefully supervised by the Agency. The young Driscoll had been schooled, rehearsed, and sent out. This is how you get people to give you money. This is how you make them afraid of you. This is how you deal with anger—your own and others. This is how you seduce an older woman. This is how you make someone talk if you mustn't damage him physically. This is how to do it if you may.

All the while, Driscoll was developing his own course of study in how to deal with his father. It had been imperfect, and only sporadically successful, but one element of it that had always worked was *never ask him about your mother*. No matter how much you ache to know.

Driscoll concentrated on relaxing his throat. "No, Father," he said at last. "I never wondered about her, much. Why? Should I have?"

The old man grunted and looked at his son through narrow eyes. "You asked me once," he said. "As I recall, I said I'd fill you in when I thought you were ready to know."

"Aha. And I'm ready now?"

"I don't know—I guess that's up to you. But in the light of the circumstances, I'm ready to tell you."

"What circumstances?" Driscoll was angry. He had been hauled in and handed a particularly difficult operation. He'd had some success, and quickly, too. Now his father had yanked him off the job for the express purpose, it seemed, of ruining his already shaky concentration.

The Congressman's lips formed a wry smile, but his eyes were sad. He picked up the folder and held it out.

Driscoll toyed with the idea of standing up and walking out. In some childish and unprofessional way, he was angry with his mother. He had learned to get along without her; he didn't need her coming along and messing him up now.

But the child who had spent those nights of tearless agony wouldn't be denied. Driscoll snatched the folder from his father's hand, put it on his lap and opened it.

He got the answer to one of his questions immediately. His mother had indeed been pretty, very pretty. The first picture, a deckle-edged eight-by-ten blowup of an old snapshot, showed a young woman in a bulky sweater. Wavy dark hair was pulled back from a smiling face.

Driscoll closed his eyes. This was the mother he'd dreamed about. This was what she looked like. Or maybe it was just the smile that matched what he'd wanted so long ago.

He looked at the rest of the pictures. There were mug shots, profile and full face, over the name Rebecca Underwood. There were pictures of a haggard woman, thin and hollow cheeked and obviously pregnant. But it was amazing. The grimmer she got, the more beautiful she got, because there was less to distract attention from the fiery intelligence of her eyes.

She wasn't beautiful in the last picture. She was naked and covered with blood, black and stark against her white skin in the monochrome picture. The blood came from the ruined top of her head and from a gash across her belly. She'd been bound hand and foot to the hospital bed.

Driscoll looked at his father. His eyes were cool and appraising and definitely unfriendly.

"Relax," his father said. "I didn't kill her. Read the report."

Driscoll read. It was all there, from his mother's infiltration of the Pentagon, to her capture, to his father's learning about her involvement in the super-secret, super-important Cronus Project.

"The Cronus Project?" Driscoll demanded. "My mother was a Russian agent involved in the Cronus Project? Why have you been trying to tell me all this time you didn't know what the goddamn thing was?"

"Keep reading, son."

He kept reading. About the General's attempts to learn

what the Cronus Project was. About his own decidedly macu-
late conception. About his mother's grim struggle to end her
life, and to deny him his. He read it all, registered it, but his
brain was defeated by the very idea of trying to assimilate it.

There was one more picture at the back, a snapshot that
seemed to have been stuck into the file as an afterthought. It
showed an infant in a diaper looking up at something outside
the picture with an innocent, round-eyed wonderment.

Driscoll stared at it a full minute before he finally realized
it was a picture of him.

Driscoll took a deep breath. He had never had so much
trouble controlling himself. He wasn't even sure what he was
controlling himself *from*.

He closed the folder and placed it very gently back on his
father's desk.

The Congressman said, "Well?"

"Well what?"

" 'Well what,' don't give me 'well what.' What did you
think?"

"Oh. What do I *think*. Well, Father, I think it's a shame the
nurse didn't show up an hour or so later than she did. I think
you should have gone ahead and called me Macduff. I never
use the name you gave me, anyway."

"I'm not—" the Congressman began, but his son cut him
off.

"I think I got a surprise today; I'd never have believed,
after what I've seen and what I've done, that anything a human
being could perpetrate could shock and disgust me, but you do,
old man. You certainly do.

"I think it's a wonderful joke to find out that you didn't just
raise me to be a monster, with no home and no friends and no
chance even to rest; you *planned* me to be one since before I was
even conceived. I'm surprised you didn't just sew me together
out of odd parts."

The Congressman's voice was sour. "You done?"

Driscoll waved a hand.

"Good," the old man said. "I wonder if in the course of
feelin' sorry for yourself, you've done any thinkin' about how
closely this ties you in with the Cronus Project."

Driscoll said nothing. He hadn't done any thinking about it; his brain refused to digest any of it. He shook his head.

"Well, think about it on the way back to Draper. *I* sure have been thinkin' about it, but it ain't done me any good. Use the 'monster' brain I gave you—and your mother gave you, too—and figure out what your bein' born thirty years ago has to do with Leo Calvin and the Russians kidnappin' the Fane girl here and now."

He pointed a finger at his son, a gesture that Driscoll remembered accompanying lectures about trusting no one or keeping his head up to see where the gunfire came from. "And figure out how they both relate to the damn Cronus Project, before it drives us all nuts."

"You've planned this all along, haven't you?" Driscoll said.

"Planned what?"

"You hunted me down to work on this case because you knew you would tell me this eventually."

"I told you because I decided it would help your work on this case. I didn't *want* to tell you."

"Right."

"I want you workin' for me, not hatin' my guts. That's inefficient. Why do you think I kept my mouth shut about it all these years, boy? I *knew* you wouldn't understand."

Driscoll started to laugh so loudly the Congressman was glad the room was soundproof.

"I knew you wouldn't; just by bein' an American, readin' the stuff you read, hearin' the music, watchin' the movies and TV, you'd soak up the 'Sainted Mother' attitude.

"Well, let me tell you something. You call yourself a monster. The woman who was your mother was no different than you are. Damn sight worse; she did it for the most ruthless bastards the world has ever seen except maybe for Hitler."

"*I* never had a choice, though, did I?" his son said.

"Sometimes you make *me* disgusted, boy. You could be something great for America. More useful than the bomb, because you can work like a surgeon instead of an exterminator. You can pick just the rotten parts to get rid of. Instead of doin' it, you fight me every damn step of the way."

Driscoll started to reply.

"Let me finish, god damn it, now that I've started, after all these years. No, you never had a choice. I made you, I raised you, as a gift to my country. Lots of men have given their sons for America."

Driscoll began to wonder if his father might not be insane; then he wondered why he'd never thought of that before.

"All the other men's sons have had to do was die," Driscoll said quietly.

The Congressman compressed his lips as if in anger, then opened his mouth to speak. The buzzing of the phone cut him off. He channeled his anger toward the phone. He picked it up as if he planned to strangle it, and yelled into the receiver, "Damn it, I said *no interruptions!*"

He listened for a few seconds. Anger had been replaced by irritation by the time he said, "Well, what does he want?" Another pause. The last trace of irritation had vanished—the Congressman was back at work.

"Okay, patch it through." He punched a button on the phone so that his son could hear, too. "Miles," the old man explained. "Code Green."

Driscoll raised a brow. Code Green was the second most serious alert in the Agency codebook. It meant that the operation was in imminent peril, but that no agent was currently in risk of his life over it.

Wonderful, Driscoll thought. *I'm down here learning my entire existence is a madman's joke, and up in Draper all my work is falling apart.*

Miles came on the phone, gave the proper identification, and began his report on the results of his ideas of placing the alarms and phone taps. He scrupulously avoided taking credit for the ideas, since that would be unprofessional. Driscoll felt a peculiar sort of affection for Miles. He envied him his illusions.

Miles concluded his report by saying, "If we move quickly, sir, I think we can salvage the situation. It involves steps I'm not authorized to undertake on my own."

"What did you have in mind, Miles?" the old man asked.

"Destruction of the building where Keith has his apartment before the police can arrive. This will remove, or at least delay the discovery of the fact that the tapes have been removed."

"I know what it will accomplish, Miles," the Congressman said drily.

"Sorry, sir."

The old man looked at his son. "What do you think, Driscoll?"

Driscoll couldn't resist. "You've asked me that once before this morning, Congressman."

His father didn't turn a hair. "This is a new situation."

Driscoll replied directly to Miles. "No one dies in that fire, Miles. Have you got that?"

"I'll do my best."

"Just do what I told you."

The Congressman spoke again. "There's something else to be taken care of, Miles, isn't there?"

"Yes, sir. The potential source of the information to the regular authorities should be eliminated."

"That's it. Can you get past the guards on his room?"

"It should be fairly easy, Congressman. The Draper Hospital is not designed for secur—"

"*No!*"

Driscoll's shout was so loud he startled even himself.

His father looked at him in surprise. He said, "Miles, wait a minute," then put the agent on hold. To his son, he said, "What's the matter with you, boy? The news today turn your brain? That's an absolutely necessary step."

"It is *not*. No wonder you want me around. You've gotten to enjoy power so much, you don't think anymore. Keith doesn't have to die."

"He's got to, and soon."

"You like it, don't you? Ordering people killed."

"I don't like it. It's something that has to be done, sometimes, that's all."

"Not this time."

"Hell of a time for you to go all moral on me."

"Morals have nothing to do with it. I can use this. Listen to me, and I'll give you Leo Calvin's head on a platter."

"How?" the old man demanded.

"I'm either running this, or I'm not. You sent for me, remember?"

"How do I know you're not just jerkin' me off to save this young idiot's life?"

"I'm running it, or I'm not. Make a decision, you're wasting time."

"What if I decide to open the line again and tell Miles to do what he has to do?"

"Then I walk out of here."

"No you don't. Don't be foolish son; I couldn't let you do that. Not under circumstances like these."

"I'm walking. You'll just have to order me killed. Maybe even do it with your own hands. How long has it been since you've killed somebody in person? Only been about a year since I have. No feeling like it."

"Shut up!" the old man snapped. He gave his son a hot stare that lasted a long time. Still holding the stare, which Driscoll met, he reached for the button the phone.

"Miles!"

"Yes, sir."

"Orders, Miles. Listen closely."

Driscoll's face was expressionless. He held his father's eyes.

"Do what Driscoll tells you to do. Here he is now."

Driscoll kept himself from showing triumph by sign, expression, or tone of voice. He gave Miles a set of instructions, calmly and completely. He finished by saying, "Tell Vi, and get started right away. I'll be back there as soon as I can."

The connection was broken. The Congressman said, "Go. The chopper will be on the roof waiting by the time you get up there. I'll have someone bring your car up to Draper."

Driscoll rose to leave.

"Oh, and son," the old man said.

"Yes?"

"This *could* work."

"I know."

"Killing him would *definitely* work."

Driscoll said nothing.

"You speak a lot of truth sometimes, boy. You should listen to yourself now and then."

"What do you mean?"

"I mean you've been pushin' me pretty hard. I take it because you are who you are, but more because of what you are for the country, what you *can* be. For the sake of that, I can take a little pushin'.

"But son, you push a man like me, *you'd better be right.*

"You mess up this operation; you make me decide you're just an interesting experiment that didn't work out, and I am perfectly capable of havin' you killed. Son or no son. Got that, boy?"

Driscoll smiled. "Loud and clear, Father. But the way I feel about it, that's not really much of a threat."

It took Vi longer to get to the hospital than she had planned. Traffic had been re-routed to allow fire equipment to get to the building where Lindsay Keith had his apartment. The kid on the local radio station, the one who'd made Driscoll look bad at the press conference, said that several fireman had been treated for smoke inhalation. In the negative language of news reporting, that meant nobody else had been hurt. Miles had done his job well.

Now it was time for her to do hers.

It had taken a long time to get around to this—she'd been freelancing for the Agency for almost ten years. She'd done things for them, of course. Making the tape, on this mission. Switching those files with Driscoll. But none of that was her real job, any more than getting a cat out of a tree is a fireman's real job.

Vi was wearing makeup today. First time since God knew when. She was supposed to be a visitor at the hospital, there to see a cousin, Franklin Pertwee, who'd been injured at his garage when a winch failed.

There really was a patient at the hospital named Franklin Pertwee, and he really did have the injuries, but Vi was no relation to him. She probably wouldn't even lay eyes on him, today—she just wanted the visitor's pass to his room on the fifth floor. Franklin Pertwee, so far as Miles had been able to find out in the short time they'd had, was the only black patient on the fifth floor.

So Vi dressed up as his cousin. She had a picture in her mind of the perfect would-be middle-class black girl. She'd done a little quick shopping at a mall far enough away from town so she wouldn't be recognized (it wasn't time for that yet), and come away with a pink short-sleeved blouse, matching twin ribbons to adorn her natural, a tight pair of jeans, and enough cosmetics to give her a moderately made-up look.

She used to hate people who looked the way she did now. It was a function of the hate she used to have for white people. If you followed white styles, the argument went, you didn't hate them enough, you were a traitor to your race, and maybe even worse than the whites themselves.

Vi didn't hate anybody anymore. Not even herself.

She told herself she was doing her best, that she was using the vast sums of money she received from her job as a lamb to help her people, and that made her feel good. But now the hour had come for the lamb to be sacrificed, and Vi was scared.

Okay, part of the deal was, and had been from the very beginning, that if she had to be given up for the sake of the operation, the Agency would see to it that she was acquitted. Or, if they couldn't do that, that she would be busted out of jail. They'd been pretty straight with her until now, about money, obligations, things like that, but this was a whole 'nother league. Maybe once her function was fulfilled they'd just as soon have her locked up for keeps.

There was no way to know their track record on this sort of thing. Obviously, a lamb people knew about was going to be no use at all, so Vi had no idea who the other lambs were or had been, or how the Agency had treated them.

And even if the Agency was one hundred precent straight with her right down the line, what if some blond crew-cut right out of the Police Academy had been reading up on his post office wallpaper, saw what she was wanted for and that she'd been on the Ten Most Wanted List for thirteen years, and started blazing away? She was supposed to make her capture look good, but Vi didn't want it to look *that* good.

The questions didn't get settled by the time she got to Draper Memorial, so she packed them away for the time being, parked the car in the visitors' lot, and went to work.

The Pink Lady at the visitors' desk, a stout woman with beautiful white hair and glasses hanging from a cord around her neck, smiled at Vi and asked her what she could do for her.

It was amazing what some new clothes and a little makeup can do for you, Vi thought. She gave the woman what she called the Credit-to-Her-Race-look, a gaze of sober innocence and determination to be a Good Citizen.

"Pertwee, please," Vi said. "I think it's room five-thirty-five."

The volunteer leafed through the cards in the box on her desk. "Here it is. You were right, five-thirty-five. Elevator to your left."

"Yes, I see it. Thank you, ma'am."

"Visiting hours are until two, you know."

"Oh, I'll be out of here long before then, ma'am." *I damn well will,* Vi thought. *One way or another.*

Vi took the visitor's pass from the woman behind the desk and walked to the bank of elevators. She carried the pass in her hand because she didn't want to risk opening her purse and letting someone see the hypodermic and the rubber-topped glass bottle inside.

An elevator came and opened up. Vi stepped inside, pressed the button for five. On the way up, she speculated about just what she was doing here.

Agency logic, as she had come to know it, dictated that Lindsay Keith be killed, and Miles was the logical one to do it. Miles obviously felt the same way—it had been blatant in his face and voice and attitude as he was briefing Vi about his phone call to D.C. He even went out of his way a couple of times to remind her that it was Driscoll's idea and Driscoll's orders.

Miles didn't add that he thought they were stupid, danger-ous, and damn near treason, but he didn't have to.

All this was pretty uppity behavior for a good soldier like Miles. Either he was *really* pissed off, or he had some heavy duty backup for his opinion. Or both. And since Miles acted most of the time like Driscoll was Jesus Christ, the backup had to be God Almighty Himself, the head of the Agency. Vi had never met him, never seen him, didn't even know if he *was* a him. He could be a woman or a computer, or he could even really *be* God for all Vi knew. All she knew was that he had power enough to call off the FBI, the Treasury Department, and the police of twenty-two states long enough to pull her out of a situation that would have led to her certain capture and a lot of hard time in prison. And he was persuasive enough to get Vi, who used to write "Death to the White Race" on walls in the blood of policemen killed by her man Hamilton, and mean it, to go to work for him.

If Driscoll was bucking that, he had guts. And crazily enough, he was putting those guts on the line to save some-body's life instead of take it. Somebody who wasn't even too popular.

Vi was all for it. As she'd told Miles, she was tired of killing. She'd do what she could to give Driscoll's plan a shot.

As the elevator opened in front of the fifth floor nursing station, Vi wished that Franklin Pertwee's room was a little closer to Lindsay Keith's. Keith was in five-fourteen, at the other end of the hall from her "cousin."

It wouldn't do to stand there thinking about it, either, or one of the nurses, or an orderly, or somebody would ask her if she needed help. Then she'd have no excuse for wandering the wrong way. Things might get inconvenient for her just walking down the hall, if anybody in authority asked to see her pass. The guard on Keith's room, for instance.

Come on, foolish woman, she scolded herself. *Get moving. You're wasting time.*

Vi got moving. Already a nurse was looking at her in a very strange way, almost astonished. *What's a matter, honey, never seen a nigger before?* At that, Vi gave the nurse a fairly close look; she seemed kind of familiar.

But that was *enough.* Vi got hold of herself, made the turn in the hallway, and started walking toward five-fourteen.

Candy had come back to the nurses' station to check out for the day. She was frantic to get downstairs. A minute ago her mind had been filled with getting back to the hideout to tell Leo about her day's work, but what she wanted now was the pay phones, and fast. She stood there, going over charts with the three-to-eleven nurse, talking about enemas and sleeping pills, slowly going crazy.

If it lasted thirty more seconds, Candy was going to abandon her cover and just run for the phones. This was too important. She was sure Leo would agree. If he didn't he'd be wrong.

The briefing was over. Candy was set to take off when she was stopped again by one of the other day-shift nurses who asked her if she wanted to go out for a cup of coffee.

"No, thanks," she said. "I've got to run." And run she did, to the stairs and down to the lobby. She picked up the phone and called the Draper Police Department.

Because she'd recognized her! She'd matched that black woman's face with that voice on the tape. Viola. The co-founder of the Committee for Black Justice. She'd been underground and invisible for years. Candy had met her briefly, just before she'd disappeared. It was down in Mexico—Vi had come to see if she could form a coalition between her group and Peter's Puerto Rican independence movement. It hadn't worked out, one important reason being Candy herself. Vi hadn't thought it was proper to have Anglos (meaning any American whites) in the kind of movement she was thinking of.

Now, here she was, fronting some kind of bogus terrorist group, heading down a hallway toward the one person who could prove they *were* bogus.

"Draper Police," said a voice.

"Yes. I work at the hospital. There's a woman heading toward Lindsay Keith's room. She's got a gun." The gun was to add urgency to the appeal. She wanted the cops there *immediately*. She knew there was a guard outside the room, but somebody like Viola wouldn't have come here if she didn't have a plan for taking care of the guard.

Of course, the cop had to waste time asking her who she was.

"There's no time for that now!" Candy's voice held an edge of hysteria that wasn't entirely feigned. "She's a black woman. Pink blouse. Afro. Pink ribbons in it. Hurry!"

The only thing Candy could do to add further urgency to the call would be to hang up, so she did. She sat in the stifling phone booth, too nervous to move.

It seemed to her she'd never cared about anything as much as she did right now about Lindsay Keith's life. She'd made him talk; she'd arranged for him to ensure the success of the plan. She would do anything so that her work wouldn't go to waste.

She wished she was a woman like Georgia or even Viola; physically able, a skilled fighter. Then she'd go and deal with the problem herself. But Candy knew her prowess was personal and psychological; if she tried a frontal attack on the black woman, all she'd get out of it would be some spectacular newspaper stories. It would have to be up to the police to stop her.

Candy decided to leave the air conditioning in the lobby for the hot, wet air outside. She wanted to see the police the second they came into view.

The guard at the door was a black policeman. Vi used to have a special hatred for those, too, but right now, all she felt was regret it was a black man she'd have to get in trouble.

He was doing a good job, too, keeping a close eye on her while she pretended to search for the right door number. She knew he wasn't doing it because she was pretty.

Vi kept coming down the hallway, the policeman kept looking at her. When she got close enough, he said, "May I help you, miss?"

She smiled at him and came a little closer. "I hope so," she said. "I'm looking for room five-fourteen."

The policeman smiled back at her, then moved aside, revealing the doorplate. "Right here," he said, "but you can't come in."

Vi looked hurt. "Why not? It's still visiting hours, isn't it?"

"Not for this fellow," the policeman said. "No visitors. Orders from the top."

"But my mama told me to come visit him while I'm around town. He's my cousin."

The policeman's grin widened. "There's got to be some mistake, miss. The fellow inside isn't your cousin."

"I don't get it. Isn't this Franklin Pertwee's room?"

"No, no. No Franklin Pertwee here."

"Well, who *is* in this room, then?" Vi made it a challenge, but a friendly one.

"Can't tell you, miss. Orders."

Vi wasn't looking at him. She had her head down to reread the pass. Every now and then she'd shake her Afro in bewilderment. "I just don't understand," she said. "It says right here, 'Pertwee, Franklin, room five-fourteen."

The policeman put out his hand. "May I have a look? Their handwriting isn't too good, down there where they make these things up. And sometimes they get the floor confused, write five-fourteen when they mean four-fifteen. That happened once to the other cop on duty here."

"Anything you could do to help me out," Vi said. She went to hand him the card, but she let go of it before he could get a grasp of it. The card fluttered to the floor between two shiny black policeman's shoes.

His mama had raised him right; he immediately bent to pick it up. When he did, Vi kicked him in the head with one of her heavy, square-toed shoes.

The policeman dropped to his knees and groaned, holding his temple and shaking his head to try to clear it. Vi didn't give him a chance. She chopped him with the edge of her hand on the side of the neck, then again, then twice more until she'd cut off enough of the flow of blood to his brain for him to pass out.

She took a second to make sure that she hadn't ruptured anything on the poor man and killed him. That would make this all kind of stupid, going through all this not to kill Lindsay Keith, then wasting his guard instead.

Reassured by her examination, Vi opened the door to the room, and dragged the policeman in behind her. A quick glance showed that the figure on the bed was sleeping. That was fine with Vi. The fewer eyes she had to look into today, the better she would like it.

She dragged the policeman into the toilet, then used his handcuffs to chain him to the drainpipe of the sink. She gagged him with his tie, then went back into the room.

She took the hypodermic from her purse. It contained insulin at a high concentration, enough to send Lindsay Keith, who was not a diabetic, into shock, coma, and eventually death. The plan, though, was not to have him go past shock. That was dangerous enough.

Instead of plunging the needle into his vein, she followed instructions and stuck it into the intravenous drip that fed medicine slowly into the body. It was a delicate line. She wanted to get enough into him to make him sick—the plan wouldn't work if she didn't. Yet the whole point was not to kill him. Miles had gotten (probably from experts reached by the computer-woman-God-whatever who ran the Agency) a whole list of numbers and measurements she had to match for best results. All she had to do was increase the drip slightly, then deliver herself up to the cops like a good little lamb in seven minutes or less.

Then a thought crossed her mind. Maybe she didn't have to. Maybe she could just leave. Call the nurses on this floor from a phone outside, get on a bus, disappear. No having to worry about a trigger happy cop. No having to worry about the Agency living up to its word.

Just running.

That wasn't so good. She hadn't run in a long time, and she hadn't liked doing it when she had. The life wore her down, made her old. She felt like an old lady all the time.

Of course, prison can make you old, too, she thought.

On the one hand, she owed the Agency for ten years of freedom, more or less. On the other hand, having seen how the Agency worked, she knew that trusting them was not usually *anybody's* best bet.

She was still undecided as she went to leave the room. Her last thought on the subject, for now, was: *The Agency ain't gonna like it if I split, and if I start running now, I'll be running from Miles and Driscoll, and the whoever who controls them. Do I fear them more than I distrust them, or what?*

Then she stepped outside the room and learned the whole

thing was academic. Immediately, Vi dropped the plans she had for various ways to draw attention to herself. They wouldn't be necessary.

A squad of policemen, eight or nine of them, was coming down the hall toward her, guns drawn. They were led, if Vi's eyes told her the truth, by Police Chief Fred Anderson.

Vi wanted to laugh. *Don't underestimate Driscoll,* she thought. He'd probably called the cops on her himself. Didn't want to trouble her with these tough decisions.

The cops saw her now. Eight or nine guns came up, most of them in the way of one or more or the others. Besides, the chief was telling them not to shoot—they might hurt one of the patients. So the chief, at least, was no fool.

All right, then. Let's make it look good for the considerate Mr. Driscoll. Vi pushed open the door to the fire stairs and started down. Once she was in the stairwell, of course, the cops would fire away to their hearts' content. She'd go down three floors and leave, go back into the hallway, then down the stairs at the other end of the hall.

As she sprinted down the second floor hallway, she began to think she still could get away if she wanted to, and she was half inclined to try, if only to teach Driscoll a lesson.

Then a notion crossed her mind: What if it *hadn't* been Driscoll? What if somebody in the hospital had recognized her? Like that nurse who'd stared at her, maybe. Who *did* she remind Vi of, anyway?

She was so rapt by these thoughts, she almost missed the door of the other firestairs. When she went through, she wished she had.

She was staring into the gun of a policeman. Just as she had feared, it was a blond crew-cut. Blue eyes, too. She didn't like the way the gun was shaking.

It came out later that the young cop, whose name was Dan Halmar, had been told by Chief Anderson to "watch the exit to the fire stairs," and had inadvertently chosen the wrong stairs. He was just heading up to check when he'd heard the ruckus on the second floor, drawn a gun, and stepped into his moment of glory.

"Drop it!" he barked. The bark had a little waver in it, as did the gun.

The only thing Vi was carrying was a purse. She dropped it. Raised her hands, too, so he wouldn't have to go through the trouble of remembering to say it.

He thought of something else to say. *"You're under arrest!"*

Vi's answer surprised her. It was foolhardy, under the circumstances, but the ten-year-old reflex was too strong.

"Eat shit, motherfucker," she said.

Then she sighed. It didn't sound the same. The words were there, but the music they played to had left her a long time ago.

On the seven o'clock newscast that evening, Tom Ivery had four major stories:

The arrest of a young black woman who had committed some unspecified vandalism at the hospital.

The movement of Lindsay Keith from Draper Memorial to another facility somewhere else in the state. The authorities wouldn't say where, nor would they discuss rumors concerning the young man's health.

The fire that had destroyed the building Lindsay Keith lived in. Fortunately, no one had been seriously injured.

The arrival of a new tape.

If you wanted to believe Rines and Anderson, only the first two items were connected. The fact that a mentally disturbed person (so they called her) had gotten onto the very hospital floor where an important person in a sensational case was recovering, pointed to a need for greater security and secrecy.

The fire, they said, was a coincidence.

The tape was the most interesting item, as far as Tom was concerned, aside from the official coverup that was obviously going on. Tom hinted at the coverup on his broadcast, but he had no proof, so he had to go easy. He followed the advice of a new friend from NBC—if you've got an opinion about something, go ahead and put it in the story. Just attribute it to "an observer." That way you've got your speculation out in the open, without really violating impartiality. After all, if a reporter wasn't an observer, what was he? Tom's "observer" felt that far from being unable to identify their prisoner, the officials in charge were keeping her identity a secret for some obscure political reason.

Nobody he called was willing to comment on what the "observer" observed. Well, Chief Anderson had had a few comments, but Tom decided not to use them. They hadn't really been relevant, just some personal remarks about Tom. Besides, they didn't make any sense; things like, "You're drunk with power, boy," and "If I can't make you take it a little easier, maybe this will do it: You keep this up and you're going to get somebody killed. Could you live with that, Mr. Anchorman?"

Incredible hyperbole, of course. Tom could have made the chief look very bad, but he decided to go easy on him. The chief was under a lot of pressure and obviously out of his depth. The press always made a convenient whipping boy, but Tom still liked the old guy.

Besides, there were other things to think about. The new tape for instance. It had arrived at the station while Tom was out covering the fire and the hospital business, although by the time he'd arrived at the latter, the excitement was all over.

He'd returned to the station and found the tape. It looked exactly like the first one, same envelope, same simple address. The only difference was that this one had been picked up by Evelyn, the secretary at WLTN who had somehow managed to hear absolutely nothing about either the Fane case or finger-prints, Tom wasn't sure which. She'd put it in his tray without a second thought, and gone back to whomever it was she talked to on the telephone all day.

Tom went through the same procedure he had with the first tape. He even called Vince, the night engineer, to come in for some overtime (such was his new status at WLTN) to run it for him; Vince was much more competent than the day engineer.

It was from LEO again. He smiled in excitement as he listened. It was the person claiming to be Liz Fane again, saying that fingerprints or no fingerprints, she had nothing to do with the New America Liberation Army or anybody like them.

"The League to End Oppression decries this fraudulent attempt to thwart their demands for justice," the strangely flat voice intoned. "They reiterate their demands, and insist they be met in full."

Then came the cute part. "As indisputable proof of my identity, proof that cannot be falsified as fingerprint records can be, I offer the following facts, which can be known only to me and the Pig Fanes.

"When I was six years old, Herbert Fane bought a black Labrador retriever which I wanted to name Bootsy. He ignored my wishes, and called the dog Prince.

"Herbert Fane once called my mother Donna, which was the name of his first wife, instead of Sheila, which is her name. This happened on their anniversary. I was listening outside their room. Until now, even Herbert Fane did not know I knew this.

"Herbert Fane reads the Sunday newspaper in the following order: Business, Sports, News, Lifestyles, Arts, Magazine, Funnies.

"I challenge Herbert Fane to put questions for me through the media to prove that I am the real Elizabeth Fane. The answers—the real answers—will reach you. Once that is determined, Fane will meet the demands of the League to End Oppression, and I will be free to go."

Tom pointed out that "be released," as the first tape had it, and "be free to go," as it was recorded in the second tape from LEO, were not exactly the same thing. "Free to go" implied that she could stick around if she wanted to. Tom noted the parallel to the Patty Hearst case, where Miss Hearst had been brainwashed into remaining with her tormentors.

Chief Anderson wouldn't be too happy with that, either, Tom thought. It had taken the authorities over two years to find Patty Hearst.

But there was another sound on the tape, something in the background. It was faint, almost subliminal, but Tom was sensitive to it for some reason—it stuck in his mind and made him pay attention.

He had Vince play the tape for him a few times; finally Vince heard the sound too. Tom asked Vince if he could do something with the controls to make the sound more prominent.

Speaking in an unprecedented whole sentence, Vince said, "Sure, but I think we ought to let the cops in on this first."

Tom agreed, reluctantly, but as before, he had Vince make a copy. The police had come, heard, left. They didn't even try to keep Tom from playing the copy of the tape on the air. Tom had to forget his background noise for a while, until after his newscast.

The consensus was that the tape had already been en route when this morning's festivities occurred at the hospital and apartment house. At least that's the way Tom's "observer" had felt about it. The "observer" said that if the two incidents today had been terrorist inspired (and his tone said, Let's forget that *if*) they had been the work of NALA, because LEO would not have sent the tape until they had been accomplished if they were the ones who did them.

What with the chief's angry phone call, ("I'm warning you, you irresponsible twerp!") and congratulatory calls from "old friends" who had ignored him completely during his tough times, he didn't get back to Vince and the tape until eight o'clock in the evening.

Vince had been working in the meantime.

"Listen," he said as Tom entered the booth. The sound of the tape as Tom had originally heard it came from the speaker.

Vince punched a button and moved a slide-rule control. The woman's voice became muted, and the background noise became a rhythmic series of thumps. Another button, the voice all but vanished. Slowly, Vince increased the volume.

The thumping became constantly louder, but so did the hissing and other extraneous noise picked up when the tape was recorded. Vince turned to another row of buttons. "Filters," he said. As he hit each one, the hissing was reduced, the thumps remained. When he hit the last filter, the sound was quite recognizable on the tape.

Amazing, Tom thought. *My subconscious was so attuned to that sound, I picked it up right through everything else. Not another person in the world would have been able to do what I've just done. Not for any special reason; it's just that nobody else has had exactly the past I've had.*

He listened to it some more, considering what it might mean. *Fsssssh-chka-BOOM-chk, Fsssssh-chka-BOOM-chk.* Only one thing in the world made that noise. The Obscene Machine. The casing former out at the Fane plant.

This tape had been recorded somewhere near the sound of that ridiculous noise. Somewhere on land owned by Herbert Fane himself. Tom was sure of it.

He thought about the implications. Fane might know all *about* this, might be a party to some monstrous deception, as the NALA tape charged. What a story, for God's sake.

Or Fane might know *nothing* about it. The terrorists might be hiding out under his very nose, having left their first hideout for a new one in a place the authorities had already searched and forgotten about. That was an even *better* story.

Tom thanked Vince and ran for the newsroom. He was in the middle of the opening paragraph of his story—he'd given himself a promotion to "informed observer"—when a terrible thought hit him.

What if he turned out to be wrong? He didn't see how he could be. He *knew* that sound. But still, what if? He'd better go out there and have a discreet look around, first. The story would wait; the story was absolutely his. Nobody else could get on it even if they thought to, which they wouldn't.

Besides, if Tom were to come back with confirmation, he wouldn't have to be an observer, informed or otherwise. He would be a goddamn *hero*; he could write his own ticket to New York. He could walk right into CBS News as a *correspondent*.

But if he went off half-cocked on this, and turned out to be wrong, what would he be? A kid who got too big for his britches and got knocked back to size. People would laugh at him; he'd be through in Draper, let alone New York.

Tom wouldn't allow that. He'd chewed on failure for almost three years, from the time he left college, through the factory and WLTN until this week. He hadn't gotten the last of it spit out yet, but it was coming. He wasn't going to take the chance of biting off any more. Not just now.

No, best to check it out. *Nobody's going to beat you to the air or into print with it,* he told himself. *If you're right, the world is yours. If you're wrong, we'll just tear up this little sheet in the typewriter, and make believe "informed observer" never said a word.*

Having made his decision, Tom put the possibility of failure out of his mind. He wished Vince good night, told him to refer all calls for him to his home, where he would be in about an hour, then left to find the last jewel of his fortune.

It was rather primitive compared with the cozy little house they'd stayed in previously, but Leo rather liked it here. There was no air conditioning, but it was cooler out in the country, anyway. They did have electricity—Leo had tapped into one of the power lines that fed the factory, but Leo had no worries that the electricity would be missed. He used it exclusively to power the television for the nightly news, which he watched under his sleeping bag, using headphones, to keep the light and sound from giving them away. The sleeping bags on concrete floors were uncomfortable after the soft bedding in the home of the late Roy, but the plumbing was hooked up here, so there was no need to use any of the bottled water they'd brought with them. The sanitary facilities worked, too, but they made sure to flush them only at night.

There was, unfortunately, the incessant noise of the factory, just across the way, but Leo treated that as an incentive to accomplish his mission that much sooner. One consolation was that the noise next door covered the noise of the chain hoist that ran through the shaft in the heart of this building. It had made getting supplies up here a lot easier.

The best part about hiding out in the abandoned coke mill, though, was that there were many places in it Leo found conducive to thought, odd little corners, or windows with exceptionally nice views he could gaze at while he considered things.

Right now, Leo was looking (being careful at the same time not to reveal himself) from a window on the forest side of the factory, away from the buildings active in Fane's business. The side away from the town, away from the parking lot.

He was thinking about Candy, and how sad it was that her efforts had failed. If she had succeeded, the whole job would have been done; as it was, there were still serious obstacles. If Candy could be believed (and there was no reason to doubt her), the authorities had bagged themselves a real live terrorist, this Viola (Leo had heard of her) who had been the speaking voice (as opposed to the groaning voice, which, as Candy had revealed, belonged to their little Daisy Mae in a moment of sexual joy) on the diabolically masterful bogus tape.

Having caught her, they would think a terrorist in the hand was worth an unlimited number of them on tape, and would henceforth take the word of NALA for gospel. Unless Leo could do something about it.

Leo sighed. It was useless to waste time in regrets, of course, but it would have been nice if Candy had been able to inform him of some of what she'd found out today before he'd gone ahead and sent the challenge tape. They had no phone— that was an incidental inconvenience of this place.

Leo looked up at a sudden light in the woods. That was an incidental *convenience* of the place. From the fourth floor, where they had established their quarters, they could see anyone who might wish to pay them a visit. Not that this was necessarily someone paying them a visit. It was a warm summer evening, and the woods was a popular spot for juvenile lovers.

Leo picked up his train of thought. The adversaries, whoever they were, had done an excellent job. Quick and ruthless, quite unAmerican. The torching of Lindsay Keith's apartment had been brilliant. It would take investigators (if there were to be investigations this thorough) weeks to determine if there even *were* video tapes in that apartment. The tapes themselves were lost for good. And the investigators, unable to prove it, would be likely to forget all about Candy's tip.

That, and the sudden inaccessibility of Lindsay Keith, wrote the end of Keith's video tapes as a useful resource. A secret communication from the local deep-cover agent had told Leo about two things. First (and this was mere reassurance), that Herbert Fane knew nothing of any counterplot, and was involved in none. He was as puzzled as Leo was, and so was the deep-cover agent. Secondly, it had been Clifford Driscoll's idea, that elusive man from the Defense Department, to move Lindsay Keith, telling no one, not even his family, where.

Leo knew from Candy, who had heard it from an acquaintance at the hospital, that it had been a fairly simple matter to save Keith's life. Because of the way it had been administered, the insulin had not reached a sufficient concentration in his blood to do anything more than place him in a mild shock that was reversed by giving him large injections of sugar solution. Leo smiled. For the good he could do them now, Keith might as well be dead.

Leo felt, fatalistically, that the personal-knowledge challenge was his best chance to achieve this project's success. They *did* have custody of Daisy Mae, all stratagems by the adversaries to the contrary, and while you might be able to counterfeit someone's fingerprints (though Leo would still like to know how) you couldn't counterfeit her memory. Herbert Fane would ask his questions and be convinced.

If that didn't work, there was one last way to convince him. It would work, but it was extremely dangerous, both to the mission itself, and to Leo's personnel. Leo didn't mind the danger, but he didn't especially want to die. He was realist enough to know, though, that he would be much more likely to die at the hands of his employers if he were to be responsible for the failure of the Cronus Project.

There was another flash of light in the woods. More than a flash. It shone right on the building for seconds at a time. Once or twice, the light in Leo's eyes changed shape from a cone to a point, which meant that the light had played directly over the window he watched from.

That was enough for Leo. He left the window, and went back to the interior rooms, foremen's offices during the plant's active days. The rooms were blind to the outside, so it had been safe to fit them with lights.

There was light only from Waldo's room right now. The move had upset him, and the rooms were enough like closets for Waldo's damaged brain to imagine that Leo was going back on his promise. Leo would never do that. He depended on

Waldo's trust; it made it possible to control the giant. Leo had let Waldo have a light; therefore, the room wasn't a closet. Waldo had remained tractable and quiet.

Leo passed Waldo's room, and the room shared by Candy and Daisy Mae. He stopped outside the room closest to the stairs, the one Georgia had insisted on occupying. He knocked softly—it didn't take much to wake her—in the code they'd agreed on.

"All right," Georgia said. When she opened the door, she was fully dressed in army fatigues. Her dark eyes were already alert. A very valuable person to have around.

Leo brought Georgia to the window and showed her the woods. The light had moved considerably closer to the building now, but it flashed less and less frequently.

Georgia nodded. "Hide him in the woods?" she asked.

"No," Leo said, "bring him here, first. We have to find out if anyone is going to come looking for him."

Georgia nodded again, went into her room and picked up the carbine lying on her mattress, then left to do her job.

In the woods, Tom Ivery alternated between fear and irritation. Fear, because the woods at night were creepy, and that's all there was to it. Besides, he kept telling himself he wouldn't try to *do* anything about the LEO if he found them here, he would just get some evidence that they were, and beat it back to town. Hell, he would even tell the police first. He would even wait until they made the arrests before he broke the story. As long as they would guarantee his exclusive. But he wasn't finding any evidence—there were no signs the building was occupied, at least not from this distance. And the closer he got, the more fear he felt.

The more irritation, too, because what if he was getting himself all worked up over nothing? He was irritated to think he might have sent himself on a wild goose chase, and he was even more irritated to discover this fear in himself. A reporter on a story wasn't supposed to be afraid of anything.

So Tom crept closer to the building. It occurred to him at one point that he really ought to be zigging and zagging through the woods. He rejected the idea; he was already finding it hard enough just to follow the path without using his flashlight too much.

He had decided he would go another twenty yards closer to the building and take a good hard look. If he couldn't see footprints on the path, or a recently forced lock, or *something* that would suggest someone had been here recently, he would forget the whole thing and go home. That is, if he could *tell* when he'd gone twenty yards in this damned jungle.

That was when he heard the voice. It was a woman's voice, and quiet. All it said was, "Don't make a sound," which was superfluous, anyway, because the second after he heard it, a hand was clapped over his mouth. Nothing that had happened in Tom Ivery's life scared him as much as that voice.

Not even when the hand let him go, and the short, nasty-looking firearm was poked into him instead.

He was a born newsman, Leo had to give him that. From the moment Georgia ushered him into Leo's presence, Tom Ivery had asked questions.

How long had they been here? How did they know the layout of the place so well? Did they really have Liz Fane here with them? *I guess I'm a hostage, now, too, huh?*

"Not that you'll get the kind of ransom for me you'll get for the Fane girl," he added. Leo could see that the boy had part of his brain reserved for calculating percentages on movie deals for the book he would write about his experiences.

Leo smiled blandly. "Well, we can answer one of your questions, Mr. Ivery, but you'll have to answer ours."

He got a rueful smile in return. "I don't have much choice, do I?"

"None at all, Mr. Ivery. Bring your flashlight, please."

The woman who had captured him in the woods (and Tom found it embarrassing now that she was such a *small* woman) handed him back his flashlight, and Tom walked between them like the prisoner he was to a small room on the same floor.

The bony blond guy, who was obviously the boss here, threw open the door to the room and told Tom to use his flashlight.

Tom saw two women just roused from sleep. Their limbs were arranged in an artistic tangle; they squinted into the light. One of them was definitely Liz Fane. Tom said, "Liz?"

The man in charge took the flashlight away and shone it on the newsman. A woman's voice from inside the room said, "Tommy Ivery? What are you doing here?"

Tom was convinced. Those were the words, and that was the tone, that Tom had heard nearly every time Liz Fane had ever spoken to him, usually when he turned up at the Tennis Club to cover one function or another.

"Go back to sleep, ladies," the man said.

"Okay, Leo," said Liz Fane's voice. The door was closed, and they went back to another room, a big open place with a wide-open window.

"Have you got her on drugs?" Tom asked.

"Speak quietly, Mr. Ivery," the one called Leo said. "It's much too warm in here if we have to close the window."

"Have you?" Tom repeated in a whisper.

"For now. In a few more weeks they won't be necessary."

"Are you—"

"Enough questions for now, Mr. Ivery. I want you to answer some for me."

"Of course," Tom said. "I told you I would. There's no reason for this woman to stand here pointing a rifle at me."

"It's a carbine, actually. And I wouldn't think of asking her to stop. She has a very strong sense of responsibility. The sooner you answer questions, the sooner it will stop."

Tom knew when he was licked. He shrugged in resignation.

"How did you find us?" Leo demanded. "That, as you might imagine, is the question I want answered. And we'll stay here until I'm happy with your reply."

The tone was more ominous than the words; it was enough to end any willingness Tom might have had to try to fudge up a story. He simply told Leo the truth about the background noise on the tape and how he had recognized it because of his experience at the plant next door.

"You don't really have anything to worry about," Tom concluded. "There's no way anybody could recreate my reasoning." Tom hoped his face was under control, but right here, he was lying. There *was* a way, if anybody knew where to look back at the station. It was a long shot, and it would take some better-than-competent mental gymnastics, but it *might* come through. Tom had no serious objection to being rescued. That would be a pretty terrific story, too—an eyewitness account of the last days of the terrorists who had kidnapped Elizabeth Fane.

There were so many things Tom wanted to ask; his mind was so full of questions, he really had no room for fear. What did they think of these other guys, the NALA? Who had done the business at the apartment house; at the hospital? Did they expect Liz Fane to join up with them? What was their exact political philosophy, if anything? And many more.

Tom was getting so excited, he almost forgot to listen to his host.

". . . inclined to agree with you, Mr. Ivery," Leo said. "I don't think your visit will lead to a lot of others."

Leo sighed, very ostentatiously. "You know, Mr. Ivery, I wish you had found us earlier, while we were staying in that house. I would have been delighted to have let you see Miss Fane alive and well, then let you go forth to bear witness to that fact."

Tom hadn't even thought of that. His face lit up. He could have this on the air *tomorrow*. He could—

"Unfortunately," Leo said, "we have no other hiding place to go to, now. You would, of course, tell the authorities where we are, and we would still have to be here when they arrived, or simply give up our mission and scatter. You can see, I hope, why I can't let that happen."

It had been too much to hope for, anyway. Tom said, "Of course."

Leo's answering smile seemed a little sad. "I'm glad. Mr. Ivery, have you enjoyed yourself over the last couple of days?"

Tom couldn't resist a grin. "Am I that obvious?"

"Good," Leo said. "I hoped that would be the case. You have come far, and since I was the one who sent you that tape, I like to think you stood on my shoulders to get there. Mine and Mr. Driscoll's of course—he let you ask the question at the first press conference that brought you to my attention."

"Just doing my job," Tom said.

"We all try to, Mr. Ivery. But you have reached the happiest time of anybody's career, the proving of yourself, where you have opened up the most possibilities for yourself. And none of them has closed down. Not many people end their lives at such a fulfilling moment."

Leo gestured to the woman behind Tom.

It took Tom a eternal split-second for it to sink in. *End their what? End their lives? Lives? My life? But I'm just getting started. I just started living this week, for God's sake!*

Tom put up his hands as if to call time out. "No," he said reasonably. "Wait a minute." But Leo was already turning away.

Tom gave up on him, and spun around to try his luck with the woman. He turned just in time to see the nasty, square end of the rifle butt heading for his face.

No, he thought, his reporter's instinct for accuracy asserting itself to the end, a carbine butt. Then a bolt of lightning shot from the bridge of his nose to infinity, and he never thought another thing.

Chapter Nine

SUNDAY AFTERNOON, TWENTY AFTER ONE. DRISCOLL, wearing white jacket and black tie (it was amazing what the Agency could come up with on short notice) paced up and down in Chief Anderson's office like a fugitive from E. Phillips Oppenheim or Ian Fleming, waiting for the phone to ring.

He'd had to come—he'd passed on the marathon and fruitless (as Driscoll knew they would be) sessions with their prize captive from the hospital. They would have been suspicious if he'd skipped this, too.

He wasn't the only one there, but he was the only one so magnificent. Chief Anderson was close—he wore his dress uniform in anticipation of the charity function later that afternoon. Rines wore FBI standard gray suit, muted tie.

Herbert Fane looked like a slob. He wore wrinkled gray slacks and a plaid shirt. He hadn't shaved recently, and his socks didn't match. He stared at the telephone as if it were a bomb that would give three seconds warning before it went off.

Driscoll had a vision of Robin Payne, who, everyone knew, was waiting at his hotel room for this to be over with, so that he could pick her up and take her to the Community Fund bash to fill in for her aunt and uncle. What nobody but Driscoll knew was that sometime in the next five minutes, she would have to pick up the secure phone in there, call this office, and put across the riskiest charade he'd thought of yet.

They were going to the ball. Mr. Driscoll, for the record, had decided it wouldn't be too dangerous for Robin to attend. Off the record, it was simply the easiest and least suspicious way to get Robin away from her aunt and uncle at the important time.

He thought of her the way he'd left her, lovely and sophisticated in a summer gown printed with soft blue flowers that left her back and shoulders bare. Her hair was tied back in a loose ponytail, and it shone with red highlights in the hot summer sun.

She'd probably twisted her hair into a tangle by now, and sweated right through the gown. Stage fright, Driscoll had called it. Robin had said nonsense, she never got stage fright.

Herbert Fane had announced his questions yesterday. They were given to the media at eight o'clock. The media, as usual, had eaten it up, but much to everyone's surprise, one of the most familiar mouths was not there to be fed. Tom Ivery, News Demon, was not to be found.

The terrorists, if they so desired (and they had to, if they wanted their demands to be taken seriously) were invited to call today between one and one-thirty.

There were three questions:

1. Aside from the obvious meaning, what did the word Orientals *mean to the Fane family, and why?*

2. What did Liz Fane say to her mother immediately after winning her first local tennis tournament at age nine?

3. What had Liz invented in the Fane kitchen that caused a cook to quit?

Driscoll hadn't worried about coming up with the answers. Herbert Fane, who was sinking deeper and deeper into a haze of frustration and confusion every day, had had to consult his family to come up with the questions. Driscoll had a direct pipeline into the Fane family. His mythical, but highly nasty, New America Liberation Army would have the answers, all right.

It was the presentation that might be tricky. The League to End Oppression would have the answers, too. Their pipeline was even more direct—Liz Fane herself. Who would undoubtedly supply the answers in her own voice.

Who had, in fact, done so five minutes ago. The voice was as flat, zonked out, and empty as it had been on the tapes.

Driscoll, in fact, was convinced what he had just heard was a tape. The voice had talked over all interruptions and responded to no additional questions. It just reeled off the three answers and hung up. A cassette recorder held up to a pay phone, nothing more. It meant that Liz hadn't been brainwashed sufficiently yet for them to trust her with an open phone. A potentially useful piece of information.

It had been amazing, the effect that ghost of a voice had on the girl's father. Anderson had been ready to call a doctor for him. He did everything but tear his hair out in anxiety—he did clutch at his heart and wail. Driscoll hadn't thought WASPs did that.

This had all been according to plan. Driscoll knew LEO wouldn't call until close to the time limit. The wait was intended to build up the tension. And he had known the voice offering the answers would be dull, flat, drugged, lifeless. He'd planned on it. He wanted it to serve as contrast to the Liz Fane to be offered by the NALA.

If she didn't chicken out.

Robin *could* back out if she wanted to, and she knew it. Driscoll hadn't stationed Miles with her to force her to do it at gunpoint or anything. Her performance wouldn't have been worth a damn if he had. Driscoll knew that for this bit to work, for Robin to convince Herbert Fane that she was his daughter, she had to motivate herself. This would take one terrific performance. And if it didn't go over, they were sunk.

Driscoll looked at his watch, adjusted his tie for the fifteenth time. She should have called by now. Robin had been so cool when he'd picked her up at her uncle's place, he thought it would be a piece of cake for her. But here it was, the last minute—at one thirty-one now, actually *after* the last minute—and still no call.

Driscoll tried to make a plan to deal with the ascendancy of LEO in the credibility sweepstakes, but his brain was diverting itself to measures to take to get the now-useless Robin Payne out of the way without actually killing her because she knew too much.

The phone rang. Driscoll, who had been trained to be surprised by nothing, jumped.

The chief picked up the phone. "You're late," he said.

The voice came through the phone speaker husky, slightly raw, as if it had done a lot of crying. It quavered a little, as though it might start crying again any minute. "They . . . they almost didn't let me call. . . . Is my father there?"

"Herbert Fane is here." Anderson was conceding nothing to anybody.

Herbert Fane was, though. If he had been stricken by the first call of the afternoon, he was devastated by this one. He had his eyes closed and his mouth open, gasping for air. Driscoll put a hand on his shoulder and squeezed to stop him from crying out anything prematurely. The solicitous, wait-and-see official. Driscoll was playing his part.

Not nearly as well as Robin was playing hers. Driscoll was amazed. Her voice was basically similar to her cousin's, of course, and she'd had a lifetime to study the right inflections, but there was more to it. There were layers of background and personality behind Robin's interpretation—a stranger listening in could have limned the proud girl humbled and afraid, and terribly alone.

He looked at Rines. The FBI man wasn't buying it, at least not all of it. He knew what Driscoll knew, that to fall into the hands of terrorists was a mind numbing, ultimately a mind destroying experience.

The Chief seemed to be buying it, but he hadn't had Rines' or Driscoll's experience. Herbert Fane was sold. As Driscoll had figured, he needed to believe that something remained of his daughter's personality. It offered more comfort.

The questions seemed almost superfluous by now, but Robin supplied the answers anyway.

"We call Christmas tree decorations 'orientals.' The first Christmas Robbie came to stay with us, she helped decorate the tree. She—she promised not to break any orientals. Instead of ornaments. We used to . . . used to laugh about it every Christmas . . ."

Herbert Fane nodded his head. He took a pad and wrote

on it, "ALWAYS CALLED HER ROBBIE." Driscoll decided to raise his amateur agent's salary. It was a nice touch.

"When I won the junior tournament, I asked Mother if I could play for money now, or did I have to wait until I won a few more."

Again, Herbert Fane nodded.

"I don't know the answer to the third quest—" There was a thump and a little scream of pain. The voice came again, as though speaking to a third party. "I *don't.* I think it's the— Daddy? Is it the sandwiches? That Dora or Flora or whatever quit over?"

Fane was nodding his head off. Driscoll nearly had to put a hand over the man's mouth to keep him quiet. Chief Anderson told her to go on.

"I didn't invent this, though, I learned it from a girl at school. Peanut butter and . . . and dill pickles with brown sugar. It sounds disgusting but it's good, and, oh, Daddy, I want to go home and make some more of them. Please don't let them kill—"

And the receiver was banged down.

Herbert Fane took in enough air for a shout, but when he finally let it go, it was the softest of whispers. "That was Liz," he said. "That was her. The factory stays open."

Rines and Anderson didn't even bother to ask him if he was sure. Rines checked with the phone company for a possible trace, but he didn't seem surprised when they told him no chance.

Driscoll feigned a helpless shrug. "I have to go help a woman show a flag," he said.

He didn't go pick her up immediately, though. He stopped first at the radio station. They recognized him and let him in. In the newsroom, he found Tom Ivery's sister, still answering phone calls and taking notes. She was torn between worry and irritation, leaning toward the former when she found out he hadn't been at police headquarters to get the news about the phone calls his fellow journalists were receiving at that moment from Anderson and Rines.

Driscoll told her not to worry; if her brother missed that one, it was only because he was after a bigger story. It seemed to cheer her up. Driscoll just wished he could believe it himself. Ivery had taken off after something, Driscoll was sure of it. He was sure Ivery had found it, too. A boy who could attract so much attention in one week wasn't going to disappear just like that. Not when there was a big story to get.

Ivery had left a sheet of paper in the typewriter, the machine, Ivery's sister told him, no one else was allowed to touch. Driscoll reached out and touched it, ratcheting the paper up so he could read the words.

It had been intended for broadcast—the style left no doubt about that. It was the usual mixture of incomplete sentences and qualifying phrases that made up so much of the news on the air. It had been typed all in capital letters, as if to remind the announcer to say it loud and clear:

SPECULATION IN THE LIZ FANE KIDNAP-
PING, INFORMED OBSERVERS BELIEVE THAT
JUST AS LIZ FANE WAS TAKEN CAPTIVE BY
TERRORISTS BEFORE HER MOTHER'S EYES,
SHE MAY NOW BE HIDDEN UNDER HER

And that was how it ended. Under her *what*? And who was "her" that second time, Liz or her mother? Driscoll looked at the clock, and realized he couldn't go into it right now. He pulled the paper from the machine and stuffed it in his pocket.

The voice that greeted his knock at the hotel was as dead and sullen as Liz Fane's. "Who is it?"

"It's me, Driscoll."

He heard the bolt being undone, the lock turning. The door opened. Robin Payne, who's been a soft, beautiful, summer-princess when he'd left her, was now a wreck. Her eyes were red and the skin of her face was blotched. Her hair had come undone. It stood up on one side in a tangled mass. The dress had been replaced by a rumpled towel. She looked miserable.

"I was about to take a shower," she said.

"It went over perfectly," he said. "You were terrific."

He caught her hand two inches from his face. It wasn't a slap coming this time, it was claws. He reached out and grabbed the other wrist as a precaution.

"What the hell is this for?" he asked.

"You *bastard!*" she said. "You cold, miserable *bastard.* Do you know what you put me through this afternoon? What you made me do to my uncle?"

"I didn't make you put in the business about 'Robbie,'" he told her. "Or the little bumps and thumps that made it sound like Liz being beaten while she was talking to him. Even the real terrorists didn't do that."

"The scene demanded it," Robin said simply.

Driscoll looked at her for a second, then started to laugh. Robin squirmed, but she wasn't nearly strong enough to break her hands free of his grasp. The anger cleared her eyes, though, and the agitation shook the towel free.

"You *bastard!*" she said again. "I'm an *actress!* I can't do a bad job, or a half-good job, I have to do my *best!* I can't just *pretend* to be somebody, I have to *be* her! I have to feel the feelings. Today I had to be Liz. I had to be trapped; tortured. I had to take off my pretty things and my makeup and let down my hair before I could do it, too. Laugh at that, if you want to."

Driscoll did not laugh. "I told you, you did a terrific job."

Anger left her unaware of her nakedness, unaware of her relative physical weakness. It didn't matter—she was lacerating him with her eyes.

"I *hate* you for making me feel these things! I must have had my uncle half insane. More. He's already half insane with fear for Liz. Maybe I've pushed him across the finish line."

"It's like the crisis of a fever," Driscoll said.

"You have a phrase for everything. I'm through listening. I know I'm trapped. I know you'll probably kill me if I try to pull out—"

"Nobody's going to kill you, Robin. For God's sake, stop it." Driscoll wished he knew if he were lying.

She snorted at him. "I won't risk it. I'm too much of a coward. But I hate you for making me experience these things, and I hate you for making me manipulate my poor uncle that way!"

Driscoll looked into angry eyes. "And you hate yourself for enjoying it," he said.

"*No!*"

"Yes," Driscoll said quietly. "You're too good at it not to."

She denied it so vehemently she cried. She jumped up and down, and twisted her body in an effort to get her hands free, then cried some more in frustration.

"Just look me in the eye and deny it," he said. "Be honest with me, be honest with yourself; then tell me you didn't feel like strutting with power even as you pitied your uncle for what you were doing to him."

She looked him in the eye. "I hate you, God damn you! If you're what our country needs to win, maybe we *deserve* to lose! You stinking—"

"I said deny it."

She stared at him. Tears ran down her face, off her chin, down between her breasts. She was showering herself with tears. Her mouth opened, then closed. It opened again. This time she made a sound, a little "ah—ah." She closed it again. She stared and cried some more.

"I live with it every day of my life," Driscoll told her. "And they won't let me stop doing it. I'm not sure I could now, even if they'd let me. I know how you feel. If you want to hate me, get in line. I'd hoped you'd feel a little sorry for me."

She looked at him for a second. Then she said, "You twist *everything*! Sorry for *you*! I hope the Russians kill you, you lying, cheating—"

He closed her mouth with a kiss, a hard and intense one. She fought it, then gave in. She never stopped crying. Driscoll's face was wet with her tears. He let go of her hands, and put his arms around her, touching the hot, smooth skin of her back.

She didn't claw at him again, she just held tight to him.

Driscoll decided they would be a little late to the charity dinner. He backed off and undid his tie.

Waldo caught a rat for him, and Leo gave him the knife back as a reward. Waldo was not to go near the body of the reporter with it. Leo warned Waldo that there was going to be a loud noise soon, so Waldo shouldn't be alarmed.

Waldo thanked Leo profoundly and promised he'd obey. He cast a wistful glance at the unbloodied body on his way back to his cubicle, but he turned his eyes from it resolutely and contented himself with watching the way the light gleamed off the blade of his knife.

Leo forgot about him for the time being. He felt the rat squirm in his gloved hand, looked at it with distaste. He hurried to get on with his demonstration.

"Daisy Mae," he said to Elizabeth Fane, "I want you to pay close attention to this."

Liz started when he said her name. It would be her name from now on. She was going to become Daisy Mae irrevocably and forever this afternoon.

She was functioning under only a light dose of drugs this afternoon, because she needed to be aware enough to absorb the warning he was about to give her. There would be instructions later, too, and she had to be able to follow them to the letter. The demonstration he was about to give her would get that point across.

It wouldn't have been necessary if the damnable *adversaries* hadn't topped him (again) at the personal question game. More tapes on the radio. Another loss for LEO, and for Leo as well. Herbert Fane saying he was more convinced than ever that NALA was the real group, and he and his lawyers were working on meeting their demands.

It was a conspiracy to make Leo look like a fool. They kept taking away his options. They would, perhaps, without even knowing what they were doing, shoot down the pilot operation for the Cronus Project. To make Leo fail.

He couldn't afford to fail! His employers wouldn't allow it. Leo didn't analyze the feeling he had when he realized that his life now depended on something that he did not control. He didn't have to. It was unfamiliar, but he knew what it was. It was fear, and he didn't like it.

Well, he thought, *it wouldn't last long.* Today, he would take back the initiative, with a vengeance, and Cronus would succeed. Leo would succeed. *This* plan couldn't fail, if he prepared carefully, and concentrated on it one step at a time.

So. On with the demonstration. He fastened a cardboard cylinder about two inches long and an inch in diameter to the rat with a rubber band. The cylinder had a small metal device taped to one end.

"Daisy Mae, watch closely." Daisy Mae reached for Candy's hand for support. That was all right, Leo wanted their guest to have close ties with the group.

Leo let the rat go in the middle of the big room. It ran for a wall. Leo took something that looked like a small radio from his pocket and twisted a dial. There was an explosion, and the rat disappeared in a wet pink cloud.

Leo took Daisy Mae over to look. She stared and kept wetting her lips. She held on to Candy for dear life, but she listened.

"What do we have?" Leo said. "Some bits of flesh stuck to the wall. What's this piece? Ah. That's the tail and a piece of leg and hindquarter. What's that you have Georgia, the head?"

Georgia held out a gloved hand with a blackened lump in it.

"Yes," Leo said. "A little charred, but recognizable. Quite a noise, wasn't it? We're lucky this is Sunday, and no one is close enough to wonder why the noise would be coming from this vacant building.

"But these things are easy enough to acquire. Fireworks; people call them M-Eighties, and children buy them all over the country. Georgia just added a remote detonator, and the rat suffered the consequences of an explosion equal to that of a quarter-stick of dynamite."

He looked at Georgia and nodded. Georgia got something from a paper bag.

"Daisy Mae," Leo said, "lift up your hair."

She stared at him and shook her head involuntarily from side to side.

Candy said, "Leo, go easy."

Leo smiled. "No one's going to hurt her. This is just insurance. We've accepted Daisy Mae as a sister and comrade. We're her friends. We *are* your friends, aren't we, Daisy Mae?"

She nodded.

"Say it."

"Yes, Leo. My friends."

"Your *only* friends. Everyone you knew before loves money more than you. They think you're a threat to them now, Daisy Mae. They'll kill you if you give them the chance. They're *pigs*."

"Pigs," Daisy Mae said.

"But today you'll show them. Lift up your hair."

She reached behind her and lifted the hair. There was a grace in the gesture that was part of the old Liz, Leo noticed.

Leo pressed adhesive tape to Daisy Mae's bare neck, right at the top of the spine. It bulged; white shone through the hair when she let it down again. Not enough to show up in a photograph.

"That's insurance, Daisy Mae, that's all it is. It insures you won't be weak, won't let them fool you. This is more complicated than the one the rat had. If you try to betray us, I'll set it off. If you try to remove it, *you'll* set it off. If you hurt me, I'll let go of the control, and *that* will set it off."

"I'll be good," she said. She almost whined it. It was the most animation she had shown in weeks. She reminded him suddenly of Waldo.

"We know you will, Daisy Mae," Leo said.

"Can Candy help me?"

"Up to a point," Leo said. "She will be there to help you through the beginning. But Candy can't come inside with us. She has to go to work."

"Oh. That's right," Daisy Mae said. "Candy told me."

Leo felt cheered. This was going quite well. He might have Candy permanently reduce the dosages they were giving their guest. She might become a useful member of the troupe. A little dividend from the Cronus Project.

"Now here's—*don't touch it,* Daisy Mae!"

He watched with approval as she pulled her hands away from her neck and clasped them chastely in her lap.

Leo began again. He felt good, now. It was going to work. "Now here's what I want you to do. . . ."

Chapter Ten

NEVER HAD SO MANY PEOPLE ATTENDED THE DRAPER, Pennsylvania Community Fund Annual Dinner. Driscoll knew that because he'd heard a mink-draped matron say so in the parking lot on the way in.

He and Robin were among the late arrivals, but not so late as to make an *entrance* when they got there. What had happened back at the hotel had been quick, but intense, like a thermite charge. It burned off emotions that might have been difficult to deal with during the evening in one bright flash. That wasn't to say Robin was suddenly reconciled to him or to what she had learned about herself, but she wasn't balancing on the edge of a dagger, either.

One of the reasons people were showing up so late was something Driscoll's father called the Rubberneck Factor. The phone calls and the quiz had freshened the scent of excitement about the Liz Fane case, and everyone (or many of them; a few refrained ostentatiously) with reason to be at the Lakeside Club that afternoon took a stroll around the grounds before going inside. "Look, Margaret, this is the bush that Spanish fellow shot from." "Liz fell right here, how horrible for Sheila." That kind of thing.

Robin, through some kind of magic—theatrical or just feminine—had managed to become cool and serene and beautiful again. She'd also developed a case of selective deafness, smiling politely at everyone, responding in general terms to expressions of sympathy and concern, resolutely ignoring the remarks that weren't so kind, the ones whispered just loud enough to be heard in passing. Driscoll's informal tally showed about fifty percent of the whisperers thought Robin would get Fane's money now that Liz was obviously lost to them, and fifty percent thought it would go to charity. Opinion was also running about sixty-forty against Robin's dress.

"What did they want me to wear," Robin murmured to him at one point, "black?"

Inside, everyone was elegant and charming. The volume in the room was sufficient to indicate that the early arrivals were slightly drunk.

Robin stood and looked. The thin smile was still on her lips when she said, "This is Liz's life, this kind of thing. She grew up right into this." Driscoll had a hard time deciding whether Robin was showing pity or contempt. Not envy, he thought. Robin had been raised to the same kind of life, but rejected it.

Robin was mildly perturbed when she learned she and her escort were to sit on the dais in front of the plate glass window overlooking the pool, but there was nothing she could do about it. It was her Aunt Sheila's traditional seat. Dinner was a buffet, all cold stuff, all expensive-to-extravagant. Tortellini salad (meat or cheese), crab and lobster in huge piles, vegetable salads, cold salmon mousse, white meat of some sort of poultry or other. Driscoll couldn't believe it was anything as mundane as chicken. Sorbet in champagne glasses, champagne in champagne glasses.

Then speeches. If nothing had happened later, the speeches would have been the worst part.

The emcee must have been running for something, because he refused to concede that he couldn't please the crowd's appetite for sensation and still keep a promise made to Herbert Fane not to mention the kidnapping. He tried to work around it by introducing Robin as "representing a brave family," but that wasn't enough. He was slogging his way through a mountain of circumlocutions when Driscoll tuned out.

He was thinking about Robin, and something she'd said as

they were getting dressed again. By then, she *was* feeling sorry for him (something that made Driscoll very uncomfortable, despite what he'd told her), and she'd said, "I still don't like this; I don't know how you can stand it, if you're telling the truth about yourself. It's a cliché, I know, but I feel all . . . all eaten up inside."

Eaten up, Driscoll thought. The way the smiling faces around them ate white shreds of crabmeat from the ends of silver forks. The way Liz Fane had been swallowed up by the mysterious Cronus Project. The way his father's world had consumed him, devoured his life and whatever natural personality he might have had. The way the god Cronus had devoured his children. The way he himself had sucked innocent Robin into his business because that was the most efficient way to achieve the Objective.

Because Clifford Driscoll, or whatever he happened to be calling himself that week, *always* attained the Objective. Except the objective of freedom from being who he was. What his father had planned him from a sperm to be.

His objective at this moment was simply to make sense out of Tom Ivery's last message. He remembered the phrases as he had read them, in emphatic captials. TAKEN BY TERRORISTS BEFORE HER MOTHER'S EYES, Ivery had written, HIDDEN UNDER HER— Maybe that was all there was to it, Driscoll thought foolishly. Maybe Liz Fane was hidden under her mother.

He made himself stop. What he didn't need right now was whimsy. He needed some kind of handle on Cronus. The father of the gods. The one who had eaten his children.

He stopped again, chasing a slippery notion through the wrinkles in his brain, but it was gone before he could catch up with it.

Cronus, thought by some to represent the god of Time. He had certainly blessed the opposition, Driscoll thought. That snatch was a work of art—the timing of it had baffled the FBI, the police, and Clifford Driscoll of the nameless Agency. How *had* the terrorists known their victim would be there then?

The elusive idea took another jaunt through his brain. It

moved more slowly this time, teasing him, but it stayed out of reach.

Driscoll was becoming so obviously irritated Robin asked him in a whisper what the matter was. He never got to answer her, because that was the instant the window behind them shattered.

A half hour before, Leo had told his little Gang of Four what he was thinking. "We want to arrive during the speeches, when the media people are wired up for action. We want photographs of this, and films and sound. Of course, the local radio station will not be represented." Leo smiled. "But the local newspaper will, and perhaps some of the bigger outlets will be there, too. I'm sure at least one of the Philadelphia TV stations will be there, if only to obtain films of our Daisy Mae's charming cousin." He smiled again, and went back to loading his carbine.

Georgia had her carbine. Daisy Mae had been given a small, nasty thing like a Sten gun. It fired a hundred bullets in a second. Leo had a reason for giving it to her, but Daisy Mae had no idea what it might be. The gun terrified her even more than the bomb on her neck. She would never be able to reload it. She'd told Leo so (respectfully), and he'd told her not to worry about it—they only wanted her to fire one burst, for show.

They didn't have to put the bomb on her neck, Daisy Mae thought. She understood, now. Candy had told her; and now she had seen for herself. Society fought them all the time, because they wanted to make things right for everyone. Candy had spent years running, hiding from them, forced to violence to protect herself. It wasn't *right*. Daisy Mae was *glad* to help them, to protect Candy and the rest of them, from people like her father. She needed Candy, now. Candy was a *healer*. With her medicine, with her words, with her body (and how the Liz Fane she used to be would have been shocked at *that*), Candy made Daisy Mae relax, made her understand. Made her feel close to a world of people doing important things.

Liz Fane would have been horrified, but old Liz was dead,

buried, along with her life. It hadn't been much of a life, anyway. Lindsay Keith. Tennis. Parties.

Robin had *told* her how shallow it all was; maybe she'd been afraid to say how evil. Robin had known, though, and that was good. Robin wouldn't have to be shocked into realizing how bad she had been. Oh, Leo had explained, maybe a little, but not as much as Liz had, because Robin hadn't bought the lies of Herbert and Sheila Fane and their society to the same degree.

So the bomb was just a test—a reminder of the destruction the people of her old life caused. They'd never do it to her again. Leo had promised.

Daisy Mae put out a hand to steady herself as the van turned around the corner. She was careful not to point the gun at anybody in the van, not even Tom Ivery, who lay loose as a rag doll on the floor. Poor Tommy. Even as a youngster, he'd been a jerk. She felt sorry for him. She tried not to look at the dent in his forehead.

They were doing the right thing. They were. Candy had said so.

Georgia had gotten the van, Daisy Mae didn't know how. It was the van from Ferguson's catering, who did all of Da— Herbert Fane's parties.

They had to be getting close to the Lakeside Club by now, Daisy Mae thought. As if in answer, the van pulled to a stop. The gatekeeper spoke to Georgia. "What's up?" he said.

"More food. These people must eat like pigs."

Daisy Mae could see Leo smile in approval.

"Never saw a woman driving deliveries before," the gate-keeper said.

Georgia sounded bored. "Welcome to the Twentieth Century."

The gatekeeper laughed. "Okay, I've got the message. I don't want to be one of those—what do you call them? Male show-business pigs."

Daisy Mae had to cover her mouth with her hand to keep from laughing.

Georgia said, "No hard feelings, but I'm late already. Open the gate, okay?"

"Sure, sure," the man said, and Daisy Mae heard the gate

swing open the way it had so many times when she'd driven her little TR6 here.

There was a little cough. Daisy Mae looked up, surprised— it sounded just like the cough of the pneumatic ball-serving machine her fath—that *Herbert Fane* had bought for *Liz*. She had to stop getting mixed up like this. Leo would be mad at her, and Candy would be disappointed.

There was an acrid smell in the van. Leo looked at Waldo, who was drawing the ball of his thumb back and forth over the edge of his knife in boredom. "Go get—"

There was another little tennis-machine noise. Leo looked impatient. "Are you done?"

"Sorry," Georgia said. "He was moving a little."

Leo turned back to Waldo. "Go get him and drag him into his little booth. Pull the phone out."

A light came into Waldo's eyes as he rose and reached for the handle to open the side door.

"Put your knife away and leave it there," Leo said sternly, and the gleam left Waldo's eyes. He left the truck, got back in a few seconds later. Leo told him he did a good job. They slid the side door shut and drove on to the grounds.

Outside the building, they turned on to the lawn, near the big, plate-glass windows that would be behind the dais. Georgia parked the van and got out. Candy handed her her carbine, and replaced her in the driver's seat. Candy gave Georgia a kiss, and Daisy Mae felt a little jealous. She suppressed the feeling right away, though, because they were all Sisters, and jealousy was unworthy of them.

Anyway, Candy gave Daisy Mae a kiss, too, and it was a better one than Georgia got.

Leo pushed Tommy Ivery out of the van and onto Waldo's shoulders. Waldo carried Tommy toward the window, to a specific spot, directed by Leo, and lifted the corpse high over his head. Then, with a sudden effort of his huge body, Waldo hurled Tommy through the window.

It made a remarkable crash; pieces of glass made a light show in the sunset as they fell. Daisy Mae heard gasping and screaming from inside, then crunching as Waldo, then Leo, stepped over the low sill.

Georgia was standing beside her, poking her with the barrel of her carbine. "Let's go," she said. "Sister."

"Yes," Daisy Mae said. She forgot all about the weight attached to her neck. Really, she did. She took a firm grip on her weapon and stepped in.

They grabbed Robin and had her out through the window before Driscoll could move. It was as if they'd known *exactly* where she'd be sitting. Incredible. Impossible. Not even the gynecologist had known about *this*.

You're being stupid, he told himself. He was acting stupid, too. He stood up to try to save Robin (though it was already too late—the red-haired giant had picked her up and thrown her like a doll to someone waiting outside in two seconds flat) and rose right into a descending carbine butt.

Driscoll saw it coming in enough time to twist his body and avoid the full impact of the blow. There was still plenty of impact. He went down, pretending to be stunned worse than he was. He wondered why they didn't shoot him. Probably didn't want to take the risk of shooting each other.

Driscoll's glasses had come off when the blow struck, but even through his myopia, he could see blond hair and a prominent nose. Leo Calvin, he thought. In person. We meet at last.

Calvin turned his attention to somebody else, yelling above the panic of the crowd, "Do it! Do it now!"

Driscoll rolled over, found his glasses, scooped them up, and sprinted for the cover of the kitchen. It was suicide to try anything else, and Driscoll decided he wanted to live. He felt a cold fury he had never felt before. Fury was unprofessional, but he felt it now. Fury at Calvin for what he might do to Robin. Fury at himself for making it possible.

And while he was at it, he found a little room for some minor self-contempt for not having brought a gun.

The kitchen was a good vantage point. He could keep the door open a little, the better to see the carnage. And carnage there was. The emcee had had his throat cut by the smiling red-haired giant, the same one, no doubt, who had been in the ambulance that had taken Liz Fane.

The woman was here, too, if the witnesses' descriptions were worth anything. She was the one firing an occasional carbine round into the crowd scrambling for the exits to keep the panic level high.

There was another woman, the one Leo Calvin was screaming at. "Do it, damn you. The police will be coming. Do it or I'll set it off!" The other woman had a Sten gun; what Leo Calvin wanted her to do was shoot it. Driscoll swallowed hard. A Sten burst into this crowd would be absolute slaughter.

She turned toward Leo, and therefore toward Driscoll. The first thing Driscoll noticed about her was that she looked absolutely miserable. The second thing was that it was Liz Fane. Leo Calvin's stern posture never varied. Liz Fane raised the gun. Driscoll considered a suicide charge, but his training won out. Suicide missions are only justified when they have a chance to work. He stayed put, and wished for a miracle to put a gun in his hand.

Liz Fane squeezed off a burst that raked down the buffet table. Pieces of asparagus and champagne bottles flew. When the roar of the gun was over, Liz Fane herself roared.

"Silence!"

It didn't work. She fired again, into the ceiling this time. Pieces of acoustical tile floated down. She yelled again for silence, and this time got it.

"I was Elizabeth Fane before The League to End Oppression liberated me from that life! Look at my face. You know me. You know my voice. *Ignore impostors.* Stop work on the MENTOR missile guidance system! I say this to Herbert Fane. Stop, or the other victim of your capitalist brainwashing will die.

"Spread the word. *Death to Pigs!*"

And those last words, in other mouths now so much of a cliché as to become a joke, raised the hairs on the back of Driscoll's neck. There was nothing funny about them.

And perhaps the words he heard next, spoken too quietly for the stunned mob to hear, were even more frightening. Liz

Fane turned to Leo Calvin and said, "I'm sorry, Leo, I was nervous for a minute. Did I do all right?"

Leo Calvin grunted assent, and they disappeared through the window. The red-haired giant followed, licking blood from his hand. The woman brought up the rear.

He waited a few seconds, then went to the hole in the window. A van was burning rubber away from the club. He'd never be able to catch them, even if his car were parked right outside. He looked down at the floor, and found Tom Ivery staring up at him. The broken glass was slippery with the emcee's blood.

Two more swallowed up by Cronus. And Robin, whose torments were still ahead. Robin was *his* victim. He'd gotten her into this. *His* responsibility. She'd been snatched out of her aunt's traditional place of honor under his very nose.

Under his nose.

He sat down on the table, still watching the van recede. Tom Ivery's last story. Before her mother's eyes. *Under her father's nose?*

He thought about it, about what it could mean, and rejected it outright. Then he thought, *the way they want me to.* So he sat amidst the carnage, and thought some more.

He had it all figured out before the van was completely out of sight in the hills around Draper.

Chapter Eleven

"WHAT HAVE YOU DONE?" HERBERT FANE DEMANDED AS Driscoll walked in the door. "You crazy son of a bitch! You said she'd be safe! *What have you done?*"

Very distinctly, Driscoll said, "Shut up," and pushed past him. It would have taken Heironymous Bosch to paint the look of imbecility that appeared on the industrialist's face. Driscoll noted it, then ignored it. A time like this came in every operation; masks off, gloves off. The time when deception, for the most part, had to give way to force. Driscoll hated it, but there was no other way.

"Keep quiet, and keep out of my way," Driscoll told the older man. "I'll get your niece back. Your daughter, too. I need the phone. You go somewhere and wait. Stay with your wife." Driscoll looked suddenly grim. "Yes, that's exactly what you do. Stay with your wife. Stay away from the phone, both of you. And don't try to listen in on any extension, either. You'll ruin everything."

"*I'll* ruin everything. What do you call it when—"

Driscoll made his voice as cold as he could get it. "I have told you," he said, "what it is I want you to do."

Fane wasn't about to argue with that voice or the face that went with it. He retired, backing away like a servant. This latest shock, that of seeing the urbane and helpful Mr. Driscoll of

Defense turning into a snarling martinet, had left him able to do nothing more effective than open and close his mouth.

He'll get over it, Driscoll thought. He watched Fane until he was out of the room, then went for the telephone. First he called Miles, at his headquarters.

There was no need to say hello. When Miles answered the phone, Driscoll said two words: "Wide open." That let the agent know that security was no longer a major priority. All Miles needed to know now was what to do.

"The abandoned building just outside the modern factory grounds," Driscoll said.

"What about it?"

"That's where they are."

Miles never broke Agency discipline, but he came close this time. Driscoll could hear the effort it took Miles to keep the incredulity out of his voice when he said, "That close to occupied Fane installations?"

"Yes, god damn it, that close. Right under her father's nose. It took a kid to see it, though I'm damned if I know how he did it. I assume you heard about the mess at the party this afternoon."

Miles had; he summed up to prove it. "Three dead, four if you count the Ivery boy. Twelve injured, most by trampling. They knew just where to go. Apparently Liz Fane was directing them."

"As well as a near-zombie can. Look, we're wasting time. Get over to that building, scope it out. Go armed; bring enough for the two of us to get inside there if we have to. I know your car; I'll meet you there. I shouldn't be far behind you. Under no circumstances do anything without me. Got that?"

"I've got it." His voice was bright with enthusiasm. This was the sort of thing he liked. Driscoll envied him. He didn't like *any* of what lay ahead, and the assault on the terrorist stronghold was in some ways the least of his dreads.

The first thing he had to do was call his father. He let go of the disconnect button and dialled an 800 number in Washington. The idea was that an agent in the field might not always have a pocket full of change in case of emergency. A side effect was that Herbert Fane wouldn't see a nickel of this call on his phone bill.

As always, a machine answered the call. Driscoll waited for the beep after the innocuous message (in case a civilian got through to the number by mistake), then gave a number and words "bright red."

That ought to get the old bastard's attention, he thought. A bright red message meant disaster, with an agent's life at stake. Driscoll had made Robin an agent for the occasion. He had never sent this sort of message before. It was supposed to reach the Congressman instantly, no matter what. It would pull him off the floor of the House, out of a conference with the President.

Apparently, nothing that dramatic had been necessary. It took less than a minute before he heard his father's voice on the line.

"What is it? Sounds like things are a little out of control up there, boy. I warned you about that."

"Yeah, you warned me. I've got it."

"Got what?" He expected one of his father's patented Southern sarcasms, then realized that no one would fool around after having been sent a bright red message. Even Driscoll, frustrated rebel that he was, had never felt the thought cross his mind.

"All of it. Where they've got the girls—that's the easy part. What Cronus is—"

"*What?*"

"You heard me. What Cronus is. Why it took so long to develop. How it's supposed to work. How they worked it here. Why it's more important than any *six* missile guidance systems. I suspect it was the brainchild of your old friend, the Chairman."

"Hell, that was a foregone conclusion. Give me *details,* boy!"

"No time. Besides, this isn't a secure phone."

"Not secure?"

"I told you, no time. I don't think there's anybody listening in right now, but who knows? I need you up here. Immediately."

"I'm buzzing for my jet helicopter right now." Driscoll

reflected that this was the first time in his life that his father had ever responded when he'd told him he needed him.

"But, son," the old man went on, "don't you dare get killed before you get a chance to talk to me."

"I'll be careful." He told his father to come to the Fane house and wait. "Bring enough men to make sure nobody gets in or out. This would be a hell of a time for anybody else to be caught by the opposition."

"Don't waste time on the obvious, boy."

Driscoll grinned. Just for that, the old man deserved something suitably obscure. "One more thing, Congressman. Remember that nurse you told me about? The one who wanted to name me Macduff?"

"I remember. What about her, for God's sake?"

"She had the right idea, but the wrong name. You should have called me 'Zeus.'"

Driscoll hung up. The Congressman would be here within the hour. His father would be angry, and maybe even a little confused and frightened. Good. Let *him* know what it felt like for a change, just as Leo Calvin was learning.

With any luck, Liz and Robin would be free by the time the old man arrived. All Driscoll had to do was figure out how to do it.

Behind him, a voice said, "Zeus?"

Driscoll whirled to see Special Agent Fenton Rines holding a gun on him.

I've got no time for this, Driscoll thought desperately. "Private joke," he said.

Rines nodded soberly, like a banker approving a loan. "Right," he said. "A private joke with a congressman. Care to tell me *which* congressman? Or should I guess?"

Driscoll said. "I don't know what you're talking about. Shouldn't you be out chasing kidnappers?"

"We need information to do that, Driscoll. I think you've got some for me."

"How'd you get here, anyway?"

Driscoll was playing for time. Rines knew it, but he didn't seem to mind. The FBI man had the air of someone enjoying a pleasure long delayed.

"Mrs. Fane called me. Said you were terrorizing her family."

"Ah," Driscoll said. "I told her husband to keep her away from the phone."

"If he tried, I don't think it did him any good. You both underestimated that lady."

"You'd be surprised," Driscoll told him.

"I'd be surprised about a lot of things. How about that Jane Doe corpse you stole?"

This was supposed to be a bombshell, and would have been if Driscoll's mind hadn't been taken up with short-term scheming. Now that Rines was staring closely at Driscoll's face to gauge his reaction, Driscoll had his chance.

It was not a good chance, just an only chance. Any sensible expert would say Driscoll was doing nothing more than committing suicide. He was jumping an armed man—not just any armed man, but an armed FBI agent. Instant death. The FBI always shoots to kill.

Driscoll wasn't sensible—desperate men rarely are. And he was better trained (and more experienced) than many experts. Besides, as he kept telling himself, there was *no time*. So he tried it.

He didn't use any martial art—Rines would have been ready for those. In the split second the FBI man had his attention full on Driscoll's face, Driscoll let his legs shoot forward in front of him, snaking into Rines' ankles in a low, dirty soccer tackle.

The bullet missed his head by perhaps an inch. Driscoll made sure the agent didn't get another shot. He grabbed Rines by the throat as he fell, and hit his head against the floor until Rines was unconscious. Driscoll picked up the gun and looked at the fallen agent.

Agency rules of procedure would have him kill Rines now. He had made Driscoll, and learned at least one detail of the operation. Driscoll knew Rines was a deadly danger to him—to him *and* the Objective. Driscoll raised the gun toward Rines' head.

Then lowered it again. To hell with it. In another hour the

Objective would either be accomplished, or such a mess that nothing could save him, Rines or no Rines.

Still, no sense being foolhardy about it. If Driscoll didn't want to kill Rines, he could still slow him up. He went through the FBI man's pockets, removing money, ID, car keys, and anything else that would allow Rines to function when he woke up.

Driscoll found one more thing in a breast pocket. It was a small tape recorder, the kind executives use for dictating notes. Driscoll took it with him. He wanted his father, or somebody, to know about Cronus if he didn't make it. Leaving a tape behind would take care of that.

Driscoll wouldn't kid himself—he knew there was a good chance he wouldn't survive the hour it would take his father to get here.

I won't panic, Robin thought. *I will not panic. If they wanted me dead, they would have killed me already. They didn't kill Liz.*

No, Liz was alive, all right, sitting right beside Robin on the floor of the van that they'd trundled her off to through the shattered window of the Lakeside Club. A van was the last thing she'd seen before they put the oily-smelling cloth bag over her head, and tied her hands and feet, all the while getting the van in motion. They stopped, got out of one van and into another, and took off again.

Robin couldn't see or move or breathe too well, but she could hear. What she heard, aside from the occasional grinding of a gear, was the voice of her cousin. It was the kind of voice that could only come through an idiot smile, the voice a Moonie used to try to sell you a flower.

Liz was selling something different, though. She was pushing the party line for the League to End Oppression, reciting it like a proud child. Every once in a while, Liz would stop and ask someone if she'd gotten some part or other of the rhetoric exactly right. A man would tell her she was doing fine, then Liz would go on. Eager to please, eager to be liked and understood by everybody within earshot.

It was pathetic. To Robin, it was the beginning of her own torture. And the things they had to do to Liz to make her this way in such a short time—Robin could barely imagine them.

She knew one thing. If nobody rescued her, and soon—if Clifford Driscoll was willing to sacrifice her life and sanity for some bizarre government priority—she wouldn't stand for it. She'd think of some way to kill herself before she let them do to her what they'd done to Liz.

She might have felt better (or she might not) to know that the man Liz consulted had no intention of doing anything of the sort to her. Leo had nothing more to prove. Now he would make demands, period. Or, rather, Robin Payne would make them on his behalf. Leo was not too proud to take a lesson from his adversary. The undrugged, naturally terror-filled voice of the victim worked better; so be it. Give the public what it likes. He had hostages now both in mentally modified and in untampered-with condition. He could use either as the occasion demanded.

Of course, not drugging today's catch made certain things necessary. In the unlikely event Robin Payne were ever released, he didn't want her remembering where she'd been taken. Having Daisy Mae burble in her cousin's ear served a dual purpose—it kept the new hostage from picking up cues to her location, and it showed her by example what they could do to her if they wanted. From the body language, and the motions visible inside the dirty sack, Leo was sure she was getting the message.

He was quite as sure she was getting nothing else, but he let Georgia continue her zigzag course for some time. They were in the plain van now. The specially-stolen liquor store vehicle had been abandoned long ago, at the same time they dropped off Candy to let her make her way to the hospital.

Leo almost regretted it when he decided it was time to go back to the mill. He was enjoying the ride. It had been years since he'd participated in a raid in person, and there was something special about it. There was something extra special about this one. This time he'd defeated somebody *worthy of him*.

Somebody (he could admit it now) who'd had him frightened, and very badly at that.

He would cherish this afternoon for a long time. The Russians would pay him well, for perservering and saving their precious operation. He had gained great personal satisfaction in the bargain. Leo hoped the Russians would use him in further operations like this. It offered so many possibilities. The terrorist scenario was just one of them. And he almost hoped as well that he'd get to match skills with his adversary once again. Leo's only regret was that he would never get to tell his adversary to his face how much he'd enjoyed beating him.

Waldo felt happy, too. He had gotten his big knife back, and had had a chance to use it. He had seen more blood than he ever had before. He was sorry that Daisy Mae wasn't a better shot. Even Waldo couldn't have missed that many people with that many bullets. Still, the man had looked so funny when Waldo had used his big knife on him. That made up for everything.

Besides, there was a New Girl with them now. Daisy Mae was now their Sister, so he wasn't allowed to touch her anymore. Only Candy. Waldo didn't know why. But he knew it was the Rule. But there was a Rule about New Girls, too. Waldo couldn't wait until they got back.

The Congressman got a chance to practice some of the fast-talking he used to get himself re-elected every two years when he arrived at the Fanes' house early that evening. It was hard to tell what-all was going on, but there was no doubt about the fact that his son had left things in one incredible hell of a mess. He'd busted in; the lady of the house was still in a righteous rage. The man of the house was in a stupor—they ought to get a doctor to look at him, the Congressman thought. Mrs. Fane had called the FBI on his little Clifford, but whether Rines had left, or even been here at all, nobody could say. The Congressman noted that the rug was mussed, as if there'd been a struggle here. What the hell could *that* mean?

Fortunately, with all this other crap going on, nobody'd bother to take too close a look at his own story, a little something he'd tossed together about being so concerned about the musical-comedy way the authorities were handling this business that he'd come out here in person to see if it warranted a Congressional investigation by his committee. Of course, if the press found out he was here, he'd have to go ahead and hold one, but that was what happened when you tried to work without adequate planning.

So here he was, summoned by his son; the chief ordered around by an Indian, and how did you let *that* happen if you're so smart, he asked himself. Ordered not to let anybody in or out of the house—he had some good boys stationed outside to see to that, brought them up from Washington with him in the helicopter. Ordered to wait till his son showed up. So he'd wait. He didn't get to be a general without being able to follow orders. He worked things so that Fane got sent off to bed with a sleeping pill, then listened to Sheila Fane complain about this high-handed young swine from the Defense Department.

The young man in question took longer to find Miles' car than he might have, because Miles had been especially conscientious about concealing himself and because the day had surrendered to a royal blue twilight that complemented the stars to perfection, but made unilluminated objects on earth hard to see.

Driscoll found the car hidden in the woods off the side of the road that led to the Fane Industries complex; the back side of it, where the abandoned coke mill was. Once there, he turned in a slow circle until he saw Miles' signal—two flashes of a penlight across the road about halfway up the wooded hill.

When he got close enough to where he'd seen the light to speak quietly and still be heard, Driscoll said, "All right, Miles, I'm alone."

Miles stepped out from behind a tree, holding a gun on him. All according to the book. Miles used his eyes and ears to verify for himself that Driscoll was alone, then lowered the gun. They sat under cover on the soft earth of the hillside and spoke in whispers. Miles handed infrared binoculars to Driscoll. "Switched to these from the optical ones about twenty minutes ago," he said.

It was a different world through those glasses. They measured heat instead of light, so that trees glowed redly, and the hood of his car was nearly white, shining through the woods where he'd hidden it. Miles's car was already· cold, and therefore invisible.

Their position gave them a view of the Fane complex; Miles had chosen it for that reason. Driscoll turned the glasses in that direction. There was a red glow, like coals in a fireplace, coming from the main plant, warm even on a relatively inactive Sunday night. The old coke mill, which would have seemed white as the sun through this instrument in its golden days, was dark. No glow through any window. No warm residue along the road of the passage of a vehicle or the step of a human.

"Nobody in the factory," Driscoll said.

Miles nodded. "Nobody's driven along here, either. Except for you, of course."

"How long have you been here?"

"Since about ten minutes after you called me. It was still light out."

"Sorry I took so long," Driscoll said. "I had to borrow some equipment."

"Nothing happened," Miles said. "They wouldn't come back before dark, anyway."

"No, of course they wouldn't." Quietly, Driscoll spat. "What did you bring in the way of armaments?"

The question was intended to kill time. Miles had brought things useful for the nighttime ambush of a moving vehicle with (Driscoll clenched his jaw as he thought it) expendable hostages aboard. A high-powered sniper-scoped rifle for shooting out tires. Sten guns (Why be armed less well than terrorists, the Congressman always said). Bayonets. Flares. Tear gas. Driscoll had stopped at the hotel and picked up his own handgun.

It took twenty minutes to examine it all, a needless exercise, since Miles would have made sure everything was in perfect shape. They wouldn't use half the stuff, anyway. And when Driscoll was all finished playing, Leo Calvin and company still hadn't shown up.

"Maybe they're not coming back," he said. He could hear the strain in his own voice. His father would be ashamed of him.

"They're driving around to keep the Payne girl from getting a fix on the location when they bring her here," Miles offered. "It's a place she's very familiar with, and they don't want to take any chances."

"They don't want to take any chances," Driscoll said, "so they're not coming back at all. They've outsmarted me. *He's* outsmarted me."

Miles had too much discipline to ask out loud who *he* was, but he looked the question intently. Driscoll ignored him, looking the other way to spit.

It didn't do any good. Nothing could remove the coppery taste of failure from his mouth. It was a strange and unpleasant sensation. It had a slight tang of fate to it, as well. He had never failed before. And it had never mattered a damn to him before.

He wondered what he would do now. Kill Miles and run for his life? Or just stay put and let the man who'd brought him into the world against his mother's will take him out of it? Or should he just take one of the guns and handle it himself?

He was leaning toward option three when he became aware of the quiet roar of a large well-tuned engine coming up the road. Toward the property of Herbert Fane. The naked eye could see headlights; the infrared showed a van, hot in the front, warm all through. A hot cargo. Human bodies, maybe, living ones this time.

Driscoll's feeling of failure was replaced by hope. Maybe Miles was right, and Leo Calvin and friends had spent all this time riding around, giving him and Miles a chance to get in position. They did that now. Miles went up the hill with the rifle; Driscoll took up a position near the rusty gate.

Maybe they hadn't outsmarted him, after all.

Maybe they'd just outsmarted themselves.

First a tire went, then the windshield. Leo heard Georgia curse as she fought the wheel, ducked and squinted to see through a hole in the ruined safety glass. Leo was glad he'd assigned her to drive—she was the better driver by far. He would have had them in a ditch by now. Georgia had the car back on course, speeding along quite efficiently on three tires and a rim.

There were noises of fear in the back of the van with him. Robin Payne screamed. Daisy Mae whimpered. Waldo bellowed. Leo snapped at them to shut up, but that was pure reflex. When his brain was working this rapidly, he could be distracted by nothing.

It was obviously an ambush. The boy Ivery had somehow left word of their hideout behind him. It was not some "other terrorists." Those, he knew, had never existed. There was a hole in the roof of the van. The bullet that had shattered the windshield had been steel-jacketed and high-powered enough not to ricochet inside the vehicle. The bullet had been fired from a low angle, so that no one but the driver would be endangered and she not very much. This was someone who wanted the hostages back alive. The adversary.

Leo faced two important facts. The first was that the Cronus Project, at least as far as it concerned him, was over. The second was that as soon as he was separated from the hostages, his attackers would shoot him down as mercilessly as he would have shot them. As he *would* shoot them, if he got the chance.

Time to cut his losses and run. If he made a quick escape, he could empty one of his secret bank accounts and have a little traveling money before Moscow found out about his failure and came to look for him. Leo allowed himself one small twinge of regret, a coming attraction of the anger and fury that would follow in the days and weeks ahead. Someone, he promised himself, would pay for this.

But now he had to get away. He closed his eyes and thought for ten seconds. He couldn't take the Fane girls with him. He couldn't shoot them down, or he was a dead man himself. All right! He had it. He just hoped the adversary was hero enough to go for it. He might even get to learn who he was.

He barked orders. "Georgia! Crash the gate. Drive through the grounds right up to the entrance of the mill, *side doors in.* Can you do that?"

Georgia didn't bother to answer—she just did it. Preoc· cupied as he was, Leo still had to admire her skill. She'd placed the van just far enough from the door of the building so that both van and mill doors could open freely. The whole thing could be worked from inside the van.

Waldo, Georgia, and Daisy Mae looked at Leo expectantly. They didn't know it, but they were about to hear their last orders from him.

He took the machine pistol from Daisy Mae, who'd been holding it across her chest like a rag doll ever since she'd forced herself to fire it at the Tennis Club, and handed it to Georgia. Then he gave her carbine to Waldo and watched his eyes light up like a child looking at a birthday cake with his name on it. Waldo had not been allowed to handle guns before, except under strict supervision.

"Hold them off as long as you can," he told them. "Daisy Mae and I will load our new friend into the Plymouth." The Plymouth was kept by the loading dock in back of the building. "I'll warm up the engine. When they get too close, come inside, run through the building and join us. We'll beat them yet."

Georgia nodded; Waldo said, "How about blood?"

"As much as you want," Leo said, and Waldo squirmed with excitement. Leo smiled. He might almost miss Waldo.

He turned to Daisy Mae. "Let's go." Daisy Mae was shaking with fear, but she was still eager to please Leo. She took one of her cousin's arms, Leo took the other, and they disappeared inside the building.

The hard way, Driscoll thought. *Always the hard way.* One driver in a thousand could have avoided rolling that van, what with

a tire out and the windshield spiderwebbed. The woman at the
wheel for the League to End Oppression was apparently that
one. Now they were holed up in that huge building, and he and
Miles had to do something about it. They'd discussed the
contingency. Even now, Miles was circling the building, to make
sure there were no vehicles ready to take them away.

Driscoll's job was to run right up their tails and keep them
busy. He retrieved his car from the woods before the rubber
laid down by the skidding van had time to cool off. He laid
some of his own down on the weed-cracked macadam that led
to the mill.

He decided to come in with high beams blazing for
psychological effect, but their main effect was to save his life.
The first thing he saw in the light was the woman who'd been
driving the van. She hadn't run inside. She raised a weapon.
Driscoll ducked below the dashboard. There was a harsh noise
of a weapon being fired, shots too close together to be
differentiated. Almost simultaneously, there was the buzz of
vaporizing glass. Pebbles of safety-glass showered down on
Driscoll's back.

Idiot, he told himself. *You* knew *they had a Sten gun.*

He was already in the safest place he could be, crouched
down behind the thick metal of the engine block. He brought
the car to a stop—a combination of luck and instinct found it
still pointing more or less in the right direction.

Driscoll stayed down. He could feel the hum of the motor
through the floor. It wouldn't run much longer—the radiator
was undoubtedly perforated in a hundred places, leaking water
and coolant into the night.

He didn't have much longer, either, so it didn't much
matter. Driscoll shifted his weight. Another blast raked the car,
at hood level this time. She'd seen the car rock slightly when he
moved.

Every once in a while, there'd be a single shot that sounded
as harmless as a firecracker compared with the automatic pistol.
Each shot would be followed by laughter that would have
sounded like a child's if the voice weren't so low. None of the
single shots ever landed.

Driscoll had his head pointed toward the left of the car

now. Carefully, he eased open the door latch, then pushed the door open. He dove back under the dashboard before the expected burst of gunfire hit.

As soon as it was over, he peeked through the crack between the door and the body of the car. He took a quick look, then pulled back in and burned the details into his memory. The small figure was on Driscoll's left. That had to be the woman, shooting over the nose of the van. There was a much larger figure at the other end, but Driscoll couldn't identify him because the headlight on that side of Driscoll's car was shot out. He'd worry about him later.

He was just about the right distance from them for his idea to work. He wouldn't drift too far off course, even driving blind. He could pick up enough speed. And the woman had already shown herself to be the kind who stands and fights.

Driscoll got down as low as he could. He held the steering wheel steady with his left hand. With his right, he pushed the accelerator to the floor.

The engine revved mightily. The car didn't move.

Driscoll came as near panic as he ever had. What was he going to do *now*? Then he looked up and saw what he was going to do. He was going to take the car out of neutral. *Idiot*. He'd done it unconsciously when he first brought the car to a stop.

He moved the gearshift to drive and tried again. This time, the car shot forward like a rocket sled. Very much like a sled, in fact, because Driscoll was dealing with at least two, possibly three flat tires. The bouncing at the speed he wanted nearly shook his teeth loose. The automatic pistol was roaring almost continuously, the car was filled with a blizzard of metal and rubber.

Driscoll stayed with the car until he couldn't stand it anymore, and three seconds after that. The next split second between bursts, he battered open the driver's side door and jumped.

He felt his right arm go numb as it scraped the wall of the building. He heard the crash as he hit the ground.

Waldo had never seen anything like it, not even the man who'd been hit by the car. He could hardly stand up for the thrill of it. The car had hit the van, and the van had pushed itself into Georgia, and she was squashed between the van and the wall, and Waldo had never seen so much blood. Bright and red and splattered everywhere, oh, my God.

Georgia was so little, too. Where did it all come from? Waldo got closer and closer to her, trying to figure it out. Every time she opened her mouth to cough or try to talk, there was a whole new flood of it, like a red beard. Finally, though, he could hear croaking words from her—"Tell . . . Leo . . ."

Then her head fell over at a funny angle, as if she didn't care if it hurt her neck or not. That meant she was dead. Waldo had seen a lot of dead people, and that was what they did.

Then he realized he had to tell Leo, the way Georgia told him. He took one last, round-eyed look at the pretty redness that had been Georgia, then went inside to look for Leo. He hoped he could remember the way.

But when he got inside the shaft of the mill, he saw something he didn't understand, something strange that no-body had prepared him for. It drove Leo right out of Waldo's mind. Waldo looked at the strange scene in front of him, finally deciding it was none of his business.

His mind kept going back to Georgia. He remembered the man who had shown him all of Georgia's blood. The man was way bigger than Georgia—he probably had a lot more blood in him. Waldo almost cried with the need to see it. And he would, he decided.

But he wouldn't go outside after the man. The man had beaten Georgia. That meant he was smart. Waldo would be smart, too.

Oh, Jesus, Robin thought. *Oh, Jesus, please get me out of this. Whatever it is, please get me out of this.*

Somewhere back in her head, a voice intoned, *"Let her be crucified!"* She tried to laugh behind her gag, under the hood that blinded her, but she choked instead.

Robin's shoulders ached. She could tell Liz's did, too, because she could feel Liz's muffled moans against her hood. Liz was gagged now, too, betrayed by the people who'd warped her mind. She could feel the length of her cousin's body against hers. Both of them were stiff with pain and panic, tight as rolls of cable.

They were suspended by their handcuffs (Robin had heard Leo tell her cousin to put out her hands, heard Liz's hurt protests until the gag had gone home) on the hook of a hoist that ran down the shaft of the abandoned mill. She didn't know how high up they were. Their feet didn't touch the floor at any point of their spin or dangle. They wouldn't touch, Robin guessed, until her arms pulled loose from their sockets and the rest of her body fell to the floor.

She heard someone come into the room, right after the shooting outside and the crashing metal. Her ears told her it was Waldo, mumbling stupidly about having to be smart, and for all Robin could tell, ignoring them completely.

If only she could *talk,* for God's sake. Or even Liz. If either of them could *talk* to him, she could convince him to let them down. Liz could. Even drugged and damaged, Liz had to be smarter than a moron. She'd say . . . she'd say . . .

But she couldn't say anything. She cursed the world, God, and man. She cursed Driscoll, and she cursed herself for listening to him. She didn't want to die like this. She didn't want to die at all.

She didn't want to cry, either, but she did.

Driscoll rolled over on his back and tried to breathe. A wheeze and a feeling of panic were all he accomplished.

The panic he handled easily; he'd had the wind knocked out of him before. It was a dreadful feeling, but it wasn't dangerous. If that was the worst thing wrong with him, he was lucky. Still, the emptiness in his chest was the top priority. Driscoll forced his hands under his hips and used them to help him arch his back, changing the shape of his chest, and drawing air into his collapsed lungs.

He took a few hungry breaths, and decided he hadn't been badly hurt in his landing. He got to his feet and walked around his impromptu junk sculpture and the mess he had made of the woman. He took a few more deep breaths, drew his gun, and made for the entrance.

He didn't have to climb in; when his car had smashed the nose of the van into the building, it had kicked the back of the van away from the wall at the same time. Now there was a narrow wedge of space. He had to squeeze through, but he could get to the door.

When he stepped inside, the first thing he saw was Robin and Liz, suspended from a hook at the end of a long chain, their feet about four feet from the cement floor. There were black puddles of freshly spilled, but old and dirty, motor or machine oil all around the room. Driscoll wondered what *that* was all about. He wondered what *all* of it was all about. Until he was jumped.

Leo Calvin watched from around the edge of the door that led off to the loading docks on the other side of the building. It pays, he thought, to notice your surroundings, and it pays to plan for contingencies. He'd noticed the oil days ago, tucked away in a forgotten drum in a corner of the room. He never dreamed he'd find a use for it.

But he had—and now it was part of a new plan. Leo had waited when he'd first entered the mill; waited and listened for a few seconds. If it had sounded as if Georgia and Waldo were going to fail absolutely to keep intruders out, he would have had no choice but to shoot both the Fane girls and run.

When he realized he would have some time, though, he quickly cuffed and gagged Daisy Mae. It seemed a shame to discharge her from the League to End Oppression after they'd gone to such trouble to make her an enthusiastic recruit, but right now her major value was as a distraction. And she would constitute an unignorable one, strung up on the hoist along with her cousin. The oil on the floor was an added touch, designed to lend urgency to the proceedings and help to mask Leo's retreat. Ignited in the enclosed space, the old oil would make a stinging, acrid, and ultimately blinding smokescreen for Leo to hide behind.

With that kind of security, Leo thought it worth the risk to wait a few moments more to see who walked through the door. When the first one through was Waldo, who took up an ambush position alongside the doorway, Leo felt safer still. With Waldo, the dangling damsels, and the soon-to-be-fire, whoever was coming for him would have plenty to occupy his attention while Leo got a look at him.

Leo waited. He watched Waldo while he waited. He wondered what had happened to Georgia. It undoubtedly had something to do with the crash he'd heard.

Leo was about ready to move. It was waste of time to wait to see an enemy who'd crushed himself inside a ton of mangled steel. He would just light his rag and drop it in the nearest black finger of oil, thereby tying off the cousins as loose ends. Probably Waldo, too, though Waldo really wasn't smart enough to do Leo much harm. Leo took out his lighter and spun the wheel.

He was touching the flame to the rag when Driscoll walked in.

Waldo was proud. He hit the man in the arm first, so he'd drop his gun. Waldo thought of that all by himself. Waldo raised his big knife. He wanted to see a lot of blood. He wanted to make a lot of cuts, especially a big one in the man's middle. He brought the knife down with all his strength.

But something was wrong. The man wasn't afraid. He didn't put up his hands to block the knife. People did that, but even Waldo knew it wasn't very smart. The blood from hands was just as pretty as the blood from anywhere else.

But this man didn't do that. Waldo wasn't sure just *what* he was doing. The man had started to spin even before his gun hit the ground. He caught Waldo's wrist, the one that powered the knife. Instead of fighting it, the man *pulled*.

Waldo lost his balance and stumbled forward, and while he did, the man stuck out his leg and tripped him.

Waldo was hurt. "Hey," he said, "that's not fair. You—"

Waldo hadn't even gotten back to his knees yet, and the man was kicking him again, this time in his hand, making him drop his big knife into a smelly black puddle. Waldo leaned over to pick it up, but it was slippery and fell from his fingers. The man pushed him away. Waldo fell in the puddle. Some of the black stuff got in his mouth. It tasted bad.

Waldo was really mad. He started to get to his feet again, but before he could reach his knees, the man attacked him again. This time, the *man* had Waldo's big knife.

It didn't hurt when a knife went into a person. Waldo was glad to know that. He never wanted to hurt anybody, he just wanted to see blood. He wasn't hurt now. It didn't feel any worse than being punched, and Waldo was big and strong enough for a punch not to hurt him.

There was a funny noise inside him as he fell back to the floor, like splitting pants or sharing a piece of chicken by ripping it apart. But Waldo hardly noticed because of the blood. It was beautiful, the way it poured through his shirt and his fingers and made red islands in the black puddle. All this bright red beauty inside him, and he was sharing it with the world.

Waldo remembered the first time he had had the warm feeling when he saw blood. That was his own blood, too. Waldo lay down, feeling the warmth in him. He thought of his Ma. It had been so long since he'd seen her, but he could feel very close to her, now. He smiled and closed his eyes.

Driscoll. Leo could hardly believe his eyes. The suit-and-tie man from the Defense Department. Leo had all but discounted him; he was the tight-assed official Tom Ivery had put on the spot back at that press conference.

Yet here he was, and he'd handled Waldo in seconds, opening him like a Christmas parcel. If Driscoll wasn't the brain of the adversary, he had enough physical prowess to be equally dangerous to Leo at this point. It was time to light the fire and run. Leo dropped the rag and started toward the back. There was undoubtedly another agent waiting for him there. Leo began formulating new contingency plans.

There was one contingency he didn't plan on—the bottom of his shoes were slick with oil, and it destroyed his traction on the scored-metal walkway in the passage. He fell with a clatter. He rose cursing.

Driscoll wiped blood and oil from his right hand onto his pants. A soft crackling noise and an unpleasant tingling in his nose made him aware of the burgeoning oil fire.

That removed any choice he might have had. He could have chased Leo Calvin and left the girls hanging on the hook. All it would have taken was some casual brutality. He couldn't leave them there in the thick smoke as if they were a couple of sides of bacon; they would be dead in minutes.

Leave Leo to Miles. It would make Miles very happy. Driscoll would rescue the women. If he could.

The noise of a body hitting metal roused him. Driscoll peered down the hallway through thickening smoke. He saw the tall, bony figure topped by the thatch of blond hair.

Driscoll almost smiled. He could sacrifice a second or two more for the Objective. He found his gun and snapped off three shots. He heard a groan, and saw Calvin grab a shoulder. Then the fire leaped to a new level of intensity. Fat yellow flames were visible now, and the smoke was thicker. He could no longer see the hallway.

When he reached the center of the room, he was glad to

find Robin was closest to the open end of the hook. Glad, because she was conscious. Her body was wiggling strenuously, fluttering the rags of the summer dress around her. Muffled coughs were audible through the bag on her head.

Liz wasn't moving. Her head hung forward, her eyes were closed. Every once in a while, her cheeks would be puffed out by an unconscious cough into her gag.

Driscoll was coughing himself, by now. He had to fight to get enough air to make himself heard over the noise of the flames.

"*Robin!*" he said. The hooded head rose. "It's me. Driscoll. I'll get you out of there, but you have to help me."

She nodded rapidly. The motion set the chain to swaying. Driscoll wrapped his arms around the girls' calves (their feet were level with the bottom of his ribcage) to steady them. Then he shifted his grasp to Robin's legs alone.

"Make your body stiff," he told her. "Absolutely stiff. Tighter! Every muscle, now."

Driscoll crouched, taking a firmer grip just where the calf began to swell. He would have liked to have gripped her lower, but it would have been impossible to keep her balanced that way. He felt the trembling of straining muscle and the smoothness of nylon against his cheek. Driscoll held tight, then rose from his crouch.

Robin had already figured out what Driscoll was trying to do, and she did all she could to make sure it worked. As if she were doing him a favor, she thought. As if it weren't *her* life that was at stake here. Her shoulders and arms no longer existed, but they'd left pain behind to remember them by. Still, when she felt her rigid body being lifted, she sent messages to her arms, stretching her already overextended ligaments more from anger than from hope.

Hope came when she felt the chain of the handcuffs go slack, and grew as she felt the metal of the manacles grate against the metal of the hook. She was rising. She ignored the pain and pushed harder. Below her, Driscoll coughed and groaned. Robin slipped down, jolting to a halt that almost made her pass out.

"Again!" Driscoll's voice cut through her stupor. "Again, goddamn it!"

Again, Robin stiffened her body, forced her arms up as Driscoll lifted her. The cuffs rose, and suddenly Robin felt herself going over backward. There was a snag—a link of the cuffs caught on the very point of the hook. Robin cried out behind her gag, and with a sudden furious effort, she was free.

For a second, she had the sensation of flying. Then Driscoll let go of her legs and caught her again around the waist. He didn't stop her from hitting the floor, but he kept her from being dashed hard against the concrete.

Robin felt herself being lifted and carried outside, then placed down again. The air of the summer night was blessedly cool against her skin. She felt hands at her neck, and jumped in sudden fear, but Driscoll said, "Let me get this thing off you."

She started to cry the minute she could see him; when she took the gag from her mouth, she began to babble thanks mixed with curses. Then her throat closed up, and it was harder to breathe than ever. It was coming home to her—*she was out of that hell.* She was going to live. After that, there was nothing big enough to say. She pressed close to Driscoll and trembled against him.

Driscoll said, "Catch your breath. We have to go back in there."

It was the bravest thing Driscoll had ever seen or heard of. It took awhile; longer than Liz Fane could afford, really. But Robin came back in.

She'd refused flatly, at first. She'd told him her cousin was already dead; that she'd joined the other side, anyway, and had been making fools of them all along. Robin didn't care, she wasn't going back in there. And she wasn't going to let him go either.

Driscoll had just smiled and shook his head and gone back inside. He had to do it. For him, bravery didn't enter into it. He had discovered that he and Elizabeth Fane had a strange kind of kinship. They were both monsters born of Cronus, and he owed her something because of it.

But he couldn't help her alone. With Liz unconscious, he couldn't lift her off the hook—there was just too much slack in her body for him to do her any good. He couldn't climb over her. Driscoll's lifting had led him to believe that Liz already had a dislocated shoulder, and possibly worse in the way of internal injuries. He couldn't take a running jump and grab the chain above her hands, because the floor was too slick with oil for him to get up enough speed.

He could barely see now. The fumes were too thick. The flames grew higher, though he was in no immediate danger from them. His eyes felt like meat being grilled in his head. He'd grown used to the taste of his own tears, and he timed his movements around the coughing fits that shook his body.

He heard Robin by her coughing first, then he heard her calling his name.

"Over here!" he shouted. "Follow my voice!" He didn't worry about her walking into the fire itself; the black and yellow flames were the only things visible now.

"Wha-what can I do?" she asked when she reached him. She held her cuffed hands in front of her like a penitent. She raised them to stifle her coughs.

Driscoll kissed her quickly on the forehead, then said. "You'll have to give me a boost."

"Me?" Robin was skeptical. "Lift you?"

"Simple engineering. It won't take a second. Just do what I tell you, and we'll get Liz out of here, and we'll all go home. All right?"

Fear had made her face loose, almost idiotic, but when her lips stopped trembling enough to speak, what she said was, "Okay."

Driscoll had her kneel on the ground just next to the plumb line made by the chain as weighted by Liz. "Now bend over," he told her. "All the way over. Head way down. Good. Now make fists against your chest, and brace your elbows against your knees. Good and tight, now."

He was making an arch out of her, the classic form to make materials support much more than their own weight. In this case, Robin didn't have to support the weight for too long. Driscoll took one quick step across the floor for momentum, one on the small of Robin's back for lift, and sprang upward through the stinging fumes. He grabbed the hoist chain three fat links above the hook, then pulled himself up with his arms.

It would have been easier if Driscoll could have used Liz to support some of his own weight, but that would be as bad as climbing her. Instead, he twined his left arm around the chain and took firm hold with his left hand. With his right hand, he reached down and grabbed the chain that connected the handcuffs on Liz Fane's wrists. And pulled.

Driscoll felt as if he were tearing himself in half; the handcuff chain threatened to saw his fingers off. He could feel tendons pop in both forearms.

But Liz Fane began to rise.

"Only a few more inches, come on . . ." Robin's voice. Ignoring instructions. He had told her to run outside as soon as he had attached himself to the chain.

Driscoll's mind echoed Robin. *Come* on, *for God's sake*, he told himself. *You still have work to do. You want to see the look on a few faces when you explain about the Cronus Project. Especially your father's. His and one other. Let's get on with it.*

Driscoll gave out with a groan that was almost a scream, and suddenly Liz Fane was free of the hook; he was holding her in the air as if she were a shopping bag. Then his grip gave way, and she fell unceremoniously to the floor. Robin ran immediately to help her, apologizing to her unconscious cousin for not wanting to come inside.

Driscoll untangled his arm from the hoist and dropped to the floor beside them. "Let's apologize outside," he said. He coughed, picked up Liz Fane and carried her outside as Robin led the way through the smoke.

Driscoll had to push past Robin—she had finally become aware of the carnage inside and outside the doorway. She stood staring at it. One shock too many.

Driscoll brought Liz away from the building, laid her down gently, removed her gag, and made sure she was breathing. He heard sirens and saw blue and red lights flashing some distance down the road. Someone had seen the smoke and turned in an alarm.

Driscoll led Robin away from Georgia's body to Liz's.

"Take care of your cousin," he said. "She needs you, and she's going to keep needing you."

"What are you talking about?" Robin blinked, trying to take it all in.

Driscoll kept trying. "Just remember this, because nobody else is going to. *None of what happened was Liz's fault.* She's been abused. Mentally. Physically. Chemically. Emotionally. By an expert. When an expert wants to break you, you will break. I would. Anybody. Don't let anybody forget it."

"Why don't *you* tell them? You seem to know all about it."

"I know too much about it."

"Then *help* me, Clifford." Robin was more herself again, irritation had cleared her brain. "I know you're right. I had only one afternoon of it, and I'm about to break myself."

"I can't."

"Why not?" Robin demanded.

Instead of answering the question, Driscoll said, "Robin, I've never said this honestly to another human being. I love you." He took her in his arms and kissed her hungrily; then gently. "I love you," he said again.

Driscoll sat Robin down next to her cousin and told her to let herself be taken to the hospital.

"Come see me later?" she said.

Driscoll smiled and said, "Sure."

In a life filled with lies, that was the hardest one Driscoll ever told.

Driscoll was tired, sore, and sick from oil fumes, but he had to run around the building to meet up with Miles. It was impossible to get inside now, and he couldn't just hang around in front and wait for the cops to show up. Not after what he'd done to Rines.

If all had gone according to plan, Miles had already

delivered Leo Calvin to the Congressman. He'd get his glory. Then Driscoll could walk in on the celebration with his own news and make it just about a perfect day for the old man.

Unfortunately, he might have to walk in all too literally. His car was destroyed, and Miles had probably left in his own car, leaving Driscoll without wheels. Driscoll shrugged. He'd walk if he had to. He'd been through worse. Leaving Robin, for example. But it would be unhealthy for him to think about that now.

When he reached the far corner of the building, he slowed to a walk. He didn't know who might have been sent around to the loading dock, and he didn't want to run into some engine-and-hose company dashing through the back way to get a better shot at the fire with their foam.

No fire truck was there, though. Miles' car *was*. Miles was in the front seat. There was a neat red hole where his nose joined his forehead.

Driscoll felt tears come to his eyes, which was ridiculous. He hadn't even liked Miles. It had to be an after-effect from the fumes. Had to be.

There was a piece of paper propped up in front of Miles on the dashboard.

"*Driscoll,*" it read. "*I know how you work now. I know your face. You have made things difficult for me. I resent it. I will see your face again.*"

It wasn't signed. Driscoll guessed Calvin thought the way he'd taken Miles would be signature enough. And so it was. Miles was no amateur.

Driscoll grabbed the note and stuffed it angrily in his pocket.

"I guess it's not even worth looking for him," said a voice. "We'll try, of course."

Driscoll whirled, reaching for his gun, but it wasn't there. He'd lost it inside.

Special Agent Fenton Rines had the drop on him. But good.

"I got here too late to help your friend," Rines said. "Sorry. The black gal's one of yours, too, isn't she?"

Driscoll said nothing.

"She hasn't talked or anything. You people are well trained. I'm mostly guessing. But I think I know what you've been up to. I know you're working for the government in some way. I don't have it all yet. But I've got a truckdriver with one corpse too few. And I've got you."

Driscoll nodded. His mind was racing. "You've got me," he said.

"The question is, what am I going to do with you?"

Driscoll said, "I have a suggestion about that . . ."

Chapter Twelve

RUMORS SPED THROUGH DRAPER MEMORIAL HOSPITAL like the vector of a new disease. No, I heard it directly from Agnes, who heard it from Ted, who got it directly from Harriet, the ambulance dispatcher. Or from the head of Emergency Medicine. Or from the head of the Custodial staff. Honestly, I did.

It didn't matter—everybody had a version of it.

Both of the girls were dead. Both were alive, but they'd been totally brainwashed and were holding the ambulance attendants hostage, demanding a flight to Algeria and the release of the black woman the police had in jail. They were both pregnant. One was the prisoner of the other—both combinations had adherents. One or both of them were imposters.

Nurse C. Barton, wing 5J, managed to hear all the rumors. She believed none of them; she was ready to accept any of them. She'd heard nothing from Leo since she'd left them just before the kidnapping of Robin Payne from the Lakeside Club; Leo was supposed to slip out to a phone shortly after they got their new hostage back to the mill to tell Candy what, if anything, she should bring back when her shift was over tonight.

There had been no phone call.

Candy decided to arrange things so she'd be in the

neighborhood of the emergency room when the ambulance arrived. It would only be a matter of minutes. The crowd in the elevator showed her that it was a common idea. Hospital people were no less curious than anybody else. Any patient who happened to need a bedpan in the next twenty minutes or so would be in dire straits.

The guards weeded out most of the crowd en route, but Candy was sweet and competent and smiled resignedly. She had no trouble getting through. She arrived just as they brought the cousins in.

They were on stretchers. Robin Payne looked as though she didn't really need to be, but her Daisy Mae certainly did. Both were filthy, both were exhausted and nagged by some kind of pain.

Daisy Mae was only semi-conscious. Candy listened as the doctor examined her. "I want X-rays on this shoulder. Make it both shoulders. Wrists, too. How we coming on the blood series? I don't want to give her any medicine until I know what she's already on. Kid's got more needle holes in her than a pincushion. Let see if we can sit her up . . ."

They sat her up very easily. It give her a clear line of sight directly to the face of nurse C. Barton.

Daisy Mae's eyes opened wide. She started to scream.

"*Candy!*" she cried. "Candy! Candy!"

Nurse Barton froze in place, expressionless, watching as the woman on the stretcher tried to lift her arms to point. Daisy Mae began to cry when her injuries kept her from doing it.

"All right," the doctor said anxiously, "lie her back down."

Candy didn't even sigh. As always, she faced it. It was over; another section of her life had come to an end. Candy's rubber-soled white shoes made a soft squeaking noise as she turned and walked briskly away from the emergency room. She wondered if it would be worth the risk to return to the fifth floor and take some salable drugs with her before she left. Leo had kept all the money; Candy would be walking out on almost two weeks of hospital pay. She thought it over, then decided against it.

The terror-stricken voice still came from the emergency room, competing with voices trying vainly to soothe it. People the guards had kept away were throwing a sop to their curiosity by hanging around the hallway to listen. Nurse Barton heard them talking as she walked by.

"What is she saying now?" a voice asked. "I can't make it out."

"She's still begging for candy," someone replied.

"Oh," the first voice said. "Well, I don't see why the hell they don't *give* her some. The poor girl's been through a lot."

That was the last thing Candy heard before she left.

Sheila Fane had sworn she would never let Clifford Driscoll back into her house, yet here he was, as conciliatory now as he had been intolerable the last time. He even looked different. His hair was wet from a recent shower, and he'd changed into casual clothes from the summer formal wear he'd had on before. Physically, though, he had been through *something*. There were raw patches of skin on him; his eyes were red and swollen. His voice was hoarse, and he coughed frequently. His movements were very stiff, like those of a man twice his age.

It was his news that had gotten him back in the door; that and the assurance of the Congressman that the young man would answer to him personally if he misbehaved.

Sheila Fane had been astounded to hear that the girls were safe, and the terrorists routed. She had, to be brutally honest, given both her daughter and her niece up for dead.

"Rines got them out. They were being held in the old building on your property," Driscoll had told her husband. "I got there just in time to see the end of it. The girls are shaken up, but a week or so in the hospital should take care of the physical part of it."

"My property?" her husband had said. Poor Herbert. The happy news of the rescue seemed to be shocking him as much as the terrible events of the kidnappings had. It was a mercy, perhaps—he seemed to have missed completely the implications of the last part of Driscoll's "good news."

The Congressman had taken charge then; Sheila Fane

hadn't known just what to do. "Why don't you folks get down to
the hospital and see them right away? I'll have my driver take
you. Mr. Driscoll and I will stay here and keep an eye on things.
Besides, I want to know what he's been up to."

"I—I want to know what happened!" Herbert demanded.
"Driscoll, come with me and tell me all about it. Rines did this,
you say?"

"Absolutely. And he's still at work, searching for the leader
of the terrorists. That's why I can't come along with you—I'm
waiting for important news from Rines."

"But . . . but . . ." It broke Sheila Fane's heart to see
Herbert like this.

"I know you want to see your daughter, Mr. Fane," Driscoll
said. Somehow, his hoarseness seemed to add sincerity to his
voice. "So you go along to the hospital. Take the Congressman's
car—Mrs. Fane, if she likes, can stay here with the Congressman and me. I'll tell her all about it, then as soon as Rines calls
in, I'll bring her to the hospital personally, and she can tell *you*
all about it."

Herbert was torn. "Your behavior earlier today hardly
. . . hardly makes me want to entrust my wife to you."

"We were all under a lot of pressure earlier, Mr. Fane.
Things had to be done in a hurry. I apologize for letting the
urgency of the situation get the better of me."

Herbert Fane turned to his wife. "Dear . . . if you can
wait a little while . . ."

Sheila Fane had smiled indulgently at him. "Of course.
Give them my love; I'll be there soon."

Herbert wasn't out the door five seconds when Driscoll
said, "At the risk of seeming impertinent, Mrs. Fane—"

"Somehow, I don't think that's a risk that really deters you,
Mr. Driscoll," she said.

"I think you might like to call the hospital and suggest they
take a close look at your husband when he arrives. It seems to
me he's been walking around in shock for several days."

Sheila Fane had to concede he had a point. Herbert would
be much better off in the hospital. She placed the call. When
she was done, she said, "Now, Mr. Driscoll, I think you were

going to tell the Congressman and me what has happened to Elizabeth and Roberta."

The Congressman cleared his throat. "Mrs. Fane," he said. "You are a very brave woman, but do you think it's wise to listen to what may be a harrowing story at a time like this? Mr. Driscoll is *enthusiastic*"—and here he shot the younger man a curiously exasperated look—"but in his eagerness he may upset—"

"No, Congressman," Driscoll said. "Mrs. Fane deserves to hear this. More than anyone. Is there someplace we might sit down?"

She led them to the parlor and remembered to offer refreshments. She wanted to laugh at herself. With her emotions churned up inside her and her entire world in turmoil, she hadn't forgotten her training. The perfect hostess, no matter what the circumstances.

Driscoll began to speak. "I have to start my story a long time ago, Mrs. Fane. Of necessity. Because this story starts with a woman known as Becky Underwood."

"*Driscoll!*" The Congressman was violently agitated. Sheila Fane was afraid for a second he'd attack Driscoll physically.

Driscoll remained calm. He turned his reddened eyes on the older man. "Yes, Congressman?" he said blandly.

"You may be giving away dangerous—classified information!"

"It will be all right, Father," Driscoll said, and the Congressman's face went from red to white.

Now that the word had been said, Sheila Fane could see that the men were father and son. They didn't talk alike or look alike, but the intelligence in their eyes was the same, the deadliness in their looks toward each other. Their determination, and their pride. All the same.

Sheila Fane began to be afraid.

"Becky Underwood," Driscoll repeated. "It wasn't her real name. We don't know her real name, but it was a Russian one. She was a spy for the Soviet Union. She was caught stealing secrets from the Pentagon during the Korean War. She was already in place at the Pentagon, so she was used in that capacity when the fighting broke out.

"That wasn't her original assignment, though. She was working on something—American intelligence intercepted several messages that referred to it—something called the Cronus Project."

"I don't understand, Mr. Driscoll. I doubt you were even born while the Korean war was on. Besides, what does this have to do with my—with my daughter?"

"I'll get to that in a moment, Mrs. Fane. First, though, I have to tell you a story. A myth, really. None of this can be understood without it."

And he went on to tell her the story of Cronus, the father of the gods, later identified as the god of Time. How he ate his children, but was thwarted by the one who got away. Sheila Fane didn't know how to react; she looked at the Congressman for help, but he was watching his son with deadly hooded eyes and was no assistance whatever. Perhaps it would be wisest to say nothing.

"The one thing we knew—yes, I'm with an intelligence agency, not the Defense Department—the one thing we knew was that your daughter's disappearance was part of the Cronus Project, the same thing 'Becky Underwood' had been working on so long before.

"When I learned that, I couldn't get the element of *time* out of my mind. What kind of project could take so long? How could they have been setting up the kidnapping of a young woman who wouldn't be born for years? To borrow a phrase, the time was out of joint.

"And there was the timing involved in the various terrorist operations. They knew just *when* to be in position to shoot your daughter with the tranquilizer gun. Only the two of you and your gynecologist could have known that, it seemed.

"They knew exactly when and *where* to strike to get Robin today, too. It was uncanny.

"And then I realized, Mrs. Fane, that I was focusing on the wrong part of the myth.

"It was of no consequence that Cronus is considered the god of Time. What mattered was something else altogether.

"What mattered—the key element that led the poets in the KGB to name the project 'Cronus'—was that *he ate his children.*

"How does it feel, Mrs. Fane," he said, "to know you turned your own daughter over to be raped and brainwashed by an animal like Leo Calvin?"

Driscoll watched her reaction carefully; it was perfect. Her whole being transmitted a feeling of refined disgust.

"You are a maniac," she said. "I want you out of my house. Congressman, if this madman is really your son, as he seems to claim, I'm going to hold you personally responsible for this incredible accu—"

But the Congressman wasn't listening to her. He was putting it together for himself, and getting the answer Driscoll had. How no one but Sheila Fane could have fingered Elizabeth Fane for the kidnappers. How Sheila Fane had been among the very few who could have fingered Robin for them.

But she could do, and undoubtedly had done, more. Driscoll could see the wheels moving in his father's head as he added it all up.

"You've got a hold of something, son," the old man said. "Don't let go."

"No death squad for me yet, eh?" Driscoll couldn't help asking.

"Keep talking. I want to see her wiggle a little. After thirty years, I deserve it."

Sheila Fane's face showed shock and hurt. "Congressman!" she gasped.

Not unkindly, Driscoll said, "Save it. You're stuck with the two men in America it wouldn't work on. No, Mrs. Fane—I'll keep calling you that—you probably don't want to tell us the name you were born with, and it might sound strange to you after all these years—once somebody sees through that arrogant name, and what it means, the rest of the project becomes obvious.

"But of course, that's what the Chairman counted on, all those years ago, didn't he? That no American would see through to the answer. We'd be blinded by that famous

American sentimentality for Motherhood. The 'Sainted Mother Attitude,' I once heard a man call it. I'm surprised the Chairman didn't think to call it 'Operation Apple Pie.'"

Driscoll was playing a part now, cold, in command, and implacable. But deep in his memory, a little boy who used to wonder who his mother was, and why she didn't love him enough to be around, was crying.

"Let me tell you how the Cronus Project was designed to work. Correct me if I'm wrong."

The woman known as Sheila Fane said nothing.

"The Chairman, who at that time was the head of the secret police, made good use of the relatively free flow of information during World War II, as well as his own spies in the States.

"He gathered information on promising young Americans. Politicians. Soldiers. Industrialists. Herbert Fane for instance. You probably know how many more."

"I know you are both in terrible trouble if you repeat this madness to anyone."

"We won't," Driscoll said.

Sheila Fane's eyes widened. It was the first thing she'd really reacted to—he'd finally said something she wasn't ready for.

Driscoll showed her a small smile. "Then he sent a special class of agents through the famous American Town training camp. They studied how to talk and react and even think like Americans.

"But they were studying something else, too. Each was assigned one of the Chairman's promising young men. You were assigned Herbert Fane, the young mover and shaker in the world of microelectronics. You learned what he liked in a woman, and more importantly, what he *needed*. You could talk about what he liked to talk about. If he wanted someone who could run his home flawlessly, you learned how to do that. You were, undoubtedly, one of the top people available, or you wouldn't have been assigned to the project.

"A few at a time, you were sent to America. There couldn't be a flood of you—all your papers had to be perfect; your background had to check out. Birth certificates had to be planted in registrars' offices all over America. You made opportunities to meet your targets. Since you were fully briefed, that wouldn't be too difficult.

"I think that's how Becky Underwood may have been sidetracked. She was assigned to some up-and-coming military person at the Pentagon, but was more useful in an immediate capacity when the Korean War started."

He looked in her eyes, and found them unreadable. "How about it, Mrs. Fane? Am I right? How well did you get to know the other girls?"

No answer. The Congressman said, "Okay, son, that's enough. There'll be plenty of time for her to answer questions."

"No, Congressman," Driscoll said. "I want to finish this. It's important."

The Congressman nodded. Driscoll turned back to Sheila Fane.

"There had to be quite a few of you, it seems to me. Statistically, some of you were bound to fail.

"But some would succeed. Even a handful would be a triumph.

"Because there you would be, perfect wives to dynamic young men. Smiling at their sides in all the Sunday-magazine articles. If there was an incumbent wife when you showed up, she could be taken care of with impunity. You had *no motive*; hadn't even *met* the people involved yet, had you? What was it the first Mrs. Fane died of? 'Food poisoning?'

"Once the Chairman's girls became the incumbents, they would be in an ideal position to pass along good, solid, useful, everyday intelligence. But I don't think you did too much of that, if you did any at all. It was a risk, and Cronus was too big to risk over everyday matters. If you were caught, you'd be stopped from completing your real task."

Sheila Fane spoke for the first time in minutes. "And," she began, then swallowed and began again. "And what would that be, Mr. Driscoll?"

Driscoll smiled grimly. "Breeding hostages, Mrs. Fane. Conceiving, bearing, and raising sacrifices for Mother Russia.

"Isn't that why Liz was an only child? To make her all the more precious when her time came? I'll bet Robin was a nuisance, when she came to live with you. I'm sure you did what you could to keep up the famous friction between her and her uncle.

"I must admit, I admire the Chairman's patience. He must have been tempted to test out Cronus many times over the years, but he waited until *one* of the targets was in a position to make *one* decision that would affect the balance of power in the world. It took a long time, but it came down at last to the MENTOR system, and to your husband. Your daughter.

"So you and Leo Calvin put Cronus into effect. You could do so many things—really, you were in a position unique in the history of crime. You not only served as finger man at your own daughter's abduction, you told them how they could hide, if necessary, on your husband's own property. And you could be of such *help* with their brainwashing of her. You knew your daughter was fastidious, so you told them to keep her filthy. You knew all her fears, all her hangups; you told them all to Leo Calvin and had him pump drugs into her to make it easier to bring them to the surface and drive her insane."

"It's all lies," Sheila Fane said. She was unnaturally calm, almost defiantly so. "Every word of it. Besides, it's all speculation. You can't prove a thing."

Driscoll grinned.

The Congressman said, "He doesn't have to prove anything. We play this game with Russian rules. We never made Becky Underwood talk, true, but we've learned about some drugs in the meantime. You'll tell us everything you know about Cronus. Every single thing."

"I—I'm calling my lawyer." She stood up and started to walk angrily from the room.

Still sitting, Driscoll caught her by the wrist and pulled her back to her chair. "You are calling no one. No one in this town is ever going to hear from you again. You are going to Washington with the Congressman, and you are going to talk, and you will live as long as you have interesting things to say, and if you weren't so potentially valuable, I for one would gladly kill you right now.

"You are worse than the terrorists; worse than Leo Calvin. He was merely a traitor to his country. You are a traitor to your

own blood, your own genes. You brought a child into the world
to be a *thing*. A monster. A pawn. I wish—I—"

Driscoll felt a hand on his arm. "Hold on there, son," the
Congressman said softly.

Driscoll's eyes flashed hot anger at the man who had done
the same thing to him.

"Take it easy, son," the Congressman said.

With a great effort, Driscoll swallowed the lump of hatred
that had been choking him. "Yes," he said, "Father. I will take it
easy."

"I want to say something," Sheila Fane said. The defiance
was gone. They heard resignation in her voice.

"Go ahead," the Congressman said.

"It—it wasn't easy, what I had to do. The mother in a
woman is very strong. *Very* strong. Stronger than I ever
suspected when I signed up for the project. I—I have cried at
night over this, knowing it was coming. I hoped it never would.
You must believe that."

"My heart bleeds," Driscoll said. "Why didn't you contact
somebody in the government?"

"I had my duty as a soldier," she said. Her voice was proud.

"You sent your own child to have her body and mind
fucked. That is nobody's *duty*, Mrs. Fane."

"Clifford," the Congressman said, "let it go, will you? She's
a soldier, okay. But I'll be gettin' more than her name, rank,
and serial number out of her. Bet that, son. What we've got to
do now is figure out a way to get her out of here with nobody
knowin'." The Congressman's accent always got thicker in the
moment of triumph. "And let's do it quick. I don't want her
pullin' a cyanide capsule out of her brassiere or anything."

The woman they knew as Sheila Fane began to laugh. "I
have no cyanide capsule," she said. "Your son was right—we
never dreamed you'd suspect. After all, I am her mother."
Then the laughter became hysterical screaming. "*I am her
mother*! No mother should have to go through what I've been
through! I made the choice before I knew! Who could have any
idea what it would mean! You don't under—"

The Congressman slapped her hard across the face, then
again. It worked, after a fashion. At least, it reduced her

screams to trembling whispers. She looked at Driscoll. "Is my daughter going to be all right?"

"She's not going to die," Driscoll said. "Whether that's a blessing or not is up to the god of Time."

Driscoll turned to his father. "I've already taken care of the way we'll get her out of here. No one will ever look for her."

"How's that?"

"Our Jane Doe is out in the trunk of my car. She goes to the seat. My car crashes between here and the hospital; the body is burned beyond recognition. You put the fix in with the coroner's office—some version of the Jake Feder trick—so that they overlook things like age difference and missing fingers."

Sheila Fane sat staring. Her lips were tight. Brave soldier to the end.

"What about you, son?" the Congressman asked. "You're supposed to be drivin' her, ain't you?"

"I also die in the crash."

"Oh? Who've you got in mind to play that part?"

"Miles. Leo Calvin got him and escaped."

"Calvin's nothing compared to the woman here." The Congressman pursed his lips. "Shame about Miles. He was a valuable man."

"Yeah," Driscoll said. *And he loved you, old man,* he thought. *He deserved better from you.*

"Let's get on with it, son. I want you back in Washington with me right away to help interrogate the prisoner."

"No," Driscoll said. "I quit. Forever. Don't come looking for me." He put his hand on his father's shoulder. "But hear this, Father. If Vi isn't sprung in a week; if you ever bother Robin Payne or Herbert Fane again without a solid reason; if I ever find your men hounding me again; I, old man, will come looking for you."

"Vi will be out in three days," the Congressman said. "Insufficient evidence. I've been workin' on that already. But you're talkin' mighty big again, son. You shouldn't do that unless you can back it up."

"I can back it up." He raised his voice. "Come on in now, Rines."

Fenton Rines walked in, wearing a huge, small-town

banker's grin on his face. In his hand, he held his little tape recorder.

"About time," he said. "I was getting lonely out there."

The Congressman was cursing the men he'd brought with him, promising revenge for their letting Rines past them.

Driscoll said, "*I* got him past, Father. When a member of your family is in on it, all sorts of plots against you can work. Ask your prisoner."

The Congressman nodded slowly. "Yep. I just taught you too well. More fool me." He turned to Rines. "What do you want from me?" he asked.

The Chairman lay in his bed and worried. The reports were bad. Elizabeth Fane had been rescued; her mother, his agent, was dead. No word from Leo Calvin—he, apparently, had disappeared. He would do well to disappear. The minute he appeared, the Chairman would see to it that he disappeared for good.

More than thirty years, *wasted*. His last gift to the Motherland, destroyed. At least tainted in the minds of others.

Because this was only *one* failure; only *one* Cronus-child lost to them. There were thirty-one more. Thirty-one more possible turning points. A different crisis, a different approach. It could work. He knew it could. The *idea* of Cronus was sound—he had just run into the one American clever and ruthless enough to stop it.

He would have to make up a plan that would work without attracting the General's attention. Something quiet, private. He could do it, given enough time.

Time. That was Cronus' domain.

He sighed. It had been such a good name for the project. True, the sexes were confused. It was women, and by extension Mother Russia, who were to devour their children, not a father. Unless the Cronus Project itself was to be considered the father. And why shouldn't he be? He was also known as Father Time, wasn't he?

The Chairman felt cold and tired. He knew the man with the scythe would come for him soon. There was no time to waste. He closed his eyes. He would begin the new start for the Cronus Project as soon as he woke up.

If he woke up.

No. He called for pencil and paper. He was old; he was sick. He would think of it *now*.

Robin cried when she heard the news about Driscoll. About Aunt Sheila, too, of course, but in all the years she'd known her, Aunt Sheila had never told Robin that she loved her.

But Driscoll had.

Poor Clifford. She had hated him, loved him, pitied him. He had been so unhappy. Robin could have changed that.

She rolled over in her clean white hospital bed to hide her face in the pillow. It made her arms hurt like mad, but that wasn't what made her cry.

She could cry for a long time without anyone seeing her. She had a private room, and the nurses were especially busy today. One had apologized for not checking on her as often as she wanted to, but they had just had a nurse walk out on them today, in the middle of the shift. Imagine that.

Everybody's got troubles, Robin thought.

The thing of it was, Driscoll was *keeping his promise*. He had been on his way to the hospital with poor Aunt Sheila, coming to visit her as he said he would.

Robin knew that in a very short time, she would have to stop crying and be strong. Poor Uncle Herbert was going to be a wreck when he learned the news. Liz would need understanding and help. Some moron was talking about putting Liz on trial for taking part in the massacre at the Lakeview Club. Shades of Patty Hearst. People refused to believe what terror and despair could do to you. It was so much easier to blame the victim. Clifford had warned her it would happen.

Poor Liz.

Poor Aunt Sheila. Poor Uncle Herbert. Poor Clifford. Poor Robin.

She decided she could allow herself one more good cry before she had to be strong.

Driscoll looked at the smoke rising from the wreck. Rines and his father's men had done a good job of staging it. The skid marks alone were works of art.

He apologized to the unknown woman whose body was now being reduced to ashes in the passenger seat. *You were another victim of the Cold War,* he thought. *Take consolation from the fact that you suffered all your indignities after you were dead.*

Miles, he was sure, would be pleased. He had finally achieved what he'd always wanted. He had become Driscoll. He'd become the Congressman's son. He'd been a good soldier to the end.

More than you could say for Driscoll. He was determined, this time, to make his resignation stick. Fenton Rines was his insurance that it would. Rines knew everything now. He'd been horrified at some of what the Agency did, but he saw the necessity for it. He said he would "consult" with the Congressman, and Driscoll's father had swallowed that, especially when it was pointed out to him that even now documents and tapes were secreted in places that would be accessible to the press should anything happen to Rines.

His father had been angry, but admiration shone through. Maybe he was glad his son had learned the last lesson—total ruthlessness to achieve the Objective.

Rines shook Driscoll's hand and said good-bye. His father ignored him and got into the car. Rines joined him. Driscoll got one last look through the glass at the stone face of the woman called Sheila Fane. She stared unblinkingly ahead at a short, painful, and dismal future at the hands of a man who never let go of anything until he squeezed some value from it.

Driscoll watched them drive off, Washington bound, and cursed his life. His father might not resume chasing him (although he wasn't absolutely sure about that, despite all his precautions), but he would still be running. That's all there was for him to do.

A normal man would have been able to settle down with the brave and beautiful Robin Payne. Driscoll wasn't, and could never be, a normal man. It was much too late for that.

He was a monster; a thing; a tool, if no longer of his father, then of Fate. This time around, he played the role of Zeus—the child of Cronus who'd come back to thwart the god of Time. He smiled at the irony of it.

He was haunted, though, by the idea of all his brothers and sisters out there. How many were there? How imminent was their danger? If his father learned anything from Sheila Fane, Rines would know of it, so Driscoll could learn it, too. He would try to do something about it.

And immediately? He would go somewhere and rest, pretend to be somebody. Meet new people, try to learn what it felt like to be normal. Try not to think of the innocent people killed and maimed in the latest secret battle in an undeclared war; try to ignore the fact that Leo Calvin was out there somewhere, with revenge on his mind.

No, it would be dangerous to ignore it. Work out some plan to deal with it.

He watched the smoke rise and the flames shoot up. *Time to get moving, Driscoll,* he told himself. No. He wasn't Driscoll anymore. That identity was going up with the smoke. He'd have to think of someone else to be.

He got in the car Rines had arranged for him. He wouldn't keep it long—he didn't want to be too easy for anybody to trace.

He started the motor and drove north, the opposite direction to the one his father had taken. In the rear view mirror, he watched the smoke obscure the lights of Draper until the darkness of the warm Pennsylvania night swallowed him up.

November, 1982–January, 1984
New York—Port Chester—London